December 2011

To Mark & Hilde

With my best wishes,

Shaul Ezer

P9-AEX-305

The Nubian Princess
The Second Wife of Moses

by

Shaul Ezer

A Biblical Novel

Shaul Ezer
50 Elgin Avenue
Toronto, Ontario M5R 1G6
Shaul@ShaulEzer.com

This book is a work of fiction. Names, characters, places, and incidents either are products of the author's imagination or are used fictitiously. Any resemblance to actual events or locales or persons, living or dead, is entirely coincidental.

Copyright © 2010 by Shaul Ezer
All rights reserved,
including the right of reproduction
in whole or in part in any form.

ISBN-13   978-1-452-850-504
ISBN-10   1-4528-5050-X

www.ShaulEzer.com

To my sons – Jonathan and Isaac

Map 1

Egypt and Nubia

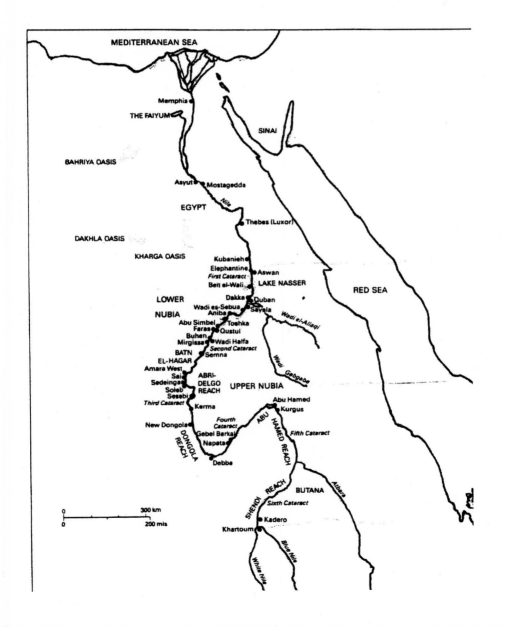

Map 2

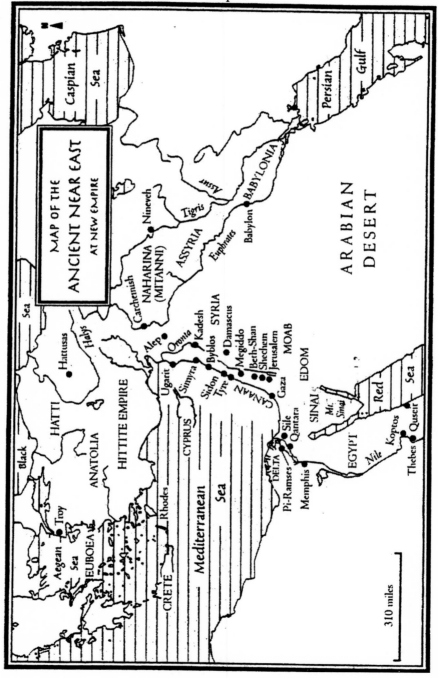

MAP OF THE
ANCIENT NEAR EAST
AT NEW EMPIRE

Caspian Sea

Persian Gulf

ARABIAN DESERT

Nineveh

NAHARINA (MITANNI)

ASSYRIA

Assur

Tigris

Euphrates

Babylon

BABYLONIA

Carchemish

Sea

Halys

HATTI

Hattusas

ANATOLIA

HITTITE EMPIRE

Black

Troy

Aegean Sea

EUBOEA

Rhodes

CRETE

Mediterranean Sea

CYPRUS

Ugarit

Simyra

Sidon

Tyre

Byblos

Alep

Orontes

Kadesh

SYRIA

Damascus

Megiddo

Beth-Shan

Shechem

Jerusalem

MOAB

EDOM

CANAAN

Gaza

SINAI

Mt. Sinai

Red Sea

Sile

Qantara

DELTA

Pi-Ramses

Memphis

EGYPT

Nile

Koptos

Quseir

Thebes

310 miles

Map 3

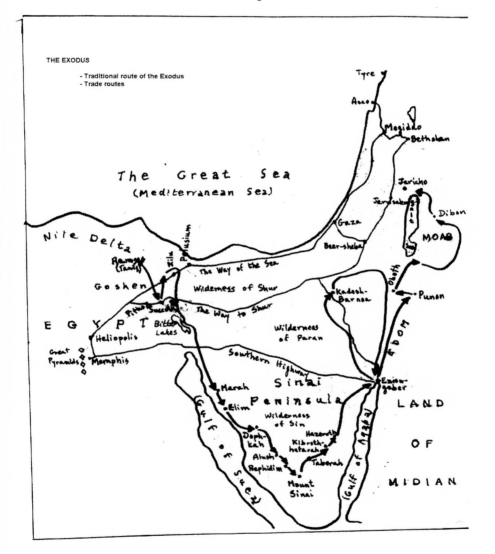

THE EXODUS

- Traditional route of the Exodus
- Trade routes

The Great Sea
(Mediterranean Sea)

Tyre
Acco
Megiddo
Bethshan
Jericho
Jerusalem
Dibon
Gaza
MOAB
Beer-sheba
Nile Delta
Pelusium
Zilu
Rameses (Tanis)
The Way of the Sea
Goshen
Wilderness of Shur
Kadesh-Barnea
Oboth
Punon
Pithom Succoth
The Way to Shur
EGYPT
Heliopolis
Bitter Lakes
Wilderness of Paran
EDOM
Great Pyramids
Memphis
Southern Highway
Sinai
Ezion-geber
LAND
Marah
Elim
Peninsula
OF
Gulf of Suez
Wilderness of Sin
Dophkah
Hazeroth
Kibroth-hataavah
Gulf of Aqaba
MIDIAN
Alush
Rephidim
Taberah
Mount Sinai

"AND MIRIAM AND AARON SPOKE AGAINST MOSES BECAUSE OF THE CUSHITE WOMAN WHOM HE HAD MARRIED; FOR HE HAD MARRIED A CUSHITE WOMAN".

BIBLE, BOOK OF NUMBERS 12:1

PREFACE

The Mystery of the Black Woman

In Bible study, one wonders at the mystery of the Cushite (or black) woman whom Moses, the Hebrew leader and prophet, married in the wilderness of Sinai after the Hebrew Exodus from Egypt (Numbers 12:1). Who was this Cushite woman? How did the Hebrews in the Sinai wilderness come in contact with Cushites? Why did Moses' older siblings Miriam and Aaron speak against him for marrying her?

In Biblical commentaries, there are two views about the identity of Moses' Cushite wife. The first view is that she was Zipporah, the daughter of the Midianite priest Jethro whom Moses married in Exodus 2:21. The novel *Zipporah, the wife of Moses* by Marek Halter (Three Rivers Press, New York, 2005) is based on this view that Zipporah was the same as the Cushite woman. The other view is that the woman whom Moses married in Exodus 2:21 (Zipporah) was different from the one he married in Numbers 12:1.

I prefer the second view, for several reasons. Firstly, the context of Exodus 2:21 is separated from the context of Numbers 12:1 by both place and time. The Bible states that Zipporah was from Midian, whereas the woman in Numbers 12:1 was from Cush. The Biblical Midian was where Moses spent 40 years between the time that he fled Egypt (after killing an Egyptian who had been beating an Israelite) and his return to lead the Israelites. During those years he married Zipporah. The Biblical Midian is generally considered to be located in northern Arabia near the Gulf of Aqaba. However, Numbers 12:1 describes the events during the Israelites wandering after the Exodus from

Egypt, which occurred many decades after Moses' sojourn in Midian. The Biblical Cush is generally considered to be the southern part of ancient Nubia in the present Ethiopia or Sudan. While some scholars have suggested that "Midian" and "Cush" could have referred to the same geographic region, it is more likely that these are two different places. In deference to sacred texts and works of enduring value, words in them should be given their full effect, unless the result would be repugnant to the general context. If the author of Numbers 12:1 meant "Midian", then he or she would not have used "Cush".

Secondly, the text of Numbers 12:1 places an emphasis on Moses' marriage to the Cushite woman ("for he had married a Cushite woman"). This emphasis indicates that this marriage was a new event. If the reference was to the marriage to Zipporah of years ago in Exodus 2:21, then an emphasis would not have been appropriate.

Thirdly, the text of Numbers 12:1 states that Miriam and Aaron spoke against Moses because of the Cushite woman whom he had married. It is unlikely that his siblings would speak against Moses for a marriage that took place years ago in Exodus 2:21, unless this was in the context of a new marriage.

Finally, proponents of the view that the Cushite woman is Zipporah state that there is no reference in the Bible to Zipporah's death. The answer to this point is that the deaths of many other Biblical figures are not recorded in the Bible.

Assuming then that the Cushite woman in Numbers 12:1 is not Zipporah, the next question is how the Hebrews in the Sinai wilderness could have come in contact with Cushites or Nubians. History books shed some light on this question.

Nubia was the homeland of Africa's earliest black culture with a history traceable from 3800 B.C. onward. Settling along the banks of the Nile in northern Sudan and southern Egypt, the Nubians developed one of the oldest and greatest civilizations in Africa. Nubian customs and traditions were adopted by ancient Egyptians. Sometime in the reign of Thutmose III (ca. 1479 – 1425 B.C.), the Egyptians conquered and fully annexed all of Nubia.

It is generally considered that the Pharaoh at the time of the Hebrew Exodus was Ramses II (ca. 1279 – 1213 B.C.) or his son Merenptah. Egypt, then the only major power, ruled Libya to the west, Nubia to the south and Syria-Palestine, including Canaan, to the north and east. These frontiers were threatened by internal revolts from the Libyans and Nubians, as well as by external powers such as the Hittites from north of Syria.

At the time of Ramses II, the Egyptian Pharaohs relied on Nubian warriors to help defend their frontiers. So it is quite possible that Nubian generals and soldiers in the service of Pharaoh could have been patrolling or defending the Sinai Peninsula at the same time as the Hebrews, led by Moses, were wandering there after their Exodus from Egypt.

The next question posed above is: why did Moses' siblings speak against him for marrying the Nubian woman? Neither biblical texts nor history books shed light on this question. The answer is a matter of speculation. For instance, some writers have suggested that this connection of Moses upset his siblings because it tended to injure his prestige in the eyes of race-proud Hebrews. In my view, this is unlikely, for two reasons. Firstly, it was not uncommon then, as well as at the time of Abraham, Isaac, Jacob and Joseph, for a Hebrew to marry outside the tribe. Secondly, at the time of the Exodus, the Nubians were a part of the Egyptian nobility and were working and dreaming of regaining their supremacy. (In fact, five centuries later, they succeeded and a Nubian king Piankhy or Piye (ca. 743 – 712 B.C.), "the Black Pharaoh", became the ruler of Egypt.) On the other hand, at the time of the Exodus, the Hebrews were a small tribe of former slaves without territory. Thus, it is equally likely that at the time of the Exodus a Hebrew, in marrying a Nubian, was marrying into a higher social and political level.

This novel is about who the Nubian woman was, how Moses met her, why he married her and the reasons that Miriam and Aaron spoke against Moses. I have tried to bring these exceptional individuals to life, describing their daily lives, motivations and quest for leadership and spirituality in an unsettled time when their existence was continually threatened.

Shaul Ezer
Toronto, Canada

LIST OF CHARACTERS

HEBREWS

Aaron	High Priest and elder brother of Moses
Ahiezer	division commander
Bezalel	architect and Miriam's son
Caleb	Miriam's husband
Captain	
Debra	Miriam's assistant
Eldad	old man
Elizur	division commander
Elishama	division commander
Guards	
Gueul	wounded man
Haggar	leprous woman
Joshua	general and second in command to Moses
Leah	seamstress
Medad	old man
Miriam	elder sister of Moses
Moses	leader and prophet
Nahson	division commander
Ohaliab	architect
Rivka	Havilya's assistant
Shooly	Joshua's scout
Zabad	Hebrew deserter

NUBIANS

Havilya	Princess of Nubia and Sebakashta's daughter
Sebaha	Havilya's mother
Sebakashta	Viceroy of Nubia
Shabitqo	aide to Sebakashta
Taharqo	aide to Sebakashta

EGYPTIANS

Black Knights

Essau	administrator of Etzion-geber
Jalam	spy for Reyes
Omar	spy for Reyes
Pharaoh	
Ramentop	Prince and head of the Black Knights, Pharaoh's secret service
Reyes	administrator of Gaza
Tasiris	aide to Ramentop

PART I

PROLOGUE

It has been more than two years since the Exodus of the Israelites from Pharaoh's rule in Egypt. This is circa 1200 B.C.E. in the rule of Ramses II, who has sworn to capture the Israelites and bring them back to Egypt as slaves again. The Israelites are wandering in the wilderness of Sinai, trying to avoid the armies of Pharaoh while at the same time searching for the way to the Promised Land in Canaan.

ONE

Shooly reined in his horse in the shadow of a ridge overlooking Pharaoh's southern highway, a trade route across the middle of the Sinai Peninsula connecting Memphis near the Great Pyramids in the west with Ezion-geber in the east. A Hebrew and an orphan, he had chosen to work as a scout for Joshua from the time of the Exodus when they fled from Egypt. He enjoyed the life of a scout more and more. Not quite 20, he could not qualify for military service in Joshua's army. As a scout, he was given a horse, generous rations and some freedom to roam. The young women admired Shooly for his adventures, certainly more than the other men who stayed in the camp to study the new laws of Moses.

Working directly for Joshua gained Shooly the respect of the other Israelites. Joshua was the son of Nun and was originally called Hosea, but later Moses renamed him Joshua (meaning "God saves"). Moses quickly saw in Joshua the qualities he sought in a military leader. He impressed Moses with the daring and originality of his strategies. The test of Joshua's abilities had come quickly. The Israelites were about to face the Amalekites, the first of many adversaries, at the battle of Rephidim. It was to Joshua that Moses had turned and issued a clear and sharp command: "Choose us out men, and go out – fight with Amalek," Moses had ordered. Early the next morning, Joshua had gathered his soldiers and marched out of the camp to meet the Amalekites in battle. Joshua and his soldiers had prevailed, as they overwhelmed the people of Amalek with the sword.

This battle of Rephidim against the Amalekites was the first Israelite victory after their Exodus from Egypt. For the first time, the Israelites organized themselves in close formations, met a fierce enemy in pitched battle, and held their positions without breaking and running. The slaves had become warriors, and the warriors had won their first battle. While many more battles would be fought before the Israelites could become a nation, none of them would forget the day the sword of Israel had gained its first bloody victory.

Now Shooly tied his horse to a rock to take a rest. He had been riding north in the hot sun since dawn of that day when he left the camp at Hazeroth in the Sinai wilderness. While his horse rested, he reflected on the task ahead of him. Before it became too dark, he had to find two mules that were to be left for him by the Nubians. Two bales of sweets and dry foods were to be tied to each mule. These were gifts from the Nubians to Moses for his wedding to the Nubian princess.

The wedding was in three days, and Shooly did not intend to fail in his mission. He liked to be considered faithful to his duties. To be entrusted with a mission involving the Nubians and the wedding of Moses was a good sign.

Miriam had told Shooly God was watching over him. His fellow Hebrews had a special love for Miriam. This was not just because she was the elder sister of Moses. Her work as a mid-wife endeared her even more, especially to the women.

The story of Shooly's birth was told many times. His father Isaac was killed in a construction accident at one of the temples. He and other Hebrew slaves had been building the temple for Ramses II in the Pharaoh's new capital, Pi-Ramses. All the Hebrews grieved for his mother Sara, who was pregnant with Shooly at the time. Then, when only in her seventh month of pregnancy, Sara's water broke and Miriam rushed over to Sara's house. When Miriam arrived at Sara's bedside, Sara had started contractions, but the contractions were not strong enough. After hours of pain, and in spite of Miriam's valiant efforts, Sara died in Miriam's arms.

With the presence of mind that made her renowned, Miriam immediately cut open Sara's abdomen and delivered a strong baby boy. She called him "Shelumiel," which means, "My friend is God." He became known as Shooly, for short. Now, as a free man respected in his calling, Shooly thought that God was truly his friend.

In spite of his premature birth, Shooly grew up to become thin, lanky but tall and strong. His body seemed to be made entirely of bone and muscle. He towered over most of the Hebrews, having to look down on them when he spoke. This created a slight hunch in his back but also gave him an air of authority. His skin was fair, but his hair jet-black. The girls found him irresistible, especially when he boyishly brushed his straight hair away from his face, showing a clean and high forehead and innocent black eyes.

Shooly carried no weapons, except a sharp dagger sheathed and hung from the waist on his left. He also carried a wooden staff, not thicker than a boy's wrist but as long as his own height. Some Hebrew fighters considered the staff unwieldy, but this was a weapon uniquely chosen by Shooly. Wielding it with agility and moving with speed, Shooly could use its length to keep a prey or enemy at bay. As well, if swung with full force, its weight could knock down a foe instantly.

Sheltered behind the ridge, Shooly looked north at Pharaoh's highway and beyond for any sign of the mules. This was the most southerly of Pharaoh's trade routes and less traveled than the others. Nevertheless, the occasional caravan passed by, as well as Pharaoh's scouts. He had to find those mules before someone else did.

Shooly started to doubt whether he was in the right place. There was another trade route a day's ride to the north. This was the Way to Shur, which was also an east-west route roughly parallel to the southern route he was sent to. The Way to Shur started from the Egyptian cities of Pithom and Succoth in the west, curved north of Jebel Helal and ended in Beersheba in the east. Perhaps it was the Nubians who confused Joshua, Shooly thought. But Joshua could not have meant to send him to the Way to Shur, which was yet another day's ride, without additional provisions. Besides, there was not enough time to ride from Hazeroth to the Way to Shur and return in time for Moses' wedding.

Shooly was intrigued by the Nubians. He had heard about their ancient civilization to the south of Egypt. The women were renowned for their beauty, the men for their fighting prowess and the land for its wealth in gold and agriculture. When the Pharaohs subdued Nubia, they made it an Egyptian province and used its gold to adorn Egypt's temples.

The fighting prowess of the Nubians became a legend. In Hebrew, they were the *nefilim* or giants. That is why Pharaoh conscripted the Nubians in his armies, Shooly thought. Only the Nubians and Egyptians were assigned patrol duties in Egypt's frontier colonies – particularly the trade routes across the Sinai Peninsula.

Joshua had assured Shooly that on this mission, he would likely not run into Pharaoh's patrols. The Nubians were to disappear as soon as they left the two mules near the ridge on the trade route. Even if he met up with the Nubians, Joshua told him, they were likely to be friendly. "I hope so," Shooly thought. "I don't want to tackle with Nubian *nefilim*."

He now stopped looking at the highway and retraced his steps back to the ridge. He realized that the Nubians would not leave the mules in the open space near the highway. He ran to one side of the ridge and then the other, with no mules in sight.

With his feet aching and his mind tired from anxious thoughts, he needed a rest from the late afternoon sun. He lay in the shadow of the ridge where he had tied his horse, and closed his eyes.

TWO

To Sebakashta, the Viceroy of Nubia, Aniba had been the city on the Nile in Nubia that served as the residence of the viceroys of Nubia. For many decades, a line of twenty-five Egyptians had been viceroys. However, as they became more secure in their control of the southern colony, the Pharaohs had looked to the Nubians for administration.

That is how Sebakashta had been appointed Viceroy. He was the descendant of a well-known Nubian family that traced its ancestry to the ruler of Nubia who had defended it at the battle of Kerma. The Pharaoh Thutmose III had launched a major campaign at that time, overwhelmed the Nubian forces and burned and destroyed the city of Kerma.

His noble birth ensured that Sebakashta would be educated in Thebes with the princes of Pharaoh. He received added instruction in government and military affairs in Memphis. In later years, Sebakashta displayed skills in varied affairs that had enabled him to perform the many duties expected of the Viceroy, and eventually to gain Pharaoh's confidence.

Sebakashta knew that the territory that the Pharaohs, now at the zenith of their power, prized the most was Nubia, which the Egyptians called "the Southern Lands" or "Cush". Its rich deposits of gold, copper and other precious stones were within easy reach of the Nile, the great river that flowed northward and made a garden out of Egypt and Nubia, which were essentially without rain. "We are the earliest culturally advanced and settled civilization," he mused to himself. "As the link between Africa and the great empires of the Mediterranean, we the Nubians can be independent and prosperous again." He had learned his history well – twice before in their history, the Nubians had been independent. Now his people ached to become independent again, and it was his destiny to liberate his beloved land from the Pharaohs.

As Sebakashta pondered how the Pharaohs ruled their empire, he could see a way for the Nubians to free themselves. The wars of the previous (Eighteenth) Dynasty of Egyptian pharaohs had left Egypt in possession of a vast empire. By the time of Ramses II, his immediate superior, the empire included Nubia and Syria-Palestine including Canaan.

Sebakashta noticed that these two territories presented a contrast in Egyptian goals and methods. The Pharaohs were attracted to Nubia for its resources (especially gold) and its manpower, and considered its territory suitable for colonization. The Pharaohs determined at the outset to destroy the Nubian power structure, Egyptianize the Nubians, and replace Nubian rule with an Egyptian administration. To consolidate their hold on Nubia, the Pharaohs created and maintained fortresses and colonial settlements along the Nile to serve as a transit corridor.

Syria-Palestine, however, was valued for its strategic location and trade routes, and less for its natural resources. It was important to subdue the native Canaanite political institutions, but not necessarily to replace them. In Canaan, two transit corridors already existed, namely, the "Way of the Sea" along the coast and through Gaza and secondly the "King's Highway" through Transjordan. The Pharaohs did not need to settle these corridors. They merely had to seize and maintain control over them. To do that, they used the Nubians.

Thus evolved two distinct Egyptian administrations for the new "provinces" of Egypt – direct colonization of Nubia, and control of existing political institutions in Syria-Palestine.

To Egyptianize the Nubians, Nubian princes were sent to Pharaoh's court where they were educated with the royal princes. When they returned to Nubia, they were expected to be Egyptian in manner and thought and loyal to Pharaoh. Sebakashta understood well that to Pharaoh, the security of the Nubian kingdom and Egyptian control over Syria-Palestine depended on the loyalty of the viceroy. And that, Sebakashta reasoned shrewdly, presented him and his fellow Nubians with an opportunity to advance their cause.

For all daily purposes, Sebakashta was the local King of Nubia, except for edicts from and reports to Pharaoh. He maintained his office at his mansion on the Nile in Aniba, the Cushite city of his birth. From there, he supervised all the major building projects – including the construction of the temples at Abu Simbel, a short distance to the south. He had done so well for Pharaoh in Aniba, that when the Pharaoh faced unrest in Syria-Palestine, he looked to Sebakashta for help.

"My dear Viceroy," the Pharaoh had told him after he had summoned him to Thebes. "You have everything under control in Aniba. I can put someone there of lesser ability. I need you to be in Gaza. We are facing unrest in our colonies in Asia and possibly war with the Hittites."

Sebakashta hated to have to leave the culture and sophistication of Aniba for a rowdy frontier town like Gaza. However, he had no choice. No one said no to Pharaoh.

"Of course, your Majesty," he had said to Pharaoh. "I shall be at your service, as always."

"In deference to your family's ancestry," the Pharaoh told him, "you will be allowed to keep your Nubian titles. But you will move permanently with your family to Gaza. We will need you there for a long time."

"Of course, your Majesty."

Such are the rewards of loyal service, Sebakashta had thought as he bowed to the Pharaoh. If I had been merely inept, my family and I would have continued to enjoy the comfort and pleasure of Aniba.

That is how it came about that he and his wife Sebaha and his daughter Princess Havilya had moved to Gaza.

For a long time, Gaza had been a sleepy and dusty provincial town – one of many along the Way of the Sea. It was a resting place for travelers, caravans and military patrols between Egypt and Syria. Recently, however, the military threat from the Hittites north of Syria had intensified. Pharaoh's military staff chose Gaza as a base for supplies and soldiers. From this base, Pharaoh could launch his attacks against the Hittites.

The sudden swell of population made Gaza a rough and boisterous town. Sebakashta's role was to head Pharaoh's military forces in Gaza, maintain civil order, patrol the trade routes along the Sinai Peninsula and defend Pharaoh's interest in any uprising from local tribes – Edomites, Moabites and, of course, the Hebrews.

Pharaoh would consider any commander a national hero if he could find, subdue and return the Hebrew slaves to Egypt. Pharaoh's military advisors had no doubt where the Hebrews were. There were no reports of the Hebrews turning up on either side of the Salt Sea. Except for a few deserters and

9

stragglers, the Hebrews did not come near any of the Pharaoh's trade routes in the Sinai. From various scouting missions, Pharaoh's chief of staff concluded that the Hebrews were on the move in the mountains of southern Sinai. With the Hittites threatening an invasion from the north, the forces of the Pharaoh were spread too thin defending the two other frontiers of Egypt. Thus Pharaoh's army could not afford the large force that would be required to find, chase and subdue the Hebrews in the hot Sinai mountains.

Even before he had moved to Gaza, Sebakashta had been intrigued by the Hebrews and their leader Moses. Word of their escape to freedom from slavery in Egypt had traveled quickly through Pharaoh's empire. As much as Pharaoh and his courtiers tried to suppress it, the story of the Hebrew escape captured the imagination of Egyptian slaves and commoners alike. None of the tribes under Egyptian rule managed to free themselves. How did the Hebrews do it? Surely their God Yahweh must be more powerful than Pharaoh's God Amun. This became the widespread belief in the empire.

After he became the commander in Gaza, Sebakashta received more reports of the exploits of the Hebrews. Small patrols of Egyptian soldiers would be subject to surprise attacks and brutally massacred. All their clothes, food and weapons would be taken. The attackers left no trace of their identity. All reports strongly indicated that this was the work of the Hebrews.

As more and more of these reports arrived in Gaza, Sebakashta began to admire the Hebrews. Perhaps the Nubians who long for their freedom from Egypt have something to learn from this wandering tribe of former slaves. The Nubians have an old and glorious history, he thought. How much longer can we endure as vassals of the hated Egyptians? As long as we merely endure! And take no action, he thought. And so he resolved to use his post in Gaza to make contact with the Hebrews.

Such a dangerous mission could be entrusted to no one except his aide Shabitqo and his daughter, the Princess Havilya.

The gods had not provided sons to the Viceroy and his wife Sebaha. Their only child was Princess Havilya. It did not take long for them to find out that this was a special child. Her green eyes were framed with high cheekbones and dark arching eyebrows. Long, black hair cascaded down and glistened against her smooth skin. Her shiny, white teeth provided a sharp contrast with her black complexion.

Few qualities surpassed her beauty, except perhaps her mind and her ability. Even as a young girl, she showed intense interest in her father's affairs of state. When she could not travel with the Viceroy – which was seldom – she pined for his return so she could hear all about her father's projects. Rich and powerful men in Aniba showered Sebaha with proposals to marry Princess Havilya. But the Princess had her own mind – she was interested only in matters of state.

"The men can wait," she would tell her mother.

Sebaha, sensitive to her failure to provide a male heir for the Viceroy, would say to him, "She is the boy the gods did not give us, and a lot prettier than any boy would have been."

THREE

"Malcontents and ne'er-do-wells!" Miriam shouted at the wounded men under her care.

"Worse. You are thieves and charlatans!" she railed bluntly at them, as she fed them and tended to their wounds.

They were in the Annex now, so-called because among the Israelites it became known almost as a part of Miriam's place. Back in Egypt, the Annex had been a small hospital or ward that Miriam founded and worked in as a midwife, even though it was several streets from the hut where Miriam lived with her husband Caleb ben Yefuneh and their son Bezalel.

Now in the desert, the Annex was a tent at the edge of the camp, far removed from Miriam's tent. A rectangular structure, it was supported by two posts in the middle and made of a patchwork of thin canvas and cloth. One entered from the middle of the short sides of the rectangle and faced a narrow corridor. Makeshift beds were on either side of the corridor. Only twenty beds were set up on each side, for a total of forty. Patients lay with their heads on the wall side and their feet nearest the corridor. A small space was left between each bed for a way to the patient. A bed was merely a piece of cloth placed on the sand.

Miriam had learned her medical skills in Thebes. Egyptian medical men were renowned, but devoted no attention to the Hebrew slaves, many of whom were frequently injured at building sites. Miriam saw that there was no limit to Pharaoh's projects and no end to Hebrew injuries. She was determined to learn what she could about the healing arts so that she could help her people.

At first, it was easy for Miriam to post herself as a Hebrew slave in an Egyptian maternal institution. There she learned midwifery. As her skills became recognized, she was assigned to more difficult wards – tending to broken bones and soldiers wounded in Pharaoh's wars. Now her skills were in such demand that she had trained Debra, a young kinswoman, as her assistant.

When Miriam came to the Annex that morning, she found Debra exhausted and overwhelmed. All the beds in the Annex were filled with wounded men.

"What happened?" asked Miriam.

"They came in last night, and I didn't want anyone to disturb you."

"You should have come to get me. This is too much for anyone to handle, dear, especially one as young as you."

Debra was only eighteen, and with a fair, almost pale, complexion. Her mid-sized robust frame conveyed more maturity. Her thick eyebrows were long and wide, arching over her oval black eyes generously spaced apart. Her nose was small but slightly winged, and her wide wavy mouth and ample hips added to her sensuousness. Her shoulder-length hair was parted in the middle of her forehead. Miriam urged her to wear a scarf around her head to hide Debra's allure from men's salacious glances.

Talking to Debra and the wounded men, Miriam pieced together their story. The men were from the tribes of Simeon and Gad. They had set off several days ago to Pharaoh's southern trade route, hoping to intercept some caravans leaving west from Ezion-geber. Their plan was to attack and raid a caravan carrying food and gifts westward to Egypt.

Miriam remembered a fierce argument between some of these men and Moses a few days ago. "We are fed up with eating just manna – raw manna, cooked manna, flat manna," they had shouted at Moses. "In Egypt, at least we ate meat and fish and fresh fruits and vegetables. We are starving in this horrible desert. Yes, we were slaves, and now we are free – free to starve, free to eat manna only or the lizards scurrying behind the hot rocks." They had told Moses of how they planned to get food. Moses had been distraught. He had on so many occasions tried to explain, but it seemed no one listened. It was left to Miriam to exhort the crowd of hungry men.

"What you plan to do is against the laws of Moses," she had told them. "Those laws were given to us by God. You may not attack innocent tradesmen carrying goods from one place to another. We are not at war with these caravans. You will be committing theft or murder or both. Besides, you cannot be sure that the meat and other food you find is fit to eat. The food itself may kill you. What is more, many of you are not fighting men yet. If the caravans are armed or put up resistance, you could get killed or wounded."

She did not have to repeat what she and the more sober elders feared most – that Pharaoh's agents and spies would find them, capture them and return them as slaves to Egypt.

Now in the Annex, a heavy-set man was moaning with pain. A blow to his right leg had shattered his shin and a bone protruded through the skin. "Quick, Debra, give me a splint and some rope." Miriam set the broken bone in place, placed a stick on the injured leg and tied both legs together. Geuel, the son of Machi of the tribe of Gad, had a flesh wound on his left thigh. He also suffered from pains in his stomach. It must have been the quail they had grabbed from the caravan. He and the other men could not help gorging themselves on it.

Miriam hurried from one wounded man to another. She could see that at least two had died overnight from the bleeding that Debra had tried in vain to stop. Another's arm was becoming soft and bloated. She washed the wound and dressed it with a clean cloth.

Miriam shook her head. "I now have no more space to look after the women and children that may need help today."

Miriam's anger terrified the stricken men. Although in late middle age, she was tall, hefty and strong. She dressed simply in a plain, long brown dress, and one's gaze almost instinctively fixed on her face. Her complexion was fair and smooth, her forehead long and ending in straight grey hair that flowed down to her shoulders. Her face shone with the radiance that glowed in those who know who they are and where they belong. The Hebrew mystics referred to this look as the *shekhinah,* the Presence of God.

Her manner was as simple as her appearance. Her plain speaking endeared her to the common folk, who appreciated hearing the truth, however unpleasant it might be, and who felt elevated to her as equals with a leader from a priestly family. Yet, others resented her outspoken ways as tactless and muttered that Miriam always blurted out the first thing that came into her head.

Debra now was dressing the wound on Geuel's left thigh. At the same time, he lay on his right side vomiting incessantly.

Geuel could not tell which made him suffer the most – his flesh wound, his stomach sickness or Miriam's wrath.

* * *

Those who wanted to see Miriam knew where to find her, for she was almost always at the Annex. Her son Bezalel came to tell her about the latest furnishings of the sanctuary, which was housed in what the Hebrews called the Tent of Meeting, or Tent of Revelation. He and another architect, Ohaliab, were commissioned to arrange the Tent. Bezalel and Ohaliab were paired together for another duty – to act as scouts for Joshua in the same squad as Shooly's. Moses had called upon the people to donate precious metals, yarn, skins, wood, and cloth to help build the sanctuary, including the holy ark, the menorah and the altar where offerings are brought to God. The response from the people was so generous that Moses had to tell them to stop. Now Bezalel was telling Miriam about his excitement in having so many gifts and objects to choose from for the decorations.

Moses told his people that the Lord had asked them to make for the Lord a sanctuary so that the Lord might dwell among them. Its main purpose was to wean the Israelites from idolatrous worship and turn them toward the thought that God was in their midst. As well, as God was holy, His presence in the sanctuary made the sanctuary holy, and so this reminded the Israelites to make the sanctification of their lives the primary aim of all their endeavours. For the less spiritual among them, the sanctuary provided a sense of a place with roots – not a small relief for a semi-nomadic people, wanderers looking for a permanent place to inhabit. For others, who were engaged in the constant labour of packing and unpacking the sanctuary as they wandered from place to place, it was a privilege to expend their labour for the sake of the Lord, and not as slaves erecting buildings in Egypt for the pharaohs. And so their labours became an affirmation of their freedom.

The sanctuary was housed in a special portable tent with a wooden framework. The entire tent had three parts. Firstly, there was the outer court supported by wooden pillars and enclosed by curtains. It was rectangular in shape, 100 by 50

16

cubits (each cubit was about half a metre). The entrance to the tent was from the eastern side. Secondly, inside the court and facing the entrance, was the altar of sacrifice and further west was a laver for the priests. Thirdly, in the western portion, was the tabernacle, or the sanctuary proper. A hanging curtain divided the tabernacle into two chambers. The first, which only the priests might enter, was the holy place containing the table, the candlestick and the altar of incense. The second chamber was called the Holy of Holies, containing the Ark of the Covenant, which only the High Priest would enter once a year on the Day of Atonement or for making sacrificial offerings.

There was a gradation of holiness peaking at the Holy of Holies and declining until one reached the entrance of the tent. The objects nearest the Holy of Holies were made of gold and rarer and costly materials, those further away being made of bronze and ordinary woven cloth. This gradation was also emphasized by the type of persons who might enter the various chambers. Moses could enter the Holy of Holies at all times, whereas Aaron was admitted only under special circumstances, such as for making sacrificial offerings, and from there on, the priests, the Levites and the people at large were admitted to assigned areas. The priests were clothed in garments of varying importance. Finally, there were gradations of colour: blue was the most sacred, followed by purple and finally crimson.

Proud of her son's achievement, Miriam's eyes shined with joy as Bezalel talked about the sacred task assigned to him. That is one of the many blessings God had given me, she thought, as this gives me strength to deal with the sick and wounded people before me.

By now many of the relatives of the wounded men had come to the Annex to help. Miriam looked at Debra, who seemed to be faltering from exhaustion.

"You must go and rest now," Miriam told her. "You have done more than your fair share."

With all the excitement and tension of the night, Debra's thoughts had been absorbed with the emergencies facing her. Now she paused for a rest in the area immediately behind, and shaded by, the Annex. She allowed her mind to wander – and to wish...

To wish that Shooly would visit her at the Annex, as he sometimes did. He would share his rations with her, and tell her stories about his scouting adventures. In some quiet afternoons, when most people were resting in their tents to escape the desert sun, they would sneak out together for a ride on his horse. As she rode behind him, with her arms around his slender waist and her cheek on his back, she would feel safe and content.

Now, suddenly she felt alarmed. Shooly had told her he was going on a special scouting mission. He could not tell her the purpose, because Joshua swore him to secrecy. But he did tell her he was going to Pharaoh's southern highway. This is where Geuel and his friends met with trouble. Would Shooly run into the same caravan and get wounded, or possibly killed?

No, she thought. He had no reason to go near the caravan. He is a trained scout. He will spot them before they spot him, and he would not try anything violent against a number of travelers. Geuel also said they had attacked just outside Ezion-geber. She thought Shooly's mission would be further west along the trade route nearer to the middle of the Sinai Peninsula.

"Shelumiel, Shelumiel," she repeated. Now she knew why Miriam had chosen that name.

"God," she prayed. "Please, always be his friend."

FOUR

Soon after moving to Gaza, the chance to make contact with the Hebrews presented itself to the Viceroy. He had been on one of his frequent tours of the administrative towns in the area. On his arrival at Ezion-geber, he was told that the local militia had just encountered a group of Hebrew deserters and killed all of them except one, spared for questioning. He ordered that the Hebrew be brought to him at once.

Frightened and hungry, the Hebrew said he was Zabad the son of Tahath of the tribe of Ephraim. He told the Viceroy that he and a group of friends had become disillusioned with life in the desert and the promises of Moses. They escaped from the camp of the Hebrews and left on foot to return to Egypt. They had hoped to join a caravan along the Pharaoh's southern highway west of Ezion-geber. When they were discovered by the soldiers from Ezion-geber, there was a fight. All of his friends had been killed. He did not know why he had been spared.

He had told his captors all he knew about the whereabouts of the Hebrews – that they were encamped somewhere in the mountains, that they were ordered to move every few days or so, and no one except Joshua or Moses knew in advance where they were to move next.

Sebakashta thought long and hard. Here was a chance to make contact with the Hebrews. If it failed, he thought, the Viceroy of Nubia, and his family would surely be dead at the hands of Pharaoh. If it succeeded, it would be the first step to a free Nubia. Would he dare to entrust this mission to this bedraggled Hebrew? What other chance would he get? How would Nubia become free if its leaders did not dare to take a chance?

Sebakashta dismissed all the officials, except his aide Shabitqo.

"Hebrew," he said. "Do you want to live?"

"Yes, yes, your Highness," Zabad muttered.

"Then listen carefully."

"Do not kill me, your Highness," Zabad begged. "I know how much your Pharaoh hates the Hebrews, but I will do anything you ask."

"If you want to live, Hebrew, then be quiet and listen to me."

Pointing to Shabitqo, he told Zabad, "This is Shabitqo. He is my trusted aide. He will take you, give you a horse and rations for two days. He will escort you to the outskirts of Ezion-geber and let you go. You are to go to your leader Moses. Tell him that the Viceroy of Nubia and Pharaoh's Commander of Gaza has sent you."

Zabad's eyes opened wide and gazed motionless at the Viceroy.

The Viceroy continued, "Tell him that the Viceroy pays homage to the great Hebrew leader and wants to meet him."

Zabad could hardly believe what he was hearing.

"If it would please your Highness, may I sit down?"

"Yes. Tell Moses to meet me in exactly four weeks at a spot outside Ezion-geber that Shabitqo will show you. Any questions?"

"Your... your Highness, what if your soldiers catch me or I am lost before I find Moses?"

"If you are caught, I will not know you and you will be killed. If you are lost, then the vultures will make a good meal of your corpse."

"And if Moses refuses?"

"He will not. He will want some relief from the bedraggled Hebrew slaves he is leading."

"How will he know he will not be captured?"

"He can come with two armed men. They can scout the meeting place before Moses reveals himself. They will see that we will mean him no harm."

"What if Moses brings a force large enough to capture you?"

"Then Moses will face the full anger and attention of Pharaoh. Now Pharaoh is distracted by other affairs. But if Moses captures one of his top commanders, Pharaoh cannot afford to ignore that."

"Do I have a choice, your Highness?"

"Yes. You can refuse, and then Shabitqo will have you executed at once."

"I understand perfectly."

Looking at Shabitqo, Zabad then asked, "When do we leave?"

* * *

Six months had passed since that fateful day when the Viceroy had faced Zabad, the lost and frightened Hebrew, and sent him on his mission. Since then he had had five meetings with Moses, four weeks apart. Each time it was in the hills outside Ezion-geber; each time he and his two aides were present; and Moses always brought Zabad and Joshua.

* * *

As Sebakashta and his two aides Taharqo and Shabitqo walked into the administration building in Ezion-geber in the Sinai, Shabitqo announced his master's entrance.

"His Highness Sebakashta, Viceroy of Nubia, Overseer of the Southern Lands, Pharaoh's son of Cush, Commander of the District of Gaza."

Sebakashta was short and slightly chubby. His high forehead merged with a balding scalp, but with greying hair remaining on both sides. He had large round black eyes with heavy eyebrows, a long nose and thick lips which he usually kept pursed together. His walk was quick, purposeful and energetic, and none who saw him could mistake his high authority.

All the officials stood and bowed to the three travelers.

The Viceroy had been travelling with his two aides Shabitqo and Taharqo. Two days had gone by since they started their ride from the Palestine town of Gaza, and the Viceroy was tired and irritable. After exchanging brief pleasantries with the local officials, he was left alone with his two aides. Taharqo sat in the corner, uncomfortable in his clothes, and anxious to unpack their belongings.

"Your Highness, you are not enchanted with this place," said Shabitqo.

"Nothing compares to our beloved Aniba," the Viceroy said.

Taharqo finished unpacking, and Sebakashta and his two aides settled down for the evening. The Viceroy thought he should review their progress with his aides. He preferred to press Shabitqo while Taharqo listened.

"Now that we are in Ezion-geber again, what is next, Shabitqo?" the Viceroy asked, testing Shabitqo.

"Your Highness," began Shabitqo, "tomorrow morning, as planned, I will leave Ezion-geber alone. I will travel west along the southern route and then off the highway to the south. I will look for any sign of the mules or the Hebrew scout."

That afternoon Shabitqo had broken away from the Viceroy and Taharqo to leave the mules at the spot agreed with Joshua. Joshua was to send a Hebrew to pick them up early this evening. Shabitqo intended to look in the hills tomorrow. If he found no sign of the Hebrew or the mules, then it would be likely that all had gone well and the Hebrew scout would be on his way with the mules to Hazeroth.

"What else?"

"I will also look for signs of Egyptian troops or patrols."

Pharaoh's generals in Thebes had been sending troops to reinforce the Egyptian armies in Syria. These troops were not under the Viceroy's command, and he preferred not to run into them.

"Yes, yes" the Viceroy said nervously. "What next?"

"Then you and Taharqo will meet with the local officials, discuss the day's events and receive their reports. By the time that is done, I will have returned. Then we will tell them we are leaving for Memphis, and take the southern highway west in the direction of Memphis."

"We will have to make sure no one is following us," the Viceroy said.

"Yes, of course, your Highness. After half a day's ride, we will turn south off the highway. Then we head to Hazeroth for the camp of the Hebrews."

"How long will that take, Shabitqo?" This was a question whose answer the Viceroy did not know. None of them had been to the camp of the Hebrews.

"I am not sure," Shabitqo continued. "If you remember, your Highness, at the last meeting, Joshua had told us that when we arrive there in two days, the Hebrews would be at Hazeroth. We should arrive there a day before the wedding."

"We have a lot ahead of us," the Viceroy said. "Let us try to have a good night's sleep."

The Viceroy gave a soft smile for Taharqo, stretched out, and turned his face toward the wall.

* * *

As he tossed and turned unable to sleep, Sebakashta reflected on the monumental events of the last few months. As a Nubian, he had formed a secret alliance with the Hebrews and his only child, his Princess Havilya, was about to marry Moses. If this shepherd could liberate the Hebrews from Pharaoh, why couldn't Sebakashta, Overseer of the Southern Lands, do the same for the Nubians? But if Pharaoh found out, all would be lost.

He could not bear to think of that possibility. I must think of Nubia, of the future of the Nubian people, he thought. We cannot allow Pharaoh to be our master much longer.

FIVE

Aaron, the High Priest, came to see Miriam late at night. From his anxious look, she thought this must be about their brother Moses. The three siblings were of Levite lineage, offspring of Amram and Yokheved. Miriam was the eldest of the three, and Moses the youngest. When Aaron was born, Amram and Yokheved doted on him because he was their first son. But Aaron was soon eclipsed by the circumstances of Moses' birth.

The Israelite slaves in Egypt were multiplying faster than the Egyptian population. Someday, the Pharaoh worried, the multitude of slaves would rise up and overthrow Pharaoh from his throne. And so the Israelite slaves were conscripted into hard labour, some of it for building temples and pyramids, but much of it in meaningless and heavy work so that the Israelite men would exert themselves to death.

When slave labour was not enough to reduce the birthrate of the Israelites, Pharaoh took a more direct approach at killing them. He issued an edict to slay the firstborn male offspring of every Israelite family. The edict was to be performed by midwives. While attending the birth of the slave baby boys, the midwives were to serve as executioners of the firstborn at the moment of their birth.

Two such midwives were Shifra and Puah, both Egyptian women conscripted for this task. But as they spent more time with the Israelite women, they discovered something new about them. In a world where infanticide was a familiar practice, and where some tribes sacrificed their own children to the pagan gods, the Israelites instead delighted in their children. This reinforced Shifra's and Puah's natural instincts, and so they could not bring themselves to obey Pharaoh's edict and execute babies.

Enraged that the midwives had not followed his orders, Pharaoh then summoned them before him. "Why have you done this thing, and saved the men-children's lives?"

And the midwives replied, "Because the Hebrew women are not as the Egyptian women; for they are lively, and deliver their babies before the midwives could come to them."

Here these two ordinary Egyptian women dared to make excuses, if not lie, to their king, who was regarded as the incarnation of the god Horus, child of the sibling gods and lovers Osiris and Isis.

"We are sorry," these valiant and righteous women told Pharaoh. "We arrive too late to strangle the baby boys."

When Pharaoh could not rely on midwives to carry out his edict, he turned to the Egyptian populace to form death squads that would hound the Israelites and kill their newborn. This was the edict in effect when Yokheved, the Hebrew slave woman, gave birth to Moses. She then hid her baby for three months. When she could no longer keep him at home, she set him adrift on the Nile in a basket of reeds. Miriam was only a young girl, and she watched the basket for one hour. This sisterly act helped ensure his safety. Then Pharaoh's daughter found and adopted the baby. She also hired Yokheved as his wet nurse, not knowing she was the baby's mother. She named her Hebrew son Moses, meaning "drawing out," as in from the water. That was how Moses grew up in Pharaoh's palace, where he was known as the Child of the Nile.

Aaron and his wife Elisheva had four sons. Not long ago, the eldest two, Nadab and Abihu, had died in a fire in the sanctuary. They would not leave when the fire broke out, for they were trying to salvage the holy objects. They were burned alive inside. Even though he had two sons remaining, Eleazar and Itamar, their father Aaron had not been the same since his two elder sons died. His face became drained of colour, his hands trembled and he stared into space. Miriam wondered how much of Aaron's judgment had remained.

"I heard about the wounded," Aaron began. "You must be tired and ready to go to bed, but I thought I would take a few minutes to talk about the wedding."

"I hear everything is in place," Miriam said.

"Yes," replied Aaron. "But I wanted you to know that there will be a celebration after the wedding. Moses is inviting all the heads of the twelve tribes and their wives. I wanted to make sure that you and Caleb would stay for the celebration."

"Of course, we will," Miriam said.

Aaron hesitated.

"I, I... also wanted to make sure you are agreeable with the seating arrangement. We will also be sitting in a rectangle. The heads of the tribes and their wives will be seated more or less in the same order as the tents of the tribes are arranged around the sanctuary."

"That sounds all right," Miriam said.

"Good," he said. "I pray that all will go well."

Then he paused, and they were both silent. Suddenly, Miriam broke the silence.

"Are you sure that is all there is?" she asked. "There must be something else on your mind. Surely, you did not come to see me this late to talk about seating arrangements?"

"No, there is nothing," he said.

Miriam pressed on.

"What about Eli?" Miriam asked about Aaron's wife.

"Of course, she has never been the same since the fire. I thought she was going to die out of pure suffering. But God has blessed us with two other sons, and they bring us solace and joy."

"And what about you, dear Aaron?"

"One never stops mourning one's lost children. The pain lingers. But we must endure. The Lord has made a covenant with us. We must be there to play our part."

"Yes, of course," Miriam said, encouragingly. "And how should we play our part now?"

"Well, I wanted to talk to you about the marriage of Moses. There are rumours that you are distressed about it. Are you? Can you tell me about it?"

"Ever since Zipporah died, I felt that Moses was finding his terrible burdens harder to bear." Miriam was referring to the first wife of Moses.

"You and me, and all the others. We are trying our best to help. But I think Moses needs a soul mate, a wife, someone to ease the daily agitation of the soul," Miriam said.

"Well, you think that a young Nubian wife will help him?" he asked.

"I think she will. I have not seen her. I have heard she is tall, black, beautiful and of noble birth. An exotic new wife could give him new zest for life."

Shaul Ezer

"What then? Is there something else to worry about in the marriage?"

"What gives me pause, Aaron, are the Egyptians. Pharaoh rules Nubia. The Nubians are Pharaoh's vassals, courtiers, soldiers, spies – they are everywhere, the eyes and ears of Pharaoh."

"But surely you don't think that the Egyptians care who Moses marries?"

"No, no, probably not. But any connection to the Egyptians makes me uneasy."

"Perhaps Moses can find happiness with a Nubian wife without the Egyptians becoming a thorn in his side," Aaron said. Then he brightened up and continued. "The ancients said that you can pluck a rose from a bush of thorns. Maybe our dear brother Moses can do that."

"Yes, maybe – maybe he can," Miriam said.

SIX

Before he could fall asleep, Shooly was startled by a soft thud on his head. As he opened his eyes, he saw a little girl, not more than eight years old, giggling and running up the ridge.

She had hit him on the head with an orange, which was now rolling down the ridge.

He caught up with her on the highway where a merchant and his wife, with two camels, seemed to be waiting for her. The merchant sat on the front camel, and his wife sat impassively on the back camel which also carried a load of oranges.

"Baba, baba!" the little girl cried, as she looked back at Shooly while she raised her arm to her father to be lifted on to his camel.

The merchant folded his arm and laughed at his daughter. "I told you to stay where I would see you. You disobeyed and disappeared down the ridge, and now you have this young man to contend with."

As the little girl screamed with fright, Shooly lifted her from her waist and onto the camel in her father's lap.

"She is lively and restless," the merchant said. "We stopped so she could run and play with an orange."

Shooly smiled and bowed toward the merchant and then toward his wife.

"What brings you here young man, without a horse or camel?"

"My horse is tied below," Shooly said. "I tend some animals for my tribe," he said, gazing away from the merchant.

Shooly changed the subject. "And what brings you here, sir?"

"Trade, my boy, trade. I go to Etzion-geber, buy what I can find. Bring it to Gaza. In a town preparing for war, one can sell anything. Today, it's oranges."

"What else can one find in Gaza?"

"Other foods. Clothes. Livestock. Sometimes weapons."

Shooly nodded.

"The villages nearby make what they can, and bring it to the market at Etzion-geber."

Shooly had heard of the small sea port there and asked about it.

"Well, yes," the merchant continued. "The market at the sea port also has goods from other nearby shores, as well as fish brought daily by the fishing boats."

Shooly was grateful for the knowledge the merchant was imparting, but he said nothing.

Suddenly, the little girl started to buck, signalling she wanted the camel to move.

"She is anxious to go to Gaza," the merchant laughed. He raised his stick and hit his camel on the side.

"Peace be with you, young man."

"And to you, sir," Shooly said.

As they rode, the woman gazed at Shooly. She had not dared to acknowledge him before, and now as her camel strode past Shooly, she looked at him. Shooly gazed back, and her eyes betrayed a sad longing.

Now he returned down the ridge to his horse. The little girl had distracted him for his urgent task, he thought, which was to find the mules of the Nubians before nightfall. He was getting hungry and the sun was setting. Perhaps he could find the orange. After he would feast on it, he would then look for the mules.

He walked further down the ridge where the orange must have rolled. He descended deeper until he reached a dry bed where a brook had once flowed. He found the orange, glistening among the grey rocks. He squatted on the ground to eat the orange, when he noticed that to his right the dry bed continued into a carvenous canopy.

Wiping his hands on his clothes, he rose and walked to follow the dry bed. Suddenly, to his relief, he saw the beautiful sight he had imagined – two mules tied to a ledge inside the canopy. They were chewing on hay that must have been left for them by the Nubians.

The Nubians had picked a good hiding spot, he thought as he stroked the mules. Almost too good. He brought his horse beside the mules, removed the load from the mules to rest them, and settled down for a good night's sleep. Early the next morning, he would set out for the return trip to Hazeroth.

As he lay down gazing at the stars, he thought of the little girl and wondered whether he would have found the mules so quickly if she had not hit him with her orange.

* * *

"Well, it's about time!"

"Hush, he will hear you."

For days the Hebrews had been lining up outside the small tent that Moses used as his tribunal, grumbling and complaining loudly as they waited. Now as their leader approached, the crowd of about fifty people became quiet.

The crowd separated respectfully to let Moses in the tent. When inside, he walked to the middle of the small tent where a knee-high chest made of wood was placed on the sandy floor. The rest of the floor was covered with pieces of thick canvas. The crowd formed a line to his left and another to his right.

Moses sat on the chest with a wooden rod in his right hand. A legend had formed around the Rod of Moses. This was the rod that was stretched over the Red Sea, pointing a pathway through its depth. It was the same rod that turned into a serpent that then swallowed Pharaoh's serpent.

This morning Moses was dealing with disputes, and his scribe Sofer stood beside him at his left.

"My Lord," Sofer said, "we have many cases today that require your wisdom and your prophecy."

"Yes, I see that."

"Some have been waiting for days to see you."

"I know, I know."

Somehow, Moses thought, he must hasten the hearing of disputes. How can they learn the rule of law when there is only one man to rule on their complaints, and they have to wait many days to see him? These delays cause loss of faith among even the learned and more so among former slaves.

"Please, let us start with the first one," said Moses, motioning to the front of the line on his left.

"The first in line, my Lord, are Shem and Lamech," the scribe said. "They have been waiting here since dawn." The ordinary Hebrews called Moses "My Lord" in deference to his upbringing as a prince of Egypt.

"Without quarrelling, I hope," Moses said, looking at the two men. "Please step forward."

The two men moved in front of Moses.

The first one said, "My name is Shem, my Lord. I am from the tribe of Zebulun. No, my Lord, we have not been quarrelling. We have agreed to bring our quarrel to you for settlement."

Shem was a short and thin young man. There were black stains on his hands and face.

"Is that correct, Lamech?" asked Moses.

"Yes, my Lord," said the man called Lamech.

Moses looked at the scribe and said, "Well, then we can begin."

Sofer then motioned to Shem. "You can begin to tell your story."

"I am a labourer," Shem began. "I started to work with Lamech two days ago making candlesticks. He agreed to pay me two baked manna pies each day. After two days of making candlesticks for him in his tent, he refused to pay me..."

"I have not refused," shouted Lamech.

"Please, please," Sofer said. "You will have your turn to speak. Let Shem finish."

"After two days of making candlesticks," Shem continued, "Lamech refused to pay me the four manna pies. I saw with my own eyes that his wife had baked many of them."

Moses was quietly pleased to see the beginnings of some commerce, however small and primitive compared to what he had seen in Egypt.

"Anything else?" asked Moses.

"Yes," said Shem, "When he did not pay me after two days of work, I stopped working unless he paid me for four days. I told him that, from now on, he must pay me for two days in advance."

Turning to Lamech, Moses said, "What do you say to this?"

Lamech stepped forward. A tall and burly figure, he wore an apron in the front, covered by a thick coat of black waxy grime.

"I am Lamech, of the tribe of Issachar. I always sell the candlesticks the day before the Sabbath. That is when our people come to buy them from me, which is another five days from now."

Moses thought of Jacob's final words to his son Issachar. He said that Issachar's descendants would be possessed of great territory; that rather than take up the sword, they would prefer to remain with their ploughshare and submit to tribute. Thus they would prefer comfort to freedom. But, Moses thought, he must dispel these reflections and not permit them to influence the hearing of this dispute.

"It is not possible for me to pay until then," Lamech pleaded. "I am known as a person of honour, and I will surely pay him for all his work in five days, if he continues to make candlesticks for me."

Turning to Shem, Moses said, "What do you say to Lamech?"

"I worked for Lamech in the camp because I did not want to work in the field looking for manna. My wife is expecting a child, and I need the baked manna to feed my family. Lamech may be a man of honour, but his honour will not feed my family."

The crowd erupted with laughter.

Motioning to the crowd, Sofer said, "Quiet, please. You must not interrupt."

Moses then paused for a few moments. He then raised his staff and brought it down, just hard enough to make a sound that silenced the crowd.

"I find Lamech must pay Shem now for the two days of work he has done. If Shem insists on payment in advance for his future labour, it is Lamech's choice to agree or not because Shem may not come back to make the candlesticks, or if he does, he may not make them properly. Lamech may choose to wait until after the work is done to pay Shem. But given the needs of Shem's family, Lamech must pay Shem before the end of each day of labour."

Shem and Lamech bowed and left the tent.

Moses turned to the scribe and said, "Sofer, you know, this is not the first time we have seen this kind of quarrel. I have given judgment in a similar case before. In that matter, I said that the wages of a hired servant had to be paid before the end of each day of labour. How soon can you write down these decisions for the people to see? It could reduce these crowds, if they learn what the judgment will be."

Sofer blushed and he bowed before Moses.

"My Lord, you may recall that our first priority was to write down the 613 commandments, and then the judgments that you have rendered. All the scribes over twenty years of age have been conscripted into the army. We only have a few aged and infirm scribes working to copy the laws and your Lordship's decisions. Our stock of writing materials is almost depleted. The papyrus we brought from Egypt has been used up. We are not making much leather parchment, as we are keeping the animals alive for carrying burden. As well, the frequent movement of the camp is slowing down the work."

Moses looked at Sofer and then at the crowd. He realized that he had embarrassed his scribe in front of many in the tent. Moses thought that he had unfairly judged Sofer's speed of work by what Moses had seen in Pharaoh's court. In Egypt, scores of academies with hundreds of scribes produced manuscripts on law, government, history and many other subjects. These academies had been established centuries ago by the Pharaohs. How could he compare the scribes of Egypt with a few old Hebrew scribes? How much could Sofer do with a few such writers, wandering in the desert and pitching their tents on sand in a different place every few days? He shook his head at the chasm between the Egyptians and his people the Israelites.

But he could not allow himself to become dejected. He then said to Sofer in a loud voice, so that all could hear, "I misspoke myself, my friend. You are doing your best under harsh conditions. The Israelite people will thank you for copying the laws given to them by God."

Moses paused to let the effect of his words sink in with the crowd. Then he said, "Next in line please."

As two other men stepped forward, suddenly a soldier in military garb rushed into the tent.

Everyone recognized Joshua, the chief aide of Moses. He was short and stocky. Muscles were visible in his chest and thighs. His pale but weather-beaten skin offered a sharp contrast to his full head of black hair and his beard. It was easy to trust him because of his soft blue eyes and benign face. Now he was in full battle dress, with armour on his chest and a sword at his side.

"My Lord," he said to Moses. "I have some bad news. I was in training camp with the soldiers this morning when a scout brought me the news. I rushed here at once."

Joshua looked at the crowd in the tent, and Moses motioned to the scribe to clear them out.

"We have to end this morning's session," Sofer told the crowd. "Come back tomorrow."

Howls of protest erupted. There was jostling among the crowd.

"What is the bad news?" one shouted. "Why doesn't anyone tell us anything?"

It was not hard for Sofer to prevail on them to leave Moses and Joshua alone. They knew the trust that Moses placed in Joshua, who alone could interrupt Moses in a public gathering, and would not do so unless the matter was of urgent importance. They could not forget that when Moses was asked to go up Mount Sinai to receive the Law, Joshua was invited to be part of a small party to accompany him. Aaron and Hur were with Moses, and as Moses set off in the direction of the mountain, only young Joshua, the hero of the battle of Rephidim, followed. It was said that Moses preferred Joshua as a confidant over his own brother. Then Moses continued alone to the peak of Mount Sinai and even the trusted Joshua went no farther. During the forty days and nights when Moses was in the mountain receiving the Law, Joshua was selected to look after the sanctuary.

Finally, at the end of the forty days and nights, Moses had turned and went down from the mountain. He carried the two stone tablets on which God had inscribed the divine law. It was Joshua who had met Moses on his way down the mountain, and the two of them had descended together to the camp of the Israelites.

A strong bond developed between Moses and Joshua, and few Hebrews understood it well. Both were men of courage but they came by their courage in different circumstances. When Moses was forty years old, he was still living in luxury as a prince of Egypt in Pharaoh's palace. To the Egyptian rulers, he was still a Hebrew, and largely ignored whenever important

military or political positions needed to be filled. Even though
he was bright, alert and able-bodied, he was nonetheless
inactive, and his idleness gave way to brooding, moodiness and a
feeling of being unloved by his Egyptian family. So his brooding
led to thinking of his Hebrew family and their oppression. One
day he saw an Egyptian smiting a Hebrew, and in a sudden
outburst of anger, Moses struck and killed the Egyptian
taskmaster, and hid his body in the sand. The Hebrews had
resented his royal upbringing while they toiled as slaves, and
now when they discovered his crime, some had treated him with
contempt. Moses realized that word of his deed would spread
from the Hebrews to Pharaoh's court, so his rash attack had
turned him into a fugitive from Pharaoh's justice. Thus he fled
from Egypt and dwelt in the land of Midian, where he worked as
a shepherd for Jethro the priest and married his daughter
Zipporah. Joshua, on the other hand, grew up as the son of a
Hebrew slave. Life for him was a struggle in hard labour and
hunger. And so, it was said by the wise men, that while Moses,
unloved by both his Egyptian and Hebrew families, came by his
courage to seek love, Joshua came by his courage in order to
survive.

When the last person in the crowd left the tent, Joshua
began.

"The men of Simeon and Gad, my Lord, do you
remember?"

"The ones who wanted to attack a caravan for food?"
Moses asked.

"Yes, my Lord."

"Miriam and I forbade them."

"Yes, but a hundred of them went anyway. They
attacked a caravan which was heavily armed. Most of them were
killed. About 40 survived, and managed to reach Miriam's tent
at night."

The face of Moses became red. He held his rod with both
hands, raised it above his head and brought it crashing down on
the wooden chest. Joshua held Moses' trembling hands. Joshua
was the only one who knew Moses well, a meek man of few
words who could sometimes erupt in uncontrolled anger. There
was a war raging in the soul of Moses, Joshua thought. Not one
war, but many. To be brought up in Pharaoh's palace, and then

to become an outcast in Egypt. To become a shepherd in Midian, then to lead massive construction projects in Egypt. To rub shoulders with the learned in Egypt, then to lead a horde of slaves. To live under the oppression of one Pharaoh, then to build a nation on the rule of law. To teach justice and mercy, then to learn to fight wars with hostile tribes. To bring together a jealous and demanding God with an impatient and thankless people.

Joshua tried to calm down his master. "Miriam and her helpers are caring for the wounded. I will order more drilling and training for the men, so that they will not stray in their missions."

Moses nodded.

Joshua thought that he must not let the mourning for the dead Hebrew renegades delay the wedding. He knew that Moses needed the love and soft touch of a woman. The Nubians had put themselves in great danger to travel to the camp of the Hebrews. No matter what happened, the wedding of Moses must go on.

"The Nubians will arrive on the evening after tomorrow," Joshua said. "Everything is set for your wedding the following day."

Moses went into a deep, thoughtful silence. He thought of his dear Havilya. A smile crossed his lips as he thought how terrified they had been just before meeting the Nubians. He remembered how he, Joshua and Zabad had ridden their horses near the spot that Shabitqo had shown Zabad four weeks earlier.

"Take us to a high spot, Zabad," Joshua had told him. "As near as possible to the meeting place. I want us to wait and watch."

They had stood silently for what seemed an eternity. A mirage had formed in the distance in the hot afternoon sun. Suddenly, three moving specks had become visible in the horizon. Then three riders on horseback had come into view, and had stopped just past where Zabad said they would. They had remained on their horses with one hand on the bridle and one hand held high above their heads pointing at the sky. This was the signal Zabad had been waiting for. He had told Moses and Joshua that they were to approach from an open space in a similar manner. As the Hebrews approached, the Viceroy had dismounted and he and his two aides bowed low.

The Viceroy had spoken first.

"O, Liberator of Slaves! Prophet of the Divine God of the Hebrews! We have come to pay homage to you."

Moses remembered how moved he had been by the deference to him, a leader of a band of former slaves. He and his two companions now had bowed to the Nubians, and Moses said, "O, Son of Cush, Mighty Commander of Gaza, we are humbled by the graciousness of one so powerful. We offer you the peace and friendship of our people."

Shabitqo had pointed to a shady spot nearby, hidden from view, and the six of them had sat down on the rocky ground.

The Viceroy had got to the point quickly. "We are in danger of being discovered. So we must make haste. My people have been suffering for centuries under Egyptian rule. They long to gain their freedom. The liberation of the Hebrews has inspired the Nubian masses. We admire the Great Hebrew Liberator and seek his counsel as teacher and ally."

Joshua had nodded.

Moses had then said, "My people have been slaves for many centuries. We are small in number against the hosts of Pharaoh, and are not trained in the arts of war. But to become a nation and to defend ourselves, we must learn. And we are learning. But how can we help the Son of Cush and his people?"

"Pharaoh is now engaged in a major war in Syria with the Hittites. If we start a revolt in Nubia, and at the same time the Hebrews open another battlefront against Pharaoh from Sinai, we can break Pharaoh's hold."

Moses remembered how elated he had become when he had heard those words. Here was the leader and warrior of the great Nubian nation desiring to form an alliance with the Hebrews against Pharaoh. Could it be, Moses had thought, could it be that Israel will really become a nation to be reckoned with? Moses had told the Viceroy that he agreed with the proposal.

Moses smiled to himself as he thought about that first meeting with the Nubians, and how intrigued he had been with the young Taharqo. The Viceroy's aide had seemed older and wiser than his age. Initially Taharqo had talked about Egypt's recent history, especially about the Pharaoh Akhenaten, who had ruled only three generation ago. This heretic king moved the capital from Thebes to a new city in Nubia called Amarna, closed all the major temples and forced Egyptians to abandon the old gods and follow him in the worship of the sun disk, the Aten. Akhenaten settled within the borders of his new city and swore never to leave it. The old priesthood, angry and dispossessed, led a rebellion against the king and his new religion. With the unrest, the populace neglected the fields, causing widespread famine and plagues. When Akhenaten died, his city was destroyed by order of the priests of Karnak who were determined to eradicate all traces of the heretical pharaoh's new religion. He was succeeded by several young and weak kings.

During this period of chaos, neighboring peoples to the north seized this chance to claim Egypt's foreign possessions in Syria – Palestine. Some like the Hebrews managed to gain their freedom and escaped from Egypt.

"Why do you tell me all this, Taharqo?" Moses had asked. "I, too, have studied Egyptian history."

"Because you seized the moment of Egyptian weakness to free your people. I wish we Nubians had done the same." Moses remembered Taharqo's look of admiration tinged with affection toward him.

Moses and his Hebrew companions had then parted from the Nubians, to reflect and to meet again four weeks hence.

As if awakening from his deep thoughts, Moses said to Joshua, "Yes, of course the wedding must go on."

Moses paused, and then said, "And another thing, we must speed up the hearing of the disputes and complaints. I want you to summon seventy of the most learned elders and bring them to me."

"Yes, of course, my Lord," Joshua said with a bright smile. He liked to see his master in control again.

Hebrew Encampment at Hazeroth

N
W ✝ **E**
S

Dan Division

Asher   Dan   Naphtali

Ephraim Division

Benjamin

Ephraim

Manasseh

Levites

Merarites

Gershanites

Tent of Revelation

Sons of Aaron

Kohathites

Judah Division

Issachar

Judah

Zebulun

Gad   Reuben   Simeon

Reuben Division

SEVEN

To avoid recapture, the Hebrews needed to stay clear of Pharaoh's spies and soldiers. After receiving the Law on Mount Sinai, the Hebrew encampment wandered in the area they called Hazeroth, which was located about two days' march north of the mountain. Further north and another two days' march away lay the east-west highway, called the southern highway. Except for scouts and adventurers, the Hebrew encampment had not yet reached the southern highway. The Hebrew scouts had discovered that, after traveling due north from Hazeroth and reaching the southern highway, it was only another day's ride eastward to Ezion-geber, a dusty and bustling provincial town with cool breezes from the sea. None dared travel too far westward along that highway, for that was the direction toward Memphis where they would be in danger of encountering Egyptians or their Nubian soldiers. Thus the Hebrews, numbering about twenty-five thousand, were encamped in a valley surrounded by low hills in the middle of a desert wilderness far from a highway and hidden from travelers.

The central portion of the encampment was called the Camp of the Shechinah, or Camp of the Divine Presence. This comprised the tents of the Levitical families, including Moses and Aaron, and the Tent of Revelation. God had told the Hebrews that this would be the place "where I will meet with you."

A protective cordon of camps surrounded the Camp of the Shechinah. These were the camps of the Levites which also included the Gershonites, Kohathides and Merarites. They were responsible to protect, furnish and administer the Camp of the Shechinah. The Levite tents formed an inner square around the Tent of Revelation. When the Hebrews were on the move, the Levites dismantled the Tent of Revelation and carried its parts and accessories in the march with the other tribes.

Surrounding the protective cordon of the inner square of the Levite camps were the camps of the Twelve Tribes. These were arranged in an outer square in accordance with an arrangement prescribed by Moses. The Annex where Miriam treated the wounded was located just outside the camps of the Twelve Tribes.

Word of the wounded in the Annex had spread through the Hebrew encampment. The crowd had also heard that Joshua had brought news to Moses that had shaken the Hebrew leader. The horde from the Annex had merged with the one outside the tent of Moses, resulting in a large and noisy throng near the Tent of Revelation. This crowd wanted some answers, and they knew their leaders Moses, Aaron and Miriam, would likely be found in this vicinity.

Outside the Tent of Revelation, the crowd was becoming louder. Joshua had implored Moses to go back to his tent, and the Hebrew leader reluctantly consented. He was then spirited away to his tent with two soldiers. Joshua had them send for Miriam and Aaron to help defuse the situation.

Joshua wanted Aaron beside him because as the High Priest, Aaron could reassure and console those who were grieving. Aaron was also seen as the priestly representative of Moses, through whom their prayers could reach God.

But it was Miriam, Joshua thought, whom the crowd needed to see. When they were sad and dispirited, she was the one who would lead them in song, as she did when they were escaping from Egypt. When they were sick, she took care of them. They felt that she was watching over them, as she had watched over the baby Moses in the basket until Pharaoh's daughter found him. This is the time, Joshua thought, when the Hebrews needed Miriam's buoyant spirit.

As Aaron neared the sanctuary, it took him little time to join Joshua in front of the crowd. The two of them waited for Miriam to arrive from the Annex. Voices from the crowd could be heard clearly.

"Why are there wounded in the Annex? Are we going to be killed by the soldiers of Pharaoh?" one shouted.

"Did we leave Egypt to become food for vultures in the wilderness?"

"Either we are going to starve here or be killed by the long arm of Pharaoh!"

To get near the sanctuary, Miriam had to walk through the camps of the Judah division. The Annex was as far as it could be from the sanctuary and still be in the Hebrew encampment.

The twelve tribes were split into four divisions, each comprising three tribes. Each division was named after its leading tribe. The Reuben division consisted of the Reuben, Simeon and Gad tribes and its camp was the south side of the outer square. The Judah division consisted of the Judah, Zebulun and Issachar tribes. Their camps formed the east side of the outer square. The north side of the outer square were the camps of the Dan division of the Dan, Asher and Naphtali tribes. Finally, on the west side was the Ephraim division comprising the Ephraim, Manasseh and Benjamin tribes. Miriam was married to Caleb of the tribe of Judah, whose camp formed the east side of the outer square. In order to be close to Caleb's tent, the Annex was pitched just east of the camps of the Judah division.

Miriam hurried between the various tents in a firm and dignified gait, as the crowd continued voicing complaints, many all too familiar. The dry wilderness was making it more difficult to find the occasional oasis and short dry grass to feed the oxen, mules, sheep and horses that the Hebrews kept with them. The Hebrews themselves were usually hungry, sustained mainly by desert manna and what they could steal by raiding caravans. They longed for the abundance of food in Egypt, then rich from the farms on the Nile. Many dreaded the savagery of the foreign tribes they might encounter in the wilderness. Gaining their freedom now paled in importance, as they faced starvation in the desert and massacre by giants who would kill and devour them.

Now Miriam stood in front of the crowd between Aaron and Joshua. She had an apron over her dress and both were bloodstained from tending to the wounded. She raised her hand, signalling for calm.

"Listen to me," Miriam said. The crowd started to quiet down. They knew that Miriam would not hold back, that she would tell them what she knew.

"There were one hundred men from the tribes of Simeon and Gad. They went off on their own to attack a caravan for food and booty. Moses had warned them not to go. But they did not listen. So they went ahead. But the caravan they attacked was armed. Only a few managed to return."

A murmur went through the crowd.

"Yes, the others are all dead."

Joshua then stepped forward. "I will send some soldiers to find the dead. Aaron the High Priest will send two priests with them. They will give the dead a proper burial."

"God bless their souls," someone in the crowd said.

"What will become of us?" another said.

"Everyone, please go back to your business," Miriam said. "Have faith in Moses and in God."

This was not the first time that Miriam resorted to the laws of Moses to calm down the people. She sensed that many were finding it tiresome and austere. She had to admit to herself that she was also starting to resent her younger brother. As one of the women grumbled to her, "Your younger brother Moses goes out in the wilderness, comes back after a long absence, and he tells us he has been speaking to God. Then suddenly we must obey dozens of new commandments that only Moses has heard about? Enough!"

Slowly, the crowd started to disperse. Miriam, Joshua and Aaron lingered so that any who wished could speak to them.

A woman spoke to Miriam and Aaron.

"Both my son and my husband are missing," the woman sobbed. "They went off with the others, and neither of them is in the Annex with the other wounded."

Aaron put his hand on her shoulder in sympathy.

"I cannot go on until I see their bodies and that they are given a proper burial."

Miriam put her arms around her. "As soon as Joshua's soldiers find them, they will take you to the grave site to be with them."

Joshua nodded.

Miriam continued, "What is your name?"

"I am Leah of the tribe of Simeon."

"I will send one of the women to be with you at night," Miriam said. "During the day, you must come to see me in the Annex. I don't want you to be alone."

"God bless you, Miriam."

The women then gathered around Miriam. Some wanted to touch her, others just to be near her. Another man stepped forward to speak to Joshua.

"When will my complaint be heard? I have been waiting to see Moses for months. Is there any purpose in waiting anymore?"

"Be patient," Joshua said. "Moses will hear you. If he cannot hear you soon, he will arrange for another wise elder to hear your matter."

The man gave Joshua his name and his tent location.

Joshua then turned to Miriam. "The multitude does not know where to turn," he said. "They are preoccupied and fearful."

After a long silence, she said, "You know, Joshua, there is no alternative to optimism."

EIGHT

"Breakfast is served, your Highness," said the cook.

The Viceroy and his two aides Shabitqo and Taharqo had just woken up. After washing and putting on fresh clothes, they walked into the dining room. They were greeted by Esau, the local commander of Ezion-geber.

"Good morning, your Highness. I hope the gods brought you pleasant dreams last night."

"Good morning, Esau. Not as pleasant as the food you have prepared for us."

The Viceroy pointed to the food on the table. The cook had prepared a sumptuous meal, including two types of bread, a thin dark Syrian *lavash* and a thick white Persian *berberi*. A large plate of goat cheese was placed beside each bread, with date syrup and honey. The Viceroy recognized the famous local fried pancake called *arok*, made of eggs, ground beef, onions and parsley.

The Viceroy picked up an *arok*. Taking a bite, he said, "Delicious. I smelt the fried oil this morning."

"May it please your Highness," Esau said. "We also have a nice surprise for you." As he motioned to the cook, he said to him, "Tell us about the new dish."

"Yes, my Lord," the cook said, pointing to a pot of hard-boiled eggs. "These eggs have been browned as the Hebrews cook them."

"It seems the Hebrews are not just builders," said Esau. "That's why Pharaoh wants them back," he continued, laughing, "for their cooking."

The Viceroy kept silent. Then Esau said, "If Pharaoh had them only cooking eggs, maybe they would not have escaped."

They all laughed, as they took their seats around the dining table.

"I will start with a hot drink," the Viceroy said. The cook had prepared a pitcher of hot goat's milk. The Viceroy then said to the cook, "You have prepared a feast. I may have to order Esau to transfer you to Gaza. We could use your cooking talents."

"I am at your service, my Lord," the cook said bowing.

Shaul Ezer

"Now Esau, what is the next task?" The Viceroy liked to work while dining with his officials.

"Your Highness, as you know, Pharaoh is mobilizing to fight the Hittites. Troops, equipment and supplies are on their way to Syria. Both northern highways are busy with the preparations for war." Esau was referring to the Way of the Sea along the Palestine coast and the Way of Shur.

"Some troops and equipment are being diverted to the southern highway. Their origin is Pithom and Succoth. Ezion-geber is their main resting point before they turn north toward Syria."

The Viceroy got to the point. "You need more money to look after the new influx of troops in town."

"You are prescient and wise, your Highness," Esau said.

"You must have a budget prepared."

"I do, your Highness."

"Well, we don't need everyone here to deal with that."

This was the signal for Shabitqo to leave. He got up and bowed.

"Thank you for an excellent meal. This will do me till dinner time."

As planned, Shabitqo would go to look for signs of the two mules and the Hebrew scout. He would also look for Egyptian troop movements. He would then return to Ezion-geber to join the Viceroy and Taharqo. From there, they would travel west along the southern highway, ostensibly for Memphis.

The Viceroy was now alone with his aide Taharqo and with Esau. The cook brought in more food – some sweets and fresh fruit.

Biting on a peach, the Viceroy said, "Let's take a look at your budget, Esau."

Taharqo's mind started to wander. Of course, among the Egyptians and the Nubians, only Shabitqo and the Viceroy knew his secret – that Taharqo was a male aide in Ezion-geber, but really the Princess Havilya at home in Gaza. She enjoyed the double life. As a woman and a princess, she was courted by all the eligible young nobles. As an only child, her mother and father doted on her.

But cooking and sewing was not for her. She wanted to be with her father, learning the affairs of state. It had been a struggle to convince her father that she wanted to travel with him on business.

"The life of a court official is not for a woman," he had said. "It is bad enough for men – the cunning court snakes professing to be in the service of the King. Their sole aim in life is to advance their cause and destroy their rivals."

"Father, remember the stories you told me as a child. How for centuries Nubian warriors have been fighting Egyptians for freedom and for control of the Nile settlements."

"If you can survive the snakes in the court, then there are the real snakes in the wilderness, to say nothing of thieves and brigands. Traveling from outpost to outpost is full of danger."

"You have gone through all of that yourself, father. Why is it different for me?"

"Because you are a beautiful young woman. That makes you a more enticing target."

"The Nubian warriors you told me about were not just men. Great women fighters became leaders of Nubia."

"That may be so. But I hate to see you become vulnerable."

"Father, the fight for Nubia is not for Nubian men alone. You cannot do it by yourselves. The women must do their part. I want to do mine. This is what I want to be. Am I not my father's daughter?"

This was what her mother Sebaha called her – "your father's daughter" – because Havilya wanted so much to be like him.

He had gone silent for a long while. Then he had said at last, "We will try it. But you must be disguised as a man. It is the only way for you to be safe."

Havilya had been elated. "The name for my new persona will be Taharqo, after the ancient Nubian warrior."

"Of course, Havilya," he had said with a smile. "I am starting to enjoy being with my new warrior aide."

Havilya now noticed that the Viceroy finished checking the budget line by line. Then he asked Esau, "Is there any excess in this budget. I trust you to be candid with me."

"Maybe yes, maybe no. It all depends on how many troops come through Ezion-geber. I have no control over that. As you can see, I have made certain assumptions about the level of troops moving through the town.   If your Highness has knowledge of the size and timing of the troop movements, we can change the budget accordingly."

"You are an honest administrator, Esau. I will go with your numbers."

* * *

Sebakashta liked dealing with the small town officials in Ezion-geber. They were innocent, forthright and undemanding, unlike the officials he left behind in Gaza. He was always uneasy about being away from Gaza for too long. Reyes, the former governor of Gaza, had been seething with resentment ever since Pharaoh had appointed Sebakashta to become the commander in Gaza. This meant that Reyes, a proud Syrian, was subservient to him, a foreign Nubian.

Reyes was the descendant of an old Syrian family. Except for a few wealthy merchants, most of his ancestors had been warriors and generals. His family had been the local rulers for a long time. Even when an outside power conquered Syria, the conqueror looked to the Reyes family to govern.   The Pharaohs had always appointed a Reyes to be governor of a region like Palestine or Syria. Until now.

Sebakashta had sensed Reyes's quiet anger.

"Pharaoh sent me here to help with the threat from the Hittites. As soon as that is over, I am sure his Majesty will re-assign me and restore you to your position."

"Hittites, Egyptians, Nubians. They all come and go. But the Syrians will always be here. Justice is our ally and eternity our guide," Reyes had scoffed.

Sebakashta knew he could not appease the Syrian, unless he resigned his position to him, an act which would certainly offend Pharaoh.

"We can work together, can't we?   Until we defeat the Hittites. I will see to it that Pharaoh will reward your loyalty."

"My loyalty is not in question. I will be at your service, and Pharaoh knows he can count on my devotion."

The Syrian had bowed low to him. But he had learned to be wary of excessive grovelling.

NINE

"This is incredible!" exclaimed Shooly to himself. "Is this a nightmare?"

No, he had just woken up. He stretched his arms and rubbed his eyes as he looked north from the ridge toward the southern highway. Several platoons of Egyptian soldiers were camped just below on the other side of the highway.

As his heart pounded, he ran frantically to the drop behind him. The two mules and his horse were just as he had left them the night before.

The sun was rising over the horizon to his right in an orange ball. The cool morning air was quickly giving way to a warm haze. He crawled to the top of the ridge to get a better look at the overnight visitors. There were about seventy soldiers and twenty-six horses. Twenty cavalry seemed to be leading fifty infantry and six supply horses.

Many of the soldiers were black Nubians. He remembered what Joshua had told him about the ferocity of the Nubians, and he could imagine what they would be like. Now, for the first time he was looking at black Nubian warriors under Pharaoh's arms.

From the tracks on the highway, it looked as though they were moving east toward Ezion-geber. He and Joshua had known for a long time that Pharaoh was reinforcing his troops in Syria for a major assault against the Hittites. Most of those troops seemed to be moving toward Syria along the coast through Gaza.

What were these Egyptian and Nubian warriors doing so far south in the Sinai? They were not routine patrols or scouts. They carried too many arms and supplies for that mission. Shooly had no time to speculate about the soldiers. He needed to calm down and get back to camp. Make haste, Joshua would have said, but slowly and carefully. Shooly quietly packed his mules and led them out of the drop with his horse. As soon as he was a safe distance south from the soldiers, he galloped the mules as fast as he could.

As he and the animals traveled over the world, he thought of Debra. Suddenly, he wanted so much to hear her talk and laugh, and feel her touch his arm, as she liked to do when he told her his jokes.

If I make it safely, the first thing I will do is see Debra, he thought.

* * *

"Good work, Shooly," Joshua said as he watched two of his men unload the two mules. "The wedding guests will eat well."

He put his arm around Shooly's shoulder.

"Tell me about the Egyptian soldiers again. Everything. How many men, animals, arms, the whole thing."

After Shooly told him what he had seen for the third time, Joshua said, "We can't be sure if they are moving north to fight the Hittites. As you said, they may stay around Ezion-geber to look for us. We have to watch them. We don't want to stray anywhere near them."

Joshua became silent for a while. Then he said, "Another thing, Shooly. Keep all this to yourself. Not a word to anyone, understand?"

"Yes, sir."

Joshua did not want word of the Egyptian force to spread through the Hebrew encampment. Their morale was in any event low, with the constant wandering, inadequate food and shelter and the dead and wounded still to contend with. Word of the Egyptian soldiers could turn dejection into alarm, which Joshua did not want to deal with, especially with Moses about to marry a Nubian princess.

Joshua was now deep in thought. What were the Egyptian and Nubian soldiers doing there? The Viceroy had not mentioned there would be an Egyptian or Nubian force nearby. But his last meeting with the Viceroy was almost four weeks ago. If there had been a change in plans, surely the Viceroy could have got word to him. On the other hand, the Viceroy might have thought it too dangerous to send a message. If the messenger was intercepted by Pharaoh's spies, their secret alliance could be exposed.

Maybe Pharaoh was sending this military force to gather troops against the Hittites. A force assembled east of the Salt Sea and the Mountains of Moab could march north of the Sea of Galilee and out flank the Hittites from the east. The Hittites would be facing Pharaoh's forces from two fronts – the main force from the south, and another from the east.

A more frightening thought occurred to him. What if Pharaoh sent this force to look for the Hebrews? Could it be that Pharaoh was making good his threat to find and capture the Hebrews and return them to Egypt? If so, this force would likely remain at a base in Ezion-geber. He would need some help from his spies.

The Viceroy will be here tomorrow, Joshua thought. He will at least tell us if this force is under his direct Gaza command, or under the command of Memphis. Then we will decide what to do.

"Shooly," he said finally. "Take two days of rest. You have earned it."

* * *

"Miriam, have you heard the latest?"

Aaron had rushed over to see her as soon as he had heard the news.

"What?" asked his older sister from behind a curtain.

Miriam was equally surprised. She did not expect him to find her where she was now, at the tent of Dinah and Seth. Dinah was in labour, and Miriam and Debra had been called.

"A new organization. Seventy Elders. All of them are to become judges."

"Yes?"

"This will be headed up by a Chief Judge."

Miriam had drawn a curtain over the bed. Dinah was moaning with pain, about to deliver her child.

"Everything looks fine, Dinah," he heard Miriam saying. "Just keep pushing. Debra here will watch you. I will not be far away."

She left Debra holding Dinah's hand as the woman screamed and pushed. Miriam then came out from behind the curtain.

"How did you hear?" Miriam asked as she wiped her hand in a towel.

"From one of my aides who heard it from Joshua's assistant."

"What of it?"

"The rumour is that Nun will be the Chief Judge."

"From the tribe of Ephraim?"

"Yes."

"Seems like a fine person to me."

"But Nun will report directly to Moses."

"Is that a problem?"

"Well, this will take away from my authority."

"But you will continue to be High Priest."

"I think so, but..."

The screaming from behind the curtain became louder.

"It is coming out," shouted Debra. "Miriam, Miriam, please hurry."

Miriam walked back behind the curtain.

"Keep pushing, dear. It is almost there."

The fierce crying of a newborn baby pierced the air.

"It's a girl, it's a girl," said Debra.

As Debra held the baby, Miriam cut the umbilical cord and then examined the baby.

"Ten toes, ten fingers, two eyes, one nose and one mouth. The most perfect baby girl. May God bless you and your mother."

Miriam washed and wrapped the baby as Debra tended to Dinah.

"You are lucky, Dinah. The High Priest is here. I will bring him in to bless you and the new baby. Aaron, you can come in now."

The High Priest came in to see Dinah sitting upright and holding the baby.

"It is wonderful to see a new being, in the arms of her mother."

"Yes," said Miriam.

Aaron put one hand on Dinah and the other on the baby girl. Then he recited the well-known three-part Priestly Blessing: "The Lord bless you and keep you. The Lord make his face shine upon you, and be gracious to you. The Lord lift up his countenance upon you, and give you peace."

"Thank you, thank you," Dinah said with tears in her eyes as she touched Aaron's arm.

After a long pause while everyone stared at the baby, Miriam ushered Aaron and Debra out and put the baby in a nearby crib.

"Try to sleep now, Dinah. In a short while, we will wake you to nurse your new baby girl."

Miriam emerged from behind the curtain.

"What were you saying earlier, Aaron?"

"I was saying that this would take away from my authority."

"How?"

"I would have thought that the new group of judges should report to me as the High Priest."

"Don't you have more than enough to do with all the priesthood and the sanctuary under your care?"

"This is a related area."

"I don't know how related it is. The point is, do you have time to do it all?"

"What annoys me is that I have not been consulted. I had to hear it from a junior aide instead of directly from Moses."

Miriam sympathized with Aaron and his hurt feelings. They both knew that while Moses was their younger brother, he was somehow distant from them. Much of that was due to his royal upbringing in Pharaoh's palace, while they grew up in a house of slaves. But there was another dimension to Moses that sometimes made them feel like strangers to him. He usually seemed to be in a trance, and his dealings with them as siblings struck Miriam as insensitive and mercurial. She shared Aaron's resentment of Moses, but she knew she dared not unleash it to Aaron at this moment. She felt that they must maintain a semblance of family unity, for if they, Moses' siblings, questioned his ways, then so would everyone else, which could then lead to catastrophic consequences for them and their fellow Hebrews.

"Aaron, Aaron. We have known for a long time that Moses cannot hear and judge all the cases. He needs help. You and I have too much to do as it is."

"I could handle a few cases."

"One or two additional judges will not be enough. A whole group is needed. This is a whole new type of official. It requires training, record keeping and administration."

"All of these duties can be performed by clerks and scribes. They could all come under my authority."

Miriam fell silent for a moment.

"Aaron, remember the importance of what you have to do. You are to manage the sacred duties associated with God's house. Now it is the sanctuary. In the future, it will be a permanent temple. This sacred duty belongs to you only and your direct descendants."

"Yes, I know."

"If you take on too much more, you may fail both in your sacred duty and as Chief Judge."

"Do you think I should speak to Moses?"

"It is better to do one thing well than two things badly. You can always talk to Moses. But before you do, think it over."

"I will, Miriam. I will think it over."

He then kissed his sister on the forehead and left the tent.

TEN

It was late afternoon when Shabitqo had returned to Ezion-geber from his mission.   To Sebakashta, he appeared unusually tense and his face was as pale as the desert sand.   The Viceroy sensed that he must make a move.

"Well, Esau.   This has been a productive day.   You have been thorough with all your briefings.   If Pharaoh had more officials as efficient as you, his Majesty's empire would be more secure."

"You are most kind, your Highness."   He stood up and bowed.

"Now Esau, we can no longer impose on your hospitality. We must be on our way to Gaza."

When Sebakashta and his two aides had ridden a safe distance outside Ezion-geber, the Viceroy stopped suddenly.

"Shabitqo, you are as nervous as a pigeon eyeing a cat. Any problems with the mules or the Hebrews?"

"I found no sign of the mules or the Hebrew scout.   But on the way back, I saw an Egyptian force of seventy men marching toward Ezion-geber."

"These are not under my command."

"I know.   That is why I rushed back.   I wanted us to leave Ezion-geber before they arrived."

"Any reason?"

"Protocol would have required you to stay.   At least to exchange pleasantries with their commander, and possibly co-ordinate our forces with them.   That would have delayed us, or at worst prevented us from reaching the Hebrews at Hazeroth."

"Good thinking.   What else?"
"The Egyptian force is heading toward us.   We must avoid them. We must turn south toward Hazeroth right now."

The Viceroy turned to Taharqo.   "What do you think the Egyptians are doing here?"

"Well, your Highness, there are two possibilities." Taharqo was disciplined to address the Viceroy formally.   Even in the presence of Shabitqo, who knew Taharqo's real identity, Taharqo did not want to fall into a careless laxness that might one day reveal his secret.

"Either the Egyptian force is riding north to Syria to fight the Hittites, or they intend to remain in the Ezion-geber area to look for the Hebrews."

"Which do you think it is?"

"From Shabitqo's description, they are carrying a lot of armour. That is needed to fight the Hittites. If they intended to hunt down the Hebrews, they would have traveled much lighter. They need to manoeuvre in these hills and mountains to find and capture the Hebrews. All that armour will slow them down."

"A good possibility, but not conclusive."

"Why not?"

"You can't assume that the generals in Memphis will think logically. They would have made a decision by consensus, which would probably be wrong strategically."

"We are both guessing. We will need to find out more."

"Yes, and we will do so in due course."

The Viceroy knew he would learn more either in Ezion-geber or upon his return to Gaza.

What was worrying him was why Memphis was keeping him in the dark about these troop movements. Was it bad communication or some other sinister purpose?

He would find out about that, too, he thought.

It was getting dark. They camped that night at the bottom of a hill. It was the same spot they picked to meet the Hebrews. They could see the ashes from the fire they had started to cook the mutton. Tomorrow, they would see the Hebrew encampment for the first time.

* * *

As Havilya lay down for the night, she gazed at the star-lit sky. She thought of that evening when she had first discovered the side of Moses that no one else knew.

The sun had set. The Nubians had finished their talks with the Hebrews. The Viceroy and Shabitqo had been sitting around the campfire with Joshua and Zabad. Fresh meat had been cooking on several skewers. Moses had got up to walk in the nearby hill. Havilya still could not explain to herself how or why, but somehow she had gone up to walk with him. He had seemed happy to have company.

"It is a fine night, Taharqo. Good for walking to clear one's mind."

"Yes, my Lord."

"For a young man, you have good mastery of the facts and figures. The Viceroy places great confidence in you."

"It is my work. I enjoy it. Do you enjoy yours?"

"I never thought of it that way. When God gives us a task, he does not ask us that question."

Without being inquisitive, Havilya had hoped he would talk about himself.

"You have had many tasks in your life."

Moses told Havilya the circumstances of his birth and how he grew up in Pharaoh's palace where he became known as the Child of the Nile. He grew up, as a grandson of Pharaoh, to be a young man of education and privilege. He told her how those days of privilege in Pharaoh's palace ended abruptly when, to rescue a Hebrew slave from his Egyptian taskmaster, Moses beat the Egyptian to death. He then feared that he would be betrayed to Pharaoh by those who witnessed this deed.

Moses had told Havilya how he then fled to Midian, and how the Prince of Egypt had suddenly become a fugitive. He then married Zipporah, a daughter of a Midian priest. They had two sons, Gershon and Eliezer. For many years, he worked as a shepherd in the wilderness tending his father-in-law's flock.

At this point, Havilya had interrupted, "Is your family now with you in Hazeroth?"

"My two sons are now married with their own families. But my wife Zipporah of blessed memory died some time ago."

Moses had then continued to tell his life's story to Havilya.

"One day in Midian, a remarkable thing happened to me, Taharqo. I was chasing a goat up a mountain and suddenly I felt the voice of God talking to me, telling me that my people are suffering in Egypt, that I must return to Egypt to free them from Pharaoh's oppression and take them to Canaan, a land flowing with milk and honey. So I returned to Egypt with my wife and two sons, where I joined my brother Aaron, my sister Miriam and the other Hebrew slaves in the struggle for freedom from Pharaoh."

Shaul Ezer

He had then told Havilya that he found Egypt had changed since the time he had fled as a fugitive. Now it was ridden with famine and sickness, and Pharaoh's hold on his people seemed to have weakened. He found the Hebrews longing for a new way and a new leader, and they heartily embraced Moses as a leader, as one who has received the call from God and who knew the ways of the court of Pharaoh. Then he and Aaron set out from their slave quarters to confront Pharaoh in his palace. The monarch was adamant that he would not free his Hebrew slaves. Pharaoh, having to deal with the many crises facing Egypt, eventually relented. Before the Hebrews could cross Egypt's borders, Pharaoh had a change of heart and ordered six hundred chariots to defeat the fleeing Hebrews and return them to Egypt.

Havilya could hardly wait to hear what happened next. She had heard rumours of the miracle at the sea, but now she was about to receive a direct account.

Moses had then related how, with the help of God, the waters parted by means of strong east wind that blew all night and turned the seabed into dry land. He then led the Hebrews across. By the time Pharaoh's chariots could reach them, the waters had returned and drowned the Egyptian soldiers.

"At the moment of this glorious victory over Pharaoh," Moses had told her, "we all gathered in our wilderness encampment, and Miriam led us in a triumphant chorus of song. I will sing it for you, Taharqo. It is called the Song of the Sea:

The Lord is my strength and song.
And he is become my salvation;
This is my God, and I will glorify him;
My father's God, and I will exalt him.

After finishing the song, Moses had paused to catch his breath. Then he had said, with a deep sigh, "We are still camping in the wilderness, Taharqo."

When Havilya did not answer, Moses had turned to look at her.

Moses had then seen the tears streaming down her face. Havilya's wet cheeks glistened in the moonlit night. Previously,

62

she had thought of Moses as an elderly man. He was more than seventy years old and she was only thirty-three. But suddenly, that age difference had melted away.

"What is it, Taharqo? Are you distressed?"

"No, no, my Lord. Some dust must have entered my eyes."

ELEVEN

When Joshua arrived at Moses' tent that morning, he found him in good spirits.

"What do you have for me this great morning?"

"My Lord, I thought we should review the new organization of judges. Then we should go over the events for tomorrow."

The next day was his wedding day. Moses had been eagerly anticipating that, and he wanted to ensure that his new Nubian family would be comfortable.

"Before we get into that, what arrangements have you made for Havilya and the Viceroy?"

"Two tents, my Lord. One for Havilya and her Hebrew attendant."

"Who is she?"

"I suggest Rivka. She is Debra's sister who works with Miriam in the Annex. Good family, very discreet. Rivka will stay with Havilya in her tent tonight. She and the Viceroy will arrive late today."

"That's good. And the other tent?"

"For the Viceroy and his aide Shabitqo."

"Good, good. And for tomorrow?"

"In the morning, we have invited the leaders of the twelve tribes to meet the Viceroy. There will be a military briefing."

"Next?"

"We have built a new tent specially for the occasion. The military briefing, the meal, the evening dinner and entertainment will all take place in the new tent."

"Everything in the new tent?"

"Everything, my Lord, except of course for the wedding ceremony. This will be in the sanctuary in the Tent of Revelation."

"Go on."

"Of course, Aaron, as High Priest will conduct the marriage ceremony."

"We have planned ahead." This is Joshua's euphemism for the raids on the Egyptian patrols and their supplies. "We have also received two mules packed with foodstuffs as a gift from the Viceroy."

"He is a fine man with a generous spirit."

"I might say, my Lord, also very brave. He put himself in great danger to provide and send us the mules."

Moses became pensive. The eyes and ears of Pharaoh are everywhere, he thought. Anyone who helps the Hebrews will be at risk.

"Now then, what about the matter of the judges?"

"My Lord, you and I are agreed that you have not sufficient time to attend to all the cases. We have arranged that your role will be to teach the seventy elders in the laws and commandments."

"Almost all the elders are eager for the task. We have planned one training session for you. Then the judges will go out to hear and decide the disputes."

"Yes, yes. We also have to think about who will head the group of judges."

"I suggest Nun of the tribe of Ephraim. He is a learned man, my Lord, and is respected by the others."

"I will give it some thought. Now let us go back to the elders. You said almost all the elders are eager. Any dissenters?"

Moses smiled to Joshua. Nothing proposed to the Hebrews is ever greeted with unanimous approval.

"Only two, my Lord, Eldad and Medad."

"What is their concern?"

As the High Priest, Aaron had founded a make-shift academy in a tent to record and teach the laws which were being created. Scribes toiled to record them and priests toiled to learn them and to teach them to others. Eldad and Medad were minor priests in Aaron's academy. The academy became a hub of activity, as all the Hebrews, including soldiers, artisans and common folk, went there to learn the new laws. Eldad and Medad liked the academy, less for the work they had to do, but more for mixing with others and hearing the latest news and gossip. To pass their spare time, they liked to sit outside the sanctuary because this was another place to watch people, and to avoid Aaron whom they regarded as a taskmaster since whenever he saw them, he seemed to have some new work for them to do.

Eldad and Medad had been part of a group of seventy elders whom Moses, Aaron and Joshua had called to a meeting. Aaron had taken to the podium to speak to the seventy elders.

"If you recall, my Lord," Joshua explained to Moses, " Aaron had spoken to the seventy elders about prophets and prophecy. He had divided prophecy into five parts. First, to reveal the divine will of God; second, to act as a lawgiver; third, to act as a leader; fourth, to act as a judge; and fifth, to predict the future."

"Aaron has always had a precise mind. Go on."

"Aaron then told them that they will be appointed to act as judges and that they should no longer carry out the other parts of prophecy. Those will be your function, my Lord."

"What about the fifth part?"

"Not clear, my Lord. It was considered that anyone could try to predict the future, if they wished."

"Where does that leave Eldad and Medad?"

"My Lord, they are a source of unease. They wish to continue as before, prophesying in any way they desire, and so they have refused to attend further meetings of judges."

"Well, it is their choice not to become judges."

"Yes, my Lord. But they intend to prophecy as before. This will create a conflict with you and what you have to say to the people. It will diminish your authority. I recommend that we restrain them."

Moses waved his hand with a smile. He was amused that Joshua would fret about two fools, Eldad and Medad, spouting words of prophecy. It pleased Moses that Joshua was loyal to a fault and zealous in protecting his leader's position. But Moses also knew that no one could prevent the Israelites, now a free people, from saying what they wished, even if it did not please their leaders.

"I am not concerned," Moses said. "I wish all the people of Israel were imbued with God's spirit. I wish all of them were prophets."

* * *

"Look at you," Miriam said to Shooly as he entered the Annex. "You are covered with dust and you look exhausted."

She brushed the dust off his clothes.

"Where is Debra?"

"She is in the back. Here, take this pail of water. Go outside and wash up, while I find her for you."

She knew that Debra would want a few minutes to look her best for Shooly. When he came back in, Debra was waiting for him. Shooly stood taller than most men, and Debra was almost as tall as him. She wore a white cotton blouse with red dots over a skirt. To Shooly, she had never looked this beautiful before.

"I thought we could go for a picnic," he said as he hugged her. "Bezalel and Ohaliab are on scouting duty now."

"I would like that."

"Let me pack something for you to eat," Miriam said. There was always some spare food in the Annex. The Hebrews sent any food they could spare to Miriam.

Shooly mounted his horse with his wooden staff pointing forward and fastened to the saddle. Debra climbed behind him and wrapped her arms around his waist. He kicked his horse into a full gallop as they rode out of the encampment into the hills.

He took her to an ancient ruin, which he had discovered on one of his scouting missions.

"There is a legend about this place," he said as they dismounted. "This was once the home of an outcast Amorite religious sect. They had come here to escape settlement life and to live in the wilderness."

"How ironic," she said. "We are trying to escape the wilderness to find a settlement!"

"They sought austerity and abstinence. When the Egyptians conquered this area, the Amorite sect refused to worship the Egyptian god Amun. So the Egyptians massacred everyone and burned down the place."

"How do you know all this?"

"Friendly local tribes. This is their story about these ruins."

He led her to the remnants of two walls which were perpendicular to each other, and which had formed a corner of

68

the Amorite structure. He untied the two blankets he carried on his horse, placed one blanket on the floor in the corner, and then took the second blanket, held it at eye level and nailed a corner and two sides to the walls. He then tied the opposite corner to his wooden staff which he planted upright in the ground. The crude canopy provided a shade from the setting sun.

They sat beside each other under the canopy.

"This is not different from a portico in Pharaoh's palace," he joked.

"Yes, I remember it well," she said, continuing the joke.

They laughed as they unpacked Miriam's food parcel.

"All we need is the Nile beside us, and it would be as pleasant as Pharaoh's garden."

"This is better," she said. "No servants and court officials to intrude."

In Miriam's package, they found manna wafers, flat bread, dried fish and honey cake. Debra put a piece of honey cake in Shooly's mouth. He then put a piece of manna in her mouth. They alternated feeding each other, until the food was gone.

"This is the best meal I've had."

"It gets better, Shooly."

She undressed and lay naked beside him. Now he noticed that her hips were slightly wider than her shoulders, which seemed to arouse him more. He leaned to his side on his elbow, looking down on her bright-eyed expectant face. He seemed more scared than when he saw the Nubian warriors that morning. He thought of what Miriam had told him. "In love and in war, above all, be confident, because the person you will face will likely know less than you."

"Do you want me to kiss you first on your lips or your nipples?"

"If you do not stop teasing me, I will not let you do either."

"We will compromise." He kissed her mouth firmly while gently stroking her nipples.

"Shooly, Shooly, I want you now."

She sat up and gently stroked his erect organ. Then he laid her flat and stretched himself over her, supported by his elbows and his knees. As he entered her, he heard a brief

69

muffled shriek of pain, followed by gasps of delight. He then turned her on her stomach and resumed from the rear, with the same rhythm as when he rode his horse at a trot.

When they had finished, they wiped her blood from their thighs. Then she sat up and he lay with his head on her lap, as she ran her fingers through his hair.

"You look after me well, Debra."

"You too."

"From now on, I will come to the Annex pretending to be sick, so that I can spend the whole day with you stroking my hair."

"But the wounded men will be jealous and will attack you."

"They will be no match for someone like me who is not really wounded."

"Then you will give away your secret."

"You are right. That will not work. I guess I will have to keep working as a scout."

As long as they could laugh like this, Debra thought, then they would be all right together.

"Shooly, do you think we will ever be like the Egyptians?"

"What do you mean?"

"You know, with towns, streets, houses, bedding and sheets."

He hesitated. He was not sure. Then he thought of Miriam's admonition.

"Of course, we will. Of course, we will."

TWELVE

The Viceroy and his two aides woke up early the next morning. They had a full day of riding ahead of them before they would reach the Hebrew encampment near Hazeroth. They decided to forego breakfast and make their way as quickly as their horses could carry them to an oasis midway to Hazeroth. There they would rest in the afternoon before the final stretch. The Viceroy did not want Havilya to look too tired when she arrived at the Hebrew encampment. When they arrived at the oasis, they were relieved to find no caravans at the watering spot. They washed, ate a small meal and decided to take a short rest.

"Taharqo," the Viceroy said to his daughter. "We will leave when you are ready. Try to take a short nap under one of the trees."

Havilya then chose a shade beside a group of saplings. The trees were a short distance up the small stream. She liked it for its seclusion.

She put a rolled blanket under her head, lay down on the bare soil and tried to sleep in the mid-afternoon sun.

Even in the coolness of the shade, she knew she could not sleep. She daydreamed about what would happen tomorrow. And she reflected on the first time Moses had shown a faint interest in her.

It was an afternoon in the desert in a resting spot, much like this one. Moses had taken a break from his meeting with the Viceroy and their aides. He had said he wanted to take a short walk in the hills. To her surprise, he had asked her to join him. Of course, at that time, he still knew her only as Taharqo, the male aide of the Viceroy.

"Taharqo," he had said. "Would you come with me for a walk?"

"Of course, my Lord."

"Young man, I enjoyed our little conversation last time."

"Thank you, my Lord."

"Walking in the hills under a blue sky is a great joy, Taharqo. Between the hills and the sky, there is nothing but one's thoughts and the presence of God."

"Yes, my Lord."

"It cleanses the soul and leads to clear thoughts."

"That is necessary for a great leader, my Lord."

"It is necessary for everyone."

"But not lonely, my Lord?"

"Not to walk in the hills."

"But after that, my Lord. It must be lonely after you have taken your walks."

"Well, it was God's choice to take away my Zipporah."

"I heard she was a fine wife for you, my Lord."

"More than a wife. A great friend."

"Many would delight in becoming your friend, my Lord."

"But would I delight in them?"

His mood had become lighter. He had enjoyed the bantering and had started to tease Taharqo.

He laughed and then said, "Perhaps... perhaps, if you had a sister."

"Why, my Lord?"

"For your qualities, Taharqo."

"You flatter me, my Lord."

"For your poise, intelligence and ability. I admire these. If you had a sister with charm, then..."

"But I do, my Lord."

"You have a sister, Taharqo?"

"Yes, my Lord. She is called Havilya. Almost identical to me. But for my duties, we are inseparable."

"The Viceroy had not mentioned you had a sibling."

"The Viceroy is protective, my Lord."

"I understand why. If your sister Havilya is half as charming as you are talented, then men will bow down to her."

"How, my Lord?"

"As the sun, moon and eleven stars bowed down to Joseph."

"If I mentioned your sentiment to her, my Lord, perhaps..."

"Not *my* sentiment, Taharqo. That matters not."

"Why not, my Lord?"

"I am the weather-bitten leader of a weather-bitten race of former slaves."

"You are the great leader and lawgiver of a free people. The Nubians are still slaves of Pharaoh. That is cause for admiration."

"We are free but without a home. The Nubians may be slaves of Pharaoh, but they have their land."

"The earth is vast and bountiful, my Lord. There will be a home for the Hebrews. Did not your God promise that to you?"

Taharqo's insight and pointed repartee had impressed Moses.

"You are a credit to your family and your tribe, Taharqo."

"You are kind, my Lord."

"Would your sister Havilya really care about my sentiment?"

"That is very likely, my Lord."

"What matters more is the sentiment of the one she would love."

"She would love the one who loves her, my Lord."

Moses had gone into a long silence. He had smiled at Taharqo.

"I must meet Havilya, Taharqo."

Taharqo smiled back.

"Yes, my Lord."

As Havilya dozed into a dreamy trance, she thought again of what Moses had said about Joseph. "As the sun, moon and eleven stars bowed down to Joseph," he had said. How curious, she thought. In Nubia, it was the other way around, where people bowed down to the sun, moon and stars. Moses had explained that Jacob gave his most loving blessing to Joseph, the father of Ephraim and Manasseh. Joseph was a man of vision with moral and spiritual strength to withstand the fickleness of life. He had been the helpless victim of the hatred of his step-brothers who drove him from his home into exile. But he resisted the temptation of disloyalty to his God, and in time became the master of his own will and a great minister of Egypt. Now, in the wilderness, Moses had explained to Havilya, the idea was to become like Joseph – a dreamer of the ages, a dreamer of peace and justice who resisted the temptation of disloyalty to his God and his father. In the dreams of Joseph, it was the stars that bowed down to Joseph, and not Joseph to the stars. And so the Hebrew, though in the wilderness, will not bow down to the stars, but will become the captain of his soul and will himself a better life as a free person, so that the stars will bow down to him.

* * *

Now Shabitqo was watching the afternoon sun, waiting to choose the right moment to resume their journey. He wanted to let Havilya rest, but not too long as to lose too much daylight.

Havilya's thoughts were suddenly interrupted by Shabitqo's voice.

"It's time to go, Taharqo. Viceroy's orders."

"Just when I was enjoying my sleep," she muttered. She did not feel rested, but she knew that she had had some sleep as she felt a sadness that normally follows. She stood up from the bare ground and dusted off her clothes. She picked up the rolled blanket that had been her pillow and joined the Viceroy and Shabitqo for the last leg of their journey.

As they mounted their horses, the Viceroy said, "Next stop, Hazeroth and the Hebrews."

THIRTEEN

Aaron was walking through the alleyways of the Hebrew encampment. He had been on his way to see Joshua, but changed his mind midway. He did not want to talk to Joshua in front of his courtiers. So he went to see Miriam in the Annex, hoping to encounter Joshua who visits the wounded daily. Aaron preferred to have Miriam present. His elder sister was likely to support him in what he had to say to Joshua.

He wanted to talk to Joshua about the new organization of judges. He did not dare take it up with Moses. He could learn more from Joshua without appearing to Moses to be anxious or bitter.

When he arrived in the Annex, Aaron was pleased to see Joshua at the entrance. As Miriam watched, Joshua was bidding farewell to a wounded man with one bandage around his head and another on his left elbow. The man was gently touching Joshua's shoulder with his right hand.

"Hosea, thank you for coming to see me," the man was saying to Joshua. Joshua encouraged his men to call him by the ordinary name his father had given him.

The wounded man went back into the Annex, leaving Miriam and Joshua at the entrance.

"Good day, my Lord," Joshua bowed to the High Priest.

"Good day, Joshua."

After exchanging some pleasantries, it was Miriam, as usual, who sensed the moment and quickly got to the point.

"You two have something to talk about. I have to go inside now."

After Miriam disappeared into the Annex tent, Aaron said, "Actually, Joshua, I did want to talk to you about the matter of the judges. I was hoping you would tell me Moses' latest thinking on the matter."

"My Lord, you were there. I thought your presentation to the seventy elders was clear and eloquent. All but two have agreed to become judges."

"Yes, yes. I know. But I was thinking of the organizational structure."

"It has not been finalized. Moses is still mulling it over."

"What exactly is he mulling over?"

"Well, the judge who would report to Moses as Chief Judge."

"Any candidates?"

"I suggested the most qualified person of the seventy."

"Who would that be?"

"I recommended Nun of the tribe of Ephraim. Moses is still thinking about that."

"Would Nun report to Moses?"

"We did not focus on that in great detail. But that is my expectation."

"Don't you think the Chief Judge should report into the priesthood?"

Joshua finally understood.

"My Lord, I did not give it too much thought. Nor did I discuss that aspect with Moses."

"What do *you* think?"

"I think the aim is to spread the work. Moses, Miriam, you, I – we all have more than enough to take care of. The aim is to appoint more elders to share the burdens of administration."

Aaron resented Joshua referring to himself in the same class as his family.

"Nun could still report to me," Aaron pressed.

"Moses sees the duties of a judge as different from those of a priest."

"Are you sure you had no hand in this?"

"What do you mean?"

"You have never forgiven me for the incident of the Golden Bull-calf, have you, Joshua?"

Joshua was aghast. He sincerely thought a judge's duties would be different from a priest's duties. But in the past he had not been able to hide from Aaron his disdain for Aaron's conduct during that fateful incident, and Joshua was not alone in losing confidence in Aaron's leadership after that event.

Joshua could not bear to think of it. Every Hebrew remembered with dread the incident of the Golden Bull-calf, for it had resulted in Hebrews slaughtering thousands of fellow Hebrews. Few families survived without the loss of a loved one. All the survivors faced further punishment from the wrath of God.

The Nubian Princess

The incident had begun when Moses had gone up to Mount Sinai. Earlier the Hebrews had received the Ten Commandments, and now Moses had gone up to receive from God the fine points of the law. He had been followed by young Joshua, the hero of the battle against the Amalekites. Joshua had not dared to follow Moses all the way up the mountain, and waited for him below.

Moses had then spent forty days and nights on the mountain. Meanwhile, as they waited for Moses to return, the Hebrews had become restless. Without Moses to scold them and guide them, they had forgotten their pledge to follow God's laws, and had begun to fret and complain. They had turned to Aaron, whom Moses had left in charge, with their demands and grievances.

The Hebrews had demanded from Aaron a new god to worship. It had not occurred to Aaron to dissuade them from their infidelity, even though the first and most important of the Ten Commandments said: "Thou shalt have no other gods before me." The second of the Ten Commandments was even more direct: "Thou shalt not make unto thee a graven image."

Instead of reminding them of their allegiance to their God, Aaron had cowered before the angry crowd, and had helped them in the task of making an idol. Aaron had appeared to take to the task with some fervour and ingenuity. He had cried to the mob to bring him the golden rings in the ears of their wives, daughters and sons. He had melted down the gold and before long had sculpted the figure of a bull-calf, which was placed on an altar built of stone.

"This is your god, O Israel," Aaron had told them. The Hebrews had recognized the image of the bull-calf as the revered symbol of fertility and the sign of the supreme god among the gods of the pagan Canaanites. This had inspired a worshipful frenzy in the Hebrews, who had just sworn their loyalty to the one and only God of the Hebrews, Yahweh. The next morning, the Hebrews had risen at dawn, gathered around the altar to offer sacrifices, burnt offerings and peace offerings to the Golden Bull-calf. This had seemed to be a further mockery of Moses and Yahweh, for it mimicked the ritual sacrifice that Moses had offered Yahweh. The Hebrew worship of the Golden Bull-calf

77

had turned into an orgiastic scene of eating, drinking and revelry.

On his way down the mountain, Moses had met Joshua. As the two of them had then descended together, they had begun to hear strange noises from the valley. Joshua, still nursing his wounds from the battle against the Amalekites, ventured to Moses that there is a noise of war in the camp. Moses had said, "This is not the clamour of warriors, nor the clamour of a defeated people. It is the sound of singing that I hear."

Joshua had then seen the rage in Moses' face – the rage of a man who feels a double betrayal. The Hebrews had betrayed their God Yahweh in favour of a Golden Bull-calf, and Aaron had betrayed Moses in trying to supplant his leadership. Scarred in battle, having seen some fight with courage while others fled and abandoned their comrades, Joshua had understood the painful hurt of betrayal, and the consequences that in time usually follow.

In an uncontrolled frenzy, Moses had then smashed the Golden Bull-calf, burnt it with fire, ground it to powder, strewed it with water, and with the help of Joshua's soldiers, forced the men and women who had been dancing around it, to drink of the hot molten metal. He had then turned to his brother Aaron.

"Why have you brought a great sin upon them?"

Aaron had been self-serving and evasive. He had blamed Moses for leaving him alone for forty days. He had then blamed the Hebrews as being ungovernable and set on evil. He had even suggested that the bull-calf had made itself. He had said to Moses, "So they gave the gold to me, and I cast it into the fire, and there came out this calf."

The dancing Hebrews had made themselves a new leader in the form of the Golden Bull-calf. Moses could not ignore this threat to his authority. Yet, many men of his own tribe, the tribe of Levi, had remained loyal. So Moses had set the Levites to purge the idol worshippers.

The guard of the Levites had then unsheathed their swords and slaughtered their fellow Hebrews. By the time the killing had stopped, the camp was littered with three thousand corpses. The authority of Moses had been restored, and he had learned a crucial lesson – to surround himself with a corps of armed men who were loyal and ruthless.

Now beside the Annex, Joshua looked at Aaron and tried to be diplomatic.

"My Lord, let us put that incident behind us."

"It is fine for you to say that, because all the blame has fallen on my shoulders. You were equally to blame, Joshua."

"What do you mean?"

"When you left with Moses to the mountain, I was left alone to calm down the restless mob. You were not there to help."

"I was helping Moses."

"You were helping yourself. Always cozying up to the centre of power."

"I resent that, Aaron."

"Well, it is true."

By this time, the two men were shouting at each other. Hearing the noise, Miriam came out of the Annex.

"What is happening?"

"Ask him!" said Aaron, stomping off with rage.

"Please, tell me what happened."

"Miriam, Miriam, everything we do seems to enrage someone."

Joshua then briefly described his conversation with Aaron.

"You know, Joshua, I said to Aaron the same things you said to him about the judgeship. I hate to see him so angry. He has to conduct the wedding ceremony tomorrow."

"Yes, and attend the other meetings with the Nubians."

"What other meetings?"

Joshua then described to Miriam the sequence of the wedding day events.

Well, well, Miriam thought. The men will have a meeting with the Nubians, and a military briefing, too. No women have been asked. Not even she, a priestess and the elder sister of Moses. And when things go wrong, it will be the women who will have to pick up the pieces. But Miriam thought better of complaining to Joshua. Then she smiled and said, "With your usual skill, Joshua, I assume you have arranged everything for the wedding."

"Yes," he said bidding her farewell. "Everything is arranged."

FOURTEEN

During the morning that the three Nubians – the Viceroy, Shabitqo and Taharqo – were galloping toward the Hebrew encampment at Hazeroth, Joshua was briefing the four division commanders about their impending arrival.

In his briefing, Joshua had to strike a delicate balance. He knew that the Nubians would be in danger from many in the Hebrew camp. So while Joshua could say little about the identity of the travelers, he had to say just enough to ensure their protection.

"We are expecting three Nubian visitors," Joshua said to his four division commanders. They are emissaries of a foreign power coming to confer with us. They will be black and on horseback. They will be armed but friendly. First and foremost, no harm should come to them."

Joshua paused for the message to sink in, and also to gauge the reaction. When there was no remark, he continued.

"They will be coming from the north, arriving after the sun sets. It could be dark when they reach this area. So the sentries should be alerted to watch carefully for them by moonlight."

The Hebrew encampment was located in a valley between two hills, one north of the other. The Hebrew army was placed around the camp concealed behind the two hills. Sentries were placed just behind the top of each hill to watch the approaches to the valley. The north hill was guarded by the Dan division and the south hill by the Reuben division.

"How should they be approached?" Ahiezer, the Dan commander had asked. His division's position was on the north side of the encampment.

"I was coming to that. The sentries on the north hill will likely see them first. Those are the Dan sentries."

"Do the Nubians know the area?"

"No, they have not been to this part of the wilderness. I have briefed them, but they could mistake the hills and approach our encampment from any direction."

Elishama, the commander of the Ephraim division, stationed on the west side, looked up at Nahshon, the commander of the Judah division, which was stationed on the east side of the encampment.

"So they could come in toward my eastern position," Nahshon said.

"Yes, or from the west," Joshua said pointing at Elishama. Unless they lose their way, most likely they will come in from the north."

They all looked at Ahiezer.

"Now listen carefully," Joshua said, wanting to take no chances. "No one is to approach them. As soon as they are sighted, word should be brought to me immediately. I will be waiting in my tent. I want to be the first to approach them."

Joshua wanted to ensure the safety of the Nubians. His plan was to personally receive and escort the Nubians with a force of eight horse guards. As well, the Nubians would be less nervous if the first Hebrew they met after their long journey was one well known to them.

* * *

After the briefing, Joshua sat in his tent with Zabad. The eight Hebrew horse guards were standing guard outside. It was well past dark. With no word of the arrival of the Nubians, Joshua was becoming nervous.

"Sir, do you think something went wrong?" asked Zabad.

"I don't know what to think. Check once again outside the tent."

Zabad had been going outside hoping to see a glimpse of the messenger who would bring word of the Nubians. He stood at the entrance to the tent.

"Here is someone coming. He is galloping frantically."

The rider stopped at the entrance to Joshua's tent, dismounted, handed his horse to one of the horse guards and burst into Joshua's tent.

"Something terrible has happened," he said. It was Elishama, commander of the Ephraim division.

"What?" said Joshua, jumping up.

"It was twilight, sir. The Nubians came in from the west. By the time they were spotted, they were in the valley a short distance from our sentry. Two members of the Benjamin cavalry were nearby. They decided to charge the Nubians with lances."

Dismayed, Joshua placed the palm of his right hand on his forehead.

"Fortunately, sir, we suffered only one wounded and a dead horse."

"And the Nubians?"

"They did better, sir. They captured the two Benjaminites and are holding them hostage until they see you."

Joshua chuckled with relief.

"Hadn't you briefed your people?"

"We had, sir, but apparently not the sentry on duty. We had briefed the replacement sentry, but he had not appeared for duty. The one on duty had been there since dawn of that day. He was tired and sleepy. He was not expecting the Nubians. Neither were the two Benjaminites."

"What happened then?"

"The two Benjaminites must have been spoiling for a fight, sir."

"Typical of them."

The tribe of Benjamin had a reputation for violence. The Hebrew elders say that the tribe carries the violent nature of their ancestor. According to them, when Jacob was giving his final words of blessing to Benjamin, the youngest of his twelve sons, he had referred to his warlike temperament by describing him as a "ravenous wolf."

"To protect their master, the two Nubian aides unsheathed their swords and galloped to meet the charging Benjaminites. The stocky Nubian aide managed to avoid the Hebrew lance and slashed the Hebrew lancer on the arm. The Hebrew dropped his lance and fell off his horse holding his wound."

Joshua recognized the stocky Nubian to be Shabitqo.

"The other Nubian, the taller one, rode low and plunged his sword deep into the chest of the Hebrew's horse. As the horse fell, the Nubian master helped his aide overpower the Benjaminite."

Good for you, Havilya, Joshua thought. But not a great way to be received for your wedding.

* * *

Joshua, his aide Zabad and the eight horse guards escorted the Nubians. Taharqo was shown to the bride's tent. Then the Viceroy and Shabitqo were shown to their tent. Each tent was watched by four horse guards. At Taharqo's suggestion, Joshua and the Viceroy had agreed not to mention the incident to Moses. There was no need to do so, Taharqo had said. It will only anger him before the wedding.

"Your Highness, Zabad will stay with you and Shabitqo," Joshua told the Viceroy. "He will attend to your needs."

"Thank you, General."

"Again, your Highness, please accept our most humble apologies for the unfortunate incident."

"Don't think of it, General."

The Viceroy looked at the horse guards near his tent. With a twinkle in his eye, and a wry smile, he said, "And thank you for your hospitality."

* * *

Rivka was waiting impatiently in the tent of the bride-to-be. She had been there alone since the early afternoon, waiting for Havilya to arrive.

Joshua had asked Rivka to become Havilya's attendant. When he had mentioned that Havilya was a Nubian princess about to marry Moses, Rivka could scarcely contain her excitement. Joshua has also sworn Rivka to secrecy.

"You can count on me, Joshua," Rivka had told him.

It was now well past dark. Rivka had arranged and re-arranged the meagre furnishings of Havilya's tent several times. Suddenly Taharqo entered the bride's tent. Rivka was shocked to see a figure dressed as a man covered with blood.

"I am Havilya and I am told you are Rivka," she said crisply.

Rivka was flustered. "Yes, my... my... Lady?"

"I will need a lot of water," Havilya said as she cast away her clothes.

"You are covered with blood, my lady."

"Don't worry. I just got too close to a bleeding horse."

84

FIFTEEN

Shooly felt spirited and refreshed that morning. The boost from Joshua's praise and the glow from love-making with Debra had enlivened him. Although he still had one more off day, he rode his horse to the training camp for soldiers.

He watched as young Israelites practiced marching and attacking in formation. Another group was engaged in hand-to-hand combat with swords and daggers. As much as possible, Shooly avoided doing anything in groups, except when ordered to do so. At the edge of the training camp, he had set up a dummy with sticks and rags, where he would practice alone. He would attack the target on his horse at full gallop with his wooden staff. Then he would dismount, and on foot, he would smash it again with wide swings of his wooden staff and then would stab it with his dagger.

That morning, he repeated his routine three times. As he paused to catch his breath, he watched the group doing hand-to-hand combat. When they finished, a young soldier approached Shooly, while wiping the sweat from his brow with a rag. Tall and heavy-set, he towered over Shooly.

"Fighting alone again, Shooly?" he sneered.

"What? What?" Shooly asked, taken aback.

"You think you are too good to fight with us."

"It is my off day, and I like to do my routine."

"Yes, yes, you are going to defeat the Amalekites by yourself. That's good. We can now all go to our tents since Shooly is our army."

"I have certain skills that I want to improve by myself."

"Yes, God gave these skills only to you, while we are but sheep to be herded in groups."

By now, a crowd of soldiers had gathered nearby to watch the quarrel. Some started to shout and curse. Emboldened by the attention he was receiving, the young soldier pushed Shooly hard on the chest. Shooly stumbled back, then regained his composure and pushed him back. Now the young soldier lifted his right arm and brought his fist hard on Shooly's face. He fell on the ground, his jaw bleeding. Shooly unsheathed his dagger and rushed at the young soldier. Just then, a group leader jumped in the fray and separated the fighters. He ordered Shooly to give him the dagger. Shooly complied.

The group leader led Shooly away.

"I don't want to see you drilling alone while the others are drilling in formation."

"It is my off day."

"I know, I know. They resent it."

"I drill with the groups when I am not scouting."

"It does not matter. They don't like it. If you want to practice alone, do it when there is no one."

Shooly tried to explain that this was not always possible or convenient. But the leader gave no heed.

"Remember, Joseph. God had endowed him with a quality of foretelling the future that he had not given to his brothers. Joseph flaunted it. As skilful as he was, yet his brothers hated him, because he thought he was above them."

"It is true. He *was* above them."

"Yes, I know. But they did not like to be reminded of it."

The leader put his arm around Shooly and walked him outside the training camp.

* * *

Havilya was in the bath as Rivka stood nearby with towels in her hand. The floor of the tent was covered with several thick burlap carpets. On one side was a bed made of a thick cotton mattress placed on a knee-high series of wooden boxes. At the head of the bed two sticks were bent across in parallel semi-circles and covered with a lace material. This was to be the canopy over Havilya's head as she would lie on the bed.

Beside Havilya's bed were a chair, a table and some writing materials. This was a sign that she was being treated like an Egyptian royalty. No one else except Moses had the use of a table and a chair. At the other end of the tent was placed a narrow mattress on the floor. This was Rivka's bed.

Havilya got up from her bath and stepped into the towel Rivka was holding up for her.

Her legs were long and thin and her thighs firm. Her waist was narrower than her shoulders. Her long neck and erect posture made her ample breasts look bigger than they were. She stood at least a head taller than her Hebrew attendant. Rivka had never seen a woman as stunning as Havilya.

"You are beautiful, my Lady."

"Thank you, Rivka. I hope Moses will think the same."

As she finished dressing for bed, Havilya asked, "What is the plan for the morning?"

"Leah the seamstress will come early. She will bring your wedding dress. Joshua told her you are my size, but I see you are much taller. Leah had said she would make your dress big for me, in case it did not fit you."

"Wise lady." She paused and then said. "Rivka?"

"Yes, my Lady."

"I have an important question to ask."

"Yes, my Lady."

"I know that to make Moses happy, I must become like the Hebrews."

"Yes, my Lady."

"What advice would you have for me?"

"Our ways are not hard to learn. Be yourself and follow your instincts."

"Anything to fear?"

Rivka thought for a moment.

"You should fear the women more than the men."

Havilya lay on her bed as Rivka was cleaning the bath.

She smiled to herself as she remembered the first time that she realized that Moses loved her. It was at the end of a long meeting. Moses had excused himself, saying he needed a rest. The Viceroy, Joshua, Zabad and Shabitqo had continued the meeting. They had been discussing the number of men each could deploy in the event of a war with Pharaoh.

Moses had gone to sit alone in the shade of a nearby rock. Havilya had then followed him.

"Details and numbers tire me, Taharqo."

"It has been a long day for you, my Lord."

"For everyone else, too."

"You have much more to think about, my Lord?"

"I try not to, Taharqo. Not thinking is the only relief I get. But even that is hard to do."

They had both laughed at the irony. Then a long silence had followed. To ease the awkwardness of the moment, he had stood up to face her and had broken the silence.

"How is your sister, Taharqo?"

Havilya remembered gulping for breath.

"O fine, fine, my Lord. Havilya is fine. I spoke to her about you."

"Yes?"

Havilya had looked down on the ground away from his gaze, as she had continued.

"I told her that you were born of a Hebrew slave woman in Egypt; that even as a baby your life was threatened by Pharaoh's edict to drown the Hebrew babies in the Nile; that you were saved by Miriam's watchful eye until Pharaoh's daughter found you and made you her own."

Havilya had then raised her head to look at Moses and assess his reaction. She had found him smiling, pleased at what she was telling him, even though the story could hardly have been more familiar to him.

"Yes, Taharqo," he had said.

Looking at him straight in the face, she had pressed on.

"I spoke of the boy who was brought up as a Child of the Nile and a Prince of Egypt, but who remained devoted to his people; how that devotion led to an act of violence to rescue a fellow Hebrew; and how that act of violence turned the Prince loved by Pharaoh into a fugitive fleeing Pharaoh's henchmen.

"I spoke to Havilya of how you lived in Midian, as a humble shepherd and a stranger in a strange land; of how the God of the Hebrews chose you to lead the Hebrews out of their oppression in Egypt.

Then she had stepped slightly closer to him close enough to touch him. She could not remember whether she had touched him then, but she knew that if she had, it had been inadvertent. No longer able to meet his gaze, she had continued as she looked at his chest.

"I told Havilya how you struggled with Pharaoh until at last the Pharaoh relented and let your people go.

"I spoke of how Pharaoh had a change of heart and ordered six hundred chariots to defeat the fleeing Hebrews and return them to Egypt.

"Of how, with the help of the Hebrew God, the waters parted by means of a strong east wind, and how you then led the Hebrews across the sea.

"Of how Pharaoh's chariots had chased you and of how the waters had then returned and drowned the Egyptian soldiers.

When Havilya's voice started to break, Moses had put his right hand on her left arm. Havilya had then continued.

"She then said she wished Nubia would find a leader as great as Moses to free them from Pharaoh's oppression.

"I sang to Havilya the Song of the Sea that you sang to me, and she learned it and we sang it together.

"I told Havilya that you are building a great nation based on freedom and laws; that you are training a vast army to fight for and hold the Promised Land given to the Hebrews by their God.

"As I finished my story, with tears in her eyes, she said, 'how can a woman not love such a man?'"

Moses had then said, "You are crying now, Taharqo?"

"Yes, my Lord," Taharqo had said sobbing. "Forgive me, forgive me. I am Havilya, daughter of the Viceroy of Nubia. Taharqo and Havilya are one and the same."

She had then untied her hair which fell to her shoulders, and took off her riding cloak to reveal her breasts under her shirt. She kneeled and bowed to him.

"Forgive my cowardice, my Lord. If I am a coward, it is the fear of showing my love."

He had then touched her shoulders with both hands and gently pulled her to him and embraced her.

"Havilya, Havilya, if love is an offence, then I am guilty, too."

PART 2

SIXTEEN

When Princess Havilya woke up the next morning, she found Rivka sitting beside her bed, with a bemused look of wonder on her face.

"It is your wedding day, my Lady. You look so beautiful, I could not help looking at you."

Havilya touched Rivka on her cheek.

"You are sweet, Rivka."

"Forgive me, I hope I did not startle you."

"Not at all. But I thought I heard voices outside the tent. Was I dreaming or hearing the sentries outside?"

"Neither, my Lady. You had an important visitor."

"Who?"

Rivka smiled coyly and hesitated.

"It was Moses."

"What?"

Havilya sat up on the bed with her feet on the floor, directly facing Rivka.

"One of the sentries came in to say that Moses was outside and that he wanted to see me."

"Yes, go on."

"I went outside to speak to him. You must have heard our voices."

"What did he say, Rivka?"

"He wanted to make sure you are fine."

"No one told him?"

"Joshua had told him last night that you and his Highness the Viceroy had arrived safely. But Moses said he wanted to check personally with me this morning."

Havilya smiled. She knew Moses wanted to be close to her, but he could not enter her bedchamber until they were married.

"Why didn't you wake me? I could have seen him outside the tent?"

"He didn't want to wake you. He said you needed a rest from your long journey."

"That's all?"

"No, my Lady. He also left this letter for you."

Rivka handed her a roll of papyrus tied in a leather string. It was the finest writing material Havilya had seen. Moses must have saved it from his student days in Pharaoh's court, she thought. This type of papyrus was used exclusively for important communications by the Pharaoh and his princes.

Havilya stood up and unrolled the papyrus. She paced up and down the tent as she read the letter from Moses.

"My dear Havilya,

Yesterday was the longest day for me. Night fell and I had still not received word of your arrival. I worried about you, his Highness and the brave and loyal Shabitqo. You can imagine my relief and happiness when Joshua came to see me early this morning to report that you are all safe in your tents.

I chose not to disturb you or his Highness, in order to allow you to rest from your long and arduous journey.

As for today, we will also not see each other until the wedding ceremony. It is an ancient Hebrew tradition that on the wedding day, the groom-to-be must not see the bride-to-be, until she walks to meet him under the wedding canopy. As I wait longingly for that moment, I know I will cherish it more and more. In preparing for your conversion, you have learned a great deal in a short time. If this comes as a surprise to you, it is the fault of your humble teacher!

With all my love,

Moses"

"I wish I could have seen him last night. Now I won't see him until later today."

Havilya handed the letter to Rivka.

"It is in Egyptian hieroglyphics, my Lady."

94

"Moses wanted to make sure I understood it. My Hebrew is still, well, tentative, though I can read the Hebrew scrolls of law that Moses writes. Can't you read hieroglyphics?"

"Yes I can, my Lady. My father made sure we learned as much about Egypt as possible, even when we were slaves."

Rivka looked at the letter, and continued.

"You are going to let me read your letter from Moses?"

"Only because I know you are discreet."

As Rivka read the letter, Havilya sat at the table to comb her hair. She wore a loose white night gown, as she combed her hair straight to her shoulders. Rivka finished reading the letter.

"I think he really loves you."

"I hope I will deserve his love."

"I am sure you will. Come, let me help you wash up."

Havilya held her hands over the bath as Rivka poured water from a pitcher. Havilya washed her face and arms. Rivka then gave her a towel.

"What does he mean by the word 'conversion'?" Rivka asked.

"As a Hebrew, Moses can only marry a Hebrew woman. Since I was not born a Hebrew, I have to be converted to a Hebrew."

"I have never seen that done."

"Of course not. Moses told me that in the time of the Hebrew patriarchs Abraham, Isaac and Jacob, many who married into the tribe converted, but when the Hebrews were slaves in Egypt, not many wanted to be converted to the Hebrew religion. There have not been any conversions since you left Egypt. I am probably the only one."

"What do you have to do to convert?"

"I have to learn about the religion of the Hebrews. Moses helped me study. He gave me the Hebrew writings since the time of Joseph, and of course some of his own writings."

"Was it hard to learn?"

"Some of it was hard. But it became easier as time went by. Moses gave me the writings in both languages side by side – hieroglyphics and Hebrew. In this way, I was able to learn Hebrew, and at the same time, learn Hebrew history, beliefs, worship practices, ethics and ritual, prayers and commandments. There is a lot to learn, but I think I have made a good beginning. At least Moses thinks so."

"Is that all you need to do to become a Hebrew?"

"No, there is more. I must come to believe as a Hebrew."

"It is strange that as a born Hebrew, I must ask you, a Nubian, what those beliefs are."

"Well, they are fresher in my memory. It is the belief in the one and only God; that we have the personal choice to follow God's commandments; that there are consequences for moral misdeeds; and that we are each responsible for our actions."

"How different is that from Nubian beliefs?"

"The big difference is that Nubians have many gods but the Hebrews have only one. The main Nubian deities are Osiris, Isis and Amun. These are the same as the Egyptian gods. The Nubians have another one called Apedemak."

"I have seen the temples of these gods."

"Yes, Rivka. The Pharaohs have built many temples to the gods in Nubia. This is another new thing for me in the Hebrew religion."

"Our Hebrew God is hard to visualize. Sometimes I wish I could see what he looked like."

"Moses said that we must not build images of God to worship. It is important to concentrate on following God's commandments, and not to try to build images of what he looks like."

"Will you still keep the Nubian gods?"

"Of course not. I must stop worshipping all other gods. I must completely reject all previous beliefs in other gods. That is why becoming Hebrew is called 'conversion'."

"Well, you seem to know a lot about Hebrew beliefs. Is there more you have to do to be... how do you call it... *converted*?"

"Tomorrow before the wedding, two things will happen. First, I will be immersed in a pool of water. This ritual bath is a symbolic act of purification. "Moses called it a *mikveh*."

"I hope they brought in more water from the oasis. I had to fight to get enough for your bath."

Havilya laughed.

"You are very practical, Rivka. Then after being immersed in water, I have to appear before a *beth din*, a court of three priests. They will ask me questions about my intentions and sincerity. They will want to make sure that I have basic knowledge and a commitment to Hebrew beliefs."

"If Moses thinks you have that knowledge and commitment, isn't that enough?"

"Moses wants other priests to make that judgement."

"What will the priests do?"

"If they are satisfied with my answers, they will give me a Hebrew name and recognize me as a Hebrew."

"Did you choose a Hebrew name?"

"I discussed this with Moses. He had an intriguing idea. He thinks that my Nubian name Havilya can also be considered as my Hebrew name."

"Really? How could it be?"

"Moses told me that one of Noah's grandsons was called Cush, who had two sons named Seba and Havilah. Moses thinks I could be a descendant of Noah's grandson Cush. Even if I am not, he said 'Havilya' is a close enough female version of the name 'Havilah'."

"Well, at least you will get to keep your name. You must find all the changes difficult, don't you?"

"Not with the love and guidance of Moses, and the kindness of people like you."

"Thank you, my Lady." Havilya's generous praise embarrassed her Hebrew attendant. Rivka now tried to change the subject.

"I have a small breakfast for us. Let me place it on the table before Leah the seamstress arrives."

Havilya helped Rivka set the table for breakfast. Rivka had brought goat cheese, manna wafers and goat milk. From another parcel, she unwrapped dried apricots and dates.

"I hope you will like your first breakfast with the Hebrews."

"This is more than I usually eat."

"You must have the dates. My mother always insists I eat the dates. She says they have magical things in them that give strength."

Havilya took two dates and placed them on a manna wafer.

"I will listen to your mother. I think I will need my strength today."

Just then, they were interrupted by the sentry. They heard his voice from outside the tent.

"You have a visitor, Rivka. Leah the seamstress."

"Let her in," said Rivka.

A woman carrying a load of clothes walked into Havilya's tent.

"Rush, rush, rush," the seamstress said. "Everything is rush these days."

"Leah, this is Princess Havilya, the bride-to-be of Moses."

"My pleasure, my pleasure."

Leah was short, stocky and strong. She looked up at Havilya who was at least two heads taller.

"My goodness, you are taller than I thought. Good thing I provided lots of room in your clothes. Here try this on first."

Leah handed Havilya a grey cotton dress.

"This does not look like a wedding dress," said Rivka.

"I know, I know. It is not. This is for the Princess's *mikveh.* She will be wearing it when she is immersed in the pool of water this afternoon."

"You thought of everything."

"Not me, not me. It was Joshua. He told me only yesterday about the dress for the ritual bath. Everything is last minute."

Havilya took off her nightgown and put on the grey dress.

"Why is the colour grey?" asked Rivka.

"That is the only cloth I had left. I used up all the white cloth for the wedding dress. For me, God does not drop sacks of cloth from the sky. Now, if Moses was a tailor, God might have done that for him."

They all laughed.

"Now, now" Havilya said. "I am sure God appreciates your good work."

"Thank you, Princess," Leah said as she looked up and down at Havilya.

The dress had long sleeves and covered Havilya from neck to toe. It hung long and loose on Havilya's body.

"Well, how do you feel about it?" Leah asked.

"It looks plain," Rivka said.

"I am only going to get wet in it," said Havilya. "It does not matter much. I think Leah has done the right thing."

"Thank you, Princess. Now let me help you try on the wedding dress."

Havilya now put on the white wedding dress. Leah fastened the buttons at the back.

"I made this from Joshua's description of you, Princess. That is all I had to work with."

"As long as he didn't make it," cracked Rivka.

"No, no," Leah laughed as she fastened the train to Havilya's shoulders.

"There, how does it look?"

A wide collar covered most of Havilya's neck. The rest of the dress followed the contours of her body in a loose fit around her hips and waist. The dress then widened gently as it reached her ankles. An ample train fell from her shoulders to the ground and ran several feet behind her.

"You look beautiful," Rivka said, as she walked around Havilya surveying the dress. "Leah, don't you think it could be tighter at the waist?"

"It could be more alluring. Is that what you want, Princess?"

Havilya wanted to look more attractive to Moses, but she did not want to overdo it on that score. She thought of the many priests in his family.

"No, I don't think I want it much tighter. It is more comfortable this way."

"Good, good," said Leah. "Now I only have to do some minor finishing at the edges, and it will be ready this afternoon."

"Thank you, Leah. Is there anything else?"

"Yes, yes. The head. I have something for your head."

Leah reached in her bag and brought out a gold tiara embedded with jewels. She placed it on Havilya's head just above her forehead.

The tiara was a semi-circular band of gold that clasped the head just above the ears. The bottom portion was a belt of gold, imbedded in the middle with a row of seven diamonds. The top portion was a golden triangular band, with its peak in the middle of the forehead and the two sides of the triangle gently falling above each eyebrow. At the apex of the triangle a hefty diamond was set in an oval ring of gold. Two rubies glistened, one on each side of the large diamond.

"This is magnificent. Where did you get it, Leah?"

"I will tell you in a minute. Let me see if it fits."

Leah adjusted it on Havilya's skull.

"It feels fine," she said.

Havilya took it off and gazed at it.

"Where is this from? I cannot accept it unless you tell me?" Havilya insisted.

"It is a gift from Miriam, the elder sister of Moses. It is a family heirloom. They don't know how old it is. Miriam said that her mother Yokheved gave it to her on Miriam's wedding day."

"That is most gracious of Miriam, most kind."

She handed it to Rivka.

"This is exquisite, my Lady. Now you look every inch a princess."

Rivka handed back the gold tiara to Havilya.

"You haven't finished your breakfast, my Lady. Let me help you take off the dress."

Havilya was quiet as Leah and Rivka helped her remove the wedding dress. She paced back and forth in her tent as she changed to her day clothes and ate her breakfast.

As she gulped down her goat milk, Havilya said, "Get dressed quickly, Rivka. We have to make an important visit."

SEVENTEEN

"May the plague of a thousand locusts chew into their hearts!"

Reyes raged against everyone in general, and no one in particular. His attendant listened and said nothing, lest he further provoke his master.

Reyes was short and intense. A meagre tuft above his forehead was all the hair he had on his shining head. His face was clean-shaven except for a long moustache. When nervous, as he was now, he combed the hair on his head upward with his fingers in a futile attempt to cover the rest of his bald head. Alternately, he twirled and pulled at his moustache with his fingers.

Egyptian troops on their way to Syria had overstayed their welcome in Gaza. Some had plundered the livestock of the local shepherds and the fruits and vegetables of the small farmers. An angry mob of Gazan shepherds and farmers were now outside the administration building shouting and demanding compensation.

"The Viceroy leaves me here in Gaza for days at a time with no authority. If I pay compensation to this mob, he will accuse me of exceeding the budget. If I don't and the mob becomes more unruly, he will say I cannot manage the civil administration."

The attendant fidgeted and said nothing.

"If I try to make the Egyptian commander pay for the excesses of his soldiers, they will either laugh at me or put me in chains. On top of it, the Viceroy will then say I was not diplomatic with our Egyptian masters."

Reyes had been chafing, ever since Pharaoh sent the Viceroy of Nubia to head up the administration in Gaza. As a Gazan, he had been accustomed to being the local ruler, reporting occasionally to Pharaoh or one of his princes in Memphis. Now he resented being second-in-command to the Viceroy in Gaza.

"It is bad enough that our Egyptian masters rule us from Memphis," the Gazan thought. "Now they send me a Nubian to live in Gaza and to give me orders."

Reyes paused for breath.

"He is not even here to tell me what to do, when I need direction."

By now, he was in such a rage that he pulled at the tuft of hair on his head with one hand and at his moustache with the other hand.

"What did we do to deserve our miserable fate?"

The attendant walked over to the window. The mob had suddenly gone quiet, and he wanted to see why.

"My Lord, my Lord. Come look. The Black Knights of Pharaoh are here."

"What?"

The astonished Reyes scrambled to the window beside his attendant. Three horsemen were riding toward the entrance to the building. The crowd separated to make way for them. The riders were dressed in black and rode black horses. Reyes immediately recognized Pharaoh's Secret Service, the Black Knights of the Egyptian empire. They reported personally to Pharaoh and roamed his empire at will checking for traitors and others they considered incompetents. The one in the middle was the commander, and the other two were his bodyguards. As they walked in, Reyes and his attendant bowed low to them.

"Welcome, welcome," said Reyes. "You honour us with your gracious visit."

Reyes motioned the commander to a table in the middle of a room. The commander sat at the head of the table and his aides stood at each side.

"Please sit down," the commander said to Reyes." I am Prince Ramentop, in the service of his Majesty."

Ramentop had shiny black hair compacted down from his forehead to the back of his neck with an oil that kept it glistening. He was clean-shaven except for a pencil-thin moustache. His fine features and smooth skin gave away a royal upbringing, as one who belonged to an inner circle and therefore chosen as trustworthy for his sinister profession. When he talked, he usually preferred to gaze at his fingernails, unless he wanted to make sure his listener understood his meaning. That was when his listener would face the fierce gaze of his deep black eyes.

He was meticulously groomed and dressed. He wore a black long-sleeved cape, fastened down with an elaborate silver accessory. It started as a wide ring loosely placed around his neck, from which a chain hung from his left to right diagonally on his chest, connected to a silver belt around his waist. A sheathed sword hung from the belt on his right.

"I am Reyes, the second in command in Gaza."

"I know, I know," Ramentop said, as he unfastened his ring around the neck, and let the ring, chain, belt and sword fall on a nearby table.

Reyes motioned to his attendant to get some refreshments.

"What brings you to Gaza, your Highness?"

"His Majesty's business. What brings a Black Knight anywhere?" Relieved from the silver ring, Ramentop stroked his neck now sore from rubbing against the metal during the long ride.

"Of course, your Highness. Now about the mob outside…"

Reyes tried to explain the commotion outside, but Prince Ramentop cut him off.

"I will let you deal with this local rabble. They do not concern me."

"Of course, your Highness."

"I am here to speak to the Viceroy and learn about matters that may concern his Majesty."

"The Viceroy is away on a journey, your Highness. But my staff and I will be at your service." Reyes could see a glimmer of hope of getting back at the Viceory, but he chose to proceed cautiously.

Ramentop knew about Sebakashta and the Nubian's family in Aniba. About twenty years ago, Ramentop, then only eighteen, had been choosing a career. His mother, Amunirdis, descendant from a line of lower Nubian nobility, had urged him to go to Thebes to study religion. She saw in her son a gentle side that would not thrive in the internal political and military culture of Memphis. With Pharaoh engaged in constant warfare, she thought her son would be much safer deep in the south where affairs were calmer. She was confident that her connections in Thebes would secure for her son a position as a higher clergy, with a handsome salary and several servants. So she sent her young son on a journey south to visit her family in Nubia. Young Ramentop spent many weeks in Thebes, Aniba and other Nubian cities. It was during that journey that he learned about Sebakashta's deep roots in Aniba and its Nubian surrounding. Upon his return to his father's house in Memphis, he announced that Thebes and the study of religion were not for him. Thebes was too far south and religion and the clergy did not satisfy his affinity for intrigue. This delighted his father, Piankhy, who wanted Ramentop to become a military officer, lest he fall into Piankhy's profession. Piankhy was a construction overlord, and he hated every minute of it. He was responsible for architects and designers, as well as for the slaves who erected the temples for Pharaoh. Something was always going wrong for him. If the work of the architects and designers was sound, which was seldom the case, the artisans and workers, if they arrived when they were supposed to, and were not sick from beatings and hunger, often performed shoddy work. He felt he had to be everywhere and supervise everything, for fear that a disaster would cost him his livelihood, if not his life. He could not forget the last time Pharaoh had visited one of his construction sites. His Majesty enjoyed following the progress of his pet temple projects, and would appear unannounced to mingle with the workers. On the last such visit, the Pharaoh watched avidly as two hundred workers pulled on ropes to raise upright an immense stone pillar. They pulled too hard, and the pillar, swaying out of control at an angle, smashed into a newly-built wall, and brought down the entire structure, killing half the workers. If the Pharaoh had not kept his distance, he too would have been crushed under the collapsing stones.

"Go to the military academy in Memphis," Piankhy had urged his son. "You will have money, honour and status, and you will live close by me and your mother."

"You will have him killed or mutilated," Amunirdis would protest to her husband. "Pharaoh is in war every year."

Piankhy had scoffed at his wife. "Military officers," he had said, "are never close to the actual fighting. I am more at risk of death in construction than the generals in a war."

104

The Nubian Princess

To Ramentop, Piankhy's advice echoed the boasts of some of Ramentop's young friends. They longed to join Pharaoh's army, to partake in travel, adventure, booty, glory and to satisfy what Ramentop saw as a savage thirst for blood.

Torn by conflicting advice from many directions, Ramentop studied history in a Memphis military college. He avoided military strategy, and eventually, through his mother's connections, secured a junior position in the secret service. It was a compromise – it kept him close to home in Memphis, away from actual soldiering in battles, but close enough to Memphis's politics to satisfy the ambitions of his parents. However, like most compromises, it left him dissatisfied. Something was always missing in his soul, and now many years later, he realized what it was. In trying to satisfy his parents' dreams or follow the bravado of his young crowd, he gave little thought to what he, Ramentop, actually wanted to do.

Just then Reyes' attendant walked in with a tray of food. He placed two plates on the table in front of Ramentop. One plate was full of fresh grapes and figs. The other plate contained dried almonds and pistachios. Prince Ramentop took a handful of almonds. He cracked one between his teeth.

"Reyes, tell me first about the Egyptian troops."

"Well, your Highness, as you know, thousands of them have been moving through Gaza on their way north to fight the Hittites. We try to look after their needs as best we can. Our resources are limited. Occasionally, conflicts arise between the troops and the local inhabitants. What you saw outside is one example. My attendant was just going outside to speak to them."

This was a signal to the attendant to go outside and disperse the mob as best he could. He would usually tell them that the Civil Administration was considering their request, and that they should go away and come back next week.

"The fighting with the Hittites has not begun. When it does, you should be ready for the dead and wounded coming back south to Gaza. The gods of Pharaoh will prevail over the Hittites, but there is always a price."

"Yes, my Lord."

"I want to know of any murmurings or acts against Pharaoh – actual or intended."

"We are his most loyal subjects, and our eyes and ears are alert to traitors, my Lord."

"Of course, of course, Reyes."

Ramentop picked up a grape and put it in his mouth. Then he gazed intently at his fingernails. "Now tell me about the Viceroy's travels."

"Well, my Lord, he does not tell me much about his travels. However, he said he has been to Ezion-geber several times, and I believe that is where he is now."

"I would have thought he is too important to spend much time in a small town in a corner of his Majesty's empire?"

"I do not question his decisions, my Lord."

"Has he sent you or your subordinates to Ezion-geber?"

"No, my Lord, although I would have been more than eager to go."

"His Majesty would have preferred that the Viceroy's presence and talents be used in Gaza where there are more weighty matters. His subordinates could easily deal with matters in the smaller towns like Ezion-geber."

"His Majesty knows best, my Lord. But I am not at liberty to instruct the Viceroy."

"Of course not."

Ramentop looked around him. Satisfied that the attendant was outside, he gazed intently at Reyes. "Now listen carefully. I want you to find out about the Viceroy's travels. When he goes, when he comes back, where he goes, do you understand?"

"Yes, my Lord."

"I especially want to know why he is spending so much time in Ezion-geber."

"Of course, my Lord."

Reyes was quietly pleased with himself. He himself had wanted to know why the Viceroy was visiting that small town. He had already dispatched two spies to find out. But as a shrewd bureaucrat, he chose not to tell Ramentop. If the two were successful, he would be able to impress Ramentop with the speed with which he acted and obtained results. If the two spies failed or got into some trouble, Reyes would be able to say that he had acted upon the instructions of Ramentop.

The attendant came back in the room. "I managed to disperse the crowd," he said. He failed to add that they were frightened away by the Black Knights of Pharaoh.

Ramentop rose to leave.

"I will be back in a few days, Reyes. I hope you will have some information for me."

"I will do my utmost to be at your service."

EIGHTEEN

"Come, come, let's get started," Joshua shouted irritably.

His four division commanders were now quiet. They could see that their general was under considerable strain. His well-trimmed beard joined his sideburns and thick head of hair to form a black frame around his tanned face. His eyelids were swollen and his fierce black eyes were blood-shot. It was obvious to them that he had not had much sleep the night before.

He had called his four commanders to an urgent meeting that morning. They were assembled in the military tent. It was bare except for burlap floor covering and a long carpet in the middle. Joshua sat at one end. On Joshua's right sat Ahiezer and Elizur. Nahshon sat immediately to his left with Elishama to the very far left.

Shooly stood just behind and to the right of Joshua, who wanted his young scout nearby. Shooly looked ashen and his left cheek blue and swollen from the blow he had taken at the training camp. But he stood erect and alert to the slightest jerk of Joshua's head, which would signal to Shooly that Joshua wanted something from him.

The four commanders looked expectantly at Joshua. He usually twitched his right shoulder, as if his muscles and light garment were too heavy for his back. Now they could see that his twitches were more frequent and pronounced.

"By now, you all know the identity of the three visitors who arrived last night," Joshua opined.

Word of the fight between the Benjaminite cavalry and the Nubians had
spread quickly. Although relieved that no harm had come to the Nubians, Joshua was furious at the conduct of the Benjaminites. But he thought that perhaps he had been partly to blame. He had briefed his commanders yesterday. If he had told them about the real identity of the visitors, the commanders might have been more vigilant in getting word to the sentries. At least, that is what Elishama implied, when he tried to defend the conduct of his division.

Now Joshua knew he had to be totally frank and open with his commanders, for they held the safety of the Hebrews in their hands. The more information he could give them, the better they would be able to discharge their duties.

"Just so there will be no misunderstanding, the Nubian leader is the Viceroy of Nubia. He is Pharaoh's commander in Gaza. Moses and I have been in secret negotiations with him for several months. He is here to conclude a secret alliance with us against Pharaoh."

The commanders fidgeted nervously, looked at each other and then fixed their gaze again on Joshua.

"You will learn more of the details of the alliance at a briefing with Moses and the Viceroy this afternoon. The other two Nubians are the Viceroy's aides, Shabitqo and Taharqo. But Taharqo is really Princess Havilya in disguise. She is the Viceroy's daughter, betrothed to marry Moses. Her formal conversion to Judaism will take place late this morning at the same time as the military briefing."

They all looked at Elishama, who was looking down on the floor.

"We all know that last night the Benjaminites in Elishama's division almost killed Moses' bride-to-be. But we are not here to blame anyone; rather, to talk openly and learn, so that this type of mishap does not happen again."

Elishama, somewhat relieved, took his gaze off the floor and looked at Joshua.

"I may have been remiss in not revealing the true identities of the visitors. I wanted to protect them. Hebrew assassins still threaten Moses because of the thousands that were killed in the incident of the Golden Bull-calf. These assassins will target the Nubians, either because the Nubians will become members of the family of Moses or because they were in the service of Pharaoh. So we must give the Nubians the same protection we give to Moses."

They all nodded.

"That does not change the fact that there were serious failures last night. At our last briefing, I did say that the visitors were friendly emissaries of a foreign power. I also said that although they were armed, first and foremost, no harm should come to them. Nonetheless, none of this information reached the sentries on guard. This must not happen again."

"Sir," Elishama said, "we have disciplined the sentry who failed to show up for duty."

"That's fine," Joshua said. "Now, the second failure was the lack of discipline of the two Benjaminites. They went on a murderous charge without orders and without knowing the identity of their intended victims."

"We are conducting an inquiry, and the guilty parties will be disciplined, sir," said Elishama.

"Good. Now there was a third failure. Having started the fight, the Benjaminites failed to subdue their opponents. Given the identity of their opponents, this was fortunate."

Joshua finally cracked a smile, to the relief of his commanders.

"The fact remains that our two Benjaminite hotheads were bested by two young Nubians – one of them a woman."

By now they were all laughing loudly. Joshua held up his hand for quiet.

"Seriously, though, it puts in question Nahshon's proposal," said Ahiezer.

Nahshon had proposed that the Hebrew forces move north to the Salt Sea. His idea was that the Hebrews were in a war for the conquest of Canaan, and that they must engage the enemy in the vicinity of Hormah. He wanted to move quickly in a surprise attack against the Amalekites and Canaanites.

Nahshon straightened his posture and looked up.

"We cannot wander in the desert continuously," Nahshon said. "At some point we must engage the enemy."

"Last night's incident is a sign that our forces are not ready," Dan said. "We must take more time to train and prepare."

"Not only that, Dan," Joshua interjected. "Moses is not in favour of an attack in Canaan at this time. He wants us to send spies into Canaan to report on the nature and condition of the Canaanite defences. I agreed with him that we will do that after his wedding. As well, after we receive the report of the spies, we will have to consider an attack in Canaan in the light of the new alliance with the Nubians."

"More information will not be amiss. But we will never have enough information. I say we attack as soon as possible."

Joshua knew they could not decide then to attack in Canaan. He had made a commitment to Moses to send spies first. So Joshua wanted to cut off the debate on this matter.

"Yes, Nahshon," said Joshua. "We will make a decision after the report of the spies."

Nahshon shrugged with resignation.

"Now," Joshua continued, "anything else before I move on to talk about our meeting with the Viceroy?"

"Who will be sent on the spying mission?" asked Elizur.

"That has not been determined. We will decide that matter together in another meeting."

Elizur nodded.

"Now, about the meeting with the Nubians later today. Moses will be there. Early this morning, I went to brief him on the events of last night. Princess Havilya had asked me not to tell him about the Benjaminite attack, so as not to vex him before his wedding. But I was uncomfortable about that. I could not sleep worrying that he might hear something about it from someone else, which could anger him even more."

"How did he take the news of the fight?" asked Elishama.

"He took it calmly, since I assured him the Princess was unharmed."

"Did he ask why you didn't tell him till this morning?"

"Yes. I explained it was Princess Havilya's wish not to tell him until after the wedding."

"What did he say about that?"

"As usual, he was thinking of everyone else but himself," said Joshua. "So that I do not lose face in the eyes of the Princess, he assured me he would not tell the Princess that I had gone against her wishes and told him about the incident."

Elishama shook his head.

"Nonetheless," continued Joshua, "he immediately went to Princess Havilya's tent to check with her attendant early this morning. He wanted to ensure personally that she was safe."

There was a murmur in the tent, as they whispered to each other. Joshua held up his hand again for them to be quiet.

"One final thing, before the meeting with the Viceroy, you need to know one more thing."

They all gazed intently at Joshua.

"My scout spotted Egyptian troops."

"What?" exclaimed Elishama.

Joshua nodded to Shooly. "Tell us about them," he said to his aide.

As Shooly began to speak, they realized that when Shooly would be absent on a scouting mission, Joshua would not be attended by any other aide. As well, it was curious to them that Joshua would permit a scout so young to address the senior commanders, when Joshua could have briefed them directly.

"There were seventy Egyptian troops camped on the southern highway," he began. He then went on to describe the location and composition of the company of cavalry, infantry, horses and other pack animals. He was factual and brief, and stopped as quickly as he could.

Ahiezer got up and paced back and forth.

"Does the Viceroy know anything about their mission?" asked Elizur.

"Unfortunately, no. They are not under his Gaza command. They seem to have been sent from Memphis."

"What could they be doing here?"

"They could be on their way to Syria."

"But that is a roundabout way for them to get to Syria."

"Not if their mission is to march to Ezion-geber, then northeast to the Salt Sea, so as to outflank the Hittites from the east."

"If this is part of an eastern flank against the Hittites, there will be thousands of other Egyptian troops to follow."

"Yes."

"What is the other possibility?"

"To look for us, obviously," interjected Ahiezer, who paced some more.

"Yes," said Joshua.

"We will have to move out of Hazeroth quickly."

"Yes, but first we have to send scouts to track their movements. Only then, will we know where we should move our camp to avoid them."

"We must avoid them at all costs. Our soldiers are not ready to meet Pharaoh's regular army in battle."

"Yes, yes," said Joshua. "Except for the scouts, whom I will personally send on this mission, the presence of the

Egyptian soldiers should be kept secret. We do not want to
alarm our people."

As the four commanders looked at each other, Joshua
said, "That will be all."

NINETEEN

"Be quiet, be quiet, here she comes!"

"We are about to see the new wife of Moses."

These were the voices from the crowd outside the Annex. They had gathered when word spread that Princess Havilya was on her way to visit Miriam.

Havilya and her Hebrew attendant Rivka, flanked by the four sentries, were now walking though the Hebrew encampment toward the Annex. Children ran ahead of them shouting, "The Princess is coming, the Princess is coming."

Havilya had taken Rivka by surprise.

"I want you to take me to see Miriam," she had told her attendant.

"This is not part of the plan for the day, my Lady."

"We will have time. Miriam is not too far away, is she?"

"No, she is not. But I am concerned about your safety."

"We can discuss that with the sentries."

Rivka had then called in the captain of the four sentries.

"Her Highness wants to see Miriam, Captain."

"Joshua had not mentioned that," the captain had said.

"I just decided now to see Miriam."

"My orders are to guard you at all times."

"Well, you will have to come with me and Rivka."

"It is safer in your tent, my Lady."

"I know, I know. But I have no intention of becoming a prisoner in my tent. I want to go out and meet with my new family."

"It is risky to walk through the encampment, my Lady. My orders from Joshua are to ensure your safety at all cost."

"Well, I am going anyway. You may accompany me or not, as you wish."

The captain had no intention of restraining the bride-to-be of Moses. Besides, he had thought of how she and Shabitqo had outfought and humiliated the Benjaminite cavalry.

"I and my three sentries will come with you, your Highness," the captain said.

As they left Havilya's tent, Rivka pointed to the Tent of Revelation.

"This is where the sanctuary is located. That is where your wedding will be."

"This is a very big tent to move from place to place."

"Not as big as any of the temples of Nubia." They had both laughed as Rivka continued.

"The Levites look after that. Of course, the entire encampment is like a small town. Everything is dismantled and moved to another location in the desert now and then."

They now entered the main alleyway in the encampment, and crossed eastward toward the Judah tents and toward the Annex.

Havilya, followed by her attendant and the four soldiers, now approached the entrance to the Annex. She wore a brown cotton gown, and a blue cotton blouse with long sleeves. Her hair fell in waves from her shoulders.

The crowd separated to clear her way to the entrance of the Annex, where Miriam now stood. Hearing the noise outside, Miriam had come out of the tent. She had her left hand on her hip and her right hand on her mouth, as she looked with amazement at Havilya, Rivka and the four soldiers marching toward her.

Havilya stopped and bowed low in front of Miriam.

"O Priestess of the Hebrews, Healer of the Sick, Comforter of Women. I come humbly before you to give you my respect."

Miriam stretched out her hand. Touching Havilya by the shoulders, she lifted her up.

"Please stand up, Princess. You are among your sisters."

"You honoured me with your generous gift, and you now honour me again by calling me sister."

"We are honoured by the visit of a brave and noble princess."

The crowd shouted, "Miriam, Miriam."

Others added, "Havilya, Havilya."

"You see, you are popular already. We all heard about your exploits last night."

"It is not as a soldier that I seek to serve Moses and the Hebrews. In the eyes of God, the gentle hand of the healer finds more favour than the strong arm of the swordsman."

"We will need both, Princess. Without the sword, we cannot conquer the Promised Land and we will remain wanderers and tent-dwellers in the desert."

"The pain of the warrior is like nothing to the pain suffered by a healer of compassion. Even a hardened general, surveying the end of a battle, will see the wounds and hear the moans of those who fell in battle for only a short time. But the healer of loving kindness, as you are, suffers daily the tears of a sick child, the pain of a woman in labour, the groans of a wounded soldier."

Moved by Havilya's words, Miriam put her arms around her, and gently guided her into the Annex.

"Come inside, and I will show you my work."

Havilya looked at the two rows of the sick and wounded, lying on the floor of the Annex. Some of them had sat up to look at the beautiful and distinguished visitor.

"Most of these men were wounded in an ill-fated raid on a caravan. They are lucky to be alive. Their comrades are buried in the desert."

"May they rest in peace."

"Midwifery is another thing I do."

"And the women and babies?"

"It is a good thing none are here. I visit the pregnant mothers in their tents and deliver the babies there. I prefer not to bring them to the Annex, unless there are difficulties."

"Outside, I sensed the love and regard the Hebrews have for you."

"They are my family, Princess."

"You look after them, as a shining light of healing and wisdom."

"You are gracious, Princess. There is a lot to do, and all are doing their part."

"Tell me more."

"Aaron is the High Priest. With the help of staff, he looks after the priesthood and the sanctuary in the Tent of Revelation."

"Including the writing of the laws?"

"Yes. But applying the laws is a growing activity. Moses has been doing the judging and the settling of disputes. But he cannot handle it all. Seventy elders have been chosen for that purpose."

"Where does the food come from?"

"That's a big problem. Scavenging for manna and raiding small Egyptian patrols and Egyptian caravans. Until we settle down in the Promised Land, we cannot farm, as you do in Egypt and Nubia."

"Moses talked to me about that."

"We have to fight our way in. But our men have been slaves for centuries. They are not soldiers. They have to learn the ways of war."

"This is a big task for Joshua."

"Joshua is a very able general. He is also Moses' trusted aide, as you know."

"How can I help you?"

"By helping Moses. He has a lot on his mind. Many of the Hebrews are miserable here. Some even want to go back to Egypt and to slavery. They grumble constantly. Moses takes all of their complaints to heart. Every grievance seems to weigh on his shoulders. He can be restive and uneasy. There is only so much any one man can take, even one as strong and meek as Moses. He needs a wife, a partner. Someone to comfort him and soothe him from the daily grinding of the spirit."

Havilya pondered at the task confronting Moses. He is a prophet and a leader, surrounded by enemies in the wilderness, while trying to build a nation. And here is Miriam, his strong and cheerful advocate, healing and comforting all who come to her, with a glow in her face, in spite of all the difficulties. She thought of how lucky she was to love and be loved by Moses, and to be part of this adventure.

"If I can be half as capable as you, dear Miriam…"

"You will be, Princess, you will be."

Moses had chosen well, Miriam thought. Havilya will not only comfort but will delight him with her beauty, bravery and wisdom.

TWENTY

"Rise up! Rise up!" shouted Shooly.

The assembled Hebrew men stood up as the two Nubians walked into the new tent.

"His Highness Sebakashta, Viceroy of Nubia, Overseer of the Southern lands of Pharaoh, Son of Cush, Commander of the District of Gaza!"

As the Viceroy took his seat on the floor, his aide Shabitqo remained standing behind him.

They were all seated around a carpet in the middle, except for Joshua and Aaron who seemed to be in a heated discussion in the corner. They were arguing about Miriam and her role – or lack of it – at this meeting. Red-faced with rage, they both finally took their seats.

They were meeting in the new tent built specially for the events of the day. The carpets and furnishings had been set up for this evening's wedding celebration, with a carpet in the middle around which the guests would sit. The three sides farthest from the entrance were occupied by the two elders from each of the twelve tribes – eight men on each side. On the fourth side nearest the entrance were the Hebrew leaders and the Viceroy. The Nubian was seated in the middle, and to his right were Moses and Aaron. To the Viceroy's left sat Joshua and his four division commanders. The aides stood behind their masters – Shooly behind Joshua and Shabitqo behind the Viceroy.

Joshua and his commanders were in full military regalia, and the elders of the twelve tribes were in their finest tribal costumes.

For each four guests, there was a set of refreshments. Each set consisted of a pitcher of water, four goblets and a plate of sweets (manna sticks dipped in honey).

This military briefing had been planned by Joshua and Moses. Its purpose was to introduce the Nubian to the Hebrew leaders and to reveal the secret alliance. Joshua thought that his commanders needed to hear first hand the strategy envisioned by the Viceroy.

The meeting held a larger purpose for Moses. He wanted to include the Hebrew elders of the twelve tribes as a gesture of confidence.   The drone of private conversations filled the tent. Then Moses raised his hand, and they were all quiet.

"Elders and soldiers of Israel," he began. "We are here to welcome our friend and ally, the noble Viceroy of Nubia and Son of Cush. He has journeyed far to meet with us, and has placed in danger his own life and that of his travelling companions."

He turned and gestured with a smile toward Shabitqo who was standing at attention behind the Viceroy and immediately to the left of Moses.

"We share with the Sons of Cush many things in common. Cush was one of the grandsons of Noah. The sons of Cush were Seba, Havilah, Sabtah, Raamah and Sabteea. Cush was the ancestor of Nimrod, who grew to be a mighty warrior on the earth. His Highness and his daughter, Princess Havilya, belong to a family of brave and noble Cushite warriors who have done battle with the Pharaohs over the centuries. We share with the Sons of Cush a common heritage through Noah, our common ancestor.

Moses looked to his left at the Viceroy and touched the Viceroy's hand.

"When the Lord God made the earth and the heavens, it is written that a river watering the garden flowed from Eden. From there it was separated into four headwaters. The name of one of these is the Gishon River, which winds through the entire land of Cush. We share with the Sons of Cush the river created by God flowing from the Garden of Eden."

Moses paused for emphasis, drank a sip of water and continued.

"It is written that God created man in his own image, in the image of God he created him; male and female he created them. God blessed them and saw that all he made was very good. We share with the Sons of Cush the common blessing of the Lord God, who created us all."

Aaron the High Priest nodded.

"For centuries, the Cushite people have been a nation with their own land, language, culture and warriors. In spite of their brave struggle, they lost their freedom to the might of Pharaoh who rules the land of Cush to this day. We the Hebrews have just regained our freedom from Pharaoh, but unlike the Sons of Cush, we have not built a nation on land of our own. To do so, to become a nation, we must have allies – allies like the noble Son of Cush. The Cushites and the Hebrews will fight against the established order that has oppressed us for centuries. Together we are making common cause against Pharaoh. Like the Hebrews, the Cushites will acquire their freedom. Like the Cushites, the Hebrews will acquire their national homeland."

When Moses finished, they banged their fists on the table in approval, and raised their goblets of water to him.

It was now Joshua's turn to speak. He was still smarting from his tiff with Aaron. He had scarcely paid any attention to the speech Moses had just finished, for his argument with Aaron was still racing in his mind.

"Where is Miriam?" Aaron had demanded.

"I don't know. In the Annex, I suppose, where she usually is."

"Joshua, you have invited all your commanders and your two aides. Yet you could find no place for Miriam?"

"Aaron, Aaron. This is a military briefing, not a gathering for women."

"Miriam can contribute more than anyone here. We need the counsel and wisdom of our elder sister."

"It did not occur to me to ask the women. This meeting would have been twice the size it is. It would have been too unwieldy."

"This is not about women and men. It is about the future of the Hebrews. Miriam is our elder priestess, an inspiration to the Hebrews. We must not exclude her from these grave deliberations."

"There was no intention to exclude her, Aaron."

Just then, Joshua had pulled away from Aaron, and both had taken their seats on the floor.

Aaron seems to be blaming me for everything, Joshua thought. For Aaron's failure in the incident of the Golden Bull-calf. For Moses appointing judges separate from Aaron's priesthood. He is now blaming me for Miriam being a woman!

As Joshua's thoughts raged on, he was startled by a nudge from Shooly, who was standing behind him.

121

"Joshua will speak to us now about the military condition of the Hebrews," said Moses.

"Yes, yes. Our military condition."

Joshua raised his goblet and drank some water.

"The population of the Hebrew encampment is almost twenty-five thousand. Every man of the age of twenty years or more is a soldier, except for the old and infirm. We have six thousand men training in the arts of war. They are divided in four divisions."

Joshua described the four divisions and introduced each of the commanders beside him.

"Our objective is to secure the Promised Land by conquest. To do that, we must wage war against the Canaanites and the Amalekites in the hills of Canaan."

"What is the state of their defences?" asked the Viceroy.

"We don't know, your Highness. Except for a few raids and skirmishes to obtain food and weapons, we have not engaged them in a major battle, save one."

"Do you have plans to do so?"

"Yes, but not immediately. While we train our soldiers in the camp, we will send a mission of spies to report on their defences. After that mission, we will make a decision on where and when to launch an attack."

Nahshon asked, "What can you tell us about the role of Pharaoh and the Nubians in the struggle?"

"The Canaanites, Amalekites and the rest of Syria-Palestine are under the control of Pharaoh. The Hebrew forces cannot defeat the combination of the forces of Canaanites, Amalekites and Pharaoh. Our only chance of victory in Canaan will arise if Pharaoh is too pre-occupied elsewhere to assist his vassal states in Canaan."

"How active are Pharaoh's forces in Syria-Palestine?" asked one of the elders.

"That is what our distinguished guest and ally, the Viceroy of Nubia, is here to tell us."

All eyes were now fixed on the Nubian leader. His forehead and scalp were shiny, and the hair on the side was neatly trimmed and combed. Soft eyes, a cleanly shaved face and a soft smile gave him a pleasant and friendly air. Nor did his medium build and height seem threatening. These features, however, belied an inner intelligence and determination. Only those who knew him well understood that those were the traits that had brought him success in the court of Pharaoh.

The Viceroy stood up and looked to his right at Moses.

"My friend, the Prophet and Liberator."

He then looked around.

"Elders and soldiers of Israel. I bring you greetings from the people of Nubia. For centuries my nation enjoyed independence and prosperity. The source of Nubian wealth has been its minerals and its trading skills between the nations of Africa and the nations along the Great Sea. Egypt has been Nubia's rival in Africa for centuries. We have fought many wars with many of the Pharaohs. In spite of Nubian resistance, unfortunately, two centuries ago, the Pharaoh Thutmose III subdued Nubia. To this day, Nubia is a conquered nation and, if Pharaoh has his way, it will be totally Egyptianized and our southern lands will become a permanent part of Egypt.

"But I am here to say to you, my friends, that Pharaoh will not succeed. Nubia will rise up and free itself from Pharaoh's bondage, as you, brave Hebrews, have done recently." He stretched his arms and patted on the back both Joshua on his left and Moses on his right.

"We, the black Nubians," he continued, "in the southern part of Pharaoh's empire, are not his only enemies. The tribes of Libyans in the western part of the Egyptian empire have been enemies of Egypt of long standing. The Libyans, a people with fair or yellow skin, have also been subdued by the Pharaoh and are now part of the Egyptian empire. The Pharaohs have built forts west of Egypt along the wells and water holes of Libya to deny them free access into Egypt. But forts will not erase the longing for freedom of the conquered. The Libyans are firmly allied with those determined to throw off the yoke of Pharaoh. They have sent secret messages to Nubia in an attempt to encourage a Nubian rebellion."

The Viceroy paused for breath and drank from his goblet.

"The Pharaohs have a third group of enemies, the Asiatics to their east. They have the same red-brown skin as the Egyptians. The Asiatics are the people of Syria-Palestine, including the Amorites, Edomites, Syrians and Canaanites. Between the Egyptians and the Asiatics, periods of enmity have been interspersed with periods of peace and trade. The Pharaohs never attempted to absorb the eastern territories, as they had Nubia. There is little formal organization of the eastern empire, and there is no equivalent in Canaan to the Nubian Viceroy who rules Nubia as an Egyptian official. The Asiatic region is divided into a series of independent city states whose kings and chiefs are allowed to retain their titles and most of their power. In turn, these people are expected to prove their allegiance to Pharaoh by taxes and declarations of loyalty. Egypt is linked to its eastern territories by the land-bridge in the north of Sinai. This is the Way of the Sea, a few days' ride to the north. This is now a route of intense military activity because of the Hittite threat to Pharaoh in northern Syria.

The Viceroy now heard murmurs from his audience. As he paused, he brushed his head with the palm of his right hand. When the murmurs subsided, he continued.

"Pharaoh is now preparing for a major campaign against the Hittites. Through our friendship with the Libyans, we hope to start uprisings in the south and in the west of Pharaoh's empire. This will provide you an opportunity to subdue the tribes of Canaan. If you engage the Canaanites, they will not be able to help Pharaoh against the Hittites. And if the Nubians and Libyans attack Egypt from the south and the west, Pharaoh's forces will be stretched. As mighty as he is, Pharaoh cannot defend his vast empire if threatened from three directions. As he defends his empire on three fronts, he will be unlikely to come to the aid of the Canaanites who will face the assault of the Hebrews."

When the import of what the Viceroy said had sunk in, the Hebrews were breathless at the audacity of the Viceroy's plan. A hushed silence suddenly erupted into a loud thunder of applause.

"There remains to consider Pharaoh's current activities in this area," the Viceroy continued. "I have mentioned the Egyptian mobilization of troops from Egypt across Sinai on their way to fight the Hittites in Syria. These troop movements are occurring along the three major routes across Sinai – the Way of the Sea, the Way to Shur and the southern highway closest to this camp. This highway connects Memphis to Ezion-geber, which is just northeast of Hazeroth, where we are now encamped.

The Viceroy then turned his head sharply to the left and nodded at Shooly with a smile.

"Joshua's scouts have spotted seventy regular Egyptian troops on the southern highway just north of Hazeroth. They are not under my command, but appear to be under the command of Memphis. They are on their way to Ezion-geber."

There were sounds of shuffling from the elders.

"We have not yet ascertained their mission. Either they are looking to engage the Hebrews, or they are on their way north to engage the Hittites. In either case, there will be more reinforcements. We will not know their mission until we find out whether they will move north of Ezion-geber to Syria, or spread out in groups to search for this camp. I have advised Joshua to send scouts to determine their movements. I will try to obtain information through my sources. Joshua and I will set up a means of secret couriers to exchange information and plan our future actions."

Some of the elders could scarcely contain themselves.

"We will surely die in this desert," they muttered under their breath. But the Viceroy tried to be reassuring.

"The fight for our freedom from Pharaoh will not be easy, short or bloodless. As much as Pharaoh has, he will want more. It is the nature of those who have a great deal and are overcome by pride and greed."

The Viceroy concluded with praise for his hosts.

"The Hebrews have stood up to Pharaoh and gained freedom from his oppression. You are now a shining example to all of the tribes enslaved by Pharaoh. As your prophet Moses just said, if we help each other, you will gain your Promised Land and we will regain our freedom."

TWENTY-ONE

"We have decided on your mission," the Viceroy told his aide Shabitqo.

The two Nubians were standing beside Joshua and his scout Shooly.

The military briefing had just ended. The Hebrews, including Moses and Aaron, were also standing beside the vacant space in the middle of the tent. They were munching on lunch that had been brought in by Joshua's aides. There were the usual manna wafers and goat cheese. But today there was something special. Shabitqo recognized the dried fish and onions that he had packed on the two mules that were loaded with gifts from the Viceroy.

"Commander," the Viceroy said to Joshua. "Before we talk about the mission, I want to entrust my wife's safety into your hands."

"By all means, your Highness," Joshua said.

The Viceroy then said that, in order not to attract attention, he had arranged for his wife Sebaha to visit her sister in Ezion-geber. After the wedding, the Viceroy would pass by the sister's house to fetch Sebaha for their trip back together to their home in Gaza. However, should anything happen to the Viceroy, Joshua should arrange to have her taken secretly from the sister's house to the Hebrew encampment. Shabitqo knew where the sister's house was located, and Shabitqo then gave the information to Joshua.

"Now as for your mission, Shabitqo, you will leave at dawn tomorrow," continued the Viceroy.

"Yes," Joshua added. "Shooly will accompany you, Shabitqo."

The Viceroy wanted to be thorough. "Shooly will lead you to the spot on the southern highway where he encountered the seventy Egyptian troops. You are to find out all you can. Are the Egyptian troops still there? If not, where have they moved to? Have they been reinforced? Are more troops coming east from Memphis along the highway? Have any fanned out into the hills?"

Shooly was biting on a piece of dried fish.

"Do we then come back?" he asked.

"No," said the Viceroy. "After you find out all you can on the highway, you will both ride as close as possible to Ezion-geber and find a hiding spot for Shooly in the hills. Shabitqo will then ride alone into Ezion-geber. He will see Esau, my second-in-command, in that town. I will give Shabitqo a letter from me to Esau authorizing Esau to answer all of Shabitqo's questions. Shabitqo will tell Esau that he is on a mission for me."

"What do you want to learn from Esau?" asked Shabitqo.

"When I met with him two days ago in Ezion-geber, we discussed Egyptian troop movements and how these will affect his budget. That should be your subject of questioning. Our main purpose is to know more about Egyptian troop movements – how many have arrived, how many are still there, how many have left, in what direction, and for what purpose."

Joshua interjected. "You are to look for any signs that Esau or the Egyptians are suspicious of our alliance, that the Egyptians are looking for the Hebrews, or that the Egyptians are merely moving north to Syria."

Shooly looked at Shabitqo and nodded.

"Shabitqo," the Viceroy continued. "You are to leave Ezion-geber, meet Shooly in his hiding spot and return here to the camp at Hazeroth."

"How many days' rations should we take with us?"

"At least three days," said Joshua.

"Thanks to the Viceroy, we have more food to choose from," Shooly said as he ate the last piece of dried fish in his hand.

* * *

Escorted by the four Hebrew sentries, the Viceroy had excused himself from Joshua and the other Hebrews and hurried over to Princess Havilya's tent. With the rush of events, he had not had a chance to speak to her since they arrived late last night.

As he entered his daughter's tent, he found her attended by two women – a very young woman and a very mature one.

"Father, this is the priestess Miriam and my friend Rivka."

Taken aback that he found himself in the presence of the elder sister of Moses, the Viceroy immediately bowed to her.

"I am honoured to meet such distinguished company."

He then bowed to Rivka.

"And you, too, of course, Rivka."

The two women bowed to the Viceroy.

"You have a beautiful and gracious daughter," Miriam said.

"Thank you."

"Miriam just came in unexpectedly a few minutes ago, father."

"Havilya had visited me in the Annex this morning, your Highness," Miriam explained. "After she left, one of the Hebrews told me that she was appearing before the *beth din* for her conversion. Of course, I said to myself, how stupid of me not to realize it. Then I thought to myself that the Princess was about to face three high priests without any help from us, except from dear Rivka."

"You are kind," Rivka said.

"Joshua may be arranging tents and meetings and sentries, and so forth. But I wanted to be present for Princess Havilya."

"I have heard of the love the Hebrews have for you," the Viceroy said. "Now I can see why."

"You flatter me, your Highness," said Miriam. "I am sure you came here to spend a few private moments with your daughter. I will be brief. Rivka and I will leave now. We will take Havilya's change of clothes to the *beth din* and prepare a changing place for her. After you are finished here, Princess, the sentries can escort you to the *beth din*. You will find me waiting for you."

"I don't know how to thank you, Miriam," Havilya said.

"It is nothing, Princess. Nothing at all. We are sisters now."

She and Rivka bade them farewell, and left the tent with a bundle of Havilya's clothes.

* * *

As Havilya was arranging her things to prepare to leave her tent, the Viceroy sat quietly on the chair at the table near her bed. He was usually exuberant. But not now. Havilya knew he had something grave on his mind.

"You have something to tell me, Father?"

"Not to tell you. Perhaps to ask you."

"I will do anything you ask, Father. Is anything the matter?"

"No, no I was just wondering."

"What about, Father?"

"You are about to face three Hebrew priests. About to change your religion."

"Yes, Father. We talked about that."

"Then in an hour or two after that, you will marry a Hebrew man."

"Yes?"

"I wanted to make sure this is what you want?"

"Is there anything I should know?"

"You know everything about them that I do. Perhaps you know more than me. They are different from us, Princess. They are fine, honourable people, but they have great struggles ahead of them."

"We knew that, Father."

The Viceroy asked her if she thought she knew Moses long enough and well enough to become his wife. She replied that many arranged Nubian marriages took place a day after the bride and groom met. By and large those marriages worked well, because of the wisdom of the elders who arranged them. She said she knew all she wanted to know about Moses. As a child, she had heard stories about Moses and the other princes in Pharaoh's palace. Moses had told her about his life at many of their meetings. She had read the scrolls of his writing. Above all, she loved him and he told her that he loved her. Would a wise Nubian elder not favour such a marriage?

"I want to make sure that this is what you want, because you are not marrying another Nubian. You are dearer to me than anything else. If you have any doubt – any doubt at all – about what you are about to do, you can ride away from this camp and go back to Nubia."

"I have no doubt, Father. But why do you vex yourself and me like this at this late hour?"

"It is not too late, if you are having second thoughts. I don't want you to do this for the alliance. If this marriage is not right for you, I don't want you to do it to preserve the alliance."

"Father, father. I am not marrying Moses to preserve the alliance. If I had any doubts about becoming his Hebrew wife, I would not be here with you, with or without the alliance."

"I wanted to be sure. I wanted to give you a way out – in case you wanted one."

"Father, I love and admire Moses. He is the best thing that happened to me since you made me your aide."

They both chuckled, as they remembered how Havilya had to persuade him to allow her to work and travel with him and how he had refused, fearing for her safety. But she had insisted until he had reluctantly agreed, but only if she accompanied him dressed as a man.

"Your new aide will be called Taharqo," she had announced, "after the great Nubian warrior."

"Taharqo is no more," she said laughing. "Going back to Nubia is out of the question for me now, as it will be when I marry Moses."

Suddenly the Viceroy felt relieved. To him, she seemed sure of what she wanted now, just as she seemed sure then when she had wanted to become Taharqo. He was relieved, too, that Havilya well understood that, after marrying Moses who to the Egyptians was an outlaw, there was no turning back for her, that she was not just marrying a Hebrew man and becoming a Hebrew wife, but that if she ever went back to Nubia, she would be regarded as a traitor and put to death by the Egyptians.

Havilya kneeled before her father and looked up into his eyes.

"My love, my life, my destiny – these are all with Moses and his Hebrew people."

He stroked her hair, as he had done when she was a little girl.

"Of course, my darling. Of course."

TWENTY-TWO

"As usual, nothing is done," said Miriam.

She and Rivka had just entered the tent assigned for Havilya's conversion, each carrying two bundles. It was the tent Moses used as a tribunal. Joshua had chosen it for its proximity to the Tent of Revelation. It was a short walk for the three priests who would have to come from the Tent of Revelation. They would form the *beth din*, the court of three priests who would test Havilya's intentions, sincerity and knowledge to become a member of the Hebrew people.

The tent was in the same condition as when Moses had left it after his last visit. It was bare, except for a knee-high chest made of wood placed in the middle of the sandy floor. The rest of the floor was covered with pieces of thick canvas. Miriam explained to Rivka that the priests would sit behind the wooden chest, and Havilya would sit in front of it facing them. In the bundles, they had brought all the oils, scents, sheets and change of clothes that they would need for Havilya's conversion. There remained water for the *mikveh*. This was the pool of water in which Havilya will be immersed in a symbolic act of ritual purification. Miriam had asked two of the four sentries guarding Havilya's tent to bring her bath with some fresh water. The sentries now arrived with the tub and pails of water, which they placed in the far corner. The sentries then left to escort Havilya to the conversion tent.

Miriam and Rivka then placed pins in the roof of the tent above the tub, and the sheets, now fastened above, fell around the tub to create a private bath and changing place. Havilya entered the tent as Miriam, standing on the wooden chest which they had moved to the corner, was placing the last pin on the tent's roof. Rivka, with pins in her hand to give to Miriam, pressed close by to prevent Miriam from falling.

As she watched the two of them, Havilya said, "I don't know how to thank you. So much to do in just one day."

"It's nothing, nothing, Princess," Miriam replied. "Have you ever appeared before three priests?"

"Not Hebrew ones."

"Are you nervous?"

"A little."

"Well, don't be. Because you are in good company."

"What do you mean?"

Miriam descended from the wooden chest which she and Rivka moved back to the middle. They began to unwrap the other bundles and place the contents beside the wooden chest.

"Here, Havilya," said Miriam, pointing at the wooden chest, "sit here and I will explain. But first we must pamper you to put you in a good frame of mind for the priests."

Rivka lit candles scented with amber. She then burned incense in a bowl. As the aroma filled the tent, Rivka stood behind Havilya and started to brush her hair gently.

Miriam then kneeled facing Havilya and started to rub oil of kaolin on her forehead, cheeks, neck and shoulders.

"We Hebrews are descendants from a long line of converts," Miriam explained. "We call a convert a *ger* in Hebrew. It means 'stranger'."

"Moses mentioned that."

"The first Hebrew was himself a *ger*."

"Abraham?"

"Yes. With his wife Sarah, Abraham left their Aramean kin and their home in Chaldea to found the new Hebrew nation."

"I didn't know Abraham was a convert."

"He was. So were the matriarchs after Sarah."

"Really? Who do you mean?"

"Rebecca, the wife of Isaac, began life as a heathen in Syria and was initiated into the new Hebrew faith. So did Rachel and Leah, the wives of Jacob, as well as his concubines, Bilhah and Zilpah."

Havilya paused and thought of the significance of what she had just heard.

"Jacob had twelve sons?"

"Yes, Havilya."

"These twelve sons were the founders of the twelve tribes of Israel?"

"Yes."

"So, Miriam, it seems that on their maternal side, each of the founders of the twelve tribes of Israel was the son of a convert."

"Yes, Havilya. In addition, two of them, Judah and Simeon, married women of Canaan."

"So the Torah, and therefore the Hebrew religion, regards these converts as flesh and blood ancestors of the Hebrews?"

"Exactly, Princess. And you forgot about Zipporah."

"The first wife of Moses?"

"Yes. Zipporah, of blessed memory, was the daughter of a priest of Midian."

"So the first wife of Moses was also a *ger*?"

"Indeed she was, Princess."

Havilya's spirit lifted from what she was hearing from Miriam. Her body was mellowing from the gentle treatments she was receiving at the hands of Rivka and Miriam. She felt even more at ease when Miriam explained what was to happen next, and that at all times she and Rivka would be by her side, and the three priests would be asked to wait outside when Havilya needed to change before and after the mikveh. Miriam also said that, for the three priests, this would be their first *beth din* since they left Egypt, so they would likely be as nervous as the convert they were questioning. Now Havilya suddenly understood why Miriam was doing all this, for she felt wholesome and a sense of belonging, even before the ritual bath and before she faced the *beth din*.

Miriam pulled a dress from the bundle that Rivka had brought, and explained to Havilya that she would be wearing it as she was immersed in the bath.

"Then they can do the *mikveh*. Then I will ask them to wait outside while we help you change back to your dry clothes. At that point, they can come back in, convene the *beth din* and ask you questions."

"You know just what and when something is needed, Miriam," Havilya marvelled.

* * *

The three priests performed the *mikveh* for Havilya, while Miriam and Rivka watched. As they immersed her in the water, they recited the usual prayers:

"Blessed are thou, O Lord, who had given us the law, and instructed us on the treatment of the ger. *There shall be one and the same law for the native and the ger. As you are, so shall the ger be before God."*

The three priests then stepped outside the tent while Havilya changed. Miriam was behind the curtain helping Havilya put on dry clothes, as the priests waited for Miriam's signal to come back in the tent.

Havilya now finished changing her clothes and was ready to face the *beth din.* She wore a long-sleeved brown dress, covering her from the neck to the floor. Miriam stood back to look at her.

"Your hair uncovered makes you too alluring. We can't send you like this before three priests."

Havilya laughed and said, "I can't cut my hair now."

"No, no. Here, I will give you my kerchief and we will tie your hair with it."

Miriam then covered and tied Havilya's hair in the cloth.

"Now we can call in the priests."

The three priests chose to stand behind the wooden chest, and Havilya stood in front of them, a short distance away.

"Princess Havilya," the first priest began. "We are honoured to convene this *beth din* for the purpose of considering whether you are ready to become part of the Hebrew people."

"Thank you," she said and bowed.

"We are here to judge not only your knowledge but also your sincerity."

"I understand."

"Our duty is not to recognize an insincere conversion that is merely a prelude to marriage."

The priest wanted to ensure that Havilya and all the other listeners understood that the *beth din* would be impartial, and not merely approve Havilya's conversion to facilitate her marriage to Moses.

"I understand fully," she said.

"What is our principal belief?"

"That there is the one and only God."

"Is this your belief, too?"

"Yes."

"There are several Nubian deities. They are Osiris, Isis, Amun and Apedemak. How will you worship these gods *and* the one and only God?"

Miriam fidgeted as she recognized the wily question. Havilya maintained her composure.

"These are not my gods. There is but one God."

She bowed and recited the familiar prayer.

"Hear, O Israel, the Lord thy God, the Lord is one."

As if to make up for the previous question, the second priest asked an easy question.

"What must we do on the seventh day?"

"Rest from work. It is the Fourth of the Ten Commandments. On the Sabbath, we must not do any manner of work."

The third priest said, "Princess Havilya, your mother and father are living?"

"Yes."

"And they are Nubians."

"Yes."

"Even after you become a Hebrew and the wife of Moses, will you have any duty towards them?"

"Yes. The Fifth Commandment instructs us to honour our fathers and our mothers."

The three priests looked at each other and seemed pleased. The first priest recited some prayers. When he came towards the end, his closing words were from the Torah:

"The ger who dwells with you shall be to you as the homeborn and you shall love him as yourself."

They could all hear Havilya softly recite these words with the priest.

Miriam was at ease. There can be no doubt about Havilya's knowledge and sincerity, she thought. Havilya has now become a part of the Hebrew people.

TWENTY-THREE

As soon as the military briefing and the meal that followed had ended, Shooly galloped on his horse to the Annex to see Debra.

"Come, let me take you away from here. You have been working too hard."

"I can't stay away too long. Miriam is with Havilya, and she could not tell me when she would be back."

"We will not be too long. There is a willow tree a short ride just west of the encampment. We can sit and talk."

"Do you have news?"

"Yes. I will tell you later."

She mounted the horse behind Shooly, and they rode to the north-western edge of the camp. It was slightly past noon, and the sun blazed on the shimmering sand. The Benjaminite sentries recognized them and waved. Shooly waved back.

"I hope they don't attack us on the way back," Debra said.

Shooly laughed. By now, everyone had heard of the rash attack that the Benjaminites had launched against the Nubian visitors the night before.

"No," he chuckled. "It will still be broad daylight when we return."

"They could still start a fight if they wanted to."

"Yes, but they have learned their lesson. They will be more careful to identify their target first."

"I hope so."

They reached the valley where a small stream fed a willow tree and the low bushes beside it. Shooly dismounted and walked toward the tree, pulling the horse's bridle behind him.

"Wait till I help you down," he told Debra, who had moved to dismount.

They were in the shade of the willow tree, as he tied the bridle to a branch. He then moved to Debra's side and held out his arms.

"Now you can jump into my arms."

She landed close to him, as her breasts brushed along his chest.

He held her firmly in his arms and looked in her eyes.

"I like it when you dismount into my arms."

"I feel safer, too."

She put her arms around his waist, as they kissed gently in the shade of the willow tree.

"It was only yesterday," he said, "that we made love in the ancient ruins of the Amorites. But it feels like a long time ago."

"Why?"

"Because I have been counting the hours to see you. They seemed like days."

"But all those meetings with Joshua and his commanders. They must have helped pass the time?"

"Not really. They seemed to pass slower than usual, because I could not concentrate. All I could think of was you, and how beautiful you are."

She held him tight and kissed him firmly on his lips.

"For me, it is different," she said. "Yesterday seems like a moment ago to me. It was my first time."

The glow of love in her face had remained. She still gave him the same adoring look with her wide, round, innocent black eyes. Shooly led her to some flat ground under the tree. He placed a blanket on the ground. She sat watching him unwrap a parcel.

"I brought us some food from the meeting. This lunch is fit for generals."

"What do generals eat?"

"Well, today they had more than manna wafers and goat cheese. Here, I brought you some of their dried fish and onions."

"Is this what you brought from your last mission?"

"Yes."

"Well, I will definitely try some."

As she bit on a piece of dried fish, she asked, "What is the news you were going to tell me?"

"I am leaving tomorrow."

"Again? You just came back?"

"I didn't tell you. On my last trip I discovered seventy Egyptian soldiers on the southern highway. I am being sent back to find out more about them."

"Alone?"

"No. I will go with a Nubian aide. His name is Shabitqo."

"Nubian? Did you say Nubian?"

"Yes, darling. I did."

Shooly then told her about the secret alliance between the Hebrews and the Nubians.

"I thought Moses was going to marry a Nubian princess. I didn't hear about an alliance."

"Yes, there is an alliance, too. Shabitqo and I will work together on this mission."

"What are the Nubians like?"

"Very much like us, except that their skin is black."

"If Pharaoh's soldiers find out about the alliance, will not the Nubians be in danger?"

"Of course."

Debra fell silent.

"Another thing. I will be away at least three days."

"Why that long?"

"Part of the mission includes Shabitqo going into the town of Ezion-geber to make inquiries."

"Are you going to Ezion-geber, too?"

"No, no. I will camp outside town and wait for him."

"Shooly, this is dangerous."

"I will be all right."

Debra said nothing. There was nothing more to say. As a scout, he had to do what was needed. Even as a soldier, he would be at risk. As Miriam had said to her, "We share the same fate. If the Egyptians attack the camp, they will treat everyone the same – men, women and children. They will enslave or massacre us all."

Shooly tried to change the subject. "How are things at the Annex?"

"Easier. We are starting to send some of the wounded to their families."

"Will you have a chance to rest?"

"I think so. Until the next episode."

These words lay heavily on him. He knew that there would be many more episodes. More than that, there would be battles for years to come. Starting soon, he thought. He dared not tell her now about the plan to send spies into Canaan. He was sure that this would lead to a major battle between the

Hebrews and the Canaanites and their allies the Amalekites. The number of Hebrews dead and wounded would be like nothing Debra had seen before.

He lay on the ground on her lap, as she stroked his hair. They were both quiet, listening only to the sound of their breathing.

"Will you miss me, Debra?"

"Or course, darling."

"If it will make it better, let us have a pact."

"Saying what?"

"The pact says that as soon as I think of you, I assume that you are thinking of me. In this way, we will never be alone, because we are always thinking of each other."

"Always?"

"Yes, always."

"Even when I am bandaging a wound?"

"Yes, even then. Even when I am looking for Egyptians, I will think of you."

"I like this pact. But what happens when we have to concentrate on something else – like something important at work, an emergency?"

"That is allowed. In fact, it means we are not suffering each other's loss. It means we are busy for the moment. But as soon as the moment stops, then we immediately think of each other, and the suffering will not start."

Debra sighed wearily.

"I don't want any suffering – for me or for you. I just want to be with you, Shooly. In your arms or with you making me laugh."

He moved and lay beside her. He kissed her on her forehead, on her eyes and then on her nose.

"There will be no suffering for you, if I can help it. I will be careful, and I will return as quickly as possible."

She squeezed him hard.

"I love you, Shooly."

They made love again and then remained embraced in the sun for a long time. They felt a wind in the air, which caught the branches overhead in a gentle breeze.

Clouds were gathering in the horizon. Overhead, a bird circled as it prepared to land on its prey on the ground.

TWENTY-FOUR

"I think we can close down for the day," Reyes said to his attendant.

"Yes, master."

They were preparing to end their work day in the Gaza administration office. It was still early afternoon, but Reyes decided to leave anyway.

"It has been a good day."

"Yes, master."

It had started badly with the mob, Reyes thought. But as luck would have it, the visit from Ramentop of the Black Knights of Pharaoh helped to scare them off. Nonetheless, Reyes liked to give the credit to his attendant. Praising your underlings costs nothing, he thought. It helps to make them loyal without having to raise their salary.

"You did well to disperse the crowd," Reyes told him.

"You are very kind, master."

"This will be remembered when the appropriate time comes."

"I am grateful, master."

Ramentop's visit was fortunate for another reason, Reyes thought. It revealed to him that he was not alone in suspecting the activities of his boss, Sebakashta, the Viceroy of Nubia. The suspicion must have permeated all the way to Pharaoh's court. Certainly, Ramentop shared it, and was taking steps to investigate the Nubian. Perhaps, just perhaps, Reyes hoped, this would be the avenue for him to get rid of the Nubian, so that he, Reyes, could again become the ruler in Gaza.

"Master, master," the attendant said suddenly, "I think we have more visitors."

The attendant was standing by the window preparing to close the shutters when he saw two men dismounting from their horses, and walking up the steps to the front door.

"Who?"

"I don't recognize them, master."

Reyes looked out and he immediately recognized the two spies working secretly for him.

"Yes, yes," Reyes said. "These are personal friends. They have come for a private visit. Please let them in."

The attendant held the door open, as the two men entered the office.

"Welcome, welcome," said Reyes. "This is my loyal servant. He was just preparing to leave, and we will not detain him."

"I can stay, master, if you wish."

"No, no, thank you. Just bring us a tray of refreshments and then you are excused for the rest of the day."

"Thank you, master."

As Reyes waited for his attendant to bring the tray, he led the visitors to sit on the chairs around the table in the middle of the room. He engaged the two men in small chatter about the weather and their families. A wink from Reyes conveyed the message that he did not wish to talk serious business until his attendant left.

Finally, the attendant came back with three goblets of rose water, a plate of almonds and another plate of soft over-ripe dates.

"Thank you. That will be all. Please lock the door behind you."

"Yes, master."

As soon as the attendant had left, Reyes sat across from his visitors and leaned forward towards them.

"Well, well, what do you have for me, Jalam?" Reyes asked eagerly.

Jalam was tall and thin, with narrow drooping eyes, a long nose and a pointed chin. He had a thin moustache and two days of growth on his face. He grimaced as he rubbed his right cheek.

"We may have found something. Omar will tell you all about it," Jalam said pointing to the other man as he reached for the dates and the almonds.

"He wants me to do the work, while he eats all the food," Omar said, as they all laughed.

Omar was a short, stocky man with a thick beard and a round, chubby face.

"Well," Omar began. "We followed the Viceroy and his two aides, as you asked us to do."

Jalam was now removing a pip from a soft date, and replacing it with an almond. He tossed the date in his mouth. Reyes could hear the almond cracking between Jalam's teeth.

"They spent one night in Ezion-geber."

"When was that?"

"Three days ago."

"Yes, go on."

"The next day one of the aides – it was Shabitqo – went out and came back several hours later. We decided to stay near the administration building where the Viceroy remained."

"Yes, I understand."

Reyes had instructed them not to separate. He thought they would be safer travelling together. As well, he did not trust them fully. If one turned out to be disloyal, the other would report him to Reyes.

"We don't know what Shabitqo did during his absence."

"Go on."

"Late that day, the three Nubians left Esau's office and rode west along the southern highway."

"How far did you follow them?"

"Well, this is the road to Memphis. Anyone travelling west on that highway from Ezion-geber would be going to Memphis."

"That's right."

"But a short distance west of Ezion-geber, they turned south and rode into the hills of southern Sinai."

"Did you follow them?"

"For a short distance."

"Did you see anyone meet them?"

"No. It began to get dark. So we turned back and returned to Ezion-geber for the night."

"Anything else?"

"The next day we rode back to the same spot. We saw nothing. We rode further west and saw seventy Egyptian troops."

"What were they doing there?"

"We are not sure. But they were moving in the direction of Ezion-geber."

They all understood the significance of this report. The Viceroy did not continue toward Memphis, as his normal duties would require him to do.

Reyes wished they could have found out more, but, still, what they told him would be of great interest to Ramentop of the Black Knights, he thought. The report of his spies clearly indicated that the Viceroy was involved in some sort of extraneous activity. Secondly, it pointed to the location where the Viceroy was active. This would allow the Black Knights to mobilize more resources and concentrate them in that particular area. Thirdly, the presence of the Egyptian troops could provide a means for Ramentop to accelerate his investigation. Eventually, Reyes thought, Ramentop and his Black Knights would find out what the Nubians were planning.

"Anything else?" asked Reyes.

"No. That is all we were able to discover."

Omar now reached for one of the plates for an almond or a date. He found that Jalam had finished them all, so he took a goblet and drank some rose-water.

"What do you think it all means?" Jalam asked.

"Well, it means that the Viceroy is involved in some activities and he is doing it somewhere in the southern Sinai, south of the southern highway."

"Are Pharaoh's people doing anything there?"

"Not to my knowledge," said Reyes.

"It is all wilderness there."

"Except for an oasis or two, there are no towns or settlements."

"Except for possibly the Hebrews."

They all knew the rumours that the Hebrews were hiding somewhere in the hills of southern Sinai. No one had been able to find them. But there had been many surprise attacks on Egyptian patrols and caravans. Reports to the Egyptian military had led some to suspect that this was the work of the Hebrews.

When Jalam mentioned the Hebrews, Reyes shook his head with a perplexed look. He took a goblet and drank some rose-water.

"Assume for a moment," Jalam said, "assume for a moment that the Hebrews are in that area."

"Yes?" said Reyes.

"Assume also that the Nubians would want to reach them."

"Yes?"

"Why would they want to?"

"That is the puzzle."

"The Hebrews need food and weapons."

"And the Viceroy has both."

"Do you think he would sell them food and weapons for private gain?"

"Possibly," Omar interjected.

"What if the Nubians do not wish to reach the Hebrews?"

"Yes?"

"Then they would be in danger from the Hebrews, because the Nubians work for Pharaoh."

"Yes, but why would the Nubians go to the wilderness?"

"Perhaps to meet secretly with others."

"Hittite agents?"

"Yes, that is a possibility."

"The Nubians may be trying to contact the Hittites."

The Hittites were the strongest active force threatening Pharaoh's empire at that time, Reyes thought. The size and experience of their armies would make them a worthy ally for anyone including the Nubians. But the Hittite forces were on the brink of a major war with Pharaoh. It seemed far-fetched that the Nubians would dare to seek their alliance. It would also be more logical for the Nubians to meet the Hittites further north. But the Hebrews were not known as a major fighting force at that time. The idea that the Hebrews and the Nubians would form a secret alliance was too outlandish.

Reyes finally stood up.

"We are now guessing without facts. Nonetheless, what you have told me is of immense value. I thank you."

"We are glad to be of service," Jalam said, as he and Omar stood up to leave.

As he closed the door behind them, Reyes was pleased with himself. He finally had something for Ramentop. His information would enable the Black Knights to search more closely in the area where the Viceroy seemed to be active. He did not much care whether the Hebrews were there or not. If they were and the Egyptians found them, so much the better, he thought. He would be even more appreciated. But what mattered more was that he had found the place where the Viceroy – his boss – was involved in some extraneous activity.

However, he could not reveal this information to Ramentop too quickly. Ramentop had been there to see Reyes only that morning. If he revealed the report of his spies now, Ramentop would know that he, Reyes, was not telling him the whole truth – namely that Reyes had previously and on his own initiative sent out the spies.

Reyes said to himself, "As my father used to say, sometimes you must not reveal everything at once."

TWENTY-FIVE

"You are going to turn their heads," Rivka said.

"And their gaze will be fixed on you as they marvel at your beauty," said Leah.

The two women were hovering around Havilya in her tent, as they made some final adjustments to her wedding dress. Miriam was sitting at the table and watching from a distance.

"Now, now," Havilya said. "You are kind, but you must not flatter me too much."

"It looks better with the veil," said Leah, who had sewn it that morning after Havilya's last fitting.

"You work quickly, Leah."

"Sometimes one has to, Princess."

Rivka placed the gold tiara, Miriam's gift to Havilya, on Havilya's head. The veil was fastened in front of it, and when folded back behind her head, covered the tiara and made it invisible.

"How does the veil look?"

"Something is not right," said Miriam, as she got up to look up at Havilya. "I think the veil is fine, it is just in the wrong place. I think the veil should be fastened behind, not in front of, the tiara."

As Miriam made the adjustments, she swung back the veil, which fell behind the gold tiara. The precious stones on the tiara, now completely visible, glistened just above Havilya's forehead.

"You are right, Miriam," Leah said. "This is much better."

"This gift means very much to me, Miriam. You have made me feel accepted, part of you."

"Havilya, it is my duty to pass down this family heirloom. I thought you should have it."

"What is its origin?"

"We are not sure. We think it is from the time of Joseph."

"That old?"

"Yes. There is a story attached to it."

"Tell me."

Havilya sat on the chair by the table.

Shaul Ezer

"Well, you know the story of Joseph. We Hebrews never tire of telling it."

"I read it in the writings that Moses gave me, but I would like to hear it from you."

Miriam then told Havilya of how Joseph, when only eighteen, was sold into slavery by his eleven brothers. They were jealous of him because he was the favourite of their father Jacob due to Joseph's talent in interpreting dreams. While he was a slave, Zuleika, the wife of his master Potiphar, had made advances which he rejected. By the way of revenge, she falsely accused *him* of making advances, for which he was imprisoned for thirteen years.

Word of Joseph's skills in the interpretation of dreams spread out of the prison walls. When Pharaoh had a dream no one could interpret, Joseph was summoned from the prison to the palace. From Pharaoh's dream, Joseph predicted that Egypt would have seven years of plenty followed by seven years of famine. He advised Pharaoh to appoint a man of wisdom and discernment to act as overseer of the lands. Pharaoh was so impressed that he put Joseph in charge. During the seven years of plenty, he collected and stored grain under Pharaoh's authority. This became a reserve for the seven years of famine. Overnight Joseph rose from prisoner to first minister. To Joseph, Pharaoh also gave Asenath, the daughter of the Egyptian priest of the city of On, whom Joseph married. They soon fell very much in love with each other. During the next seven years, Egypt prospered under Joseph's administration.

Havilya then said, "Moses told me that was the time when the Pharaohs began to appreciate the Hebrews."

"Yes," Miriam continued. "During those seven years, Asenath bore two sons for Joseph, Manasseh and Ephraim. To honour his wife and to celebrate his good fortune, Joseph had this gold tiara made for her."

"What a wonderful story."

"There is more. The seven diamonds that you see on the tiara are for the seven years of prosperity. The two rubies above the row of seven diamonds represent his two sons. Thus, Joseph gave this tiara to Asenath as a token of his love and a gesture of gratitude for giving him his two sons in a time of prosperity."

"How did the tiara come into your Levite family?"

150

"We are not sure.   Some say a granddaughter of Manasseh married a Levite and was given the tiara at her wedding.   Others think that Manasseh and Ephraim had inherited considerable wealth on the death of their father Joseph, and they distributed some of that wealth, including jewellery, to their nephews and nieces."

As Havilya listened to Miriam, she wondered whether Moses would love her as Joseph loved Asenath. She thought of the evening when she first realized that Moses wanted her to become his wife. As the six of them – Moses, Joshua, Zabad, the Viceroy, Shabitqo and herself – had sat by the campfire, she had noticed that Moses seemed distracted. The political and military discussion had seemed to hold little of his interest, and he had deferred more of the decisions to Joshua. Moses had suddenly seemed more attentive to her, to be almost watching her every step. He had fidgeted nervously and looked at the others as if he wished he could be alone with her.

In his presence, she too had become self-conscious. She had started to care more about what she wore and how she looked, even when dressed as Taharqo.   Her face would suddenly flush each time he touched her, however slightly, as when he passed her a piece of mutton that was broiling in the fire. She had begun to notice that Moses held an attraction that had nothing to do with his being a man of learning.

While Joshua had been in mid-sentence talking to the Viceroy, Moses had suddenly blurted something to her, as if oblivious to the others.

"I need to go for a walk. Please come with me."

She remembered that she too had been nervous, as they had strolled that night in the hills away from the campfire. He had been looking down toward the ground as they walked, too shy to face her.

"I don't know how to say this. I am a poor middle-aged shepherd with a sun-worn face. A leader of a young nation of former slaves. Many of them scoff at my rule. We have more promise than land. We are sustained by mere faith in our invisible God."

Then he had shifted his gaze to look directly at her.

"You are a beautiful young princess from a fine family and a rich culture. You have had your own nation and your own land for many centuries. In many ways, Nubia rivals the Egypt of the Pharaohs."

He paused for a moment, and then continued.

"I don't know whether I am worthy of you or whether I should dare to say what is on my mind."

His voice had seemed to be breaking now.

"I... I have loved you ever since that moment when you told me that you and your so-called sister were one."

She had barely been able to suppress a silent chuckle.

"I will never forget your words. You said to me: *If I am a coward, it is the fear of showing my love.* How brave you were, I thought, to love a man like me and to reveal it in such an innocent way."

She remembered that she had now touched his arm, as he had continued.

"If you still feel that way, I want you to be with me always, to share our lives together, as husband and wife."

She could not remember exactly what she had said to him at that moment, except that she had put her arms around his neck and her face firmly on his chest, sobbing uncontrollably with happiness. Later, when they had been more relaxed, he had tried to explain.

"Normally, I would have talked first to your father. I would have asked for his consent. But these are not normal times. I did not want to mix our political discussions with my love for you."

He had not seemed shy to tell her this now.

"I also wanted to know how you would feel yourself, without first talking to your father about it."

He had hesitated now, as he had seemed to realize that he was perhaps underestimating her independence.

"Not that you do not have your own mind. Especially about what is best for you."

She could not remember what she had said, or whether she had needed an explanation.

As she sat now in her wedding dress and looked at Miriam, she suddenly noticed how much Miriam resembled her youngest brother in appearance.

She thought of how attracted she was to him the very first time they had met. She had noticed that he was slender like a palm-tree and tall and strong. Later she would discover his other side – a meek nature with a shining countenance. Coupled with his physical stature, he had seemed like a vulnerable lion. What could be more lovable and irresistible to a woman, she thought. She wished that her mother Sebaha could be with her now, to see her on her wedding day.

"You were right, mother," she would have told her. "You always said to father that no one will arrange Havilya's marriage – to a Nubian or to anyone else. That is something she will arrange herself."

Suddenly, her thoughts were broken by a gentle touch on her hand.

"Come, Havilya," Miriam said. "We can't have the wedding without you."

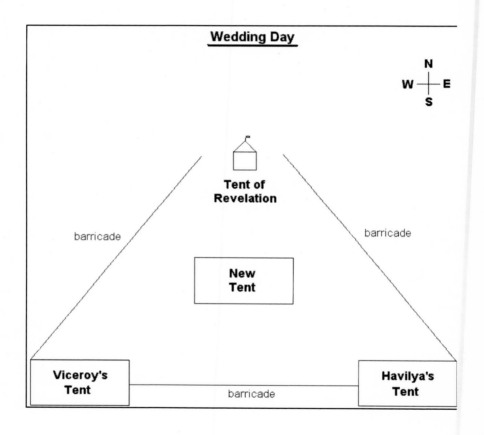

TWENTY-SIX

The marriage ceremony was to take place beside the sanctuary inside the Tent of Revelation, and the celebrations after were placed in the new tent where the Hebrews and the Nubians had the military briefing that morning. The new tent was placed just south of the Tent of Revelation. A short distance further south of the new tent were the Viceroy's tent on the west and Havilya's tent on the east. These three tents formed a triangle pointing north toward the Tent of Revelation, with the new tent at the apex and the Nubians' tents along the base of the triangle.

News of the wedding had spread through the encampment, and a crowd was forming along the peripheries of the four tents. This was cordoned off with barriers and soldiers.

It was late afternoon, and the heat was still radiating from the ground. The area inside the barricades between the new tent and the Tent of Revelation was bustling with noise and activity in preparation for the wedding. Inside the Tent of Revelation, Bezalel and Ohaliab were building the *chuppah*, under which the marriage ceremony was to occur. The roof was a square plank of wood with each side about the length of one person. Each corner was supported by a wooden stilt. The roof was covered with a white silk cloth embroidered on the edges with gold rope and blue tassels. The cloth was hanging slightly over the roof, revealing the embroidery and the tassels on the top four sides of the canopy. The north and south sides of the canopy were hollow to provide standing room for the high priest and the bride and groom. The east and west sides were draped with blue taffeta cloth laced with streaks of yellow silk material.

More elaborate preparations, under Joshua's direction, were underway in the new tent. Entrances on the east and west side were left open and on each side two soldiers were placed with large fans, which they gently waved up and down to create a breeze through the tent. Inside, the walls were adorned with the same gold rope and blue tassels used for the *chuppah*, but here, the rope was fastened to the walls in waves, and a blue tassel hung from the trough of each wave.

There was a wooden dais in each corner of the new tent, on which were placed two candles and a bowl of burning incense. Each dais was tended by two young girls dressed in the best white finery their families could provide. Along the north and south walls were placed long and narrow tables, with plates of dates, baked sweets, manna wafers and broiled lamb. Room was left open on the tables for other plates of food that the guests would bring.

The interior of the tent was arranged as it had been that morning for the military briefing. A group of carpets were placed in a square in the middle. The guests were to be seated around the square, with a short distance between their backs and the walls of the tent. Now, however, two special features had been added for the evening celebration. Cushions were placed at intervals around the square. Each guest was to be seated on the cushion or use it as an arm-rest on the side. As well, white linen was placed in front of where the guests would be seated. The cushions were sprinkled generously with rosewater which the Hebrews kept for special occasions. The scent from the rosewater and the breeze from the fans created a fresh fragrance, while a more sensual aroma emanated from the burning incense and candles.

Eldad and Medad, as had become their custom, were passing the time outside the Tent of Revelation. As priests, they were not prevented from crossing the barricades. Like most of the Hebrews, by now they had heard about the wedding, but were not quite sure where it would take place.

"What if the wedding is in the new tent?" asked Eldad.

"I think it will be in the Tent of Revelation," said Medad.

"But if it is not, the Nubians will come out of their tents, go into the new tent and we will miss them altogether."

"It is too late anyway. All the good spots are taken. If we move, we will have to look over the shoulders of the crowd and the soldiers."

Suddenly they noticed a movement just south of them. The soldiers were making an opening to let in a well-dressed man and a woman.

"This is Pagiel of the tribe of Asher and his wife."

"They are going in the Tent of Revelation."

"They are the first wedding guests to arrive."

"We really were fooled last night."

"There was no sign of a woman among the Nubians last night. Either she came later or she was disguised."

"There is Eliasaph of the tribe of Gad with Shelumiel of the tribe of Simeon."

"They are wearing black shirts."

"Their wives are not with them."

"They are mourning the dead in their family from the recent raid."

"They will likely not stay for the celebrations after the wedding."

They watched as the other guests arrived. Soon after, Miriam and her husband Caleb went in, followed by Aaron and his wife Elisheva. Moses was the last of the Hebrews to walk in under heavy guard.

"Where are the Nubians?"

"Here comes something?"

The Viceroy and Shabitqo, surrounded by four soldiers, approached the Tent of Revelation. The Viceroy was dressed in an Egyptian-style kilt made of a thick white silky fabric. It covered his body from his chest to his knees. A geometric pattern of red thread embroidered the borders of the kilt. A semi-circular ornament four fingers deep covered his chest from one shoulder to the other. This ornament was chequered in colours of black, yellow, red and blue. Two broad gold sashes were tied around his body – one around his waist and the other diagonally across his chest. His head was covered with an Egyptian headdress, with flaps behind his ears. His legs below the kilt were bare, except for gold sandals on his feet.

The Viceroy's face was freshly shaven and his black complexion glistened in the shafts of sunlight coming through the gathering clouds, forming a contrast against his white formal dress. He smiled benignly to the crowd as he looked to his left and then to his right. The watching Hebrew throng had suddenly become silent. This was the first time that many of them had been this close to a high-ranking Egyptian official.

Shabitqo did not seem to be dressed for the occasion. He wore a brown kilt and a brown riding cloak, and a white kerchief was tied around his head. The two Nubians then entered the Tent of Revelation while their escort of soldiers stayed behind outside.

"These are the two Nubians we saw last night," said Eldad.

"I think so," said Medad.

"So where is the bride?"

"As usual, you must wait longer for her."

"Someone is always fussing over the bride's appearance."

"Or her dress."

"Maybe brides like to show reluctance."

"Especially if they are much younger than the groom."

"How old do you think they are?"

"I don't know. Moses is more than seventy. I heard she is not too young. Someone guessed early thirties."

"Why?"

"Her fighting skills. She must be a seasoned warrior to outfight our sentries. That takes years."

"Not to beat the Benjaminites."

They both chuckled, as they looked south for any sign of Princess Havilya.

Suddenly they started to hear cheering noises beyond the new tent.

"Havilya, Havilya," some shouted.

Finally she emerged from the east side of the new tent. Rivka was behind her holding the train of her wedding dress and both were surrounded by an escort of four soldiers.

Havilya was holding her head high as she approached. The veil covered her face in front of the tiara and her wide collar scarcely covered her long neck. As she approached, they could see her black visage through her veil.

"We heard about black Nubian beauties, but I never saw one this close."

"Nor I."

"Now the young men have a reason to kill Moses."

They both laughed.

Soon Havilya stopped at the entrance as Rivka adjusted the train on the wedding dress. Taking a deep breath, Havilya, followed by Rivka, disappeared into the Tent of Revelation.

"Well, tonight Moses should be happy."

"If she cannot make him happy, no other woman can."

As Havilya entered, she saw Aaron the High Priest facing her. He was under the *chuppah*. Miriam had told her that this symbolized Abraham's tent which, like the couple's home, would be a place of shelter, hospitality and friendship.

She could see three others inside the *chuppah*. Her father was on Aaron's right and Miriam was on Aaron's left. Moses waited for her just outside the *chuppah* close to Miriam.

The *chuppah* was placed in front of a walled-off area of the tent. Havilya assumed that this was the sanctuary, which was accessible only on special occasions of sanctity. She realized that inside the sanctuary would be a small chamber containing the ark. This was the Holy of Holies, in which only Moses could enter at all times.

With her heart pounding, she walked slowly between the throng of guests on either side. She was only a few steps from the *chuppah*, but it seemed to her like an eternity. She felt her blood draining from her face, when suddenly she felt a strong grip on her right arm. Moses held her hand, as they walked the last few steps together.

She was now under the *chuppah* facing Aaron with Moses on her right. Her father was on her left facing Miriam.

Moses now turned toward her. He smiled as he reached over and raised her veil, looked at her face and lowered the veil again. The groom performed this ritual to avoid making Jacob's mistake. Because he didn't see the face of the bride, Jacob had married Leah instead of Rachel, the woman he loved. By dressing his bride with a veil, the groom sets her apart from all others.

Moses was wearing a simple white robe of heavy linen. He had a round white cap on his head. His black beard was neatly trimmed. Few had seen him as now, with a smiling, happy face on his rough, weather-worn complexion.

"Welcome in this house of God," the High Priest began.

Aaron was dressed with more adornment than the priests Havilya had seen in Nubia. He wore a white tunic with sleeves made of fine linen. It covered his shoulders and reached down to his feet. Over the tunic, he wore a sleeveless blue robe embroidered around the opening of the neck. The hem was adorned with balls of richly coloured material in the shape of

159

pomegranates. Between each pair of pomegranates was placed a golden bell. The bells attached to the robe indicated to the congregation when he was performing his duties.

Under his arms, his body was wrapped by another vestment. This apron-like garment was called the ephod or pinafore, woven with intricate design in gold, blue, purple and crimson yarns. The ephod was held up with two shoulder-straps, to each of which was sealed a lazuli stone.

A breastplate made of the same fabric covered his chest. The fabric was doubled over and open on all sides except the bottom, so as to form a bag or pouch. The breastplate was set with twelve precious stones, each engraved with the name of one of the tribes of Israel. The stones were arranged in gold settings in four rows, three stones in a row. Two rings were attached to the corners of the breastplate. Two other rings were placed on the shoulder-straps. Threads of blue passing though the rings tied them together, keeping the breastplate firmly on the chest of the High Priest.

A plate of gold with a linen back extended over his forehead about two fingers deep. It was held up with blue string attached at each end and tied behind his head. Finally, a sash of embroidered fabric was fastened as a girdle around his waist.

The High Priest now recited the Invocation, asking God to bless the wedding:

> *Splendour is upon everything.*
> *Blessing is upon everything.*
> *Who is full of this abundance*
> *Bless this groom and bride.*

Havilya smiled softly to her father, who was now standing erect but relaxed with his eyes fixed on the High Priest, who had just finished the Blessing for the First Cup:

> *Holy One of the Blessing, your presence fills creation forming the fruit of the vine.*

Then she heard the Betrothal Blessing:

> *Praised are you, Monarch over Time and Space, who has allowed us to share life through chuppah and marriage. Praised are you God, who sanctifies your people Israel through the covenant of marriage.*

The Nubian Princess

The High Priest took a sip of wine and passed the goblet to Moses who then took a sip. Miriam stepped forward and lifted the veil from the face of Havilya. The bride then took the goblet from Moses.

Miriam's shoulder-length grey hair was combed smoothly and tied in a ribbon behind her head. She wore a simple red gown of rich fabric, but with no ornaments or embroidery. Her face was shiny, as if she had scrubbed it hard that afternoon. Now she looked brightly at Havilya, who had just taken a sip of wine and returned the goblet to Moses. Miriam them replaced the veil over Havilya's face, and stepped back to her spot to the High Priest's left.

Moses then took Havilya's right hand, placed a ring on her index finger and said:

"By this ring you are consecrated to me as my wife in accordance with the traditions of Israel."

Havilya thought of the Hebrew belief that the index finger was directly connected by a special artery to the heart. And so, by this ring, his heart was joined to hers.

In deference to the Viceroy, the High Priest gave a short explanation of where they were in the ceremony.

"We have now ended the first part of the ceremony, in which the bride and groom are betrothed and consecrated to each other. This is called *kiddushin*, which means sanctification or consecration. The next part, called *nissuin*, consists of the seven blessings of marriage. Those blessings reflect the splendours of creation and the joys of marriage. They hearken to the time of Adam and Eve. Since they were created together as male and female, theirs was the most compatible marriage."

Aaron now held another cup of wine, and began to recite the Seven Blessings:

Blessed is the creation of the fruit of the vine.

Blessed is the creation which embodies glory.

Blessed is the creation of the human being.

Blessed is the design of the human being. Developing our wisdom, we may become God-like. We are assembled from the very fabric of the universe and are composed of eternal elements. Blessed be and Blessed is our creation.

Rejoice and be glad you who wandered homeless. In joy you have gathered with your sisters and your brothers. Blessed is the joy of our gathering.

Bestow happiness on these loving mates as would creatures feel in Eden's garden. Blessed be the joy of lovers.

Blessed is the creation of joy and celebration, lover and mate, gladness and jubilation, pleasure and delight, love and solidarity, friendship and peace. Soon may we hear on the streets of the city and the paths of the fields, the voice of joy, the voice of gladness, the voice of lover, the voice of mate, the triumphant voice of lovers from the canopy and the voice of youths from their feasts of song. Blessed Blessed Blessed is the joy of lovers, one with each other.

The High Priest now drank from the second cup, as did Moses, who lifted the veil from Havilya's face so she too could drink. Moses then took the empty cup, placed it on the ground and smashed it under his foot. Moses had warned Havilya about this custom. The broken glass, marking the end of the wedding, was also a reminder. While the wedding had provided a taste of happiness, it was a reminder that the Hebrews were still in exile, a broken people in need of a house.

After the ceremony, Moses took Havilya to a private room. It was in the walled-in area, just outside the sanctuary and the Holy of Holies.

"This is my private study," he said.

The room was bare, except for two chairs and a small table. There were some writing materials on the table – a reed pen, a knife to sharpen the pen, a jar of ink and blank papyrus. At one side was a half-finished scroll.

"I could hardly wait to hold you in my arms," he said.

He unfastened her veil and her tiara, and put them on the table beside his writings. He then put his arms around her waist and kissed her on her forehead, her eyes and her lips.

"When we met, God must have been smiling, for he surely meant us to be together."

She felt secure and loved, as though she had always belonged in that small, austere and stuffy room. Although warm and comfortable in his embrace, a cold sensation enveloped her, as if she was in the presence of a fear-inspiring force. She knew that, as husband and wife, they would face ecstasy and pain, but theirs would have a rare and extraordinary reach. She had never had any doubt that she wanted to be a part of his destiny. She smiled to herself now as she thought of her father's words earlier that day, asking whether she had any doubts. Her head was on her husband's shoulders, as the sound of the merrymaking outside reached their ears.

"Come," he said finally. "We are expected to join the festivities."

* * *

"They are gone, Shabitqo."

Shooly pointed at the location where he had spotted the Egyptian troops.

"There were seventy Egyptian soldiers camped there with twenty-six horses."

"Are you sure this is the place?"

"Absolutely."

They were standing on the ridge looking north toward the southern highway. Behind them was a sharp drop in the land.

Shooly turned around and looked at the drop behind them.

"Is this not where you left the two mules for me, Shabitqo?"

"Yes, it is."

"Well, I spent the night here with the two mules and my horse. The next morning, I looked toward the highway, and found the Egyptian troops camped there."

They had been riding since dawn when they had left the Hebrew encampment. It was now early evening. As they faced north toward the southern highway, the sun was at an angle on

163

their left. Shabitqo thought for a while, as he paced to the left and the right of the ridge, looking for any sign of the Egyptians.

"Shooly, there is still some daylight left."

"What do you suggest?"

"That we split up."

"How?"

"We will both ride near the highway. You go toward the setting sun in the direction of Memphis. I will go in the opposite direction toward Ezion-geber."

"Then what?"

"We will look for the Egyptians. We will meet here at dark."

"It is dangerous to ride in the open highway alone."

"It is. We will ride in the hills but close enough to see movements on the highway."

"All right. Anything else?"

"In your direction, Shooly, you are less likely to run into the local inhabitants. In my direction, as I get nearer to Ezion-geber, I could meet some locals, but as a Nubian, I will not be unfamiliar to them."

"We will avoid contact in any case."

"That is right."

Shooly looked up at the sun.

"We don't have much time, Shabitqo."

"We must make haste."

They quickly mounted their horses and galloped in opposite directions.

TWENTY-SEVEN

"Havilya and Moses ben Amram!" shouted the sentry, as the newlyweds entered the new tent. As if on cue, the two young girls in each corner quickly stoked the burning incense and then each held high a lighted candle in her hand.

Suddenly the music and dancing stopped, as all eyes were now on Havilya and Moses. She had discarded the veil and the train behind her dress. She was still wearing the wedding dress that Leah had made for her. They could see her height and shape more closely. The tiara that was Miriam's gift remained on her head, and it made her look taller than her husband.

Moses looked cheerful and boyish. He was still wearing the white robe of heavy linen, but he was without a head covering. His left arm was on Havilya's back, as he gently guided her into the tent.

Moses and Havilya started to walk toward their seats on the side furthest from the entrance. They could see two empty seats between the Viceroy and Miriam on his right. To Miriam's right sat her husband Caleb, then Aaron's wife Elisheva, then Aaron. To the Viceroy's left sat Joshua, then Joshua's wife. Shabitqo stood behind the Viceroy. Havilya sat beside her father and Moses sat between Havilya and Joshua.

The remaining three sides were occupied by the four commanders and their wives, and the elders of the twelve tribes and their wives. However, the tribes of Gad and Simeon, who were in mourning, were not represented.

As the musicians began to play, Miriam rose with a plate of henna in one hand. This was in deference to the Nubian custom of applying henna, considered by the Nubians to be a symbol of life and blessing, to the fingers of the bride. The custom had been adopted by the Egyptians and became well-known to the Hebrews. On a signal from Miriam, several Hebrew women surrounded Havilya, and applied the henna dye to her fingers, in an act that symbolically blessed and adorned the bride.

Then Miriam pulled Havilya briskly to the middle. Prompted by Miriam, several of the women, including Havilya, started to dance.

At first, Havilya felt shy and awkward. Her movements were slow and tentative. But the other women, led by Miriam's energetic movements, were confident and brisk. Soon the other women joined them dancing, and there was hardly any room left in the middle for all the gyrating bodies.

As the ambiance of the decorations and the candlelight and the scents in the tent wafted over her, Havilya soon regained her confidence. Suddenly the other women moved back from her, leaving her alone in the middle of an empty circle. Now all eyes were fixed on Havilya as she danced alone in the middle of the tent.

At first, her smooth spinning and circular arm movements had a gentle and modest quality. But then as the music became louder and faster, she responded in kind. Her pirouettes became more abrupt and alluring. She held her arms high in a seductive, plaintive twirl that left the men gasping. Two seated women eyed her closely.

"Well, the Nubians can dance," the first woman said.

"As well as any woman in the fleshpots of Egypt," said the other.

"Now, now, is this bothering you?"

"Only that she married one of our men."

"But she and her father seem to be fine, upright people."

"Yes, but Nubia and Egypt are full of men. Were none good enough for her?"

"Moses seems very happy."

"I don't like these foreign women stealing our men. They always seem to get the best."

"Come, come now, enjoy the evening. Isn't the food exceptional?"

"That is another thing. It is the work of Joshua."

"I also hear the Viceroy brought gifts of sweets and other foods."

"Joshua's soldiers always have the best food. They never seem to have any for the women and children."

The music started to wind down. As it stopped, Havilya also stopped her dance and bowed low to loud cheering. Miriam then embraced her and led her back to Moses, who was watching at the edge of the dancing throng. He kissed her and led her to their seats beside the Viceroy.

Havilya took her seat, with the Viceroy to her left and Moses to her right. Miriam also took her seat to the right of Moses.

Moses leaned over to the Viceroy.

"Your daughter has many talents, your Highness."

"She has always treated me and her mother with delightful surprises, my Lord."

"I regret that her mother is not with us to see her daughter's marriage."

"I am sure there will be other opportunities for her to enjoy your hospitality."

"Your Highness, much of our hospitality has been made possible by your kindness."

Moses now motioned to the sumptuous foods in front of them, most of which were gifts from the Viceroy. At every short interval, there was a large tray, each with four plates. A plate of sweets contained manna wafers and honey cake. Another was full of almonds and pistachio nuts. A third contained parsley and onions, with the fourth full of dried Nile pike. Beside each tray was a bowl of fruit with grapes, figs and pomegranates.

The Viceroy smiled as he looked at the foods in front of them.

"The markets of Ezion-geber are rich in their varieties. Isn't that right, Shabitqo?"

His aide, who had purchased and packed most of these foods himself, smiled.

"Yes, my Lord."

"But they don't make manna wafers like the Hebrews. Here, Shabitqo. Try one."

The Viceroy passed a manna wafer to Shabitqo.

"No, they don't, my Lord," Shabitqo said, as he took a bite.

Miriam got up and went to the middle again where the dancing had resumed. She whispered to the musicians, who changed their tune to a fast melody familiar to all except the Nubians.

"Miriam is now leading the women to sing the Song of the Sea," Moses said to Havilya and the Viceroy.

Miriam and the women held their hands together forming a circle. Suddenly, Havilya got up and joined the women in the circle, with Miriam holding her right hand and Joshua's wife her left.

As the lute and the oboe played the gentle melody, Miriam, Havilya and the other women sang the song celebrating the victory of the sea and anticipating the victories to come in Canaan:

I will sing to the Lord, for He has triumphed gloriously
Horse and driver He has hurled into the sea.
The Lord is my strength and might;
He is become my salvation.

This is my God and I will enshrine Him;
The God of my father, and I will exalt Him,
The Lord, the Warrior –
Lord is His name.

Pharaoh's chariots and his army
He has cast into the sea
And the pick of his officers
Are drowned in the Sea of Reeds...

Then they all stopped singing, and they gently nudged Miriam in the middle of the circle. As Miriam stood alone surrounded by all the women, one of them recited from the official account of those momentous events:

For the horses of Pharaoh, with his chariots and horsemen, went into the sea; and the Lord turned back on them the waters of the sea; but the Israelites marched on dry ground in the midst of the sea.

Then Miriam the prophetess, Aaron's sister, took a timbrell in her hand, and all the women went out after her in dance with timbrells.

And Miriam chanted for them.

Then all together they sang again with Miriam:

Sing to the Lord, for he has triumphed gloriously;
Horse and driver He has hurled into the sea.

* * *

The Nubian Princess

"Havilya, Havilya," shouted the wedding guests.

The music and dancing had stopped and the attendants had served the evening's dinner. This was broiled lamb seasoned with coriander and sage cooked with dates that were stuffed with almonds. The lamb was garnished on the side with onions and parsley.

Havilya had barely touched her dinner plate, but now they seemed to clamour for her. She quickly swallowed two morsels and stood up. She raised her hands, signalling that she wanted to say something.

As the noise subsided, she began to speak.

"Family and friends."

There was silence now, as they waited to hear for the first time the words of a black Princess who called them "family".

"Family and friends. When I was growing up, I seldom thought of marriage. I wanted to be a politician and a warrior, like my dear father, who is sitting here beside me."

She turned to her right and gave the Viceroy a soft smile.

"My mother Sebaha, who unfortunately cannot grace me with her presence, worried about her failure to provide a male heir for my father. But she was comforted that I like to do a man's work. She would say to my father, "She is the boy the gods did not give us, and a lot prettier than any boy would have been.""

The guests laughed, as the Viceroy nodded knowingly with a smile.

"When I did think of marriage, which was not often, I thought I would marry a Nubian or an Egyptian. Little did I know that my destiny would be to meet this great and wonderful man, sitting beside me as my husband. As he said to me, 'God works in wondrous and mysterious ways.' The most wondrous and mysterious deeds of God are here before us in the life and work of Moses."

Miriam turned her head nervously to the right to look at Aaron. Her face was stern, but she seemed to be trying to look unperturbed.

"As Moses told me more and more the story of his life, and the story of your great victory of liberation, I grew more and more in love with him. With every step, his love for me seemed to grow in equal proportions.

"In Nubia, love usually grew after marriage. If the wife was compatible with her husband and they established a home, in time they came to know each other better, and their love followed from shared experiences, mutual respect and the affection for children. Such was the love that our matriarch Rebekah and her husband Isaac had for each other. Her behaviour showed modesty, hospitality and kindness to her family. It is for these finest of qualities that Rebekah became known as 'very beautiful'.

"But for me and Moses, I have the good fortune of being blessed with love *before* marriage."

She now turned to Moses and looked at him, as she continued.

"Inspired by your love, I seek to follow the example of Rebekah. Just as she was a partner in the great task to which Isaac was committed, I seek to be your partner in the great tasks ahead of us."

She now looked directly at the audience and then covered her eyes.

"We were both strangers in a strange but very different land. But we have found each other, and now we are home together with our people."

She now hesitated, unsure whether to go any further. Taking a deep breath, she decided to forge ahead with what was on her mind.

"In Nubia, at banquets like this one, we always sang an old charming song, which came down to us engraved on the tomb of a Theban priest. It bids one to enjoy this fleeting life."

In a steady voice, she started to sing:

"Spend the day merrily, O priest! Put unguent and fine oil in thy nostrils, and garlands and lotus flowers on the body of thy beloved whom thou favourest, as she sitteth beside thee. Set singing and music before thy face. Cast all evil behind thee, and bethink thee of joy, until that day cometh when one reacheth port in the land that loveth silence."

There was silence in the tent as most were not sure whether she had finished. Suddenly, with tears in her eyes, Miriam got up and embraced Havilya. The soft sobbing of a woman could be heard in the distance.

Soon the stillness was broken by a soft melody from the oboe – a melody from Egypt that they all knew and loved.

As they listened to the oboe with solemnity, they were all waiting for more. They knew that there was one more person to hear from.

TWENTY-EIGHT

Their eyes were still fastened on Havilya, for the feeling forged by her words had scarcely eased. Then the Viceroy, sitting on her left, rose to say a few words.

He was still wearing his white Egyptian-style kilt covering his body from his chest to his knees. From one shoulder to the other, his chest was covered by the broad semi-circular ornament chequered in many coloured squares. But now they noticed the glitter of gold around his neck. He was wearing the much-prized golden collar. This was bestowed in Egypt upon a public servant for distinguished achievement.

He paused as he looked around the tent, and then began.

"I am Sebakashta, the Viceroy of Egypt, a Son of Cush, commander of the District of Gaza.

"I come from a proud Cushite family, who, like the Hebrews, resisted oppression and fought the Pharaohs for independence.

"My ancestors were engaged in battle against the Pharaoh Thutmose III at the battle of Kerma. That was when we lost our independence and became a part of Pharaoh's empire.

"Like Moses, I was educated in Pharaoh's court with the princes of Egypt in Thebes and Memphis. It is possible that as a student my path crossed with that of Moses. Little did we know that destiny would bring us together years later."

The Viceroy turned slightly to the right and, over Havilya's head, smiled at Moses, who was now acknowledging the Viceroy's words with a nod.

"I worked as a public official of Pharaoh for many years. My contributions were soon recognized. In Aniba, the city of my birth, I became the Viceroy of Nubia, responsible for the civil and military administration of the region.

"From there, I supervised the construction of the many temples in Nubia to complete these great monuments for Pharaoh.

"Massive projects were in progress outside Nubia to build new temples, complete or renovate old ones or build a new capital city for Pharaoh. They were in Thebes, Luxor, Pi-Rameses and Memphis. In addition, in Nubia we built at least seven new temples – the most northerly in Beit el-Wali, at Aksha, at Derr, at Wadi es-Sebua, at Gerf Hussein and the two at Abu Simbel."

"All of these were built with the labour of countless slaves and prisoners of war. Who knows if this work will ever be completed to Pharaoh's satisfaction."

Now he stopped, looked around at the guests, and feeling more comfortable in his surroundings, placed his two hands on his hips with his thumbs inserted in the gold sash around his waist.

"You know these works well," he continued, "for until your escape, you worked hand in hand with Nubians and others to complete these great monuments.

"That was not the only time that Hebrews worked for the greater good of Egypt. Centuries ago, the greatest of Pharaoh's viziers was the Hebrew patriarch Joseph. Both in scarcity and in plenty, Joseph was a peerless minister. Under his administration, Egypt and Nubia enjoyed decades of plenty that were not known in neighbouring lands. We all know the great regard that Pharaoh and the Egyptians had for Joseph. When Joseph went from Egypt to Canaan to bury his father Jacob, with him went all the officials of Pharaoh, the senior members of his court and all of Egypt's dignitaries.

"But the legacy of the Hebrews will be more than building projects and public administration in Egypt."

The Viceroy turned to his right to give a distant look at Aaron, in a gesture of homage to the High Priest.

"I have read some of the Hebrew scrolls that Havilya has been studying. Fortunately, she gave me a translation in hieroglyphics."

There was some scattered laughter.

"In those scrolls, you teach that a person's conduct must be governed by commandments. The rule by Pharaoh is replaced by the rule of law. Through the ages, you will become known as the people of the law, and these laws, and not temples of stone, will be your monuments.

He paused and looked toward Miriam.

"We have just heard the song of Miriam celebrating your great liberation from Pharaoh. That is why you will be known also as the people of freedom and liberation.

"While you have gained your freedom, you continue to struggle to build a nation on land of your own. We in Nubia, however, have our land and our nation, but we lack freedom from Pharaoh.

"As Moses said to me and all the generals of Israel this morning, we must fight together as allies. For both of us to be free in our own nation, the Cushites and the Hebrews will make common cause to fight Pharaoh. Our forces will be joined to fight against the established order that has oppressed us for centuries."

Miriam looked perturbed and glanced toward Aaron, who shook his head in surprise.

"Like the Hebrews, we the Cushites will acquire our freedom. Like the Cushites, you the Hebrews will acquire your national homeland."

He now looked at Havilya.

"My dear daughter, you told me today that you wanted to marry Moses, even without an alliance. I say to you gathered here that there would have been an alliance without the marriage."

Miriam now leaned over to the right to speak to Aaron. They seemed to have an animated conversation, as the Viceroy was concluding his speech.

"And so, both the alliance and the marriage have occurred. That is the reason we can now enjoy a double celebration, for happiness is enhanced where love meets necessity."

* * *

"Alliance? What alliance?"

These were the first words that Miriam declared as she rose to speak. All of them, Nubians and Hebrews alike, were eager and alarmed about what Miriam might say, for this was wholly unexpected. Joshua's attendants had quietly passed around the word that the Viceroy and his daughter, the new bride of Moses, would say a few words. This was to limit surprise and ensure a polite response. But they had said nothing about Miriam.

Some had suspected that Miriam would have views about the marriage. But they were not sure what those views were. One rumour was that Miriam objected to Moses marrying outside the Hebrew race; another was that she resented Moses marrying into a Nubian family of high rank; and another was that she saw in Havilya a strong rival in the leadership of the women. Still another rumour was that, as a woman, Miriam was jealous of Havilya because the Nubian princess had all the qualities that Hebrew men secretly desired in a woman – youth, beauty, bravery, a high rank in Egyptian society and exotic black skin.

As they listened expectantly, they were sure of one thing – that Miriam would speak her mind and that she would be clear.

"Alliance? What alliance?" she repeated. As she repeated these words, Aaron buried his face in the palm of his hands in fear of what she might say.

"This was the question I just asked Aaron, and he knew as much about it before today as I did – which is nothing."

Moses looked on the floor, shaking his head with dismay, while Joshua shook his head with resignation. The Viceroy and Havilya seemed amazed by Miriam's outburst, and looked at her with a blank, uncomprehending gaze.

Miriam looked to her left at the Viceroy and Havilya.

"Your Highness, dear Havilya, family and friends. I am sorry to inject politics into our celebration. But this is the first time I heard of the alliance. With his Highness here but for a short time, and all the elders and generals gathered here, this may be the only time to speak to you together.

"When I first heard that Moses was planning to marry a Nubian woman, it was before I had met your Highness and dear Havilya. I must say I had misgivings.

"Those misgivings had nothing to do with the usual rumours and gossip one inevitably hears before marriages. I will not dignify those with an answer.

"At first, I had a vague sense of peril that the marriage would bring us closer to Pharaoh. But after some reflection, reason prevailed over my fear. I asked myself why would Pharaoh, with all his might and his vast empire, care about a single marriage? Aaron also re-assured me. He reminded me of what the ancients would say, that one can pluck a rose from a bush of thorns.

"As I grew to know Havilya, I discovered just what a rose – a fine, brave, noble, charming rose – she is. I thought she would be just what Moses needs in these trying days. My memory of the years in Egypt – in the bush of thorns – seemed to recede.

"Until now. Until I heard about the alliance."

Now she could not resist a barb toward Joshua. She looked directly at him and said,

"Why is an alliance of this importance not discussed with the elders and the women? Why all the secrecy, even from all of us, the priests, priestesses, leaders and commanders of Israel? Why must we hear of this at the end of a celebration?"

She paused now to regain her composure. She took a deep breath and brushed her hair to the side, as if this act would make her calmer.

"Now," she continued, "it is one thing to hope that Pharaoh will not hear or care about this marriage. It is another to hope that he will not hear or care about this alliance.

"What is it about this alliance that frightens me? It frightens me because it puts in peril our people, as well as his Highness the Viceroy and his family. Now why do I say this?

"Our interest is to consolidate our freedom, end this wandering and settle in our Promised Land. Ahead of us is a battle – no, *battles*, many of them – for the conquest of the Promised Land. Our men have no experience in battle, and have just started to train in the arts of war. Our only hope for victory will be if Pharaoh does not come to the aid of his vassals in Canaan.

The faint sound of thunder could now be heard.

"Somehow we must hope either that Pharaoh will be engaged fighting on other fronts, such as against the Hittites, or that he will not care to defend Canaan.

"It would be folly for us to attract the attention of Pharaoh with an alliance with Nubia – which all Pharaohs have considered vital and integral to Egypt.

"Does this mean that we should have no sympathy for the aspirations of the Viceroy and his fellow Nubians – aspirations to attain their freedom from the oppression of

Pharaoh? Not at all. I have nothing but love for Havilya and esteem for his Highness and the noble Nubians. I wish for his Highness and his people the freedom they desire, the freedom that we have attained for ourselves. In years to come, the Nubians may not only be free, but may be the leaders of Egypt."

Looking squarely at the Viceroy, she thundered, "This is what I prophesy for you and your people, that one day you will overcome your enemies and Nubians will be the Pharaohs of Egypt."

The Viceroy's face flushed, and he responded with a knowing and determined nod to Miriam.

"But," she continued, "the Hebrews are a small collection of disparate tribes. Some even want to return to Egypt. Our army is a mere platoon compared to the hosts of Pharaoh. We are but flies on the back of the Egyptian camel. There is little – nay, there is nothing – we can do to help the Nubians."

The sound of thunder became louder.

"By this alliance, we are doing worse than nothing. We will bring to ourselves the attention of Pharaoh, who seems to be distracted now with the Hittites.

"This will put in peril his Highness and his family, as well as jeopardize our hard-won freedom.

"If Pharaoh were to turn his full wrath against us, the blood of the Nubians and Hebrews would flow like a river. At best, we will be alive, but slaves again, building temples in Memphis, Thebes and Abu Simbel. Everything we have gained will be lost again."

The crash of thunder seemed to engulf the small tent, and now it was mixed with the sharp crack of lightning.

Suddenly Moses rose and slammed his fists on his thighs. His feet caught and pulled the cloth in front of him, as plates of food came crashing to the side on the floor. His face was crimson with anger.

He stalked briskly through the middle, stepping on the lyre that lay on the ground. As the instrument cracked under his feet, its strings sounded their discordant notes. Sentries and guests who had milled together bolted from his path, as he aimed for the tent's entrance.

After he left the tent, they all rose in an uproar. Those who had seen him in such a state before knew that some fearsome horror would surely ensue.

TWENTY-NINE

"Miriam, we must speak to him now."

These were the words that Miriam heard from Aaron, as she sat stunned and bewildered at Moses' harsh reaction.

Her face was pale and her spirit downcast that the celebration had ended in turmoil. She felt embarrassed, as well, that their squabble erupted in front of the elders and commanders of Israel and their wives; even ashamed that foreign dignitaries – now their family – had to witness the sibling wrangle; but also angry that a mere questioning of the policies of Moses, policies that might be critical to their future, could not be tolerated and could elicit such a violent response.

"We must find him and calm him," Aaron said. "He must not go to his wedding bed in anger."

She could barely remember how Aaron led her from her seat. He guessed that Moses would be in the Tent of Revelation. He usually went there, especially in times of crisis, to think, to pray and to communicate with God.

She vaguely remembered the crowds jostling outside for a view of them, as she and Aaron crossed from one tent to the other. The sounds of the lightning and thunder seemed to intensify. At last, she thought, we might finally get some rain.

When they entered the Tent of Revelation, they found Moses down on his knees just outside the sanctuary. The curtain to the sanctuary was open, as was the inner curtain beyond that normally sealed off the Holy of Holies.

They sat behind him and remained quiet so as not to disturb him. Eventually he would sense their presence and speak to them when he was ready.

As Miriam sat there with Aaron, she stared at the bare interior of the tent and the elaborate religious ornaments in the sanctuary. At one level, she loved and revered her youngest brother Moses. She knew that he had sacrificed more than anyone for his people. Much of what they had achieved was due to his vision, his tenacity and his faith that God would stand by them, as He had covenanted that He would.

But at another level, she felt that there was still more, much more, to do before they as a people could cease their wandering and settle down in the Promised Land. She felt that she and the other elders of Israel had a role to play, a right, and even a duty, to be heard and to share in the leadership. She thought that it was their collective destiny that was at stake, and all of them would suffer the consequences of the decisions that were being made.

She wished that she could discuss these matters with her younger brothers calmly and dispassionately. She did not know why debates among siblings took on a ferocious intensity. Natural rivalry, a childhood slight, a parent's favour – all of these exist, but do not explain. Perhaps it is love, and the knowledge that, however fiercely they will fight, their love will in the end reconcile them; and that it will somehow stop them from crossing over to the brink of a lifetime of enmity.

She stared inside the sanctuary. She could see the golden candlestick and the table of shew bread (or bread of display) in front of Moses. Behind these was the altar of incense, and further back was the open inner curtain to the Holy of Holies, which housed the Ark of the Covenant.

Much of this was the work of her son Bezalel, the architect, and his colleague Ohaliab the artisan. As she gazed at their beauty, she realized that this was the first time she had viewed them closely and wished that she had let Bezalel show off his work to her, as he liked to do. She wondered whether these religious ornaments were enough to cover up the austerity of the rest of the tent; and whether the talk they were about to have with Moses would succeed in restoring harmony in their family.

At last, Moses looked back and saw them behind him. He closed the inner curtain and the curtain to the sanctuary, and sat silently near them on one of the benches. There was a long silence, as they stopped to catch their breath, to take a measure of the other, like fighters waiting for the next assault from their opponent.

It was Aaron who finally broke the silence.

"Moses, I thought we should quickly clear the air," said his older brother.

Moses nodded.

"So as to send you back to your bride."

"Yes, my bride," he said softly.

"This is perhaps not the best time to resolve matters. Except to say we should have a way – a forum – to discuss and share ideas. It may be that the same decisions will be made, for instance, to have an alliance with the Nubians. But we will avoid this kind of confrontation, if we reach these decisions together."

"The decision for the alliance cannot be changed."

"I know, I know. I am only speaking about how the decisions are made."

"What is your idea?"

"Well, I think Miriam had some good thoughts about the alliance. We, too, may have reached the conclusion to have the alliance in the end. But she should have been heard."

"I am always available to hear you."

"Well, it seems that – it appears to me that – you are consulting less and less with Miriam and me and more and more with Joshua and his aides."

"In what area?"

"Well, you know, the matter of the judges. I have not been consulted on that. It seems that Joshua was making the decisions."

"Joshua is merely my aide. With the judges, I merely needed help from others to hear the cases."

"We could have been part of the decision. This could have been my role."

"You have a lot to do looking after the priesthood. You just lost two sons. It is too much for you to take over a whole new administration."

"Perhaps, but like the alliance decision, the decision for the judges was made without consulting us."

"Our talks with the Nubians had to be secret."

"Understood. But Miriam and I could have been part of the inner circle, with Joshua and his aides. Joshua could have kept us informed."

"There is no need to blame Joshua."

"We are not blaming Joshua. He could have kept us informed and obtained our opinions."

"He was merely carrying out my decisions."

Miriam could not remain silent any longer.

"That is the problem, Moses. It is *your* decisions. We do not seem to play a part in them any longer."

"Each of the other nations has but one leader. The Hebrews cannot have several."

"The other nations are ruled by tyrants."

"I am guided by God and my conscience."

"We have our conscience, too, and we have the same God. We may have ideas that work better. We also have to bear the consequences of these decisions. This alone entitles us to take part."

His voice began to rise.

"Are you saying that my decisions have been wrong?"

"About the Nubian alliance, yes."

"What is wrong with it?"

"If we had been consulted, we might have persuaded you not to enter into it, or at least changed it."

"How would you have changed it?"

"I cannot say now because I was not part of the talks."

"Miriam, Miriam, I have a lot on my mind. I cannot consult with everyone."

"You can consult with me and Aaron."

"I consult with my conscience, and with God, who speaks through me."

Exasperated, her voice too began to rise.

"You are not the only prophet in this family. You have forgotten what I have done." "Miriam, Miriam, this is not the point."

"Is this not enough? Am I not your older sister? Am I not a prophet, too?"

Moses could not speak anymore. Enraged again, he walked toward the entrance, with Miriam shouting as she followed him.

"You cannot just run away and ignore us. Our destinies are intertwined."

He was outside the Tent of Revelation now. As he sped away, Miriam stood outside and continued to shout at him. The crowd was still milling outside. The thunder and lightning were now almost deafening, but they could see and hear her as she railed against Moses.

"You are not the only prophet in this family. Are we not also the prophets of Israel? Has the Lord spoken only with Moses? Has he not also spoken with us?"

Tears began to stream down her cheeks, as the thunder and lightning broke into a heavy downpour. She collapsed and sat helpless and alone in the wetness of the rain and of her tears, until finally Aaron came out, took her hand and led her into the shelter of the tent.

* * *

Shooly galloped toward the setting sun. The way ahead was flat and barren, so he could cover a long distance quickly before he reached a range of low hills.

As he rode beside the open road, the sun began to move behind the hills again. He wanted to get to the hills before dark. If there were any Egyptian troops in the vicinity, they would more likely be in the hills, where they would find some shade from the sun.

Ahead he could see the highway disappear between two hills. He veered to the left around the hill to find a high spot from which to scout the surroundings. He climbed to the top of the hill and dismounted to rest his horse and catch his breath.

In the distance, the sun was disappearing quickly and an orange glow now settled on the western horizon. He could see a higher range of hills beyond, but just before them, he thought he saw some shimmers of light. The sun was too low for mirages to form, he thought. Could this be reflections off the metal objects of an Egyptian army?

He had to push forward, he thought. It would be almost dark before he could start his return trip, but the sky was clear and the moon full. He felt he could find his way back in the dark.

He quickly jumped on his horse again and rode hard up and down the low hills with the highway a short distance to his right. The sun now completely disappeared behind the high hills ahead. He decided he would stop to look from behind a low escarpment just a short distance in front of him. He dismounted and walked up to the highest point overlooking the highway.

Shooly skipped a breath.

There they were. Not seventy, but more than twice the number he had seen before.

Quickly he counted two hundred soldiers and about seventy horses. At least fifty must be cavalry, he thought, and the other twenty horses appeared to be carrying supplies.

Having found what he was looking for, he turned back and rode toward the spot where he had left Shabitqo.

THIRTY

Havilya was now alone in Moses' tent, waiting for him.

After Moses had walked out of the wedding celebrations, Joshua had quickly arranged for the Nubians to be taken away. With four sentries, he had escorted Havilya to Moses' tent.

The Viceroy also accompanied them. As he watched Havilya enter the tent alone, his natural impulse was to go inside and be with his daughter while she waited for Moses. But he had thought better of it. Moses would only be embarrassed to find the Viceroy in his tent. Quite apart from the lateness of the hour, Moses might feel compelled to explain the turn of events, and the Viceroy had not wanted to put him in that uncomfortable situation.

Joshua had then left with the four sentries to walk the Viceroy to his tent. Havilya remained alone in Moses' tent, except for the special guards posted outside permanently.

As she looked around the tent, she thought it was austere but larger than the others she had seen. The floor was covered with a light green burlap cloth. She was surprised to find the large bed for two from her tent. This was placed in one corner, and she recognized the semi-circular canopy at one end under which she had slept the night before. This was to be her marriage bed; it must have been moved here during the wedding ceremony. In another corner was a narrow cot, which she surmised had been Moses' bed before tonight. In the third corner, there was a wooden tub with linens stacked nearby. This was the bath, full of fresh warm water. In the fourth corner was a table, a chair, blank papyrus, a reed pen, an ink-like substance and an unfinished scroll.

Knowing this was where she would live, she had arranged for her personal things to be brought here. She started to unpack her things, and as she arranged them in the corner where the bath lay, she reflected that this was her first night as a married woman.

She knew that Moses would come soon and that he would be upset. She thought of her mother Sebaha, who was especially adept in the art of soothing her husband when he came home angry.

"First," her mother would say, "when he arrives, you must look pretty and be pleasant."

"Even when he is angry?" Havilya had asked her.

"Yes. Remember, he is not angry with you. It is something else that is bothering him."

"How will you know he will be angry, so that you can look your best?"

"You won't know. You must try to look your best as often as you can, especially if you are expecting him home after a difficult day or a lengthy or trying mission."

"Then what?"

"Don't talk much. Except to answer a specific question, and then only say little. Be deft, discreet and pleasant."

"Wouldn't you ask him what is bothering him?"

"No. Asking questions is the worst thing you can do. He will have to answer and re-live what is bothering him. The point is to try to help him forget it and to distract him from his anger."

"But wouldn't you be curious to find out the reason for his anger?"

"Yes, but that comes later. He will tell you in his own way and at the time of his choosing. In fact, inevitably he will tell you everything, more perhaps than you would want to know."

"Would you then just sit there?"

"No. You should try to do things gently and subtly to please him. This is why you must know what he likes and do it, and what he doesn't and avoid it."

"Why wouldn't you just go away and return after he has calmed down?"

"No. He wants you to be there to help to comfort him."

"It sounds complicated, mother."

"Not after you know your man."

"You almost have to sense his needs and read his thoughts."

"Yes, you do, Havilya."

"Any words of warning?"

"The danger is that if you don't follow what I said, he will remain angry and you will make him angrier. Then the anger could be directed at you."

"That would not be fair."

"No. It would not."

The Nubian Princess

"What about the woman's wishes?"

"Your turn will come. After he calms down, if he is gentle and loves you, he will do anything he reasonably can for you."

Havilya smiled to herself as she remembered her next line to her mother.

"It really is complicated, mother. I'd almost rather be in a battlefield. At least you know what you are fighting and when you are prevailing."

"That's clever, Havilya, but no one said that being married to an ambitious man was easy."

As she unpacked her bag of personal things, she noticed items that must have been put there by her mother. She found medicinal oils and powders, including salve, a smooth ointment to put on wounds and sores to soothe or heal them; bryony, a herb which, when mixed with oil or honey and poured inside the ear, was said to cure ear aches and prevent deafness; alum, used to stop bleeding; castor oil, used as a purgative; and valerian, a herb used as a sedative.

She found some cosmetic items – a bronze razor, a wooden comb, a small mirror, a red ochre (a pigment used by women on their cheeks) and balm of Gilead (a fragrant ointment from the resin of a tree). There were other jars of rare Nubian oils and perfumes whose fragrances she recognized but could not name. The Viceroy liked his wife to give him long, slow and gentle back rubs, especially after a hard day at work. These, Havilya thought, were the perfumes and ointments her mother must have used.

Havilya now opened the jars of perfumes and oils. She applied ointment on her neck and arms, and repeated it with various fragrances. She stroked her face lightly with the fine red ochre pigment that Nubian women used. She then sprinkled the bed and the air around the bath with other fragrances. By the time she had finished, the tent was overpowered with the aromas of exotic Nubian perfumes. She smiled when she remembered her mother doing that and her father jokingly saying to her, "This place smells better than Pharaoh's palace of concubines."

When she looked at herself in the mirror, she thought she looked like the court beauties that Nubian men longed for. At least, she hoped that Moses would think so when he saw her.

When Moses finally arrived, he found her standing just inside the entrance of the tent. As he looked at her and breathed the air, his anguished frown lifted and a bemused smile came over his face.

"Havilya," he said, "you are the loveliest woman in Pharaoh's empire."

He looked at her, up and down, and then embraced her. He kissed her all over her face and neck, and held her tighter.

"Come," she said, as she led him confidently to the bath. "A bath will help you."

He untied the string on his gown and began to undress. Havilya held his hand as he slowly stepped into the bath. She stood behind him as he sat in the bath. She kissed him on the back of his head, and caressed his neck and shoulders. They remained there silent for a while, until he stirred, signalling he wanted to leave the bath.

As he stepped out, she covered him with towels and dried his body. Then she led him to the bed, and she pulled the covers as he slid under them. Then she undressed and lay beside him on the bed.

"I am sorry about what happened earlier."

He tried to explain, but she put her hands gently on his lips.

"There will be time to talk later."

As he lay on his back, she moved on top of him, kissing him on his face, lips and neck. He felt her smooth back with his hands and smelled the fragrances on her hair.

Then she turned him on his stomach, mounted him at his waist and massaged his back. Suddenly he felt the sensation of a cold liquid on his back. She quickly rubbed the oil into his skin. His tense muscles seemed to soften under her hands. She pressed on his back, and as he seemed to like it, she pressed slightly harder. This would be the moment to undress fully for him, but she thought better of it, for she sensed he needed tenderness more than sexual passion.

Then they lay face to face on their sides. He slid one arm under her side and moved down with his face between her breasts. He pulled her tightly toward him, as he buried his face in her bosom.

"This is where I want to be," he said softly, "to soothe my soul and escape from the daily turmoil."

As he rubbed his face on her chest, his cheeks touched her breasts, and she gently caressed his head.

"This will be my home now, in your bosom and your arms."

She felt his tears on her breasts, as he sobbed gently in her arms.

They stayed there locked in each other's embrace for a long time. They were silent and it was quiet except for the sound of raindrops falling on their tent. Whatever he had wanted to explain to her did not seem to matter now.

Suddenly, a sharp sound pierced the midnight air and jolted them from their wedding bed. They heard a woman's screams of terror – screams not too far away. Moses quickly rose.

"I am called by the Lord," he said to Havilya. "I must make haste to the Tent of Revelation."

PART 3

THIRTY-ONE

When Debra arrived for work at the Annex that morning, she found a captain and four sentries guarding the tent. A priest stood silently nearby. She had heard or seen nothing unusual the night before.

The previous day had been arduous for her. She had her usual chores at the Annex – cleaning the floor, tending to the wounded, and feeding the incapacitated. Although the horseback ride with Shooly had been an exciting interlude from the day's monotony, the afternoon sun and worrying about Shooly's mission had tired her. Even then, she had returned to the Annex to work late in the evening because Miriam had been busy with Havilya and the wedding. By the time she had got to her bed late that night, she was exhausted and she quickly fell into a deep and sound sleep, oblivious to the screams that many had heard in the middle of that night.

"Good morning, captain," Debra said.

"Good morning, Debra."

"What brings you and your soldiers here, sir?"

"I am afraid it is Miriam."

Debra put her hand on her mouth.

"Oh, my goodness, what about Miriam?"

"She is leprous, Debra."

"What? Let me see."

She tried to brush him aside to enter the Annex. But he restrained her.

"She is not here, Debra."

"Where is she?"

"In isolation. With the other lepers."

"She was perfectly fine only yesterday."

"I know, I know. But I am afraid it is true."

Debra collapsed sobbing. She could not comprehend that Miriam – her mentor and idol – could be stricken so quickly. Only yesterday, Miriam had seemed so healthy, cheerful and vigorous.

She felt the captain's hand on her arm, trying to soothe her and to pull her up from the dusty ground.

"Try to contain yourself," the captain said softly.

Debra got up and wiped her tears.

"Maybe you should go to your tent and rest with your family," he continued.

"No. I think it is better if I am busy."

"We have arranged for Leah to come to help here today."

"Thank you. But she is a seamstress. She can't handle this by herself."

She brushed the dust off her clothes and entered the Annex.

As she regained her composure, her first thought was to touch her own skin. She found no signs of scales. Then she looked at every one of the patients, and they too showed no signs of the disease.

Then she went up to the priest. Before she could say anything, he began: "Soon after Miriam left the wedding tent last night," the priest told her, "suddenly the Lord called Moses, Aaron and Miriam to the Tent of Revelation. So the three of them went out. The Lord came down in a pillar of cloud, stopped at the entrance of the Tent of Revelation and called out: *"Aaron and Miriam!"*

She felt a chill as the priest continued.

"Miriam and Aaron then came forward, and the Lord said: *Hear these My words: When a prophet of the Lord arises among you, I make Myself known to him in a vision, I speak with him in a dream. Not so with my servant Moses; he is trusted throughout My household. With him I speak mouth to mouth, plainly and not in riddles, and he beholds the likeness of the Lord. How then did you not shrink from speaking against My servant Moses?"*

The priest paused and looked at Debra who said nothing.

"When the Lord departed," the priest continued, "He was still incensed with Miriam and Aaron. As the cloud withdrew from the Tent, Aaron walked with Miriam to her tent. When they reached her tent, Aaron turned toward Miriam. To his dismay, he found Miriam stricken with snow-white scales."

"Is that when the screaming started?"

"Not just then. At first, she did not believe it. She would not go to the lepers' colony."

"Then what?"

"Aaron had to call Joshua and his soldiers. Her screams began when she had finally realized what had happened to her and that she was being forcibly taken away."

"Why were soldiers needed?"

"Most lepers don't want to be isolated. So they have to be taken against their will. On the way, lepers also need protection from those who might stone them to death."

"When Miriam and Aaron spoke against Moses, what did they say?"

"Aaron was not too clear on that."

"Did it have to do with the Nubians?"

"Apparently. But he did not go into much detail."

Debra tried to make sense of it all, but she could not. She kept questioning the priest. He could not explain to her many things that puzzled her: What did Aaron and Miriam say against Moses? Surely they did not object to Moses marrying outside the Hebrew faith, for many of the patriarchs had done so. Besides, Havilya had converted yesterday. Perhaps Miriam, like many other women, did not like a woman from another tribe taking their men. But Zipporah, the first wife of Moses, was not a Hebrew and Miriam got on well with her. Maybe Miriam and Aaron resented Moses marrying into a Nubian family of high rank? No, that did not make sense, for Miriam seemed to be good to Havilya, and Moses grew up as a prince, so none should begrudge him marrying into high rank. Siblings, though, her father had told Debra, can begrudge you anything.

"It was more political," the priest had allowed. "Miriam and Aaron spoke against the alliance with the Nubians. The Lord speaks with Moses and not with Miriam and Aaron. Maybe that means that the Lord does not want Miriam and Aaron to interfere with the leadership of Moses."

Debra was not quite satisfied. If both spoke against Moses, why was only Miriam punished and not Aaron? The priest merely shrugged without answering. Debra suddenly smiled to herself – obviously, Aaron would not have discussed this point with the priest.

She now thought of Shooly. As planned, he and Shabitqo must still be on their mission. She wondered whether he knew about Miriam. Even if he did, he would still have gone, she thought. He would not have looked for reasons to delay carrying out his duties.

Now a stream of people began to arrive at the Annex. They had heard of what had happened to Miriam last night. Some were kin or friends of the sick and wounded under Miriam's care, and wanted to see if the same disease had stricken the Annex. Debra had to show them through the Annex to convince them it was free from leprosy.

They could not imagine the Annex without Miriam's guidance. Previously, each family had to care of their own sick and wounded in their own tents. Some could handle those situations, but most lacked the patience and the skills needed to take care of their own. The constant wandering in the desert added to the strain. Most could not manage to pack their belongings and their tents, and then move and unpack them at another location – while also tending to family members who might be sick or wounded.

Miriam's idea was to put all the sick and wounded in one place, to be cared for and moved, if required, by skilled people trained under her guidance. That is how Miriam's Annex was born. None who had to be brought here felt they were a burden to their families or in danger of being abandoned if a sudden order came down to move the encampment. Thus both the sick or wounded and their families found a deep sense of relief under Miriam's system of care. And only those who came under her care and their families could have the deep-rooted gratitude they had for Miriam, and the sense of loss at her isolation in a lepers' colony.

The crowd grew large and noisy. They demanded answers from the captain and his sentries. Apart from the basic facts – that Miriam became leprous last night and was taken forcibly to the lepers' colony – they appeared to know little else.

The captain had not anticipated this many people. There had been the unrest a few days ago outside the Tent of Revelation. But, he thought, that had grown as a result of the news of the dead and wounded from the tribes of Simeon and Gad after they attacked the caravan.

At last, by the afternoon, another priest came to the Annex. He found a large and anxious crowd. Soon, however, they became quiet and attentive as the priest raised his hands over his head, indicating that he wished to speak to them.

The priest was young and his face was fresh and hairless. He wore a long black gown and held a scroll in his hand. He seemed hurried and eager to deliver a message.

The priest told them of the events of the previous night, why they heard the screams of terror in the night and what had happened to Miriam.

"The wrath of the Lord has fallen on Miriam," the priest said. "The Lord will not countenance those who speak against Moses."

Instead of calming them, the words of the priest made them more restless and angry. Some of the women began to wail.

"What will become of Miriam? Who will look after us?"

Other women lamented and beat their chests.

"Who will heal Miriam, our great healer?"

A man lunged at the priest, who took a blow below his ribs. As the priest bent forward breathless, the captain grabbed him by the arms. The attacker was stocky and of medium height. He had thick black hair, and a heavy beard encircled a pale and weary-looking face. His fierce, blood-shot eyes gazed angrily at the captain.

"Aaron is stupid and Moses is venal!" the man railed.

He had lost most of his family in the massacre of the Hebrews that Moses had ordered after the incident of the Golden Bull-calf.

"It was the spinelessness of Aaron that led us into worshipping an idol. And who pays for it? No not Aaron. Not the High Priest. Instead he is *elevated*! He is given high office to preach to us!"

The man shook his fist at the captain and the sentries guarding the entrance to the Annex.

"My family was massacred by Moses' henchmen for Aaron's stupidity. Instead of punishing Aaron, Moses sent his killers against my family. Why? Because Moses did not want them to bow before an idol."

The man turned toward the crowd and continued with a deep bitterness.

"And now this. Moses suddenly marries whom he wants. Aaron and Miriam say a few things he does not like. Suddenly Moses is in a rage again. Who bears the wrath of Moses? Why Miriam only, the only one of them who really takes care of us. Not Aaron, no, not him. After all, he is the High Priest. Those who hold high office are never wrong, are they?"

The captain handed the man to two of the sentries who beat the man with their fists. As the man fell, they dragged him sobbing into the Annex. The captain then looked frantically in the distance. Suddenly, to his relief, he saw a body of eight horse guards led by Joshua slowly advancing toward them.

The crowd, in no mood to tackle with this superior force, quickly dispersed into the encampment.

THIRTY-TWO

Miriam was awakened by a kick to her side. She heard the breaking cackle of a woman's voice above her head.

"Time to get up, priestess."

When she opened her eyes, she saw that she had been sleeping on the dust inside an empty tent.

"This may be a colony of lepers, priestess, but someone must clean this tent."

For the moment, Miriam could not get up to face the woman overhead. She looked at the bare wall of the tent, as she lay with her head on her arm. She remembered that it was almost dawn when the soldiers pushed her into the tent. She had crawled among the sleeping bodies to find an empty space to sleep. It must now be almost mid-day, she thought. She was still wearing the long red gown she had had on at the wedding. It was still damp from last night's rain. The sleeves on her arms, which had been her pillow, were wet from crying. She must have sobbed her way to sleep, for she felt the slight burn on her face from the salt left behind from her tears.

What a wedding, she thought, as she went through the events of the previous night in her head. After the terrible row with Moses in the Tent of Revelation, she had collapsed in tears and in the rain outside. Then Aaron had walked her to her tent. When they had arrived, she had felt a chill running through her body.

"Aaron, Aaron," she had said. "I feel terrible. Something horrible has happened."

He had looked at her in dismay.

"O my Lord, Miriam. It is scales. You are covered with them."

At first she had been calm. She thought that it might be a temporary rash.

But Aaron had persisted.

"It is leprosy, Miriam."

Her terror had barely abated when Aaron reminded her of his duty as the High Priest.

"You must be isolated, Miriam. I cannot leave you with Caleb."

They both knew the law, that to safeguard the ceremonial purity of the camp and to prevent the defilement of others by contact, lepers were to be excluded from the whole camp. Her terror was mixed with shame, because leprosy was regarded as a providential affliction in punishment for slander, tale-bearing, gossip, or any hostile talk.

Her husband had left the wedding soon after Moses had stomped out in a rage. By now, Caleb had become used to Miriam's long sessions of discourse and argument with her brothers. He could do nothing to prevent or allay them, and he could never predict how long they would last. Whenever he saw one of those arguments coming, he felt it prudent to get out of the way and go to his tent. Eventually Miriam would turn up.

Poor Caleb, Miriam thought. How terrified he was last night when he heard Aaron say those words. Caleb would not let his wife go, and Miriam also insisted she would not be isolated.

But Aaron had felt he must follow the Hebrew laws of ritual purification. He had diagnosed Miriam to have leprosy, and it was his duty to isolate her. If she would not go willingly, he had no choice but to call in the soldiers.

It had taken Aaron two hours to return with the soldiers. When they had entered the tent, they found Miriam still in her evening dress and in animated conversation with her husband. The captain had asked her to come with him peacefully. When she had refused, two soldiers grabbed her and tied her hands behind her back. That is when the screaming had started. They had forced Miriam on the back of a horse, and ridden with her to the lepers' colony. When they had untied her hands and thrown her into the tent of the lepers, she remembered rays of light were coming out of the horizon. Broken, disheartened and exhausted, all she could do was crawl to an empty space among the bodies and cry herself to sleep.

Miriam now felt another kick to her ribs.

"Come on, priestess. You must get up."

When she got up, she took a good look at the woman. She had a tall and thin but hunched figure. Her stoop made her look shorter that she was. She had a long thin nose and a wide but lipless mouth. She wore what appeared to be a disorderly clump of rags, and her head was covered with a dirty scarf to conceal her baldness. Miriam could see elevated white rashes of various sizes on her hands and face. There were also several scattered wounds on her hands. Her eyebrows and eyelashes had disappeared with the advanced stage of her sickness.

Miriam had seen this condition before and recognized the illness. She knew also that the woman must have lost the ability to sense touch, pain, hot and cold. That explained the wounds on her hands, which must have been contracted touching sharp rocks but being oblivious to the pain and bleeding. She recognized, too, the weak, clawing look of the fingers, arms and feet, as the limbs became frail and took on a deformed appearance.

"I am Haggar," the woman said.

Miriam said nothing.

Haggar now circled Miriam and eyed her up and down.

"Fine fabric. Fine fabric."

As she stroked Miriam's gown, Miriam moved away from her.

"I like the red colour. Nice party dress. Nice party dress."

A smile suddenly appeared on Haggar's face.

"If you were going to a party, priestess, you went the wrong way."

Haggar started to laugh.

"There is no party here, priestess," she said as she giggled uncontrollably.

Miriam gave her a stern look. Realizing that her humour was not appreciated, Haggar's tone became more earnest.

"I am the head leper in the women's tent. I have been here the longest."

Miriam nodded.

"I give out the food that is left for us at the edge of the pit. I also make sure the tent is cleaned every day."

Miriam looked around the tent, puzzled as to what there was to clean. The tent was pitched on bare dusty soil, and there was no floor covering or furnishing.

"Some leave their things, food, and rags. We clean this daily, because this is where we sleep."

Miriam then quickly walked out of the tent, as if to gasp for fresh air. Haggar was close behind. They squinted from the heat and brightness of the noon sun.

Miriam recognized the pit they were in. It was a large quarry east of the valley where the encampment was pitched. Some thought that the pit had been carved out by the Amorites centuries ago, when they dug out sand and stones for the nearby Amorite settlement, which now lay in ruins.

Miriam had never been at the bottom of the pit where they now stood. The women's tent behind them was in the east end of the pit. In the middle of the pit, there was another tent.

"That is the men's tent," Haggar said. "If you thought our tent was full, theirs is twice as crowded."

At the other end was a path winding a way to the top of the pit.

"That is the way in and out of this place," Haggar explained. "The food is left for us at the top of the pit at the end of that path."

Miriam remembered standing at the top when she had brought or visited one of her patients.

"Since you are new here, I should tell you a few things."

Miriam did not bother to look at her but listened anyway.

"As the newest member, it is your duty to clean the tent every day."

Miriam said nothing.

"As a new member, a priest will visit you in seven days. You are to meet him at the top of the pit at the end of that path."

Miriam looked up at the spot where Haggar was pointing.

"If the scales on your skin look better, he will let you leave the colony. If not, you will stay here."

Miriam knew these rules but said nothing. She looked at herself and at the scales on her skin. She touched her red gown, and suddenly felt ill at ease in her formal evening dress under the noon sun.

She began to notice the other lepers in the colony. Some walked alone, others in pairs. Most were sitting in the shade beside the east wall of the pit. She did not want to go near them, for she knew she could not bear to see close by the deformed figures and the vacant looks on their faces.

The lepers shuffled around like mourners, and as those upon whom death had laid its hand. Theirs was like a living death, both physically suffering from a loathsome disease, and spiritually cut off from the community of their friends and families.

Suddenly Haggar turned to her. She had an angry look on her face.

"You have said nothing to me, priestess."

Miriam was still ashamed, frightened and dismayed at her fate. She walked in a semi-conscious and listless state. She could hear and understand Haggar, but could not muster the strength or the interest to say anything.

"I know who you are. I know what happened. The soldier who brought the food this morning told me all about it."

Miriam knew that the events of last night would be told and retold, mostly by those who knew the least about what had actually been said or what had actually happened. The gossips and the hot heads would twist the story beyond recognition.

"You say nothing because you think you are better than us. You think just because you are a priestess, that we are beneath you."

Miriam could not bear to reply.

"Well, you are not better. Now you are a leper, just like the rest of us. Cast away in this pit dug for us by the godless Amorites."

Haggar's rage continued to build.

"The soldier told me all about you. You think you are even better than Moses. You spoke against Moses because of the Nubian woman he married."

Miriam turned to her angrily but continued to say nothing.

"They say you are jealous of her youth and her beauty. Or maybe you did not like her beautiful black skin."

Miriam shook her head in dismay.

"They say you think she is too dark."

Haggar now pointed at Miriam with derision.

"Too dark for you, is she?"

She was laughing and cackling so loudly that other lepers could hear. By now, several had gathered around them.

"Too dark for you, yes, she is too dark for you."

Haggar now came close to Miriam and pointed at Miriam's hands, almost touching them. The scales from her leprosy were visible for all to see.

"Of course, she is too dark for you. Well, if you prefer whiteness, you are now whiter than ever."

Haggar turned around and walked away from Miriam.

"Whiter than ever," she cackled repeatedly.

"Miriam is whiter than ever."

THIRTY-THREE

"What is this?" exclaimed Reyes's attendant, as he picked up a scroll that came flying in through the window.

The attendant was idling away the afternoon with his master Reyes in the Gaza administration office. He had opened the windows to let in the cool afternoon breeze coming in from the sea.

The attendant looked out the window as he held the scroll. He then walked over to the table where Reyes was sitting, and handed it to him.

"This was thrown in through the window, master. It was a man in black riding a black horse."

"He didn't stop to speak to you?"

"No, master. He just paused long enough to make sure the scroll came in. Then he quickly galloped away."

Reyes examined the object. It was a roll of papyrus tied with black ribbon.

"The Black Knights of the Egyptian empire," Reyes said, as he opened the scroll. He recognized the marks of Pharaoh's Secret Service.

Reyes read the letter slowly. Then he rolled it up and replaced the black ribbon.

"It is Prince Ramentop. He enjoyed our hospitality so much last time that he is coming again."

"So soon? He was here only two days ago."

"Well, he is coming again this evening. It looks like we are not going home early today."

"If it would please you, master, it would be my duty and pleasure to serve you."

"Thank you, thank you. But you will have to serve more than you did last time."

"If my poor memory serves, master, I had brought in fresh grapes and figs, and a plate of almonds and pistachios."

"Yes, of course."

"When I came in the next day, only some of the grapes were gone."

"He enjoyed a few of those, but Prince Ramentop does not seem to be a big eater."

"No, master."

Reyes paused briefly.

"Nevertheless, just in case. Prepare a sumptuous dinner. Even if he eats little or nothing, he must experience the Syrian hospitality that my family taught me."

"Of course, master."

The attendant bowed down to Reyes. But before he could leave the room, Reyes motioned to him to wait.

"Another thing."

"Yes, master."

"You will hear us talk of important matters of state."

"Yes, sir."

"They are secrets of the Pharaoh."

"Yes, master."

"You are not to breathe a word of what you hear."

"Yes, of course."

"It could be a matter of life and death for us, if we cross the Black Knights of Pharaoh."

"I understand, master."

"As we say in Syria, in one ear and out the other."

"I understand fully, master."

The attendant bowed again and hurried to the kitchen.

* * *

As Prince Ramentop walked into the Gaza administration building, Reyes and his attendant bowed low to him.

"Welcome," said Reyes. "We are flattered that you grace us so soon with your presence."

"Thank you, Reyes. You are most kind."

The attendant looked at the door for the Prince's two bodyguards to enter.

"They will remain outside," Prince Ramentop said. "I know that I am among friends."

"Your Highness may be assured of that," Reyes said, bowing again.

Ramentop was wearing the same black cloak and silver accessories he had worn during his last visit.

"Your Highness, may I relieve you of your collar and chain?" Reyes asked.

"No, thank you, Reyes, I will do it myself."

Reyes motioned Ramentop to the table in the middle of the room. Ramentop took off his black riding cloak, and hung it on the back of his chair.

As the two of them sat down, Reyes pointed to his attendant.

"Your Highness, my attendant and I are your loyal and humble servants. He has prepared for you a delectable meal."

Ramentop looked at the attendant and nodded.

"I hope that you can stay long enough to enjoy the fruits of his culinary labours."

"It will be my pleasure to do so, Reyes."

As the attendant bowed and left for the kitchen, Ramentop quickly got to the point.

"Reyes, I know I was here only two days ago. I had asked you to find out about the travels of Sebakashta, the Viceroy of Nubia, who is the governor of Gaza and your superior in command."

There was much about his job that Ramentop hated, but he revelled in the exercise of power, in going after someone like Sebakashta. He resented the Viceroy's position as a descendant of an old and noble family with deep roots in Aniba, while he, the son of a mere construction master, had to work his way up the grubby ladder of Memphis politics. Now he was in a position from which he could hound the Viceroy, and if successful, establish his reputation in Pharaoh's court.

"Yes, your Highness," said Reyes.

"I wanted you to find out where and when he goes, when he comes back, anything at all."

"I remember well, your Highness."

"I know it is too soon for you to have obtained such information."

"Perhaps, perhaps not."

Ramentop missed the hint and continued.

"Since my last visit here with you, I had remained in Gaza. I learned from other sources here that I will obtain more information from officials in Ezion-geber."

"Yes, your Highness."

"And so, I intend to ride to that town early tomorrow morning."

"I understand, your Highness."

"I thought that before I commenced my journey, I would visit you, my good friend Reyes."

"You are kind, your Highness."

"To see whether you have any information that might assist me in my journey."

"I understand fully, your Highness."

Just then, the attendant walked in with a large tray. He placed it on the table and prepared to unload the food from the tray.

He placed before each of them a bowl of hot barley porridge with wooden spoons. In the middle, he put a pitcher of water, two goblets and a plate of colourful vegetables – parsley, fresh onions (peeled and sliced), radishes, cucumbers (pickled and sliced) and sliced tomatoes.

As he watched his attendant unload his tray, Reyes was gratified at the deference that Ramentop was showing him. Suddenly he felt more esteemed, as he had when he had been governor of Gaza. Slowly but surely, he thought, they will get rid of the Nubian, and he, Reyes, will again be governor of Gaza.

"Thank you," Reyes said to the attendant.

As the attendant bowed and returned to the kitchen, Reyes replied to Ramentop.

"Your Highness, I too have my sources. I come from an old and well-established Syrian family. Little of what goes on escapes our notice."

"I am sure," said Ramentop.

"Your Highness, I do have some information that may be of assistance to his Majesty."

Reyes purposely brought the Pharaoh into the conversation. He shrewdly understood that this subtle reference to Pharaoh elevated his own importance and the information he was about to reveal to Ramentop. As well, if the Nubian were implicated, his offence would be seen as an offence against Pharaoh, deserving of the highest punishment.

"His Majesty will be grateful for your loyalty and assistance," said Ramentop.

Reyes then told Ramentop everything that his spies Omar and Jalam had reported to him.

"To summarize, your Highness, the Viceroy was spotted in Ezion-geber with his two aides. They spent the night with Esau, the local administrator. But that is not unusual."

"Yes, my friend," said Ramentop.

"The next day they traveled west along the southern highway, ostensibly on their way to Memphis. That is not unusual either."

"Of course not."

"But suddenly they were observed to turn south and ride into the hills of southern Sinai."

"That is unusual."

"Very much so, your Highness."

"It confirms that the Viceroy is involved in some kind of off-duty activity."

"Yes, your Highness. Somewhere in the hills west and south of Ezion-geber."

Reyes said nothing further, waiting for a reaction from Ramentop, who was now deep in thought. The Prince had finished his porridge and pushed the bowl gently away from him.

"Another thing, my friend."

"Yes, your Highness."

"We have reason to believe that the Hebrews are hiding out in the hills of southern Sinai. This appears to be where the Viceroy turned off the highway."

"It appears so, your Highness."

"Did your sources provide any information on the Hebrews?"

"No, your Highness. But they did report another matter."

Just then the attendant came in with more food. He put in front of each of them a large dinner plate. He served roast goose, cut in thin slices, and rubbed with rosemary, cumin, chervil, and orange. It was surrounded with grilled leeks, onions, and garlic. He picked up the empty bowls and returned to the kitchen.

"My friend, you are well served by your cook," Ramentop said as he chewed a piece of roast goose.

"He is both cook and office administrator."

"You are lucky, my friend. I, too, should get a desk job. This constant travel does not allow for good meals like this."

Shaul Ezer

"You are very kind, your Highness. I owe my good fortune to the grace of his Majesty."

"We all do, Reyes, we all do."

As he finished gulping down a grilled onion, Ramentop returned to the subject at hand.

"Now, my friend, you said that your sources reported another matter."

"Yes, your Highness. They had spotted about seventy Egyptian troops on the southern highway."

"I know about them."

"Perhaps they could assist you in your mission, your Highness."

"They will, Reyes, they will."

Ramentop paused and looked directly at Reyes. He seemed to be mulling some conflicting thoughts in his mind.

"Your information is most helpful, Reyes."

"I am glad, your Highness."

"If confirms my other sources."

"My sources are most reliable, your Highness."

"It appears so."

Reyes was satisfied with himself. Ramentop was not only enjoying the meal, but the Prince seemed impressed with the information Reyes had provided him. Reyes thought that this was an opportune moment to raise with the Prince the matter foremost on his mind.

"Your Highness," Reyes said. "I hope that you will not consider it indelicate of me."

"How so?"

"To raise a personal matter."

"Not at all. Let me hear it."

"The position of commander of Gaza."

"Yes, Reyes."

"Now held by the Viceroy of Nubia."

"Yes."

"Should it become vacant..."

"I understand, my friend."

"I would hope that you would be kind enough to intercede with Pharaoh on my behalf..."

"Yes, yes."

"... so that his Majesty may find it in his heart to reward a faithful servant..."

"Of course, Reyes."

"... so that he may grace me with the office, so that I may continue to serve his Majesty."

Ramentop knew the pitfalls of promising promotions, yet he also knew he needed Reyes and had to be encouraging without making an outright commitment.

"My good friend. As you know, these will all be decisions of his Majesty. But at the appropriate time, I will ensure that his Majesty is made fully aware of your prompt and loyal service."

"Thank you, your Highness."

As he prepared to leave, Ramentop looked directly into Reyes's eyes.

"I believe by now that I may confide in you as a friend."

"Of course, your Highness."

"And as a loyal servant of his Majesty."

"Indeed, you may."

"You mentioned the seventy troops on the southern highway."

"What about them, your Highness?"

"Well, you should know that they are under my direct command. I placed them there for just such an eventuality. They are awaiting my further orders."

"You have great foresight, your Highness."

"Thank you, my friend. And another thing. They are now being reinforced by another one hundred and thirty."

"From Memphis?

"Yes, my friend."

Reyes nodded, seemingly impressed.

"I will depart for Ezion-geber at dawn. With the help of the local officials and two hundred Egyptian troops, I will get to the bottom of the matter of the Viceroy of Nubia."

"May the gods look with favour on your mission," Reyes said.

"Thank you, my friend," Ramentop said, as he bade him farewell.

THIRTY-FOUR

When Joshua arrived at Moses' tent that morning, he found him in a solemn and reflective mood.

Joshua understood why. This was only the second morning after his wedding, so Moses had spent only one day with his new bride before resuming his duties. Moses knew the long list of matters on the agenda, even without having to deal with matters relating to the Viceroy of Nubia and the new alliance. Added to all this would be the strain from the row with Miriam and Aaron, for Joshua was sure that it continued to weigh heavily on Moses.

"What is on the list today, Joshua?" Moses asked.

"A few items, my Lord. Then his Excellency the Viceroy will arrive to confer with you."

They were silent for a brief moment as they reflected that this would be the first time that Moses would meet with the Viceroy since Moses had walked out in anger from the wedding. Joshua wondered how Moses would handle the next encounter with the Viceroy.

"Let us go through the list quickly then," Moses said.

Joshua looked at a scroll of papyrus in his hand.

"My Lord, first the judges."

"I hope that is in place."

"It is, my Lord. Except for one thing."

"What is that?"

Joshua hesitated to bring up a subject touching his brother Aaron, especially after the recent row Moses had had with Aaron and Miriam. The High Priest was still angry with Joshua for suggesting that Nun should be appointed Chief Judge reporting to Moses, instead of to Aaron.

"You were still considering who should be the Chief Judge."

"Yes, I remember. You recommended Nun of the tribe of Ephraim."

"Yes, my Lord."

"That is a good choice. Let us go with him."

"Thank you, my Lord."

Joshua hesitated, and then said, "My Lord, another matter has arisen. It has to do…"

"I know, I know. Who should Nun report to? Aaron wants Nun and all the judges to report to him."

Joshua nodded, but said nothing. He scarcely wanted to become more embroiled in the continuing squabble between Moses and his brother and sister. Joshua felt that Aaron was already blaming him for the separation of the judges from the priesthood. Joshua thought that he was trying to stay neutral and give Moses only his best impartial advice, but that did not seem to prevent Aaron from faulting him.

"I hear rumblings that Aaron was not punished as much as Miriam."

Joshua nodded again but remained silent.

"This would not be an opportune time to place under Aaron the new administration of judges. Would it, Joshua?"

"My Lord, I defer this matter to your greater wisdom."

Moses smiled.

"The Chief Judge Nun will report directly to me, and not to Aaron. Next item, Joshua."

"The next item, my Lord, is the operational failure of the Benjaminite division."

"Yes, Joshua."

"My Lord, the Benjaminite sentry was told about the impending arrival of the Nubians, but he did not turn up for duty. That is why the two Benjaminite cavalrymen, not expecting friendly visitors, attacked the Nubians."

"I know the details," Moses said smiling. "Elishama, the division head, sought me out at the wedding, specifically to tell me about it. He said he wanted me to hear about it directly from him, and that he personally took responsibility for the mishap."

"That is brave of him, my Lord."

"I appreciated that."

"My Lord, the sentry has been disciplined. The two Benjaminites have been demoted for further training."

"That is good."

"Anything else on that matter, my Lord?"

"Just that it points to the need for improving the fighting ability of our soldiers. I must say that I was very proud of Havilya. I wanted to hear her side of the story, and how she felt about being attacked on her first encounter with the Hebrew encampment."

"What did she say, my Lord?"

Moses smiled again.

"Not much. She just waved it away as a mere nothing. She did not wish to boast about it."

Joshua then looked down at the list in his hands.

"The attack into Canaan is the next item."

"Go on."

"Some of our commanders are arguing for an immediate attack into Canaan."

"What do you think?"

"I share your view, my Lord."

"Yes?"

"That we should first find out more about their defences."

"That was decided."

"Yes, my Lord. As you had proposed, we will first send in a mission of spies to investigate the Canaanites and their fortifications."

"When will you do that?"

"Immediately, my Lord."

"Who will you send?"

Joshua read off a list of men he had compiled with his commanders. They had picked twelve men – a chieftain from each one of the twelve tribes.

"The list sounds fine," Moses said. "How does this mission relate to our alliance with the Nubians?"

"At this point, it does not. The mission will tell us whether it is opportune to attack Canaan. This is independent of the Nubians. However, when the time comes that we are ready for the campaign into Canaan, we will try to co-ordinate it with any other action that the Viceroy may be planning."

"Should we discuss the mission of the spies with the Viceroy?"

"No, my Lord. At this point, it is merely a scouting mission for us. At the appropriate time, we can share that information with the Nubians."

"I agree, Joshua."

Just then an aide walked in with a plate of refreshments. Moses waved him away.

"Not for me. Perhaps for Joshua."

"Not for me either," said Joshua.

As the aide bowed out with the plate, Moses smiled at Joshua and said, "Things must be getting better. We are actually turning away food."

"Much of the credit for that is owed to his Excellency the Viceroy."

"I know, Joshua. What's next?"

"Moving the encampment."

"Go on."

"I am putting in place plans to move again."

"Why?"

"The longer we stay in one location, the more likely it is that Pharaoh's spies or troops will find us."

"That has not changed?"

"No, it has not, my Lord."

"Where do you plan to move to?"

"Somewhere else in the Sinai wilderness."

"What is the exact location?"

"I don't know, my Lord. It depends on what we find out about the Egyptian troops on the southern highway."

"Who is finding that out?"

"If you recall, my Lord, our scout, Shooly, and the Viceroy's aide, Shabitqo, are on that mission right now."

"Yes, yes, Joshua. When do you expect them to return?"

"Tomorrow night, my Lord."

"Good." Moses hesitated, then continued. "About this scout, Shooly. I hear mutterings that you favour him above others, even allowing him to address directly your senior commanders."

Joshua was taken aback. "My Lord, Shooly is trusted, eager and capable. I deliberately had him address the commanders. He shows signs of future leadership which I seek to develop in him."

"I understand," Moses nodded.

Joshua paused for a moment. This could be Aaron making trouble for him, or perhaps one of the commanders jealous of Shooly. Then he continued.

"The next item, my Lord…"

Moses looked away from Joshua as if distracted by other thoughts.

"How many more do you have, Joshua?"

"Several, my Lord."

"What are they?"

"Food and provisions. Detailed plans for moving the encampment. Whether military training is allowed on the Sabbath…"

"Joshua, perhaps we can defer these matters. We still have to see the Viceroy, and tonight is the eve of the Sabbath. It is Havilya's first. I want to be early for her."

"I understand, my Lord. I will ask the sentries to escort the Viceroy here."

* * *

As Moses waited for Joshua to return with the Viceroy, he felt strangely cheerful. The session with Joshua that had just finished had a few light moments. Although Miriam's isolation and how that would unfold still weighed on him, he managed to push that aspect to the back of his mind. What was forefront in his thoughts was Havilya. He marvelled how he had previously revelled in his work, and had seemed to enjoy the long hours with his aides and his priests. In the past months, he had had no one to go home to, so work and more work had seemed to be both a necessity and a distraction. Now all that had changed. Now he looked forward to the end of the workday, so that he could be back with his Havilya again. How he longed to be curled up in her inviting arms again, he thought.

Suddenly, his thoughts were interrupted by the loud voice of the sentry.

"His Excellency, the Viceroy of Nubia."

As the Viceroy entered the tent, followed by Joshua, Moses rose up to greet him.

"Good morning, your Excellency," Moses said.

"Good morning, Moses."

The Viceroy and Joshua sat across from Moses.

"You are my son now, Moses," the Viceroy said smiling. "Perhaps we need not be so formal anymore."

"All the more reason for me to treat you with respect and deference, my Lord,"
Moses said, bowing to him with a smile.

They all laughed, as Moses continued. "I still prefer to call you Excellency."

"I consent reluctantly, if I may call you Moses."

"That is acceptable."

They patted each other heartily on the back.

Moses began quickly.

"Excellency, I know that at the close of the wedding, my behaviour must have caused you discomfort, perhaps even some distress."

"Do not mention it, Moses."

"But I must. I feel I must apologize for that and for any discomfort that I caused you."

"Do not think of it, Moses."

"The members of my family, how shall I say it? We are strong-willed and can be volatile."

"I understand, Moses. You have all been under great strain since the Exodus from Egypt."

"That does not excuse such outbursts, especially on the occasion of a wedding celebration."

"It happens more than you think, Moses."

"Perhaps. But I do extend my sincere and humble apology."

"Moses, Moses. We are not so different in Nubia. Family squabbles do have a way of erupting at weddings and at other such occasions."

"It is unfortunate, but true."

"My wife, Sebaha, likes to say that if a brief argument is the worst that can happen, then it is a good omen for the married couple."

Suddenly Moses realized that the Viceroy was not aware of the full extent of Miriam's condition. After a brief thought, he let the subject pass.

"Excellency, I also want to thank you for the generous gifts you brought to us. Thanks to you, the wedding guests enjoyed the best meal any of us can remember."

"It is my pleasure, Moses."

Moses then turned to Joshua.

"Now, Joshua, what is on our agenda for this day?"

"Firstly, my Lords, I wish to confirm that as planned, Shooly and Shabitqo left on their mission at dawn yesterday."

"Good," said the Viceroy.

"They are expected to return after sundown tomorrow. We will convene again together to hear their report."

"What is the critical information we are seeking?" asked Moses.

"The deployment and mission of the Egyptian troops spotted on the southern highway," replied Joshua.

"That will determine the direction I will travel," added the Viceroy. "I intend to leave at dawn following the receipt of their report."

"Why so early?" asked Moses.

"I cannot impose on your hospitality much longer. Besides, I have been away from Gaza far too long. My frequent absences from the office have already raised some suspicions."

"I understand fully," Moses said. He then looked at them and asked, "Is there anything further to discuss at this point?"

Joshua had other matters that he would have preferred to discuss with both Moses and the Viceroy together, but Joshua sensed that Moses wanted to leave.

"No, my Lord," Joshua said. "You have given me the direction I need. I will, however, stay a while longer with his Excellency to review some operational matters."

"Thank you, Joshua," Moses said, as he rose to leave.

THIRTY-FIVE

"Captain, I need directions to the lepers' colony," Havilya said.

As soon as Moses had left that morning to confer with Joshua and the Viceroy, she had called in the captain of the sentries guarding their tent. He was taken aback by her request.

"The lepers' colony? Why, your Highness?"

He was a thickset and dark-skinned man of about thirty with a thick head of hair and a neatly trimmed goatee. He wore a vest of light armour around his chest and back.

"Because I want to go there," she said.

"It is forbidden, except for priests."

"Who takes food to them?"

"Family members. But they don't go inside. They leave the food at the edge of the colony."

"What happens to it then?"

"The head leper comes to get it and distributes the food inside the colony."

"Well, I have a family member there, captain. I must take food to her."

He gave her a puzzled look.

"Forgive me, your Highness. I don't doubt you. But my orders are to guard you at all times. My superiors did not mention anything about the need to visit the lepers."

"Rivka came in to see me briefly yesterday afternoon. She told me about what happened to Miriam. She said that the priests are telling everyone about it."

"Yes, your Highness. It is most tragic."

"I must visit her, captain. I want to take some food to her."

"Your Highness, I am sure that her husband Caleb and her son Bezalel are aware of their duties to her."

"I have no doubt they are."

"They must have taken some food to her by now."

"I must still visit her, captain. I am both her friend and her family. All I ask are for directions. If you do not give them to me, I will have to ask a passer-by outside in the encampment."

"Do you intend to go alone?"

"Yes, if necessary. But you may accompany me if you wish."

"Your Highness, many who go among the lepers become leprous themselves."

""Yes, yes," she said. "We have our own leper colonies in Nubia, mainly among those suffering from hunger. Divine providence strikes with many blows. But if you do not linger close and long among them, you will not become leprous."

The captain rubbed his goatee as he thought briefly about his options. He knew she was determined to go and could not stop her. He thought better of letting her go alone.

"If you insist, your Highness."

"Very well then, captain, I insist."

"I and my sentry will ride with you to the edge of the colony. You can leave food there for her, and then we will return immediately."

"I will be ready soon," she said.

The captain left the tent and waited outside while Havilya changed. She put on her riding clothes that she had used when she was the Viceroy's aide, Taharqo. Then she quickly went to the table for some manna wafers, goat cheese and dried figs. She wrapped them in a cloth and placed them in a bag tied to a strap. She hung the strap around her left shoulder, and the bag fell against her right hip. Then she covered her head and face with a large white scarf, leaving only a small opening to see through.

She walked briskly out of the tent.

"There, I am ready. No one will even recognize me."

"Very well, your Highness."

The three riders galloped quickly through the valley of the encampment. The morning sun was at a sharp angle above, shining into their faces. Soon the tents of the twelve Hebrew tribes were behind them, and they approached a large opening in the ground.

The captain pointed to the opening in the ground ahead of them.

"It is an old Amorite quarry," he said.

Soon they reached the edge of the pit. The captain led them to the beginning of the pathway leading down to the bottom and to the tents of the lepers.

"This is where we stop," he said as he dismounted.

Havilya's gaze was fixed on the lepers' colony below, as she too dismounted and handed the bridle of her horse to the captain.

"You can see two tents below. The one nearest to us is for the men. The one further back in the shadow of the far wall is for the women."

Havilya remained silent, as she continued to look down. She could see various figures below and around the tents and scattered alone in the shadow of the walls. Some were limping in pain, others seemed to look blankly ahead at nothing in particular.

"The ancients say that the Amorites had been here before," the captain continued. "They dug out the stones from this hole to build a settlement not far from here. Only some burnt-out ruins remain there."

Havilya nodded but said nothing and continued to look down below.

"Many old skeletons have been found in the pit. Some say the Amorites carried out human sacrifices here."

Havilya felt the blood draining from her face and her heart started to beat faster.

"Others say the skeletons are the remains of lepers and other sick people brought here to die."

"Or both," Havilya said softly, her voice breaking.

Sensing that the scene was too overpowering for Havilya, the captain decided to hasten their return.

"Your Highness, it is best that we return now. This is the spot where you can leave the food."

Suddenly, with tears streaming down her face, Havilya broke away from the captain's side, and ran down the pathway toward the women's tent. The captain chased after her for a few steps. Then he realized where he was going and the peril that awaited him. He stopped, and walked shortly back up the hill, with his head turned back, all the while watching Havilya running down into the leper's quarry.

"We will have to wait for her here," he said to the sentry.

Havilya raced down the pathway, past the men's tent and toward the women's tent near the back wall. She brushed against some of the lepers who looked at her with a puzzled resignation. She looked frantically to her left and to her right. Ahead she saw a woman in a colour she thought she recognized. As she got closer, she realized it was Miriam, still in the red gown she was wearing at the wedding.

She found her crouching in the shadow of the women's tent. She sat with her knees bent against her chest. Her hands surrounded her knees, and she seemed to be rocking herself gently while she flexed the muscles in her limbs.

Havilya sat on the ground in front of her. She looked up at Miriam, as she removed the scarf covering her head and face.

"My Lord, it is you, Havilya."

Suddenly Miriam stretched her legs and started to frantically beat her chest.

"Not you, not you, Princess. I cannot bear to see you stricken with this horrible disease. My Lord, my Lord, what calamity has befallen us? Havilya, a leper in the flower of her youth, a bride stricken in her wedding bed."

With both hands, Havilya reached out and grabbed Miriam's hands, and put them on her cheeks.

"No, no, Miriam, I am fine. Look, look. Look at my face."

As Miriam saw Havilya's smooth face, she seemed to calm down a little.

"Why then are you here, Princess? This is no place for you, my sweet young bride."

"I came to see you."

"What a sight I must be. Hobbling on my frail limbs. Covered with scales. Dressed in a red evening gown, waiting for death. I wish that it would come soon, Havilya. The grave is better than this living death."

"Have trust in the divine, for lepers can heal. I will take you away from here, Miriam. Come with me, now."

"You cannot, Princess. I must remain here for seven days. Then the priest will come to see me. If I am cured, he will release me. If not, I am doomed."

Havilya now looked closely at Miriam's hands and face. Her body seemed to have shrunk, and her figure was stooped and frail. All colour seemed to have drained away from her face. Whiter than her skin were the raised scales that now covered her face and body.

They both knew that in her condition no priest would release her from the colony. Unless she was cured by some miracle, she was doomed to die a slow death in that pit.

Miriam bent her knees toward her chest and began to rock herself again. Havilya sat facing her, clasping Miriam's hands against her breast. The presence of each other seemed to calm them, and they sat quietly, seemingly oblivious to those around them.

At last, it was Miriam who broke the silence.

"You would be right to reproach me, Princess," she said, as she rocked back and forth. "What a spectacle I created. What shame have I brought on all of us? Years from now, is that what you will remember? A wedding that ended in leprosy in the valley of death?"

"No, no, Miriam, Miriam, don't say that. That is not what I will remember. It will be your kindness, verve, how you took me in as a sister, and then your wisdom. Others will remember your good works and how you looked after them when they were sick."

Then she remembered the story of Moses' birth and early childhood.

"Above all, I will remember the elder sister who watched over her little brother. Didn't you, Miriam? You watched over him, Miriam. To me, it is as if you watched over him for me."

Miriam looked at her with a faint smile.

"Don't forget that, Miriam. You saved him for me. Didn't you? Didn't you?"

Havilya now rocked Miriam gently.

"Didn't you, Miriam?"

"Yes, I guess I did. That was a long time ago. But what I did two days ago must have found offence in the eyes of God."

"Perhaps, Miriam, you spoke eloquently – both for men, but especially for women."

"No, Havilya. The realm of ideas, strategies, leadership – these are not the realm of women. Women cannot cross the line to engage in these matters with men."

"But you have, Miriam."

"Yes, but look at the consequences. We work in their shadow – in the shadow of their decisions. Decisions which sometimes produce dead soldiers, wounded youths, orphaned children, widowed wives, destitution, hunger. Yet with all that, the lot of women is to care and to cure, to pick up the pieces of the wreckage of men's ideas."

"Not all of the decisions of men are bad."

"No, they are not. But good or bad, women are allowed to contribute nothing."

"You have played a part. You are playing a part. A priestess, a leader of women. Your good works will be remembered through the ages."

"Yes, yes, Havilya," Miriam said, as she pushed her gently away from her. "You must go now. This is no place for you."

"I will be back to take you from here. If the Lord creates miracles, there will be one for you."

Havilya now took out the food from her bag, and gave it to Miriam.

"Here, Miriam, I brought you something to eat. I will be back soon."

Miriam took the cloth in which the food was wrapped, but did not open it.

"Thank you, Havilya. But you must go now."

As Havilya stood up to leave, suddenly the head leper went by. She did not stop, but merely muttered as she limped past them.

"Miriam, time to clean the tent. Time to clean the tent, Miriam."

Miriam laughed.

"This is Haggar the head leper, Havilya. She has been here so long that she cannot feel anything. Most of her senses are gone."

Havilya glanced briefly at the head leper, as she wrapped her scarf around her head and face.

Oblivious to the risk of even touching a leper, Havilya hugged Miriam, and quietly ran up the pathway to the captain and his sentry waiting at the top.

THIRTY-SIX

Shooly and Shabitqo could hardly sleep that night, because of what Shooly had found and reported to his Nubian companion. By the time Shooly had returned to their meeting place, it was well past midnight. Shabitqo had been waiting for him anxiously.

"I thought you would be back before dark?"

"So did I, Shabitqo. But it was an easy ride, and I thought I could find my way back by moonlight."

"It was risky."

"But worthwhile. I wouldn't have found them if I had turned back earlier."

"I found nothing, "Shabitqo reported. "I reached close to Ezion-geber. Except for a few locals, there were no signs of Egyptian soldiers."

"That's because they have moved in the other direction," Shooly said.

"Why do you think they moved there?"

"I don't know. Remember, there were many more than I found last week."

"So they were reinforced and re-positioned."

"It seems so."

"I wonder why?"

"That is what we hope Esau will tell you tomorrow."

"Yes, Shooly, and it will be your turn to wait here. I will leave at dawn."

* * *

"The Black Knights of Pharaoh," Shabitqo muttered to himself. "What is Pharaoh's Secret Service doing here?"

As he approached the administration building in Ezion-geber, he found the men in black milling around outside, seemingly waiting for something.

He had never seen them before in such large numbers, especially in a small administrative centre such as Ezion-geber.

He decided he would be nonchalant and simply ignore them, and go in to see Esau as if on a routine visit. He tied his horse to a post outside, and walked into the building.

Esau was working alone at his desk. He looked up, surprised to see Shabitqo alone.

"Welcome, my friend. Will I also have the pleasure of greeting his Highness the Viceroy?"

"No, sir. He is otherwise engaged. I was passing through your town, and he asked me to give you this letter," he said, handing Esau a scroll.

"I believe it authorizes you to give me the information I am seeking for the Viceroy."

Esau finished reading the scroll.

"Yes, it does, Shabitqo."

Rolling up the scroll, Esau motioned to Shabitqo to sit down.

"What does his Highness wish to know?"

"Just a brief review of his last meeting with you. His Highness would like to know about troop movements, the impact on your budget, that sort of thing."

Esau was somewhat surprised. He had taken the Viceroy through the budget only a few days ago. It was unusual for him to inquire so soon about the impact on the budget. But he felt he had no choice but to co-operate. The Viceroy was his superior, and the letter – obviously in the Viceroy's style and handwriting – was clear in its instructions.

"It is too early to identify any changes to the budget, Shabitqo."

"What can I say to him about troop movements through town?"

"There have been none since your last visit with his Highness."

"Are you expecting any?"

"Perhaps."

Esau hesitated, and then continued.

"Did you notice the Black Knights outside?"

"Yes, I did."

"They are aides and assistants of Prince Ramentop, the head of the Secret Service."

"I surmised as much."

"Tasiris, the senior aide of Ramentop, spent some time with me."

"Yes?"

"Tasiris said that Prince Ramentop will be arriving shortly."

"For what purpose?"

"To take direct command of some two hundred Egyptian troops."

"Where are they?"

"Somewhere between here and Memphis. On the southern highway."

"What does Ramentop want to do with the troops?"

"I am not sure."

"At first, Tasiris asked questions about the Hebrews."

Shabitqo's heart sank.

"What about them?"

"Don't know. He wanted to know if we had seen any sign of them or whether someone had reported seeing or hearing about them."

"Did you?"

"No."

"Why is he interested in the Hebrews?"

"Apparently Prince Ramentop wants to know. It is part of his duties to find them."

"Do they have reason to believe the Hebrews are in the vicinity?"

"He did not say. I would assume so, although he would not tell me."

"When is Prince Ramentop expected?"

"Today or tomorrow."

"Do you expect the Egyptian troops to be brought into town?"

"He didn't say. He intimated that they are under Ramentop's command, and he will use them as he sees fit."

"Any hint of where the next move for the troops will be?"

"No, except that he asked a lot of questions about conditions in the area south of the Bitter Lakes."

"Any place in particular?"

"Villages such as Marah and Elim."

Shabitqo remembered that Joshua had described the route of the Exodus. He remembered Joshua saying that the Hebrews went south from the Bitter Lakes into the vicinity of Marah and Elim.

Esau hesitated again and looked furtively around him. There was no one there but the two of them.

"Shabitqo, you should also mention to his Highness..."

"Yes?"

"...that Tasiris asked many questions about his Highness, the Viceroy."

"What kind of questions?"

"His whereabouts, comings and goings."

"What did you say?"

"The truth."

"Which is?"

"That he was here with two aides recently. That we discussed routine business, such as the budget."

"What else?"

"He wanted to know where his Highness went next."

"What did you tell him?"

"That he was heading to Memphis."

"Not to his office in Gaza?"

"I believe he had mentioned you were going to Memphis."

"Thank you, Esau. Anything else?"

"Yes, please give my warmest regards to his Highness."

"I will, Esau. You have been most helpful."

Shabitqo bowed out of the office and galloped as fast as he could back to meet Shooly.

THIRTY-SEVEN

"I must speak to Aaron the High Priest at once," demanded Havilya.

She was standing outside the Tent of Revelation, speaking hurriedly to the guard at the entrance. She held the bridle of her horse in her left hand. As she spoke, she gestured with her right hand. She had galloped as fast as she could directly from the lepers' colony, with her two protectors, the captain and a sentry, barely catching up with her. It was still midday before the eve of the Sabbath and the captain had told her that Aaron would be in the Tent of Revelation preparing for the Sabbath services.

The guard gave her a puzzled look. He was tall and thin, with clean-shaven face and a long pointed nose. He wore a cloak, a kilt and sandals. He held a spear loosely in his left hand. He recognized her, but could not understand why she was wearing a man's clothes and riding a horse.

"Your Highness, the High Priest is inside," the guard said, looking up and down at her. "You are of course welcome to go inside to see him."

"I prefer to see him outside," she insisted.

Havilya thought that she was about to tell Aaron that she had just been to the lepers' colony. She did not want to offend the High Priest, lest he now considered her impure to enter the Tent of Revelation.

Her captain, sensing her deference, interceded.

"Officer," he said to the guard. "She may have good reason to meet the High Priest here. Please obey her wishes."

The guard nodded.

"I will see what I can do," he said, as he turned to walk inside.

A few moments later, Aaron came out with the guard behind him.

"What is it, Havilya?" he asked perplexed.

She handed the bridle to her captain, and took Aaron outside.

"I must speak to you – alone, in private."

"Won't you come in?"

"No, we can speak here."

They walked alone to an empty spot at the side of the tent. She realized that this was the first time she would be speaking to him alone.

"I just visited Miriam," she blurted out.

"You what?"

"I did, Aaron."

He shook his head. "It is terrible what happened to her," he said.

"I know."

"I am partly responsible. I probably encouraged her to speak against Moses."

"Aaron, this is no time to dwell on the reasons why. We have to do something for her."

"What do you have in mind?"

"She is very ill, Aaron."

"I know. I saw her. I took her there."

"That place will make her worse."

Aaron said nothing and waited for Havilya to tell him what was on her mind.

"We can't leave her there, Aaron."

"What do you suggest?"

"Bringing her into the camp."

"She is leprous, Havilya. She must be isolated from the camp."

"She can be brought closer – maybe we can empty the Annex for her, if the wounded have improved enough to be sent home. Or we can set up a separate tent for her nearby."

"How will that help?"

"I and the other women can then take care of her."

"But we cannot let you and the other women come into contact with her."

"Aaron, it is our only chance to make her better."

The High Priest paused as he thought about what Havilya had just said.

"Havilya, a priest is required to visit her after seven days. I will personally visit her then."

"That is five days from now."

"We must wait to see if she improves."

"She will not improve in that horrible pit, Aaron."

The Nubian Princess

"I cannot visit her after only two days. I will not find a change."

"I am not saying her condition improved. It may be getting worse because of where she is."

"Havilya, I cannot release her into the camp after only two days. I have to think of the other lepers and their families. They will want the same thing."

"Miriam has done so much for all of them."

"Yes, she has. But that does not mean I can expose the camp to her."

Havilya took a deep breath in exasperation, and walked back and forth in front of Aaron. Aaron took her hand and looked her in the eyes.

"Havilya, Havilya, I know how much you love Miriam. She cannot have a better friend than you."

Havilya looked down to the ground.

"I am her younger brother. I love her, too, as do most of the Hebrews, especially the women."

Havilya's eyes began to glisten.

"She looked after all of them when they were sick," she said. "Why can't we do something for Miriam now?"

"Havilya, it pains me, too. It hurts me that we cannot heal the healer."

Havilya looked up at Aaron helplessly.

"Perhaps you can pray for her, Aaron."

"Of course, I will."

"The Lord may hear a High Priest."

"The Lord hears all of our prayers, Havilya."

"And in five days?"

"Yes?"

"What can you do for her in five days, Aaron?"

"I will visit her. If I find her better, if I find that her scales are disappearing, then I can release her."

"If not?"

"Then she has to stay another seven days, and she will be examined again."

"It may be too late, Aaron."

"It is all we can do, Havilya."

Havilya shook her head quickly.

"Thank you, Aaron, thank you," she said, as she walked away with tears in her eyes.

* * *

"This will be my first Sabbath eve with Moses," Havilya thought, as she rushed back to their tent from her meeting with Aaron.

The High Priest had been rigid and uncompromising, she thought. She understood the dread that the Hebrews had for leprosy. Such attitudes were not different in Egypt or in her native Nubia. But with Miriam in a desperate state, she had hoped – even expected – that he would feel a sense of urgency to aid his elder sister. He could have relaxed the rules, and found a way for her and the other women to help Miriam.

As she dried her tears, she thought she would try something else later to help Miriam. She did not yet know what it would be. For now, sundown was just approaching and she did not want to disappoint Moses on their first Sabbath eve.

When she arrived at their tent, she was relieved that Moses was not yet there. She had learned from her mother Sebaha to be home for her husband when he arrived, especially for an important evening.

She quickly took off her riding clothes and went in the wooden tub. The water was clean. The sentries had discovered her fondness for baths, and made sure the tub had warm water. Except that they were early today, and the water had chilled.

After drying herself with the linen stacked nearby, she put on a long green dress of fine silken fabric. It covered her loosely from neck to toe, but was tight enough to reveal the contours of her figure.

She decided she would arrange for them to eat side by side sitting on the floor with a low table in front. The burlap floor covering had been cleaned. She removed the narrow cot in the corner, and placed some bedding on the floor for them to sit on. Then she placed a white cloth in front. This was to be their table. She placed three flat stones side by side, with a candle on each.

Then she took two wooden plates. She put manna wafers, dates, parsley and goat cheese on one, and dried Nile

236

pike on the other. Rivka had brought the food for her, so that Havilya would not have to cook before the Sabbath eve. Finally, she poured some wine in two goblets and placed them on the linen cloth.

"It's your first Sabbath as a married lady. You don't have to do the cooking," Rivka had said.

"But I won't learn, if you do everything for me," Havilya had protested.

"Don't worry. There will be a lot of cooking ahead of you."

Miriam had taught her that since the time of the patriarchs Abraham, Isaac and Jacob, a Hebrew custom had developed on holy days of saying blessings to the Lord for giving light. This blessing was recited before candles were lit. Four other blessings to the Lord were also recited – one over wine, for giving the fruit of the vine; another over bread; a third over a fruit from the tree; and a fourth over a vegetable of the earth.

Miriam then explained that when Moses recently brought down the Ten Commandments, one of them was to keep the Sabbath holy, which meant that one must rest from work during the seventh day of the week. The evening of the sixth day become known as the "Sabbath eve", and Moses ordained that each household must observe the eve of the Sabbath in a special celebration at home, which was to comprise three parts: the first was a reading of a brief passage reciting the story of creation, how the Lord created the heavens and the earth in six days and rested on the seventh; the second part was to recite the blessings and light the candles and eat the symbolic foods; and the third part was to rejoice during the rest of the evening and partake of the evening meal with one's kin.

Having prepared the table for the blessings and the meal, Havilya then went to the table in another corner where she had placed her cosmetics. She looked at herself in the mirror. She applied a faint layer of red pigment on her cheeks and a darker layer on her lips. She rubbed balm of Gilead on her neck and applied her favourite Nubian fragrance to her chest and shoulders.

She was now ready for Moses to arrive. As she waited, she seemed confident in preparing for her first Sabbath. At first, Hebrew custom had seemed so complex and forbidding. But now it all seemed so simple. The credit goes to Miriam, she thought, and how quickly and well she had taught her. The priestess had a talent for stripping complex matters to their bare essentials.

Suddenly she heard the sentries outside greeting Moses. When he walked in, he found her standing in the middle of the tent facing him.

"Shabbat shalom," she said, greeting him.

"Shabbat shalom," he replied, as he embraced her.

He kissed her on her cheeks and neck and squeezed her tightly.

"Havilya, you are a beautiful sight to come home to."

She turned to his side, so he could see the spread that she had prepared.

His smile widened as he looked at the candles and then at Havilya.

"I see you have prepared a double feast for me, Havilya – yourself, and now this meal."

"They are both for you to enjoy."

He kissed her again, and then they sat on the floor behind the linen cloth. She sat to his left with his left arm around her waist.

She lit the three candles, as she recited the blessing for the light.

Moses now recited the familiar Sabbath passage from the story of creation when God had finished His creation on the sixth day and rested on the seventh day. He said the blessing over the wine, and they both sipped from their goblets. Then Moses said a blessing over the manna wafers, and they each ate a piece. Miriam had told her that in Egypt that part of the blessing was done with bread. With no bread in the wilderness, Miriam – always the improviser – had advised that some form of manna would be an acceptable substitute.

Moses then took a date and said the blessing for the fruit of the tree. This was followed, using parsley, by the blessing for the vegetable of the earth.

With the blessings completed, it was time for a dinner of goat cheese and Nile pike. But Moses could not keep his eyes away from her. He held Havilya tightly in his arms.

"I could not wait to come here to you," he said. "Poor Joshua, I cut his agenda short. All I could think of was you."

"Did you discuss what was needed?"

"Yes. But work now seems more a means than an end. I feel blessed that I want to spend more time with you than at work."

"I am here to please you, my love."

"You more than please me."

"Were my Sabbath preparations acceptable to you?"

"Of course, of course. How stupid of me. I didn't even think that this was our first Sabbath. It all seemed so normal, so perfect."

"I have not done this before."

"I know. But it seems like you have always done it."

Here was her chance to mention Miriam. She wanted him to talk about his elder sister, to find out his thoughts and what could be done to save her. But Havilya hesitated, for fear that it would upset him and spoil their first Sabbath eve together.

She decided to take a chance; for she felt their love was strong enough to withstand it, and that Miriam's needs were urgent.

"I learned from an experienced master," she said finally.

"Who is that?"

"Why your sister Miriam, of course."

Moses became silent for a short moment. But a smile returned to his face.

"Yes, she is a good teacher," he said. "To all of us."

Havilya put her hand on his arm, and looked up at him.

"Moses, there is something I must tell you."

"Yes, Havilya, what is it?"

"I went to see Miriam today."

Moses said nothing. Havilya was almost frightened as to how he would react, but she pressed on.

"At the lepers' colony."

He still said nothing.

"I took her some food. But her condition is bad and getting worse."

Moses nodded.

"I know you were angry with her. I don't want us to discuss your reasons for that. I just want her to get better. If there is something I can do to make her better, I want to do it."

He continued to remain silent. He seemed like an enigma to her, a puzzle far away. She thought she knew him well, and loved him. But now he seemed impenetrable, and it was beyond her power to find out what he was feeling and thinking. She remembered her mother's admonishment – not to say too much. She felt she had said more than enough, and wished Moses would now reveal himself to her.

At last, he turned to her, and put his arms around her again. He sighed heavily, as he seemed to make a great effort to talk about a subject he preferred to avoid.

"Havilya, Havilya, I love you more now that you care for Miriam, and took such risks for her. I cannot say more."

He hesitated, and after another heavy sigh, he seemed to force out the words, as he added, "It is a time of rebellion within my people, when our hearts and minds are not one. My heart is with Miriam, as a dear sister beloved as a priestess by all who know her. But my head is with what the Lord has commanded me to do for my people. If her rebellion is condoned, one must also be merciful to the rebellion of the others. That is the way to catastrophe for our people. I have faith that our Lord will guide us along His path and do what is right for Miriam and our people."

He now stretched out and pulled her with him. They lay on their side, pressed face to face against each other. He then moved down, pushing his face between her breasts.

Her heart raced, for she now knew that what should have happened on their wedding night was at last about to happen. She was glad Moses was raised in an Egyptian court, for he would understand her and her Nubian upbringing, and thus she would not have to explain. He would know that her skills of how to please a man derived not from experience with other men, but from the teaching of the wise Nubian wives of powerful men. The Nubian wife knew that she needed to please her husband, otherwise his attention would wander to other women. And so, Nubian women taught their unmarried daughters the ways of the marital bedroom. She thought, too, that there would not be blood afterward, and that Moses would understand that as well, by reason of her horseback riding and not for having known another man. As glad as she was for marrying a Hebrew, she was relieved that he had his Egyptian side.

She sat up and removed her clothing and she began to remove his. As he lay on his back, she could see the throbbing veins of his erection. She gently rubbed her lips up and down the back of his member. He stayed as long as he could, for he had not had such pleasure for a long time. Then, as he could resist no longer, he turned her on her back.

She gripped him around his shoulders as she parted her thighs. Her eyes were open wide with a child-like eagerness. She remained alert without falling into a sensual trance, for she wanted to feel every pleasure and pain.

He entered her with a savage lunge. With each thrust, he was conscious of his ecstasy in conquering a beautiful young black Nubian princess. Her moans heightened his passion, and now he was also vanquishing the ancient civilization of Nubia and the Egyptian rulers who possessed it.

Sated, they lay together in a balmy embrace. At last, she allowed herself to drift into a supernatural trance. They stayed content for a long time, each comforted by the sound of the beating of the other's heart.

THIRTY-EIGHT

"I need a candle," Miriam told Haggar the head leper.

Miriam was sitting near the entrance to the tent of the women lepers. She was facing the setting sun, which now disappeared behind the western edge of the pit. A red haze formed a ribbon along the dusty horizon.

Miriam's tall and sturdy body still exuded some strength. But her fair and smooth complexion had given way to the scales on her skin. Her long grey hair seemed whiter now and more dishevelled, and the radiance in her face had been replaced by an ashen look. The wrinkles and dirt on her red evening dress added to her subdued appearance.

"Why do you need a candle, priestess?" Haggar asked.

The head leper was hobbling back and forth in front of Miriam. Her tall and thin body was hunched over in a steep stoop, with her back almost parallel to the ground. The rags that covered her figure and bald head seemed dirtier than before.

"It is the eve of the Sabbath. We should light a candle and recite the blessing of creation."

"How do you know what day it is?"

"I know because I came here two days ago."

"We have been here so long that all the days and nights are the same to us."

"I say to you that it is the eve of the Sabbath, and we must keep it holy."

Haggar looked up and stared at Miriam with a puzzled face.

"Every day is the same. Sabbath or no Sabbath. We don't work here anyway, so we cannot stop work."

"Have you lost all faith that you will not listen to a priestess as to what day it is?"

"The Lord has turned His gaze away from us."

"We are all His children – even the lepers."

"We do nothing. We are nothing. Nothing, nothing, priestess. Something will not come from nothing."

"Do not lose hope."

"I don't want to lose a candle. We need it to keep the darkness away."

"We also need it to make a blessing."

"You are a good talker, priestess. Talk to the Lord. He does not listen to us. Talk to Him, priestess. Talk to Him, priestess."

"I will, Haggar, I will. But you must talk to Him, too."

"You are the priestess, Miriam. Talk to Him. Find out why we are here."

"I know why I am here."

"Why, priestess?"

"As punishment."

"For what?"

"Hostile talk against my brother Moses."

"Is that all?'

"Yes."

"Much hostile talk is between brother and sister. Why isn't the lepers' colony full of people?"

"I cannot say."

"Aren't you the priestess who looked after the sick and led us in a victory song after we left Egypt?"

"I am."

"Your good works did not keep you out of this place."

"No, they did not."

"Is that just?"

"I do not know all the ways of the Lord."

"If a priestess does not, how can we?"

"Those who speak for you before the Lord will prevail."

"No one is speaking for me."

"If your cause is just, someone will."

"When is my cause just?"

"Do you know why you are here?"

"No, priestess. They took me away from a husband and four little children."

"Even as a priestess, I cannot account for the suffering of the innocent."

The head leper became silent. She came close to Miriam and looked her straight in the eye.

"I will give you a candle, priestess."

"You are very kind."

"No, no. It is not to bless the Sabbath."

"What is it for then?"

"To join me in cursing the Lord and His justice."

"I cannot do that. You must not do that. The Lord lives and He will redeem us."

"The Lord lives above the clouds."

"But He is watching over us."

"He lives above the clouds because He dares not come down to face the wrath of the innocent."

"The Lord will redeem the innocent."

"Innocents suffer and the wicked prosper."

"You must not lose faith."

Haggar moved away from Miriam and started to walk in the direction of the setting sun toward the men's tent. She was muttering to herself some phrases over and over again. Then she circled back toward Miriam, who could now hear the head leper sing:

> *Priestess, priestess,*
> *Tell me why*
> *So many innocents suffer.*
>
> *Priestess, priestess,*
> *The Lord stands by*
> *While the wicked prosper.*

Miriam stood up and gently pulled Haggar toward her. As the head leper sat beside her, Miriam put her right arm around Haggar and her left hand in Haggar's lap.

"I don't know the song you are singing. Sing with me a song we both know."

Haggar now stopped singing, and Miriam could feel the old woman's sobbing as her tears fell on Miriam's hands.

"You know the Song of the Sea, Haggar. You sing it with me."

Haggar nodded.

"Will you sing it with me now?"

Haggar nodded again. She put her hand in her burlap bag, took out a candle and handed it to Miriam.

"First," she said, her voice breaking, "first, we light this for the Sabbath."

* * *

"Tasiris, Esau! Let us review the situation," declared Prince Ramentop of the Black Knights of Pharaoh.

It was late in the afternoon when the head of the Egyptian Secret Service had arrived in Ezion-geber. It had been a long ride from Gaza without a rest stop. He had immediately gone to the administration office, and was now anxious for a report from Tasiris, his senior aide, and Esau, the local administrator in Ezion-geber.

"We have some decisions to make," he said as he dusted off his secret service uniform.

"Your Highness, where do you wish to start?" asked Tasiris.

The prince's senior aide was well dressed and groomed. His features resembled Ramentop's, and like his master, he combed back and oiled his hair into a glistening layer. Except for a full beard on his face, it was difficult to tell Tasiris apart from his master Ramentop.

"We will start with you, Tasiris," Ramentop replied. "Then we will see what Esau has to add."

"As you wish, your Highness," said Esau, bowing low to the prince.

The local administrator was short and bald. His smooth and cherubic face had never grown a beard.

"Your Highness," Tasiris began, "we have reinforced the seventy Egyptian troops."

"How many are there now?"

"Two hundred, your Highness, as you have ordered."

"Where?"

"We moved them further west along the southern highway."

"Where exactly?"

"Just east of the Bitter Lakes."

"Why there?"

"Two reasons, your Highness. To keep them far from Ezion-geber. Contact with the locals may jeopardize their sensitive mission."

"Yes. The other reason?"

"As you will hear later, they are now better positioned to search for the Hebrews."

"Explain that."

"I will make my recommendation, your Highness. But first, you may wish to receive Esau's briefing."

"Of course," said the Prince, motioning to Ezion-geber's chief administrator.

Esau sat up, and clapped his hands loudly as he glanced impatiently toward the kitchen.

"Your Highness, forgive me if you find us wanting in our hospitality."

A servant quickly rushed in with a tray of food. He placed before them plates of grapes, fresh dates and dried almonds.

"Your Highness," Esau began, "I will repeat what I told your senior and trusted aide."

Esau turned and nodded to Tasiris who nodded back.

"Questions were asked about the Hebrews."

"Yes, yes," the Prince said expectantly.

"Unfortunately, I and my staff have no information about them."

"Nothing about where they might be?"

"No, your Highness."

"What about your superior, the Viceroy?"

"As I said to Tasiris, the Viceroy and his two aides were here a few days ago."

"For what purpose?"

"A routine visit, your Highness. They stayed overnight. We discussed the budget."

"Anything else?"

"Nothing of substance, your Highness."

"Where did they go next?"

"He said they would go west toward Memphis."

"Have you heard from the Viceroy since?"

Esau hesitated for a moment. But he had already decided in his mind not to mention Shabitqo's visit. He would regard it as not a matter of substance. In any case, while he was a neutral administrator, he did not wish to jeopardize his master's position any more than was required to do his duty to Pharaoh.

"No, your Highness."

Ramentop removed the pip from the inside of a date, and replaced it with an almond. He then put the combination in his mouth. As he chewed, the others could hear the crack of the almond.

"Now, Tasiris, you had a suggestion to make," Ramentop said.

"Yes, your Highness."

Tasiris held up a large bunch of grapes, and broke off a small branch. He put one grape in his mouth.

"Your Highness, our information about the movements of the Hebrews is sketchy."

"But we know a little."

"Yes, we know that when they escaped from Egypt more than a year ago, they went south of the Bitter Lakes in the wilderness of Etham."

"Can we be more specific?"

"They probably wandered in the hills and moved south along the coast of the gulf."

"Did anyone spot them?"

"Just some shepherds, your Highness. We think they went through Marah and Elim."

"Anything there?"

"No. Just oases."

"What is your suggestion?"

"A thorough approach, your Highness."

"Which is?"

"We would use the two hundred troops."

"Who are awaiting my command, I assume?"

"Yes, your Highness."

"Go on."

"The troops would start from a point on the southern highway just south of the Bitter Lakes."

"Then what?"

"They would move south in the wilderness of Etham."

"Toward Marah and Elim?"

"Yes, your Highness."

"But the Hebrews may have abandoned those positions months ago."

248

The Nubian Princess

"That may be so. But the troops would follow the paths in the hills south of Marah and Elim into the wilderness of Sinai looking for debris that the Hebrews may have left behind."

"The Hebrews may have moved to the other end of the Sinai Peninsula."

"Yes, your Highness. But we believe they are somewhere south of the southern highway. The thorough approach I am suggesting will find them sooner or later."

"But they might move north to Canaan."

"They could, your Highness. But if we make haste, our troops may find them sooner."

"Are two hundred troops enough?"

"To search for the Hebrews, yes. But not to engage them. A small number like two hundred can move quickly in the hills."

"What happens if the troops find the Hebrews?"

"Their orders would be not to engage them, but count their strength and deployment."

"For a larger force to be then sent against them?"

"Yes, your Highness, if his Majesty so chooses."

"Very good, Tasiris."

Ramentop now tossed a small handful of almonds into his mouth.

"Now Tasiris," the Prince said. "What about the Viceroy?"

"We think he is involved in some secret activity."

"I agree."

"But we don't know if it involves the Hebrews."

"What do you suggest for the Viceroy?"

"That the troops would be alerted to also look for him."

"He is not likely to remain long in the wilderness."

"No, your Highness. That is why I also suggest that the Black Knights plan frequent patrols along the southern highway."

"To look for the Viceroy?"

"Yes. Sooner or later, he will cross or travel along that highway."

Ramentop turned toward Esau.

"What do you think, Esau?"

"I am not a military man, your Highness."

"Yes, yes, I know. But do you have anything to add?"

249

"No, your Highness, I have nothing to add."

Ramentop thought for a moment, as he picked up a date.

He looked at Esau and Tasiris.

"This matter is of the utmost secrecy. Do you understand?"

"Yes, your Highness," said Esau bowing.

Ramentop then turned to Tasiris.

"I like your plan, Tasiris. You may proceed immediately."

THIRTY-NINE

"We have terrible news!" Shooly exclaimed as he and Shabitqo burst into the military tent.

It was well past dark and the Sabbath had ended three hours before. Joshua had assembled them together to hear the report of the two scouts and plan the next move. He had called in his aide Zabad and the four division commanders.

Moses would not normally have attended but he, too, was there with Sebakashta, the Viceroy of Nubia. The Viceroy had said that he intended to leave the Hebrew encampment at dawn of the next day.

"Should you not want to hear the two scouts before you decide?" Moses had asked him.

"Moses," the Viceroy had replied, "regardless of their report, I must return. My absence from Gaza has been too long. Longer still from Memphis. I am afraid my long absence may give rise to suspicion."

All eyes were now on the two scouts.

Shooly was thinner than usual. The stress from his mission and the dust from his face and clothes made him look older than his twenty years. Though of medium height, he seemed to stand taller and with more confidence today. In his left hand, he held his wooden staff from its middle.

"Egyptian troops," Shooly gasped. "There are three times as many as before."

"And the Black Knights," cut in Shabitqo. "They are everywhere in Ezion-geber."

The Nubian scout was taller and older than Shooly. The dust that covered his face and beard gave his black complexion a lighter sheen.

"At least two hundred Egyptian troops," Shooly said.

"The Secret Service has taken over Ezion-geber," Shabitqo jumped in.

Joshua raised his hand.

"Calm down both of you. Sit down. Have some water. We will hear you slowly and one at a time."

The two scouts sat at the edge of the carpet and faced Joshua on the other side. Moses sat on Joshua's right and the

Viceroy on his left. Ahiezer and Elishama sat on the edge of the carpet to Joshua's right, and the other two commanders across from them.

Joshua then said, "Shooly, why don't you start?"

"We rode together at first," Shooly began. "We came to the ridge overlooking the southern highway. That is where I had found the two mules Shabitqo had left for me."

Shooly paused for breath.

"Go on," said Joshua.

"It was early evening. There was still some light. We decided to split to look for the Egyptian troops. I rode near the highway toward Memphis. Shabitqo rode toward Ezion-geber."

"What did you find, Shooly?"

"I rode for a long time. Past the point where the highway disappears between two hills. I went up the hill to look down on the highway. That is when I found the Egyptian soldiers. Two hundred of them and seventy horses."

"What could you see?"

"Not much more. It was getting dark. But I could see that twenty of the horses carried supplies."

"The other fifty must be cavalry," someone said.

"Then what?" asked Joshua.

"I rode back to the ridge. I found Shabitqo waiting for me."

"It was well past midnight," Shabitqo began. "I had returned earlier than Shooly. I rode toward Ezion-geber, but found nothing except for some local inhabitants."

"Is that all?" asked Joshua.

"No, no," continued Shabitqo. "The next morning I went to Ezion-geber, while Shooly waited near the ridge. The administration building was surrounded by men of the Black Knights of Pharaoh. I managed to see Esau alone, and gave him the letter from his Highness."

He nodded toward the Viceroy.

"What did Esau say?" the Viceroy asked.

"He was co-operative, your Highness. He said it was too early to tell how the budget would be affected by troop movements. Esau said there have been none that he was aware of. He told me that the Black Knights were aides and assistants of Prince Ramentop. The senior aide was Tasiris, who told Esau that Ramentop will be arriving in a day or two in Ezion-geber to take command of the Egyptian troops."

"For what purpose?" asked the Viceroy.

"He did not know, your Highness. But Esau said that Tasiris had asked questions about the Hebrews."

"Why?" asked Joshua.

"Esau did not know. He guessed that Prince Ramentop wanted to know, since it was part of his duties to track them down."

"Anything more about the troops?" asked the Viceroy.

"Your Highness, I tried to find out what their next destination might be. Esau did not know. But he did say that Tasiris asked him many questions about conditions in the area south of the Bitter Lakes."

"Where?"

"Villages such as Marah and Elim."

The Hebrews looked at each other with surprise, for those were the villages they had passed through after their Exodus from Egypt.

"Anything else?" asked Joshua.

Shabitqo looked gravely at the Viceroy.

"Yes, your Highness. Apparently Tasiris asked Esau many questions about you."

The Viceroy shifted nervously.

"What about?"

"Your whereabouts, comings and goings."

"What did he tell Tasiris?"

"Esau told him that we were there recently on routine business to discuss the budget."

"That is all?"

"No, Tasiris also wanted to know where you had gone next."

"What did Esau tell him?"

"That you and your two aides said you were going to Memphis."

They were all quiet now as the Viceroy looked down at the floor ahead.

"Anything else?"

"Yes, your Highness. Esau sends you his regards."

The Viceroy turned to Joshua with an ironic smile.

Joshua looked at the Viceroy, and then at the two scouts.

"Shooly, Shabitqo. That is most helpful. Anything else?"

"No," Shabitqo said. "After that, I rode back to meet Shooly, and here we are."

Nahshon looked at the Viceroy.

"Your Highness, what can you tell us about Ramentop and the Black Knights?"

"Prince Ramentop has the ear of Pharaoh. He leads the Black Knights, who are Pharaoh's secret service. The Black Knights, particularly Ramentop, have a reputation. They are known to be able and ruthless."

"What do you think of what the scouts have just told us?"

"We have to assume the worst – that Ramentop will use the troops to look for this encampment. I know his methods. He is thorough. He will probably order the troops to follow the path the Hebrews took after leaving Egypt. Starting from Marah and Elim. That is very near the spot where the Egyptian troops are now located."

"Your Highness," Joshua asked, "what does that mean for you."

"Ramentop is probably looking for me, too. That's what all the Black Knights stationed in Ezion-geber are for."

"Do you think that Ramentop has connected you with us?"

"I don't know. It does not matter. We must assume he is looking for all of us."

They were all silent as the Viceroy's assessment sank in. Then suddenly they all seemed to talk at once.

"I must leave for Gaza at dawn," the Viceroy said.

"Your Highness," Joshua said, "Shooly will come with you and Shabitqo to the southern highway."

"We may have to delay the mission of the spies into Canaan," Elishama said.

"This could jeopardize our alliance with the Nubians," Ahiezer said.

"We must move the encampment," Joshua said. "That is now urgent."

"What will happen to Miriam?" asked Nahshon. "Will we have to leave her behind?"

No one answered that question.

PART 4

FORTY

"Shooly will come with you."

Those words from Joshua to the Viceroy began to sink into Shooly's mind, as he

left the military tent. It was now well past midnight, and he was to leave at dawn again

with the Viceroy and Shabitqo to lead them to the southern highway.

That was just a few hours from now, he thought, as he galloped toward the

Annex. Just a few hours to spend with Debra, before he would be on the road again.

When Shooly arrived at the Annex, he found two sentries, each sitting half

dozing at either side of the entrance.

"Debra is inside," a sentry said, recognizing Shooly.

Before he could go inside, Debra came out to greet him. She had heard his horse's gallop and the sentry's voice.
"Shooly, Shooly," she said, as she put her arms around him. "It is so late. You must be exhausted."
With her arms around his waist, she led him outside the tent. Debra had arranged some bedding on the ground. She knew he would return that evening, but was not sure when. So she arranged to be at the Annex all of that evening until the following morning.
"We are sleeping here tonight," she said.

"In the open?"

"Yes, under the star-lit sky."

The Annex was located on the edge of the encampment. With their backs to the Annex, there were no other tents in front of them. All they could see was the night sky, the darkness shrouding the barren and rocky wilderness and the shadows cast by the light of the moon.

"You must be tired," she said.

"Exhausted, actually."

"Let us sit down. I brought us some food."

As Shooly sat on the bedding, he could see a small wooden plate on the side.

"What do we have here?"

"The usual. Manna wafers and goat cheese."

"I don't want much. I just want to be here with you."

"I am here, darling. But I also managed to bring us some grapes."

"Leftovers from the wedding?"

"Yes."

"The guests lost their appetites toward the end."

"Apparently," she said, putting a grape in his mouth.

"How are you managing?"

Debra then told Shooly what happened to Miriam. Shooly said nothing about Miriam, as if numbed by all that was happening.

"It is not the same without her," Debra said. "But I do get help from Rivka and my sisters."

She was looking into his eyes now.

"Did you think of me?"

"A lot."

"When?"

"All the time."

"Any special time."

"Yes, I was galloping alone in the hills. It was getting dark. I was looking for the

Egyptian troops. I was not sure if I would find them, or what would happen if I

did, or if I would be able to find my way back in the dark."

He paused, as he ate another grape.

"I knew if I thought about it too much, I would become scared. So I distracted

myself."

"With what?"

"With our pact. Remember?"

"Yes, but tell me anyway."

"Our pact was that as soon as I think of you, I assume that you are thinking of

me."

"Did it work?"

"Yes, I did not feel alone. I felt you were floating in the sky, watching over me as I galloped into the hills."

"Did I lead you well?"

"Yes, you did. You helped me find the Egyptians."

"How many?"

"Two hundred."

"I would not intentionally lead you into the hands of two hundred Egyptian soldiers."

"You didn't. You stopped me at a hill overlooking their camp."

"How clever of me."

"Better still. You led me safely back in the dark to where Shabitqo was waiting for me."

"All the way here?"

"Yes."

"In my arms."

"Yes."

They laughed at their little game of make-believe, as they now lay side by side on their backs looking at the night sky. The encampment was in a valley, and they could see hills on their left and on their right lit by the moon overhead.

She began to undress. When she was naked, she lay on top of him. She kissed him on his forehead, his eyes and his mouth, as he caressed her bare back.

Then she slowly began to undress him. She untied his sandals, then pulled away his kilt, undershirt, riding cloak and the rest of his clothes. When he too was naked, she lay beside him and pulled a blanket over them.

Now he moved to his side and looked down on her. He kissed her on the neck and lips. Then he ran his cheeks on the nipples of her breasts. He moved down and ran his lips all around her breasts.

"This is better than when you were just floating in the sky."

"Yes," she said. "It was tiring flapping my wings for too long."

They laughed softly. Now he moved on top of her and put his arms under and around her back. Suddenly, he was no longer tired. Invigorated, he kissed her firmly on her cheeks and her mouth, as he vigorously made love to her.

"I love you, I love you," she said, as she dug her fingers in his back.

They lay side by side under the blanket. They looked up at the clear night sky, gazing at the constellations.

She was the first to break the silence.

"Shooly, I hope I can see you more now that your mission is over."

"Not right away."

"What do you mean?"

"I am leaving at dawn again."

"So soon?"

"Just to escort the Viceroy and his aide Shabitqo to the southern highway. They are returning to Gaza."

Debra was now silent. To her, every one of Shooly's missions was dangerous. While he was alert and quick, he was not an experienced fighter and would have no chance if he ran into an Egyptian patrol. Shooly mentioned two hundred Egyptian soldiers, and that worried her more.

"Tell me more about the Egyptians you found in the hill."

"There is nothing to tell. There are Egyptian soldiers everywhere along the highway."

"Did you discuss them with Joshua and the Viceroy?"

"Yes, of course. That's where I was before I came to see you."

"What did they say about them?"

Shooly had long ago decided to keep nothing from Debra. He would tell her exactly what he knew, even if he thought it would worry her needlessly. He hated to lie to her. He knew their fate was tied together with that of the other Hebrews. She might as well know what was happening. She was his friend and his lover, and he needed to share with her everything he had – including his information, his hopes and his fears.

"Shabitqo and I told them what we found. And the Viceroy and the others gave their assessment."

"And what is that exactly?"

"I found the two hundred Egyptians on the southern highway. They were near Marah and Elim."

"That is where we were a few months ago."

"Yes. The Viceroy thinks the Egyptian soldiers will follow our tracks to try to find us."

Debra sat up and looked down on Shooly.

"Oh, no!"

"That is not all. Shabitqo says that the Black Knights, Pharaoh's secret service, are swarming all over Ezion-geber."

"Why?"

"Probably to look for the Viceroy."

Debra was now alarmed.

"Why are you going with them?"

"To guide them to the southern highway."

"Can't they find their way alone?"

"Yes, but it will be faster and safer if I take them. They are less likely to lose their way."

"If the Egyptians or the Black Knights catch you, they will have no mercy on a Hebrew."

"Debra, Debra. I have no choice. Those are my orders. Besides, if we just sit here in this camp and do nothing, they will find us anyway."

Debra said nothing, for she knew he was right.

"Debra, we are in a war. It is a war to keep our freedom and to conquer the Promised Land. I must do my part."

"I know, my love. I know. But I don't want to lose you."

Her head was now on his shoulder, and he had both of his arms around her.

"Debra, have faith. You will not lose me."

He could feel the wetness of her tears on his chest.

"When I come back, we will be together again. I will be yours forever."

They remained cuddled in each other's arms, warmed by each other's body. The blanket kept away the cold air of the desert night. The stillness was unbroken, except for the soft sound of their breathing, as they watched the stars and the moon in the night sky.

FORTY-ONE

"His Highness is ready," the sentry told Joshua.

Joshua had just arrived at the Viceroy's tent with four horse guards. As he dismounted, he could see Shabitqo preparing the horses, while Shooly, ready and mounted, looked eager to start the mission.

"I will wait for his Highness here," Joshua told the sentry.

"Actually, sir, he has been ready for quite a while," the sentry said, "He has been pacing in and out of the tent."

It was just past dawn. The sun was casting its orange hue in the eastern horizon. The Viceroy must have slept very little, Joshua thought.

After a short greeting, Joshua and the Nubians mounted their horses and galloped through the encampment toward the rising sun. As they galloped past the last tent at the eastern end of the camp, Shooly looked back toward the Annex. He could see the spot where he had spent the previous night with Debra.

As they emerged out of the valley, they reached the top of the first hill. Joshua, who was in the lead, halted. This was the signal that he and the four horse guards would be separating from Shooly and the Nubians to return back to the camp.

Joshua rode back to the Viceroy's side.

"Your Highness, this is where I must bid you farewell."

"You have been most kind, to rise with us so early."

"Do not mention it. You will ride further toward the rising sun."

The Viceroy nodded.

"Then you will turn in the direction of the southern highway," Joshua said, pointing toward the north.

"Joshua, you have placed us in good hands," the Viceroy said, nodding toward Shooly.

"May the Lord be with you, your Highness," Joshua said. He pulled down his bridle, as he and his horse bowed their heads to the Viceroy, turned around and galloped back toward the camp followed by the four horse guards.

Now the Viceroy and the two scouts resumed their ride toward the east. The sun was now low in the morning sky, shining its rays directly into their faces. The Viceroy rode a few steps behind Shooly and Shabitqo.

As he looked down to avoid the sun's rays, the recent events went racing through his mind. But for a moment, he blotted them out to think of his wife Sebaha. As early as it was, if she was home in Gaza instead of with relatives in Ezion-geber, she would be up by now, to make sure the servants were on their toes and doing their chores. While he was involved in matters of state, he did not underestimate the constant effort of Sebaha to make their home beautiful, welcoming and comfortable. She alone understood his needs – the need to find refuge from a disorderly world of personal betrayals, cynical politics and ruthless wars, refuge from these agonies to an orderly and loving home. He knew that his marriage to Sebaha was unique, and now longed to be back home with her in Gaza.

He hoped and prayed that Havilya and Moses would have the same kind of relationship he enjoyed with his wife – not just as husband and wife, but as friends, together laughing and crying, working and dreaming. Havilya and Moses had been to his tent late last night to bid him farewell. The signs were good, he thought. They seemed comfortable with each other and very much in love. That is a rarity, he thought, for a man and a woman so early in their marriage.

Moses had been cheerful and expansive. He talked of frequent visits, as if distances meant nothing, and he, the Viceroy, had been reassuring.

"Moses, I expect to be posted in Gaza for a long while. Ezion-geber and this region will continue to be my responsibility. From there, you will not be far away."

"And you should be able to bring mother with you on one of those trips," Havilya had added.

The Viceroy had said the same thing to Joshua, by way of emphasizing that their alliance could continue and thrive.

But as he was saying goodbye to Havilya and Moses, his heart had been heavy with doubt. Toward the end, he had felt that even Moses had seemed subdued. None of them knew where the Hebrews would be next and when they would be settled. As for him, as high a position as he might have now, he was in reality a mere administrator, at the mercy of the whim of Pharaoh and his close advisors.

The Nubian Princess

What now worried him was the news of the Egyptian troops on the western end of the southern highway. That was the highway they would soon approach. It was possible that what Shooly observed were troops on their way to Memphis. But in his heart he knew this was unlikely, and he did not wish to paint an optimistic picture for his new Hebrew allies.

Better to expect the worst and hope for the best. In this way, he would keep and perhaps enhance their confidence in him and in their alliance. That had always been the secret of his success – to analyze a matter in great detail and depth, to arrive at a correct assessment and to use the resources of Pharaoh that were at his disposal to take the appropriate steps. That was the trick – to use the Pharaoh's vast resources. And that may be the difference now, he feared. Without Pharaoh, would he now have enough resources to do what would be required? That depended on how many Nubians would join his cause.

As he looked ahead, the sun was now blazing brighter in his eyes. He squinted toward the horizon. Shooly and Shabitqo had sped much farther ahead of him. He must catch up with them, he thought, as he kicked his horse for a faster gallop.

Much as he tried to fight it, his mood seemed to become blacker. The spectre of the Black Knights alarmed him. The secret service usually worked in the larger cities of the empire. What were so many of them doing in a small backwater like Ezion-geber? Perhaps it had to do with the war against the Hittites. He hated to be in an apparently high position, but not knowing what was really going on. That is the price we pay for working for despots, he thought. That is why we must fight for freedom.

Shooly and Shabitqo had now slowed down their horses to a trot. As the Viceroy approached, they were looking down at a quarry on their left. By the time he reached them, they were stopped, gazing intently downward.

A chill went through the Viceroy's body. This was the lepers' colony. They had heard what had happened to Miriam. This must be where she was now.

As they looked down in the pit, they could see the two tents below. A few lepers were visible in their rags. Some were sitting alone in pairs in the shade of the pit's eastern wall. A few were hobbling from one spot to another.

The Viceroy had seen scenes like that in Nubia. He never stopped too long, although he knew they were suffering a living agony of isolation. As they shuffled to and fro, they seemed to be mourning their own impending deaths.

For a moment, he thought of going down to find and to speak to Miriam. Certainly they would find her, and perhaps they could comfort her.

But the futility of it overcame his otherwise good intention. He could do nothing to cure her, he would be risking his own life and that of his scouts, and the delay could imperil his mission – which was to get back to Gaza and to his wife as soon as possible.

A deep depression began to almost overwhelm him. He felt he had to get away from this place very quickly.

Suddenly, without thinking, he kicked his horse hard and galloped as fast as he could past the two scouts.

Shabitqo gave Shooly a knowing smile, as they both kicked their horses, scrambling to catch up with the Viceroy speeding ahead of them in the distance.

FORTY-TWO

Two days had gone by since the Princess had interceded with Aaron the High Priest to release Miriam from the lepers' colony. The High Priest was still haunted by the tears in Havilya's eyes when she had pleaded with him to help Miriam. She had insisted that she and the other women could care for Miriam in the camp. As the High Priest, he of course could not break the law and release Miriam from the colony while she was leprous. He had to wait seven days before he could even examine her.

During those two days, he had thought of speaking to Moses about helping Miriam, but he hesitated. The following day had been the Sabbath, and now the day after that, he thought that Moses might be busy after seeing off the Viceroy that morning. He knew that the Viceroy had left at dawn, but he thought that Moses had the rest of that morning to catch up with the routine affairs on the first day after the Sabbath. It was midday now. Perhaps Moses would be free to speak to him.

Now as he walked toward Moses' tent, he felt he could procrastinate no longer. He was not exactly sure what he would say to Moses, and deep down he dreaded what his reaction might be. As the High Priest, he was due to examine Miriam in only three days, and if he was to intercede with Moses to save their older sister, he could no longer waste time.

As Aaron approached Moses' tent, he could see Joshua's horse guards waiting outside. The High Priest slowed his walk. He disdained to speak to Moses about their private family crisis in the presence of the man he loathed. To the High Priest, much of what happened was the fault of Joshua.

But the High Priest felt that Joshua or no Joshua, he had to find the courage to speak to Moses about saving their sister. He strained to put out of his mind what he considered to be Joshua's hostile acts. Those acts seemed to diminish in importance in the face of the peril his sister now faced. It no longer seemed to matter to the High Priest that he considered Joshua partly responsible for the incident of the Golden Bull-calf, for failing to remain in the camp to help Aaron. Nor did it seem important that Joshua appeared responsible for detaching the judiciary from the High Priest's responsibilities. The High Priest still thought it was unforgivable that Joshua failed to invite Miriam to the early Hebrew discussions about the Nubian alliance. Had Joshua done that, Aaron felt, Miriam's views about the alliance would have been known and taken into account before the alliance had been consummated and before the wedding. If Joshua had given Miriam the deference due to her, the High Priest thought, then this crisis would not have occurred.

"Good day, my Lord," one of Joshua's guards said to Aaron as he approached the tent.

The High Priest nodded without replying.

For an instant, Aaron thought that the horse guards were snickering at him. But, no, he was not sure. Perhaps they were merely smiling because they were in a good mood. The High Priest felt he had to dispel these dark thoughts from his mind. He had to face Moses with a pure heart. A pure heart, like Havilya's, he thought. The words of the tearful Princess were still ringing in his ears.

"Why can't we do something for Miriam now?" Havilya had insisted.

As Miriam's brother, the High Priest felt he could do no less for Miriam than the Nubian princess.

As Aaron entered the tent, he found Moses sitting in his familiar place – on the chest with the wooden rod in his right hand. The High Priest saw Joshua with the corner of his eye to the left, and gave him a brief nod. Aaron's firm posture and intent gaze toward Moses hinted to Moses that they should be alone. Moses nodded to Joshua to leave the tent. Joshua bowed low as he walked out backward through the entrance.

"Good day, Aaron," Moses said. "What brings you here today?"

"A matter of great urgency."

"What is that?"

"Our elder sister, Miriam."

Aaron fell on his knees, as Moses looked down on him.

"I have been at the lepers' colony. Her condition is serious. I fear she may not recover."

"We live by the Lord's will."

"The Lord would have cause to lose patience with me by now."

Moses knew that Aaron was referring to his role as a collaborator in the building of the Golden Bull-calf and in arranging the festivities that had swirled around it. The Lord had been angry enough with Aaron to have destroyed him. But Moses had interceded on his behalf and saved him.

"I lacked faith in the Lord when I built the Golden Bull-calf, and now I feel shame that I and my sister have incurred the divine rebuke for our hostile talk."

Moses said nothing and let his older brother continue.

"I am overcome by guilt that the Lord has chosen to punish Miriam severely, and has spared my flesh from the same affliction."

Aaron now bowed even lower in front of his younger brother.

"My Lord, my Lord, I prostrate myself before you and ask for your forgiveness."

Aaron was now more humbled before Moses than even at the time of the Golden Bull-calf.

"In three days, I must visit her to examine her condition. I fear the worst for her, unless the Lord heals her."

Moses put his hands on the High Priest's shoulder.

"O my Lord," Aaron pleaded, "account not to us the sin which we committed in our folly."

Moses could now see the tears in the eyes of his older brother, as he pleaded to save their sister.

"O my Lord, let her not be as one dead, who emerges from his mother's womb with half the flesh eaten away."

Aaron now touched the feet of Moses.

"You have interceded with the Lord on my behalf and saved me. My lord, I pray that you do no less for our dear sister Miriam."

By now, the High Priest was sobbing uncontrollably. Moses then pulled up his older brother and stood up with him and embraced him.

FORTY-THREE

"Captain," Havilya said, "I must again impose on your good nature."

"I am at your service, your Highness."

"I wish to go to the lepers' colony."

"Yes, your Highness."

"You may accompany me, if you wish."

The Captain of the sentries guarding her tent did not want to fight a losing battle with her again.

"It will be my pleasure and my duty to accompany you, your Highness."

"Thank you, captain. I will be ready shortly."

"Yes, your Highness. If it would please your Highness, there are two things I must mention."

"Yes, captain, what are they?"

Havilya noticed that his goatee had not been neatly trimmed, as had been the captain's habit. And he still wore a vest of light armour.

"My sentry has left for family reasons. So I will ride with you alone."

"That will be fine. And the other thing?"

"If it will not offend your Highness, I would propose to ride with you to the top of the lepers' colony. As we did the last time, I will wait for you at the top of the pathway."

"Captain, I can understand why you do not wish to descend down to the bottom."

"Your Highness, I will recommend that you also stay at the top and not descend to the lepers."

"Miriam will not know I am at the top."

"You may leave the food there for her."

"No, captain, I must also speak to her. She needs companionship."

"Very well, your Highness."

Havilya already had her riding clothes on. She had put them on as soon as Moses had left for work that morning. Then she had immediately called in the captain. Her long hair was tied, and she put over her head a wide hood attached to her riding cloak.

The captain watched as she quickly went to the table to pack some dates, almonds and goat cheese.

"I am ready, captain."

"Yes, your Highness," he said, bowing to her as she walked out of her tent ahead of him.

Soon they were thundering eastward into the rising sun. The morning air blew a cool breeze into their faces, but soon lost its freshness as they approached the valley of the lepers. At last, they stopped their horses at the head of the pathway leading down to the tents of the lepers.

The captain thought he would try again to dissuade Havilya from going down.

"Your Highness, what you see below are those who are barred from all human society. Their isolation is an expression of God's displeasure."

Havilya glared at him as she dismounted.

"I beseech you, your Highness, stay here. Do not go down."

Havilya would not reply to him. She handed the captain her horse's bridle, and quickly ran down the pathway toward the lepers.

As she ran past the first tent, she looked closely at some of the lepers. Some were extreme cases with the extremities of their bodies, such as their noses and jaws, rotting away. Others merely sat, scratching their scales incessantly. Sensing that she was not afflicted, some cried to her, "Unclean! Unclean!" The lepers had been admonished to sound this cry to warn the unafflicted from touching them. Havilya pressed on to the back of the pit until she reached the women's tent. It was easy to spot Miriam. She was the only one in a bright red evening dress. Havilya found her sitting on a ledge in the sun.

Miriam had lost her eyelashes and her skin had more ridges. But she seemed to be at peace with herself. She sat calmly, looking in the distance. She made no movement, except for the occasional twitch to scratch the sores on her body. Havilya sat in front of her and removed her hood.

Miriam sat up straight and her face brightened.

"It's you, Princess. The sun shines twice on me today."

Havilya smiled at her, and began to unwrap the food.

"I brought you some breakfast."

Havilya handed Miriam a piece of goat cheese.

Miriam quickly devoured it.

"You shouldn't be here, Princess."

"I am visiting our priestess for inspiration."

She handed Miriam the rest of the cheese, which Miriam quickly ate.

"Princess, princess," Miriam said, as she shook her head. "There is no inspiration in a lepers' colony."

"The Lord is everywhere and will comfort the sick wherever they are."

"You speak like a priestess."

"I do. I heard you say that to one of the wounded men in the Annex."

"You learn quickly, Princess."

Havilya now held out her hands with her palms facing upward. On the left palm, she had the almonds and on her right palm were the dates.

"Princess, you are laying a feast before me."

Havilya laughed.

"It is not a feast. Just a few little things to keep up your strength."

Miriam picked up an almond and a date, put them together and ate the combination.

"Princess, you even took out the pits from the dates."

"Why, to make room for the almonds, of course, Miriam."

Suddenly they both started to giggle uncontrollably. Tears of laughter came down both of their cheeks. For a moment, they forgot the tragic state of Miriam's condition, and were now overcome by the absurdity of where they were and what they were doing.

After their laughter subsided, they became quiet while Miriam finished the food in Havilya's hands. Then Havilya was the first to break the silence.

"If we can laugh, there is hope."

"Princess, your presence cheers me and brings me hope."

"You must not lose faith."

"I know, Princess. To lose faith is to face the abyss."

"I have also spoken to the High Priest."

"Aaron?"

"Yes."

"What about?"

"To pray for you, Miriam."

"Prayer never hurts, Havilya. What else did you say?"

"I tried to persuade Aaron to release you into the camp. I said that I and the other women will take care of you."

"And?"

"As you know, the law forbids him. He said he must keep you separated from the camp until your condition improves."

"And in the meantime?"

"In the meantime, he will pray for you. When the seven days elapse, he will come here to examine you."

"Seven days, seven days. I don't know when that will be. The days have become blurred for me, Havilya."

"That will be in two days, Miriam."

A sad look returned to Miriam's face.

"I pray to God, too, Havilya. But I feel He has rebuked me and turned His face away from me."

"The Lord is forgiving, Miriam."

Miriam nodded.

"Miriam, I have also spoken to Moses."

Miriam was aghast.

"About what?"

"You."

Miriam now seemed distressed.

"Havilya, Havilya. You are his new bride. You must not vex him for my sake. He will be angry with you. You must not threaten your marriage for my sake."

"Our love as husband and wife is strong."

"Yes, but you must not weaken it on my account."

"I assure you, Miriam, you need not worry about me and Moses."

"Squabbles between brothers and sisters are common. Some are minor. Others like this one are serious. But they will not disappear. It is human nature."

"I know."

"I am not sure that, as an only child, you really understand."

"I do, Miriam, I do," she said emphatically.

Havilya remembered the words of Moses when she first told him of Miriam's plight in the lepers' colony. "It is a time of

The Nubian Princess

rebellion within my people, when our hearts and our minds are
not one," he had said. At first, the meaning of those words was
obscure to her. But then soon after, she remembered her
father's stories. After dinner, Sebaha and Havilya would sit on
the floor beside Sebakashta as he told them of what had
transpired at his work that day. He would describe the many
supplicants who would seek his favour by reason of their
relation with Sebakashta or with one of his friends. As much as
he was a man of mercy, he insisted on treating all of Pharaoh's
subjects equally, for he knew that if he was to seem to favour
some for the position of their family or friends, Pharaoh would
soon lose the loyalty of his subjects. As much as he, at one level,
detested the Pharaohs, he could not administer Pharaoh's
business except with integrity. And so it was with Moses,
Havilya thought. "Our hearts and minds are not one." As she
turned Moses' words in her mind, they could mean only one
thing – that in his heart, Moses wanted to see Miriam cured and
returned to her family, but in his mind he could not let Miriam
go unpunished for her rebellion while only punishing the others
who had also rebelled.

Miriam now reached to Havilya, and said, "If you become
involved in our quarrels, it will hurt you in Moses' eyes."

"Miriam, you are worrying needlessly," Havilya said, but
she thought better of burdening Miriam with what was going
through her mind.

"I don't want you to sacrifice your marriage for me.
Marrying Moses made you a Nubian outcast. If you vex him and
lose him, you will also become a Hebrew outcast."

"I merely interceded with your brothers."

Miriam paused for a while, and then looked expectantly
at Havilya.

"And Moses. What did Moses say?"

"I told him that I had come here to visit you."

"He must have been angry with you."

"No, he was not. I told him I came here to bring you food.
I said your condition is bad and getting worse."

"Did he talk about our quarrel?"

"No. I told him I did not want to talk about the reasons
for your quarrel. I just said I wanted to do something to make
you feel better."

277

Shaul Ezer

"What did he say?"

"Nothing much. He said he was pleased with me that I came to see you. He said he could not say more. He said that he has faith that our Lord will guide him, and do what is right for Miriam."

Miriam shook her head.

"What is right for Miriam?" Miriam said. "This is what is right for Miriam! A colony of lepers!"

"Do not despair. Your brothers have the Lord's ear. Especially Moses. I know he will help you. Otherwise he would have shown me his displeasure."

Havilya's report of her interceding with Aaron and Moses seemed to calm Miriam. She remained sitting, still with her knees bent against her chest, and her hands around her knees, as she rocked herself back and forth. For a short while, she seemed engrossed in her thoughts. Then suddenly she looked up at Havilya.

"Princess, you are in peril here. You must go now."

"Not until we discuss another thing."

"What is that, Princess?"

"The camp will soon be moved from Hazeroth."

Miriam shook her head. They both understood what that meant. Some of the lepers in severe condition could be left behind.

"When?"

"We don't know exactly. Everyone is packing."

"Could they move before Aaron visits me?"

"Yes, if Joshua orders it."

"Even if Aaron visits me before the move, and finds me still leprous, I could not rejoin the camp."

"Yes, Miriam. That's what I want to talk about."

Miriam looked down in despair.

"What is there to talk about, Princess?"

"As soon as the move begins, I will come and fetch you."

"Princess, sometimes you seem so young and innocent. Moving the encampment will be arduous for everyone. They will not think of the lepers."

"Miriam, I will let you have my horse. I can ride in Moses' cart, which will be pulled by oxen."

"As a leper, I cannot rejoin the camp."

"You can still remain separate, but move with the rest of the camp."

A smile crossed Miriam's face, as if an idea suddenly came into her mind.

"Havilya, you are inspired, my Princess."

"What do you mean?"

"If I can be separated and moved with the camp, so can the other lepers."

"You would move everyone here?"

"Yes, of course, Havilya."

"Most are too weak to walk."

"The stronger ones will walk, and the weak will use the carts with oxen."

"Will there be enough to carry them all?"

"That is up to Joshua. His military can be resourceful, when they need to be."

Havilya shook her head and smiled.

"Miriam, *you* are the inspired one."

"Havilya, there is no time to lose."

"What do you mean?"

"I must speak to Haggar, and to the head leper of the men."

She paused as she turned these thoughts in her mind.

"I must get them to help me prepare the lepers."

"How can I help, Miriam?"

"Speak to Joshua. Tell him all the lepers will be ready to move. Tell him we will move separately behind the main camp."

Havilya nodded.

"Tell him we will need some carts for the very sick."

Miriam now gently nodded to Havilya.

"And you, my darling, you must leave this place now."

Havilya pulled the hood over her head.

"I will do as you say," Havilya said, and she turned and hurried back to the captain waiting for her at the top of the quarry.

FORTY-FOUR

"It is dawn, and I still have not slept," Shooly muttered to himself as he tossed and turned under his blanket.

He looked for any sign of movement from the Viceroy and Shabitqo. There was none. They were fast asleep, alternately snoring, as if engaged in an animated conversation in their sleep.

Shooly was almost jealous of those who could sleep soundly in a time of crisis. He had thought that he could, too. But there was something that kept him restless and awake.

He knew it was not their snoring. He was used to that, since he was usually sleeping in a tent with others who snored louder. They had been riding all of the previous day, and, like the Nubians, he was exhausted and should have fallen asleep quickly.

He could not help thinking of the debate that had ensued the previous evening between him and the Nubians. After a day of riding, they had arrived at dusk at his usual resting place. This was the ridge overlooking northward toward the southern highway. Behind that spot was a drop in the land, a naturally excavated pit.

Shooly thought it was a good hiding spot. That is where some days ago he slept with the two mules that Shabitqo had left for him. That is also where he and Shabitqo spent the night during their last scouting mission. In addition, the high ridge nearby provided an ideal spot from which to view the southern highway without being detected by travelers.

"Your Highness," Shooly had told the Viceroy, "I suggest we camp here for the night. We can then set out early tomorrow morning."

"Yes, Shooly," the Viceroy had said. "We all need the rest. Now tell me again your thoughts for the morning."

"I would ride with you, your Highness, as far as you desire."

"You are most kind, my friend. Shabitqo and I will proceed alone on our way to Gaza in the morning. At the same time, you must return to your camp."

"Your Highness, I am at your service, if you wish me to accompany you north of the highway."

"You have done more than enough by bringing us here."

"As you please, your Highness."

While Shooly and the Viceroy had been talking, Shabitqo had dismounted and had been looking over the site.

"Shooly," he had said, "come and see this."

"What is it?"

"Fresh footprints."

"Yes, many of them."

"And, over here, some ashes."

"These were not here when we slept here about three days ago."

"No, they were not."

They had then looked at each other, as if reading each other's mind.

"Shooly, do you think the Black Knights were here?"

"Possibly, or some other travelers. We cannot tell for sure."

"Shooly," the Viceroy had said, "if the Black Knights could have been here, perhaps we should move elsewhere for the night."

"There are no better hiding spots nearby. If the Black Knights can find us here, they will find us if we camp in the open further north."

"Shooly, this may be a good hiding spot. But it is also a good trap."

In the end, Shooly had deferred to the Viceroy's higher authority. They had then crossed the highway and ridden farther north. They had found a low hill and camped beside it for the night.

The darkness was now giving way to the light from over the horizon. Trying to sleep was a lost cause, Shooly thought. Equally futile was to worry as to whether they would have been safer sleeping behind the ridge in Shooly's own hiding spot. As he had told the Viceroy, if the Black Knights were nearby, they would find them in either of the two spots.

Shooly now lay flat on his back with one arm under his head. He gazed toward the horizon where the sun was about to rise. To his left was the Wilderness of Paran and to his right was a low hill and then the southern highway a short distance beyond. At least, he thought, the hill concealed them from travelers on the southern highway.

Suddenly Shooly noticed that their horses were becoming restless. Two of them were snorting and neighing. His own horse was banging its front right foot in the sand.

Shooly sat up. As he looked around, he saw the Nubians were now awake.

"What is it?" the Viceroy asked.

"It is the horses," Shabitqo said. "Shooly is checking."

Shooly now crawled up the low hill to look toward the highway.

"O my Lord," he gasped. "Quick. It is the Black Knights!"

Eight men in black riding black horses were galloping fast toward them, with swords unsheathed and raised overhead. In an instant, the horsemen were trampling into the camp.

Shabitqo raced to his horse to pull out his sword hanging beside his saddle. Two Black Knights were quickly upon him, as one of them brought down his sword on Shabitqo's and disarmed the Nubian scout. Two other Black Knights dismounted and intercepted the Viceroy before he could reach his horse. Shooly, unarmed and the furthest away from the horses, was quickly subdued by two other Black Knights. The Black Knights worked quickly. Soon Shooly and the Nubians, with their hands tied behind their backs, were each straddled by two Black Knights. They stood facing the leader, who had not yet dismounted. Another Black Knight remained on his horse beside the leader.

The leader advanced toward the Viceroy and pushed the tip of his sword against the Viceroy's chest. "Tell me who you are and why you are here."

The Viceroy was defiant. "How dare you? I am Sebakashta, the Viceroy of Nubia, in the service of his Majesty the Pharaoh of Egypt."

"Just the person I am looking for."

"By what authority do you presume to attack one his Majesty's princes?"

"By the authority of Prince Ramentop, a Prince of Egypt and the head of the Black Knights, Pharaoh's own Secret Service."

"I order you to release us immediately. You must be making a serious mistake. Otherwise, when his Majesty hears of this, you and your henchmen will be severely punished."

"Now, now, Viceroy. I take my orders from Prince Ramentop."

He turned toward Shabitqo.

"You are a Nubian, too?

"Yes, sir," Shabitqo replied.

The Viceroy quickly interjected. "He is my trusted and loyal aide." Then the Viceroy nodded toward Shooly.

"And this one is a guide we found on the highway. My aide and I were lost. We sought this scout's help. He is guiding us through the wilderness."

The leader now moved in front of Shooly.

"You are not a Nubian?"

Before Shooly could answer, the Viceroy interrupted, knowing that Shooly's accent would give him away.

"He is a Hebrew straggler. He knows his way through the wilderness. For a small sum, he agreed to be our guide."

The leader nodded. The Viceroy pressed on.

"I insist that you release us at once."

The leader now moved to face the Viceroy.

"Save your breath. I am Tasiris, in the service of Prince Ramentop. My orders are to take you to him in Ezion-geber."

Shabitqo's heart sank. He recognized the name. Esau, the local administrator in Ezion-geber, had told him about Tasiris. He was Ramentop's senior aide who had arrived in Ezion-geber asking Esau questions about the Hebrews and their whereabouts, and about the Viceroy and his comings and goings.

Shabitqo had, of course, told the Viceroy, Shooly and the other Hebrews about what Esau had said. Suddenly, their worst nightmare seemed to be unfolding.

The Viceroy persisted with Tasiris.

"Tasiris, if you must take us to Ezion-geber, then release the Hebrew. He is no longer needed."

Tasiris looked at Shooly and thought for a while. Then a grin flashed across his face.

"I think Prince Ramentop will enjoy meeting a Hebrew. He will enjoy it very much. He may even find him useful. The Hebrew is coming with us to Ezion-geber."

FORTY-FIVE

"Why is our move delayed?" Joshua asked irritably.

He was losing patience, even as he started the meeting with his four division commanders. They were seated with him in a circle on a carpet. He had called them urgently to the military tent to review the preparations to move the encampment.

They recognized the familiar symptoms of strain in their general. His eyelids were swollen and his black eyes seemed fierce, as they were blood-shot from lack of sleep. His beard was not as well-trimmed as usual. His sideburns and thick head of hair seemed to them to reveal more than the normal strands of grey hair.

"Three days have gone by since the evening with Moses and the Viceroy. That was when we heard the report of the scouts Shooly and Shabitqo. Do you remember?"

One or two of the commanders nodded, but no one said a word.

"At the end of the meeting, I said that it is now urgent to move the encampment."

Joshua looked around the tent and at the commanders seated beside him.

"We have to move from Hazeroth urgently before the Egyptian troops find us. I have noticed a serious lack of readiness. None of the tribes is."

Still no one said a word, as each waited for someone else to engage the general.

"Well," Joshua said, "we will take it division by division."

Joshua turned first to Nahshon.

"Nahshon, according to the order of the march, your division must set out first. Are your people and your troops ready to leave?"

"I am afraid not, sir. Many families in the tribe of Judah are restless. Caleb, of course, is their kin, and he has been unco-operative ever since his wife Miriam was taken forcibly to the lepers' colony."

"Can you speak to him to console him?"

"I did, sir. It is futile. Besides, there are so many of them to console."

Joshua then turned to the commander of the Reuben division.

"Elizur, how prepared are your people?"

"Sir, I am having the same problem as my friend Nahshon. As you know, the order of the march prescribes that the Gershonites and the Merarites must take apart the Tent of Revelation and carry it themselves, marching in front of us but behind the Judah division."

Elizur was referring to the two groups of Levites who were assigned the task of safeguarding the Tent of Revelation.

"What is the reason for their delay, Elizur?"

"Lack of co-ordination, sir. They can't seem to do anything without orders from the High Priest."

"Have you spoken to Aaron?"

"Yes. He kept saying he will take care of it. But he too seemed to be distracted by Miriam's situation."

Joshua shook his head.

"What about you?" he asked Elishama.

"Very much the same, sir. We are to march behind the Kohathites. I am having the same co-ordination problems."

The Kohathites were the third group of Levites, who were assigned the task of carrying the sacred objects of the Tent of Revelation.

"Have you tried to speak to Aaron?"

"Yes. He means well and seems to be trying his best. But he is now terribly pre-occupied with his sister's leprosy."

"What about you, Ahiezer?" Joshua asked the commander of the Dan division.

"We are the rear guard, sir. We march the last. It is hard to get my people organized when those ahead of them are in disarray."

Joshua nodded.

"And another thing, sir," continued Ahiezer.

"Yes?"

"The delays are not only from the Levites. The rank and file are also grumbling, because Miriam is not here to take care of the sick in their families. No one has her presence and authority to organize the movement of the sick in the Annex."

"The army may have to do that."

"Only as a last resort, sir. We should avoid the spectre of soldiers dealing with the sick."

"What about the other women?"

"There are many, sir. But they lack the skills and rapport that Miriam has with the people in the Annex."

"Obviously, there are difficulties," Joshua said. "But you must overcome them. That is why you are commanders. Is that clear?"

They all nodded.

"Sir," Nahshon said.

"Yes, Nahshon."

"It would help if we could tell our people where we are going."

"We do not know exactly," Joshua replied.

"Is there anything we can tell them?"

"We in this tent heard what Shooly and Shabitqo reported. We also heard the Viceroy's assessment. If we assume the worst, the Egyptian troops will be following our trail starting from Marah and Elim."

"Sir," Ahiezer interjected, "if we tell our people all this, it will alarm them."

"Exactly," replied Joshua.

"What do you suggest?" Nahshon asked turning to Ahiezer.

"We should just reply in general terms."

"Fine. Where in general can we say we are going?"

"All we can say," Joshua said, "is the truth. We will move to pitch our tents somewhere else. It will be in the wilderness of Paran."

Ahiezer sat up, shaking his head.

"That will fill our people with dismay," he said. "They are anxious to settle down in the Promised Land. They are already tired and restless from living in the wilderness. To move them from one place in the wilderness to another without giving good reason will exasperate them."

"To lie to them is worse," Elishama said. "We cannot tell them they will enter the Promised Land next week."

"Let us settle this question," Joshua said holding up his arms. "Let us just say we are moving to another spot in the wilderness of Paran."

"It occurs to me now," Ehiezer said, "that Shooly is escorting the Viceroy and his aide to that area. Has he returned, sir?"

"No," Joshua replied. "Not yet."

"He is overdue, if he was just taking them to the southern highway."

"I know, I know," Joshua said dismissively. "I do not know why Shooly has not returned yet. I am worried, too."

Just then an aide rushed in and whispered something in Joshua's ear. The general quickly stood up.

"I just need to speak to someone outside," he said to his commanders. "Please wait for me here. You can discuss among yourselves how you can work together to prepare more speedily for the move."

When Joshua walked outside, he saw Havilya and her captain waiting for him. The Princess had dismounted, and was holding her horse's bridle in her hand. She still wore her hood over her head.

"I must speak to you at once, general," she said.

"What is it, your Highness?"

She handed the bridle to her captain and took Joshua by the arm to the back of the tent.

"I have just been to the lepers' colony," she told him breathlessly.

"Why? Don't you know it is forbidden?"

"There is no time for that, general. I went to see Miriam. I wanted to prepare her for the move, so that she can come with us."

"But, Havilya."

"She wants to move all the lepers."

Havilya explained that until now each family took care of the leprous members and moved with them. But now that the edict of the High Priest was in force, which was to keep them separate, then the lepers had to be moved in a separate band. Joshua looked impassively at Havilya, as he realized that he had overlooked the plight of the lepers' colony.

"What can I do about it?" Joshua asked.

"Provide us with a few carts drawn by oxen. Miriam and I will do the rest."

"I cannot spare any carts. We scarcely have enough to carry the tents, the old people and the children."

"The healthy can walk. We must make room for the sick on the carts."

Joshua now thought of the Egyptian troops and the need for speed in moving the camp.

"They will slow us down, Havilya. It will not work."

"No one needs to wait for them. The lepers will be carried on the carts behind the rear guard. The carts will catch up eventually. It is better than having their families abandon their own in that horrible pit. Do you want that on your conscience, general?"

Joshua shook his head and smiled. But his smile concealed deep anxieties. News of hundreds of Egyptian troops nearby was spreading throughout the encampment. There was talk of the dreaded Black Knights of Pharaoh, which some remembered from their days in Egypt. The Viceroy had left three days ago. If he is caught and the alliance discovered, the Egyptians will treat him as a traitor. Seemingly oblivious to this, Havilya was interceding to save Miriam. The people were incapable of action and their leaders paralyzed. Chaos is a kind of leprosy of the state. He would achieve nothing by arguing further with Havilya.

"You are persuasive, your Highness. I will see what I can do."

"Thank you, general."

As Havilya mounted her horse and galloped away with the captain, Joshua returned to his meeting in the military tent.

"Well," he said to his four commanders as he sat down. "Have you found ways to expedite the preparations for the move?"

"We will do our best," Ahiezer said.

"We will exhort our people," Nahshon added.

"Is there anything else?" Joshua asked.

When none of them said anything, Joshua continued.

"I have one final matter. I will need eight oxen-driven carts – two from each division."

"Empty ones, sir?" asked Elizur.

"Yes, empty ones."

"For what purpose, sir?"

Joshua hesitated, and then said, "To move the lepers."

The commanders looked at each other with amazement.

"That is impossible," Nahshon said.

"We hardly have room for the material we must move," added Elizur.

"I have only enough for the old people and the children," Elishama intoned.

"Why can't each family look after their own lepers?" asked Ahiezer.

"Gentlemen, gentlemen," Joshua said raising his hands. "You heard the order. That will be all. We will meet again tomorrow to review your progress."

The four commanders shook their heads, grumbling as they rose to leave the tent.

FORTY-SIX

"You must not risk your life for us, Esau."

"Your Highness, my small effort will hardly repay your kindness to me."

It was the morning after Shooly and the two Nubians had been brought to Ezion-geber as bound captives of Pharaoh's Secret Service. They had spent the previous night in the dungeons below the Ezion-geber administrative building. The three of them had been thrown into a cell without food and water. Soon after, Tasiris and his men had come in to beat them with clubs.

"This is to soften you up for your meeting with Ramentop tomorrow," Tasiris had said, as he had watched his thugs deliver blows to the three captives.

They had lain all night in the cell, with their bodies aching from the riding fatigue, hunger and the beatings of the Secret Service. Early the next morning, they heard the soft voice of Esau through the iron bars of their cell.

"I brought you some bread and water, your Highness," he said.

"Bless you, Esau. Bless you."

As the three prisoners grasped Esau's offerings, the Viceroy looked at Esau through the iron bars.

"You must leave this place before Ramentop arrives. I fear for your safety."

"This is just my administrative duty. I always arrange for food to be brought down to the cells."

"Yes, but not when the Secret Service is in charge."

"Don't worry, your Highness. My conscience will not allow me to stand by while my master is in distress." Before they could say more to him, he disappeared.

It was mid-morning when Ramentop, surrounded by four soldiers, finally came into their cell. Two soldiers carried lances, while the other two carried clubs and chains. Ramentop unfastened his neck ring, chain and belt, and clasped it in his right hand as a weapon.

Ramentop gazed intensely at Sebakashta. He had not seen him since his visit to Aniba as a youth twenty years before, when he attended a religious celebration at the temple for the god Amun. On that occasion, the Viceroy was much younger, exuding all the vigour of one in his prime. Now, on his knees with his hands bound together in chains, Sebakashta was forlorn and unaccommodated. The henna with which his hair had been dyed had faded, revealing mostly grey hair. This is the moment I have been waiting for, Ramentop thought, to have Sebakashta in my grasp. And yet suddenly a feeling of emptiness engulfed him. To hound this hopeless man further seemed pointless to him, but yet he had a job to do for Pharaoh, and he could not turn back. Ramentop then quickly got to the point.

"Sebakashta, what are you doing with the Hebrews?"

The Viceroy said nothing. He only shook his head.

You are not known to be speechless, Sebakashta. You are renowned in Nubia for your oratory."

The Viceroy did not reply.

"Perhaps this will loosen your tongue."

Ramentop nodded to a soldier with a chain.

The soldier slashed the Viceroy across his shoulder and chest. The Viceroy went down holding his stomach.

As Shabitqo kneeled to help his master, Ramentop shouted at him.

"You stay standing with the Hebrew."

Ramentop brushed his carefully oiled hair with his left hand. Then he brought his chain down hard on the Viceroy's back.

"We know more than you think. First, we observed you traveling south of the southern highway. You had no business going there. Your duties should take you to Gaza, Ezion-geber or Memphis. Yet for some reason you traveled south into the wilderness of Sinai."

Ramentop paced in front of the Viceroy, who was on the ground straining with pain.

"There is nothing in that wilderness, except for the Hebrews."

Ramentop paused for a reaction but received none. He kicked the Viceroy sharply in his stomach.

"You disappear for days. Then you turn up with a Hebrew. What do you say to that?"

"I told you many times."

"Yes, yes. You told Tasiris that he is a Hebrew straggler, that he knows his way through the wilderness, and that for a small sum he agreed to be your guide."

The Viceroy nodded.

"Well, the Black Knights are not fooled so easily."

Ramentop now took a white object and tossed it in front of the Viceroy's face.

"Do you recognize this?"

No one responded.

"Of course, you do. It is a piece of manna wafer. We found it on all three of you. Now what are Nubians doing with Hebrew food?"

The Viceroy strained to speak. "It is common in the desert."

"Sebakashta, we are not children. When did you have time to make wafers out of the manna? And when did the Hebrews teach you how to do it?"

Ramentop paced some more.

"When you were here last, I understand you were with two Nubian aides. Where's the other one?"

"Returned to Gaza."

"By himself?"

The Viceroy nodded.

"Strange that you would split up. Why would your other aide know his way when you had lost yours?"

"He is a scout," the Viceroy moaned.

"Then it was stupid of you to let him leave you without a guide."

Ramentop kneeled down and looked at the Viceroy.

"You are not known to be stupid."

Ramentop stood up, looked at the ceiling and rubbed his hand together.

"We think you made contact with the Hebrews. Making common cause with Pharaoh's enemies has always been a Nubian habit."

The captives said nothing.

"Now you have produced us with concrete evidence. This Hebrew scout and the Hebrew food in your bags."

Ramentop now turned to Shabitqo.

"What do you say to that, Nubian traitor?"

Shabitqo said nothing. Ramentop nodded to the soldier, who moved forward and slashed the young Nubian in the face. Shabitqo fell beside the Viceroy, holding his bleeding face. Ramentop now turned to Shooly, who was standing and shaking.

"Now, you Hebrew dog should be down beside your Nubian friends. But you are lucky, because I have a mission for you. You can tell your Hebrew masters that our Egyptian troops have found them. Pharaoh now knows where the Hebrews are, but has chosen not to engage them at this moment. His Majesty has other priorities at this time. However, tell your Hebrew masters that if they persist with alliances against his Majesty, then his Majesty's long arm will reach all the Hebrews. To show you what will then happen, you must now watch."

No one knew that Ramentop hated the sight of blood, for he kept it a secret. The butchering of an animal sacrificed in a temple disgusted him, and that final shudder before it became lifeless filled him with terror. Now he had to deal with human beings, and he had never actually seen the killing of a man or woman at close range, much less participated in one. He now knew it was power, not blood, that he sought, power to satisfy his sense of envy for his station in life. He knew what he had to do to those who betrayed the Pharaoh, but he was glad that he had underlings whom he could order to do the bloody work for him.

Ramentop now nodded to the two lance men.

"Finish off the Nubians."

The two soldiers rushed with their lances toward the fallen Sebakashta and Shabitqo, and stabbed them repeatedly in the chest and stomach. Shooly turned his face away, but Ramentop pulled him toward the dying Sebakashta.

"You don't like to watch, Hebrew? But you must. This will be part of your mission. You must look and tell. You must tell the Hebrews what happens to those who betray Pharaoh." Ramentop looked away as he kicked the corpses to ensure that Sebakashta and Shabitqo were dead. "Look carefully, Hebrew. Tell your Hebrew friends that the arm of Pharaoh is long, and he will catch the traitors to his Majesty's empire. And this is what will happen to traitors." Shooly broke down sobbing.

"We will let you go soon, Hebrew. Go out with the guards. They will take you to your horse." Ramentop gave

Shooly a wicked grin. As the guards led Shooly out of the cell, Ramentop shouted after him. "But before you ride away, we will prepare a gift for you to take to your fellow Hebrews."

FORTY-SEVEN

There was bedlam outside the Annex. Some of the sick had been brought outside to move with the camp. When no movement had started, they were left outside. The others were still inside the Annex.

A captain and two sentries guarded the entrance, as a large crowd pressed angrily against them. Fists were shaking in the air in anger and frustration. The crowd was looking for Miriam to help them move their sick family members, lest they would be left behind. The soldiers remained calm amid the clamour.

"Where is Miriam? We need her to move the sick," an agitated man shouted.

"She has been in the lepers' colony seven days," replied a sentry.

"Has the High Priest examined her?" the man demanded.

The sentry shrugged.

"No one knows anything," the man said.

"We are not marching without Miriam," another said.

The crowd then split into two factions. The second faction shouted back.

"We can't wait for Miriam."

"We have been ordered to move."

"If we don't pack and get ready, we will be left behind."

"Don't trample on the wounded."

"You should not have brought them outside."

Debra was trapped inside the Annex, frantic and helpless. The crowd outside pressed heavily against the sentries and their captain. She did not know whether to try to move the sick who were still inside the Annex to a location outside, just in case the march began. Even if she tried, she knew she could not penetrate the thick crowd.

At the same time, she worried that those outside might be trampled by the crowd. From inside the Annex, she could do nothing for them, either.

Throughout the encampment, the alleyways were blocked with those who were ready to march. Their belongings were packed and their tents folded in bundles. Some bundles were lying in the alleyway, others were placed on the carts tied behind oxen. But most of the encampment was not ready to move. Many would not move without Miriam; their tents were untouched. Others were not sure whether to march or not; their tents were pulled down, but left unfolded and their belongings in the dirt nearby. Unattended children were scurrying among the bales in the alleyways.

Frustrated men and women converged on Moses' tent. They found Joshua and four horse guards guarding the entrance. The throng pressed against Joshua.

A man glared at Joshua, shouting sarcastically, "What do our great leaders have to say to us?"

Joshua raised his hand for attention.

"My fellow Hebrews," he said. "We are saying now what we have been saying for four days."

"What is that?" came the shouts.

"Go back to your families. Join your division. Prepare for the march from Hazeroth. Obey your division commander."

"When does the march begin?"

"As soon as everyone is packed and ready."

"We are packed and ready," one shouted.

"We are not. We are not marching without Miriam. Why is she not with us?"

Joshua shook his head and said, "Miriam's fate is in the hands of the Lord and the High Priest."

"What about the Egyptian troops and Pharaoh's Secret Service?"

Four days had gone by since Shooly and Shabitqo had reported on their mission. Word of the Egyptian troops and the Secret Service had spread alarm throughout the encampment. Joshua felt he had no choice but to be plain and blunt.

"That is why we must move urgently. The Egyptian troops or Pharaoh's Secret Service could be upon us. We must move from Hazeroth immediately."

Cries of trepidation filled the air.

"Moses has brought us in this horrible wilderness to face starvation or death at the hands of the Egyptian troops or torture at the hands of the Black Knights of Pharaoh."

"What was wrong with Egypt? Why did we leave?"

"If I get the chance, I will go back to Memphis."

"Slavery in the towns of Egypt seems like paradise compared to the hunger and terror of the wilderness."

In the training grounds outside the encampment, the Hebrew soldiers were equally divided. The Judah division did not want to march without Miriam, her husband Caleb and their families. Their commander Nahshon was torn between obeying Joshua's command to mobilize and heeding the friends and family of Miriam who did not want to march. So he embarked on elaborate ruses and manoeuvres. On the one hand, he ordered some mobilization. On the other hand, he tolerated delays to gain time for Miriam.

Ahiezer, the commander of the Dan division, lost his patience. In charge of the rear guard, his division would be the first to be exposed to an attack from the rear by the Egyptians. He stormed into Nahshon's tent.

"Nahshon, it has been four days since the order to march. Yet your people are not ready."

"Ahiezer, packing takes time."

"It did not take this long during the last march."

"Many things have happened since that time."

"Things are happening all the time. We can't sit and wait. The Egyptians will be upon us any hour."

"My people are moving as fast as they can."

"We are facing a catastrophe."

"It cannot be helped."

Ahiezer walked out in disgust.

Near the Tent of Revelation, there was another mob scene. The packing of the sacred objects was only partially completed. The tent was still up, but the standard was down and the exterior furnishings had been removed. The crowd pressed against the Levite sentries guarding the entrance.

"Bring out the High Priest."

"Why is he inside?"

"When is he going to the lepers' colony to examine Miriam?"

"Seven days have gone by since our priestess was stricken with scales."

"This is the day that he must see her."

"If there is any justice, he too would be leprous with her."

"The High Priest also spoke against Moses. Miriam was not the only one."

"He should be punished, too."

"Miriam said nothing wrong. Her punishment is unjust."

"Miriam suffers while the High Priest waits in the temple."

"And the soldiers wait to march."

Suddenly, four horse guards and their captain came out of the Tent of Revelation.

"Make way, make way," the captain said. "Make way for the High Priest."

The soldiers pushed against the crowd as Aaron came out and quickly mounted a horse waiting outside.

"The horse guards, surrounding the High Priest, pushed through the crowd. As the throng made way for the riders to pass, the captain waved to them.

"The High Priest is on his way to the lepers' colony," the captain said. "You will soon learn of Miriam's fate."

* * *

It was mid-afternoon before Ramentop and his men were ready to leave Ezion-geber. They left Shooly outside with Shabitqo's corpse and Sebakashta's torso on the sand. As his last act, Ramentop personally handed Shooly a sack holding the Viceroy's head.

As the Egyptians rode off, Shooly waited. He wanted the Egyptians to make some distance from him. He needed to calm his agitation and to find some space for divine guidance to reach him. He took his staff and walked into the mounds of rock and sand, swaying his staff in front of him as if in search of something in the ground. He stayed in the sun and the sand for what seemed like a long time. As he lingered alone in the wilderness, suddenly the heavy weight of events lifted from his soul, and his body regained its strength and purpose.

Now he walked back to where the corpses lay. Shooly noticed that the Egyptians had left only his and Shabitqo's horse.

"Ramentop must have coveted the Viceroy's stallion," he thought. He slowly lifted the two bodies on Shabitqo's horse, and tied the sack to the saddle. He then mounted his horse and slowly rode out of Ezion-geber with the other horse and its grim load in tow.

He rode westward from Ezion-geber, along the southern highway, with the setting sun directly in his eyes. Ramentop and his men would have taken the same way toward Memphis. But soon he would be turning south toward Hazeroth and the Hebrew encampment. He and the other Hebrew scouts had marked the place with a square-shaped rock that was inconspicuous to other passersby.

It was dusk by the time he reached the square-shaped rock. As he prepared to turn to the left to head southward, he looked to his right where the land fell sharply into a shallow valley. His heart quickened as he noticed a small encampment at the bottom.

He galloped south toward Hazeroth but stopped as soon as he found a spot, invisible from the southern highway, where he could tie his horses. He then walked back to the square-shaped rock and started to crawl towards the encampment.

There were three men, with their five horses tied towards the right. He dared not look up for now, as there was still some light and the horses might sense him. He circled slowly toward the left to approach the camp far from the horses. "Wisely and slow," he remembered Joshua's admonishment, as he advanced imperceptibly. His knees and elbows bled from the sharp hot rocks, and his fresh blood mingled with the dried blood that had been splattered on his body during that morning's killings.

At last he was behind a high mound looking at the backs of the three men as they faced the horses. Two of the horses had packs on them, and the other three were for riding. The men were sitting in a circle eating and talking. He recognized Ramentop's distinctive cloak and silver collar and chain. The other two were his personal attendants and bodyguards.

Shooly quickly rolled his body down the mound away from the camp. He lay on his back looking at the twilight sky. The rest of Ramentop's men must be on their way to Memphis, he thought. But why did Ramentop stay behind? Could it be that he suspects the Hebrews to be nearby and he intends to search for them in the morning? Not likely, because he would have kept more men around him in case of a violent encounter with the

Hebrews. Perhaps he intends to turn north in the morning on another of Pharaoh's assignments? But the road north starts directly from Ezion-geber, so Ramentop would have spent the night in town. Shooly thought of what his father Isaac would have told him. While he was a simple construction worker, he had gained wisdom in the ways of people. "Don't look for complex explanations for people's behaviour. The correct answer is usually the simple and commonplace." Perhaps Ramentop, lacking the stamina of his soldiers, was simply tired and settled down for a night of rest, instead of riding hard into the night to Memphis, as he may have ordered the rest of his men to do.

As he turned these thoughts in his head, suddenly it didn't seem to matter why Ramentop was there. What was more important was that he was there at all, with only two men and apparently bedding down for the night. Even more, Shooly thought about what he himself was going to do.

By himself, he thought, he was no match for three Egyptians. He could rush to Hazeroth and seek help from Joshua, but it would be morning before they returned, and Ramentop would likely have moved on.

Shooly crawled back up to the top of the mound for another look. Ramentop had taken off his collar and chain and lay on his side. The two men were also lying down.

A thought started to form in Shooly's head. He crawled back to the southern highway and waited at the square-shaped rock. If they were following the usual scouting routine, Bezalel and Ohaliab would be coming from the west any time now.

FORTY-EIGHT

"This is the day that Aaron will examine Miriam," Havilya thought.

She called in the captain guarding her tent.

"Captain, I am going to Moses' tent." She was referring to the small tent that Moses used as his tribunal.

"Your Highness, but he just left from here this morning."

"I know, I know, captain. What I have to say is of critical importance. It will fall on his ears with greater weight at his place of work."

"Your Highness, all the paths to his tent are blocked with angry mobs. Even if you could reach his tent, I cannot vouchsafe your safety."

"Captain, captain, I am ready to go. You may stay or come with me."

Havilya covered her head with a hood, brushed past the captain and out of her tent.

She walked briskly as she wove a path through the throngs outside. The captain and his two sentries struggled to keep up with her. Soon she was lost to them, as she plunged deep into the mass of people. When she reached Moses' tent, she continued to press her way in, among men shouting and shaking their fists.

"Moses, Moses, we will die here from starvation."

"We sit here waiting to be slaughtered by Pharaoh's soldiers."

"We live like lizards in the desert."

"Take us back to Egypt."

She finally pushed her way in and was now face to face with Joshua and his horse guards who were guarding the tent.

"Havilya, what are you doing here?"

"I have come to see Moses."

"Where are your bodyguards?"

"They are coming soon," she said, as she looked back.

Joshua shook his head. "No one can keep up with you, Princess," he said. "Moses is inside working alone. Many want to see him for their personal business. But they can't get through."

Joshua pulled her in toward him, and pushed her gently inside the tent. She found Moses sitting alone on the floor, poring over some scrolls on a low bench in front of him. When Moses saw her in front of him, he jumped up.

"Havilya, what brings you here, my love?"

"I needed to see you."

"You have put yourself in danger. Could it not have waited till I returned to our tent?"

"No, Moses."

She pushed back her hood and kneeled down before him.

"Moses, I am your wife and bound to you by a sacred duty, as your mother was bound to your father and my mother to the Viceroy. My love and loyalty to you will remain unshaken."

Moses gave her a puzzled look.

"Havilya, I know, I know. You did not need to come here to tell me this."

"Moses, I beseech you to hear me." He stood back and let her continue.

Havilya remembered she had pressed Moses about Miriam at their first Sabbath eve together. For a moment, she thought that raising the subject again might annoy, even enrage, him. She thought of Miriam's warning that if Moses was vexed and thought she, Havilya, was interfering, he might leave Havilya, and she would then become both a Nubian and a Hebrew outcast. Nevertheless, Havilya took a deep breath, knelt down before Moses and continued in a shaky voice as she faced the ground.

"But I do have another duty – a duty of kinship to Miriam. I came here as a stranger, but she quickly took me in as a sister. Soon I learned of the sacrifices she has made to care for Israel's women, children and fallen soldiers. They came to her to be comforted, counselled and healed. It is not without reason that she is held in high esteem and devotion."

Havilya now looked up to him.

"Moses, while I am here to speak for Miriam, my devotion to her does not detract from my duty to you as my husband. I cherish you as my husband while I defend her as my friend."

Moses kneeled down and pulled her up to face him, as she remained kneeling.

"Moses, you have taught me that the Ark of the Covenant contains the tables of God's laws, and the condition of God's covenant with us. Those who transgress will be punished by the Lord, as Miriam has been punished."

Moses nodded.

"I now understand what you meant when you said that our hearts and our minds are not one. But, Moses, now that Miriam has been punished, and all of Israel has seen her punishment, no one can say that you punished the others but not your sister. Your heart can have mercy on her and your mind will know that Israel has seen that even the sister of Moses will be punished for rebelling against the Lord. And so Moses your heart and your mind can be one and they can be at peace, if you forgive Miriam and intercede for her in front of the Lord."

Havilya looked into Moses' eyes, as his tears welled up in them.

"When you open the ark of the Law, you first see the faces of children, so that the Law will be tempered with mercy. You taught me that pity is the virtue of justice."

Suddenly Moses buried his face in her knees and sobbed loudly and uncontrollably. A force deep within him seemed to erupt – his hurt feelings of betrayal at the hands of his people and his sister, her suffering, the Lord's wrath, Havilya's pleas. The force seemed to crash through a dam that he had built within his soul to suppress all of these thoughts at once.

They were quiet now, as she stroked his long grey hair with her hand wet with his tears.

Moses stood up and pulled up Havilya with him. He embraced her, as they stood there alone quietly in his tent.

"Havilya, Havilya," he said, as he kissed her on her forehead. "You are wise beyond your years. You speak to me as a teacher, for today I am Havilya's pupil. You have shown me what true friendship is. If half of Israel had a friend such as you, then we would have a speedy road to redemption."

He moved away from her and walked to the entrance of the tent.

"Joshua," Moses said.

His chief aide quickly walked in.

305

"Yes, my Lord," he said bowing down to Moses.

Moses looked at Havilya.

"Joshua," he said, "prepare the soldiers outside. We must leave this tent now."

"But, my Lord, the crowd is thick and angry. It is too dangerous. Let us wait till later when the throng had dispersed."

"Joshua," Moses said. "We must leave immediately."

"Yes, my Lord."

Joshua bowed again.

"Where to, my Lord?"

"Take us both to the sanctuary."

* * *

"You may be architects and scouts, but today you will become cold-blooded killers."

As Shooly was saying this to Bezalel and Ohaliab, he knew that he had never killed a man before.

He had ridden west of the square-shaped rock to intercept them as far as possible from Ramentop's camp. Then he had led them to his own horses, and described to them the location of the various elements in Ramentop's camp.

As Shooly revealed his plan, the other two scouts listened quietly and intently.

"We each have a dagger. I also have this wooden staff. We will crawl close to Ramentop's camp. On my signal, you will pull out your daggers and we will rush them. Bezalel, you take one of Ramentop's men, the one on the left. Ohaliab, you take the other. Leave Ramentop to me."

He took his dagger from his holder, and they did the same. He waved his dagger, to show that it would be visible in the moonlit night.

"If one of the Egyptians or their horses hears us, before my signal, then we rush them anyway. Each of us must succeed, otherwise we all perish."

The two scouts nodded.

"Our best hope is to stab each one of them in the neck while he is asleep. If they are awakened, we are into hand to hand combat. Then we must use all the practice and training we have received under Joshua's hand. If you stay close to them, before they can draw their swords, your daggers will prevail."

Shooly had never commanded a combat operation before. Nor did he rank above the other two scouts. All three knew it but left it unspoken. The two scouts did not question Shooly's plan. They seemed overpowered by what they had just seen and heard – Shooly's blood-spattered clothing, the corpses of the Nubians and the story of how they were killed by the Egyptians, and Ramentop's camp and its apparent vulnerability.

There was also a quality about Shooly they had not seen before. They knew he had Joshua's confidence, but today he seemed different – clear, bold, determined. He made his plan appear to them to be obvious, compelling, and even irresistible.

As the darkness deepened, they slowly crawled behind the mound where Shooly had first watched the Egyptians. In the moonlight, they could see Ramentop's sword, chain and collar, and other metallic cups and eating implements. Bezalel, Ohaliab and Shooly were positioned left to right in that order corresponding to how their targets lay, with Shooly hugging along his wooden staff. On Shooly's nod, they crawled over the mound to descend down to the camp. Suddenly a loosened rock rolled down noisily and stopped. Instinctively they paused, and as all was calm again, they continued downward on their hands and knees. Soon Bezalel and Ohaliab were a distance from their quarries no more than the length of two men. But Ramentop lay more than three times that distance to the right of Shooly. Prudently Shooly would have preferred the two scouts to stop while he crawled closer to Ramentop. But he quickly discarded that idea for fear of confusing his comrades.

He unsheathed his dagger and they did the same. Then he signalled the attack.

Bezalel and Ohaliab were either gripped with fear of death, possessed a beginner's zeal or were faced with fatigued Egyptians in deep sleep. In any event, the two Egyptian attendants were slaughtered instantly. They hardly uttered a croak, passing painlessly from sleep to sudden death.

Shooly had a longer distance to crawl toward Ramentop. The rush of the three scouts alerted Ramentop. Before Shooly could take him, Ramentop grabbed the sword lying beside him and fled into the darkness. Shooly stopped to sheath his dagger, grab his staff and then chased Ramentop under the light of the moon. He found Ramentop waiting for him, sword in hand, in front of a low wall of rocks. Ramentop was out of breath.

"Hebrew dog, you are biting more than you can chew," Ramentop said.

"Your two soldiers have gone to Amun," Shooly replied. "You are all alone now."

Ramentop lunged with his sword at Shooly, who jumped to the right, staff in hand. The sword entered deep into Shooly's left ribs. They were now almost nose to nose. With his staff in his right hand, Shooly jammed the ball of his left forefinger deep into Ramentop's left eye. Ramentop staggered back holding his eye in pain. Shooly, with Ramentop's sword still dug in his ribs, grabbed his staff at one end with both hands. He swung it as far back as he could and brought it down hard just below Ramentop's left ear. As the neck broke, the head dangled on the right shoulder by the skin under the right ear.

FORTY-NINE

"Make way for Moses! Make way for Moses!" Joshua shouted as he and his horse guards led Moses and Havilya through the encampment.

The crowd could barely see them, as the two of them walked on foot surrounded by the soldiers on horseback.

As Moses and Havilya neared the Tent of Revelation, the crowd separated to let them in the tent. A dark cloud was gathering in the sky.

Some fled as they had a sense of impending doom, as Moses had come to the Tent of Revelation to seek the Lord's guidance.

Inside the Tent of Revelation, Moses walked quickly into the sanctuary. Havilya stayed outside with the priests.

This was not the first time that Moses was pleading before God for His mercy. He had pleaded before Him for his brother Aaron, as he was preparing now to do the same for his sister Miriam. She had been leprous now for seven days. Although that seemed a long time to many, in the eyes of God, seven days was a lenient punishment. The Lord had told Moses, if Miriam had offended her own father, he would have shut her out of the camp for seven days. How could the Heavenly Father choose a lesser punishment when He had seen fit to inflict a public punishment upon her?

The rumblings of thunder could be heard, followed by screams from the crowd outside.

Moses kneeled and bowed down in the sanctuary.

"Heal her now, O God, I beseech you."

Moses knew how to pray. At one time he stood before God for forty days and nights. But there is a time to say long prayers and a time to say short ones. Here Moses said only a few words. From the thunder, they knew that the Lord was now speaking, but none except Moses could hear. Suddenly, the thunder subsided, and no voices could be heard from the sanctuary. Moses remained there for a long time in silent prayer.

As Havilya and the priests waited, suddenly they could hear fresh shouts from the crowd, as if from a new cause.

She wanted to wait for Moses. She wanted to be there when he emerged from the sanctuary. But a feeling of dread came over her body. It was the sound of horror from the crowd.

Suddenly, she rushed from the Tent of Revelation. When they saw her, all eyes seemed to be fixed on her. In the middle there was a large and empty piece of ground, surrounded by a crush of people all around. On one side stood Joshua. Facing him at the other end of the empty space stood Shooly, covered with blood. Bezalel and Ohaliab were beside him, holding the bridles of the several horses in tow, horses carrying the corpses of the Viceroy, his loyal aide Shabitqo, Ramentop and his two attendants. Between them was an empty sack and a round hairy object.

The crowd made way for her as she advanced toward Joshua. He rushed to put his arms around her.

"What is it, Joshua?" she asked bewildered.

The anguish in his face terrified her.

She looked at Joshua and then at the round object on the ground.

"O my God, it is my father's head."

She collapsed sobbing in Joshua's arms. Someone ran inside to find Moses. Joshua quickly ordered a soldier to replace the head in the sack and take it to the military tent. Soon Moses was by Havilya's side, as was Sebaha, her mother. The night before, Joshua had dispatched a small detachment to Ezion-geber to spirit Sebaha to the encampment and to Havilya's tent.

Joshua now mounted his horse to speak to the crowd.

"Soldiers and people of Israel, listen to what I have to say. The evil henchmen of Pharaoh have murdered a valiant Nubian prince and his loyal aide Shabitqo. They have spared Shooly so that he can deliver to us this message. With the Lord's guidance, our brave scouts Shooly, Bezalel and Ohaliab have avenged the murder of the noble Nubians. They have slain Ramentop and his two attendants.

"What is this message that Pharaoh's killers seek to convey? To the Nubians, it is that they must forever remain the subjects of Pharaoh, and that they shall not dare to follow the leadership of a great patriot like Sebakashta, who sought to bring freedom to his people. To the Hebrews, Pharaoh seeks to convey to us that we must not dare to make common cause with those who resist his oppression.

"My friends, I convey to you a different message. That, as our valiant scouts have shown, the Hebrews will forever fight to preserve their freedom – from Pharaoh and from any other tyrant. That the Nubians will find inspiration from the bravery of the fallen heroes Sebakashta and Shabitqo. And that someday the Nubians will prevail, and one of them will mount the throne of Egypt as its Pharaoh.

"Finally, the Egyptian troops that were nearby and threatening us are on their way to Memphis. They will celebrate the killing of the noble Nubians. However, when Ramentop fails to appear, they will come back searching for him and for us. So, my fellow Hebrews, we must immediately move this encampment. Make haste and obey the commands of the leader of your tribe."

Joshua waved them away, and the crowd started to disperse.

When Debra had heard what had happened, she immediately rushed to the Tent of Revelation. As Joshua finished speaking, she pushed her way through the crowd, looking for Shooly. Finally, she reached the middle, and found Shooly pale, bloodied and in a daze. He collapsed on the ground, as she rushed to his side. As soon as Joshua finished, he ordered that the Viceroy's head be removed, and a funeral prepared for the Nubians with full military honours. Soon the people, who only moments ago were loud and riotous, were now motionless. As time passed, some started to shuffle quietly, in tentative moves to back away from the horror. But they had barely begun to walk away when suddenly shouts of joy could be heard in the distance. Some looked at Havilya, embarrassed that there was rejoicing in the midst of her tragedy. But the happy cries became louder. Joshua, still on his horse, looked above the crowd in the distance. He could see two figures on horseback, with the crowd touching the figure on the horse in the front, as it slowly pressed its way through the cheering crowd. Then Joshua, realizing what was happening, ordered a soldier nearby to dismount. He motioned to Havilya to mount the horse and to look with him in the distance. Soon she could see the figure on the front horse, with the crowd straining to touch her feet and her outstretched hands.

The woman was in red.

"It is Miriam," Havilya cried. "She has been cured."

The Hebrews could now finally move the encampment. As the last of the twelve tribes went by, Havilya, dressed in black, walked hand in hand with Miriam. On either side of them, there was an oxen-driven cart laden with the sick and wounded. They had packed everyone in the Annex. In the distance, another eight carts followed, carrying the lepers.

And afterward the people journeyed from Hazeroth and pitched in the wilderness of Paran.

END

APPENDIX

NUMBERS XII

1. And Miriam and Aaron spoke against Moses because of the Cushite woman whom he had married; for he had married a Cushite woman. 2. And they said: "Hath the Lord indeed spoken only with Moses? Hath He not spoken also with us?" And the Lord heard it. 3. Now the man Moses was very meek, above all the men that were upon the face of the earth. 4. And the Lord spoke suddenly unto Moses, and unto Aaron and unto Miriam: 'Come out ye three unto the tent of meeting.' And they three came out. 5. And the Lord came down in a pillar of cloud, and stood at the door of the Tent, and called Aaron and Miriam; and they both came forth. 6. And He said: 'Hear now My words: if there be a prophet among you, I the Lord make Myself known unto him in a vision, I do speak with him in a dream. 7. My servant Moses is not so; he is trusted in all My house. 8. With him do I speak mouth to mouth, even manifestly, and not in dark speeches; and the similitude of the Lord doth he behold; wherefore then were ye not afraid to speak against My servant, against Moses?' 9. And the anger of the Lord was kindled against them; and He departed. 10. And when the cloud was removed from over the Tent, behold, Miriam was leprous, as white as snow; and Aaron looked upon Miriam; and, behold she was leprous. 11. And Aaron said unto Moses: 'Oh my lord, lay not, I pray thee, sin upon us, for that we have done foolishly, and for that we have sinned. 12. Let her not, I pray, be as one dead, of whom the flesh is half consumed when he cometh out of his mother's womb.' 13. And Moses cried unto the Lord, saying: 'Heal her now, O God, I beseech Thee,' 14. And the Lord said unto Moses: 'If her father had but spit in her face, should she not hide in shame seven days? Let her be shut up without the camp seven days, and after that she shall be brought in again.' 15. And Miriam was brought in again. 16. And afterward the

people journeyed from Hazeroth and pitched in the wilderness of Paran.